DIAMOND DOVE

'An amazingly accomplished first novel with a memorable heroine…Hyland's hard-hitting prose has conjured up not only the atmosphere but the spirit of this remote little community and its colourful inhabitants. He's a definite writer to watch'
Sunday Telegraph

'The writing in *Diamond Dove* is absolutely beautiful, and we are presented with a witty, angry and moving book. This is a breathtaking audacious debut novel that demands to be read, and that will remain in your mind for a long time after'
Reviewing the Evidence

'A brilliant portrait of different cultures attempting to coexist in a climate of ignorance, taboos, racism and greed. Emily's investigations take her to the heart of the conflict and lead to a denouement as impressive for its elegance as for its tension. A startling, confident first novel'
Guardian

'A clever murder story in a fascinatingly filthy setting'
Literary Review

'The book is extremely well written with extensive use of local dialect never detracting from the story…Adrian Hyland not only writes extremely well about the Australian outback, he also gives a very convincing portrayal of a restless and defiant young woman'
Crimesquad.com

After studying languages and literature at Melbourne University, Adrian Hyland moved to Central Australia where he lived for ten years, working in community development in remote Aboriginal communities and living with the Warlpiri people in the Tanami Desert. *Diamond Dove* is his first novel.

DIAMOND DOVE

Adrian Hyland

Quercus

First published in Great Britain in 2007 by Quercus
This paperback edition published in 2008 by

Quercus
21 Bloomsbury Square
London
WC1A 2NS

A CIP catalogue record for this book is
available from the British Library

ISBN 978 1 84724 377 5

For Kristin

Author's Note

Readers familiar with the Northern Territory will recognise that I've taken liberties with time, geography, even politics – if nothing else, the rednecks are no longer in office! While my portrayal of the Warlpuju is based upon insights gained during my years of working with a number of Central Australian communities, they do not exist: the people, the dreamings and the places described are inventions. The Warlpuju language is also mostly fabricated; it does, however, include some terms that are common to the languages spoken across a wide area to the north of Alice Springs.

About Skin Names

Aboriginal society is traditionally organised into 'sub-sections' denoted by 'skin names'. A person's skin determines many important aspects of their relationships with others – from how they should be addressed to whether they are eligible for marriage. In Central Australia's Indigenous communities this framework is still fundamental to everyday life.

Glossary

budju	attractive young person
Jangala	skin name
Japanangka	skin name
juntaka	bird
kalu!	an exclamation
kantiya!	stop!
karlujurru	diamond dove
kirta	owner
kurlupartu	cop
Kuminjayi	taboo name
mamu	devil
manti	spirit familiar
mijiji	white woman
Nangali	skin name
ngampartu	father
Nungarayi	skin name
papalurtu	whitefeller
parnparr	poor bugger
two-pella	two people
warriya	crazy
warlakunjumana!	come here!
wartuju	fire
wartujutu	fire-like crystal
yuwayi	yes

Fat Flies and Green Water:
the Sunlit Plains Extended

I parked my little white ute on the outskirts of the camp and sat there, looking out at the scatter of corrugated iron hovels.

There's enough people here, I thought. Boys brawling over a flaccid football, girls bouncing a basketball in a cloud of dust, young men working on a car, pensioners chewing on the cud. A bare-arsed tacker raced past pushing a pram wheel with a length of wire.

Fifty, maybe sixty people all up. The Moonlight Downs community.

They stopped what they were doing and stared at me. Every one of them.

I climbed out of my seat, stood by the door.

'Er, hello...' I called. My voice trailed away unanswered.

The only up-front individual in the place was a dog – a mangy leatherjacket with weeping eyes and a snout like a stubbed cigar which slunk up and sniffed my wheels.

A minute or two crept glacially by.

I took a look around. To the south was a row of rust-red hills, to the north the scorched yellow spinifex plains that would eventually crumble and fade into the Plenty Desert. The camp was nestled in between, its standout features a sidling windmill, a silver caravan, a long-drop dunny and a horse-yard made from lancewood posts. The amenities seemed to consist of a leaky tap and a solar-powered radio mounted on a pole.

Dust devils whirled, lifted scraps of rubbish into the air. Somewhere a child cried, somewhere a crow called. A trio of hungry-looking kite-hawks eyed me from the windmill.

We waited and watched. Maybe they knew what we were waiting for, but I sure as hell didn't. We were miles from nowhere. The nearest town, Bluebush, was four hours of rough roads away, Alice Springs another five beyond that. Even so, there was a nagging voice inside my head telling me to turn around and go back the way I'd come.

Fat flies came hounding out of the green water at the base of the tap. A toddler sat in the puddle and picked at the number eleven under his nose. A woman took out her teeth and inspected them, possibly for stress fractures or white ants. A burly, middle-aged bloke with an eye-patch, a fur hat and a T-shirt with a picture of a frog in a bun above the caption 'Cane-toad Burger' sat on the bonnet of a wrecked car and tapped two boomerangs together. The effect was more menacing than musical.

Then I realised who we were waiting for. He came crawling out of one of the rabbit-hutch humpies, scratched his pants and stretched his thin frame out to its full six feet. He shaded his eyes against the late-morning sun, squinted in my direction, then began to walk the same way. He was bow-legged and barefoot, wearing, as he'd always worn, a checked shirt, a white beard and a look of bemused anticipation.

Lincoln Flinders.

I scooped my blanket up from the seat, threw it around my shoulders, kicked away a couple of dogs and took a step forward.

When he was ten feet away he paused, examined me more closely.

What would he have seen? A short woman in a blue denim dress with a mass of wiry black hair, a tawny complexion, a pair of apprehensive eyes. Anyone he recognised? I should be so lucky.

A stubbly smile crinkled his beard.

'Why, ello h'Em'ly!' he croaked, his brown eyes beaming.

A wave of relief swept through me. The years had taken a toll on his teeth but not his powers of observation. I hadn't seen him for over a decade, and he sounded like I'd just stepped out for a smoke.

'Hello, Lincoln.'

He shook my hand, put an arm around my shoulders and said, 'I shoulda knowed you straightaway from that ol red blanket.'

When I was growing up, the blanket I was wearing had gone everywhere with me: in winter it was my coat, in summer my shade.

'I've been out the Jenny, Lincoln. Visiting Dad. He's been keeping it clean for me.'

'Mmmm,' he nodded. 'I see. Your Moonlight blanket, look like.'

He turned around and yelled at the milling masses: 'Hey you mob o' lazy myalls, come say ello to li'l h'Emily.' I smiled at the heavily aspirated pronunciation of my name. 'H'Emily Tempest! That Nangali belong ol Motor Jack. Get over an make 'er welcome! She come home!'

Which they did; and which, for a day or two, I almost thought I had.

*

3

'Li'l Emmy, *parnparr*,' said Gladys Kneebone as we sat by the fire half an hour later. 'Didn't they feed you down south?'

Gladys herself was a battleship on stilts. She wasn't much older than me, but she'd exploded in every direction. She was immensely tall, immensely fat, wearing a green dress and a coiffure that looked like it had been fashioned with a splitting axe. She thrust a pannikin of head-banging tea into my hand, fossicked through the embers with a stick and offered me a leg of... a leg of what? I wondered warily. Rabbit?

'Good tucker that one,' she exclaimed.

I took a look at the scorched carcass grinning up from the ashes. Jesus, a fucking cat! Been a while since I'd had one of those. What the hell, I decided, it couldn't be any worse than some of the crap I'd endured in roadhouses on the way up here.

It wasn't. Kind of stringy, kind of greasy, kind of... well, cattish, but I managed.

Many of the adults I remembered from my childhood – Stumpy Dodds, Spinifex, Timothy Windmill – drifted over and had a quiet word, shook my hand or threw their wiry arms around me. Cissy Whiskey slipped in through the ruck, touched my face as if it was a sacred object and gave me the long-lost-daughter spiel. Cissy was famous for her ash-baked damper. I must have eaten tons of the stuff, smothered in golden syrup and washed down with sweet black tea. Despite the damper, Cissy herself was as skinny as a picket, with piercing eyes and an aureole of white hair.

Lincoln's daughter, Hazel, was nowhere to be seen. My father had told me she was away out west, and evidently he was right. For that I was grateful.

Lincoln eventually hunted the mob away and we sat by the fire and talked, just the two of us. He was an easy feller to talk to, Lincoln. Always had been. He was the head stockman on Moonlight Downs station, where my father Jack was the mechanic, all through my childhood.

He still carried himself with the quiet authority that had made black and white respect him. He was a smooth-skinned, handsome man, skilled in the whitefeller ways of cattle-work and motorcars, but among his own people a religious and community leader.

We talked about my father, nowadays running a small gold mine out at Jennifer Creek, a couple of hundred k's to the south. I told him a little about my wandering years: Adelaide, Melbourne, boarding school, university. I'd started three degrees and finished none of them, had a dozen different jobs, most of them in grungy pubs and bars. Done a lot of travel. Somehow, it seemed, always gravitating towards the drier parts of the world.

'So all them places you seen?' Lincoln asked, shaking his head. 'China. India. Africa. Uz… whatever that one.'

'Uzbekistan. Yep. Went there too.'

'How were they?'

Jesus, where do I begin?

'Good country?' he prompted me.

I took a look around. Women were cooking tea and damper, men were playing cards, laughing. Kids were decorating each other's faces with puffballs. Two teenage girls had made a cats cradle out of lengths of hairstring, and were shyly glancing in my direction and grinning.

'Never as good as here.'

Lincoln nodded, clicked his tongue in the sympathetic

manner he had for anybody who'd had the misfortune to leave Moonlight Downs, and then told me about their own homecoming.

For decades blackfellers had been deserting their traditional country and drifting into outback towns. But in recent years, as they won their land back through the courts, there'd been a counter-attack. Blacks all over the Territory were packing their kids and dogs into motorcars held together with fencing wire and moving back out into a world of ghosts and songs.

It was the same with the Moonlight mob. For most of the time I was away they'd been squatting in a fringe camp in Bluebush, but they'd been back on Moonlight for a couple of years now. Technically, they were its owners, successful claimants of the property under the Northern Territory Land Rights Act.

When Lincoln talked about the future, though, there was an edge to his voice. The return to Moonlight hadn't worked out the way he'd hoped it would. For many, the move had come too late: the ghosts were gone, the songs forgotten.

'Still aven't scrape the bitumen from their boots,' was how he put it. The young were hanging out for computers and booze, the middle-aged for soft beds, fast food and DVDs. They scuttled back into Bluebush at the slightest excuse. Only the kids and the pensioners, it seemed, were content to be back on their own country.

While we were talking, I noticed a pack of young guys hovering in the distance but keeping a surreptitious eye on me, whispering into their fists as they mangled a rusty Holden ute. The car was balanced precariously on its side, propped up by a shaky-looking log beneath which they were nonchalantly working away. I had no idea what they were doing under there, but it didn't look like it involved fine-motor skills: their main tools were a sledgehammer, a crowbar and a length of wire.

When Lincoln looked like he needed a rest, I moseyed over to the young men, said hello. The biggest bloke, a young feller with cauliflower ears and a zucchini nose, ran a greasy rag across his mitts, shook my hand and gave me a familiar name.

'Why Bindi!' I exclaimed. 'I remember you! How'd you turn into a fucking mountain? I used to wipe your arse.'

He grinned shyly, scratching the arse in question. I hoped I wouldn't have to wipe it again.

'We goin huntin, Em'ly,' he said. 'Why don't you come along? Mebbe getta turkey, pussycat. See a bit o' country.'

'No worries, Bindi. Love to.' I took another look at their transport, now restored to the horizontal. It looked like something the Japs had dropped on Darwin. Its tyres were as bald as the camp dogs. One of them – the tyres, not the dogs – had been repaired with spinifex and fencing wire. 'I'll bring my own wheels, though, if it's all the same to you.'

It was all the same to everybody. Word travelled fast. By the time I got back to my Hilux it was staggering under a load that would have broken the back of a Shanghai bus. There were old blokes squinting down their rifles, little old ladies armed to the gums with nulla-nullas – fighting sticks – and crowbars, young mums with undies in their hair and babies on their breasts, kids with globs of snot bubbling under their nostrils. Slippery Williams, with a confidence that belied his name, was casually reclining on the roof. Lincoln materialised in the passenger seat next to me.

We completed a noisy circumnavigation of the camp, then set out across the sunlit plains extended. Bindi was in the lead. The nine or ten guys in his car belted out what I first thought was some ancient Warlpuju hunting song but which gradually crystallised into the flattest rendition of 'Six Days on the Road' I'd ever heard.

'Sik DAY-on de road an ah'm a-gunner make it ome tonight!' My own car-load bellowed from the back whenever the chorus came round, roaring with laughter and punching air. Lincoln tapped out the rhythm on the door.

'What a hoot!' I said to myself an hour or two later. 'What a bloody hoot.' I'd forgotten the pleasures of hunting with the Moonlight mob.

The trip so far hadn't been much more than an excuse to see a bit of country and make a lot of noise. They shut up now, though: we'd just rounded a bend and pulled up behind the Holden, which had pulled up alongside a bush turkey. So alongside was it, in fact, that Bindi could have just about reached out and throttled it. When you have in your hands the miracle of modern technology, however, you're obliged to use it, and to that end a rusty rifle barrel came creeping out the window. The turkey looked up into eternity with interest.

I watched Bindi's finger squeeze back and closed my eyes, not wanting to see that naïve head blown off.

Nothing happened.

I opened my eyes. Another squeeze of the finger, another agonised silence. The tension was killing me, if not the turkey. Although it was, at least, beginning to look a little suspicious.

A long black arm emerged from the passenger's window and rummaged quietly through a box on the roof. Looking for a spear? I thought hopefully. A boomerang? Even a well-aimed spanner would have done the job.

It emerged with a can of CRC. Oh god, I thought. He's gonna persist with the high tech!

The hissing of the spray onto the rifle seemed to disturb the bird more than anything else thus far. It took a step or two to the west, but kept an eye upon us, still reluctant to tear itself away from the circus.

Lincoln, sitting next to me, had been fidgeting restlessly throughout the entire performance. When the rifle clicked yet again, he roared out the window, 'More better you run the bastard over!'

The rifle swung back in our direction and I ducked for cover. If the bloody thing was ever going to go off it would be now, for sure. 'What you bin say ol man?' yelled Bindi.

That was enough for the turkey, which lumbered into the air.

'I say you better let the pensioners ave a go!' Lincoln was out of the car in an instant, rifle in hand. He steadied his aim with an elbow on the bonnet. The bird was a hundred metres away and rising, but he dropped it with a single shot.

An hour later we pulled up for a break, my under- and over-aged passengers in need of a pit-stop. I stretched back, took a long, soothing drag of Champion ruby, surveyed the scene around me through a haze of smoke. The old ladies were digging for yams and some of the younger ones were using a rake to drag a bush banana vine down from a bloodwood. The turkey on the back of my ute had been joined by a kangaroo, a couple of scrawny cats and a bucket of conker-berries.

It was their home country, all right. But was it mine?

I grew up on Moonlight Downs. Came here when I was four years old. My mother, Alice Limmen, was a Wantiya woman, from the Gulf country five hundred k's to the north-east. Of her I remember almost nothing except a thin, sweet face, a Wantiya lullaby and the enveloping breasts upon which I used to nuzzle myself to sleep. My father, Jack Tempest, was a wandering whitefeller who courted, married and buried her in the space of five years.

After Jack and I came to Moonlight I ran wild, energetically evading his half-hearted attempts to enrol me in the radio-based School of the Air. The blackfeller camp was school enough for me: I'd be down there at dawn and I wouldn't make it home till dusk. In the intervening hours my little mob and I would hunt in the hills, fish in the creeks, climb the skeletal trees, scour the countryside on horses borrowed from the stock camp.

Occasionally, when I returned from some such expedition dirty and dishevelled, wild honey dripping down my chin, lizards wriggling in a pocket, I'd catch my father glancing at me with a troubled look on his face. Presumably wondering what sort of a wild thing he'd created. But he did, at least, seem reassured by the ease with which I learnt to read, both the books on our shelves and the rocks through which he and I fossicked whenever we had the opportunity.

Jack was a part-time prospector back then, a gouger, and he reckoned I had a good eye. During quiet times on the station he'd take Hazel and me out bush for weeks at a time. The three of us would go rambling across country in his old Bedford truck, looking for traces of gold or working some little claim in the hills.

This wild, magical world came crashing down around my head the year I turned fourteen. Tim Buchanan, the station owner, died without an heir, and the property was taken over by a hard-nosed bastard by the name of Brick Sivvier. The Warlpuju, whose language makes no distinction between p and b, called him prick, which wasn't that far off the mark.

Within a month of his arrival Sivvier had turfed everybody, black and white, off the place and brought in his own people, from Queensland. For me, this meant being shipped off to boarding school in Adelaide. For my father it meant transforming what had been a part-time interest – gold mining – into the full-time occupation that would eventually make his small fortune. For the Warlpuju it meant leaving their homeland for the ten-year exile in boozy, brutal Bluebush.

Still, I reflected as I relaxed at the wheel of my ute, knees on the dash, fag hanging off my mouth, they can't be doing too badly if they can enjoy themselves this much.

Bindi's clutch had packed it in, as a result of which he couldn't change out of first gear. Nor could he stop, since he wouldn't be able to start again so he circled slowly around us like a great clanking buzzard, cracking jokes and occasionally flushing the old boys out of the bushes.

'Aaaiiyy!' yelled Bindi. 'This drivin round in circle tangle up my brain…'

My passengers gave up their various diversions and clambered back aboard. We inscribed a slow circle in the dust and headed for home, swapping insults, oranges, tobacco and, occasionally, passengers, as the kids took whatever opportunity arose to make death-defying leaps between the two cars.

We were running along the foot of Jimpili Hill, almost back at the camp, when something – a shift in the noise level, a subtle tension in the air – made me look up.

There was a row of rocks on top of the hill, or what I took to be a row of rocks until one of them moved. The figure rose to its feet and bellowed, '*Kantiya!*' – stop there! – in a voice as deep and dark as a valley full of thunder.

My heart sank as he drew closer and I recognised him: he was a tall, powerful man encased in rags, fur and army surplus, a tuft of owl feathers in his headband, a rifle across his shoulders, a pack of ratty dogs at heel.

Blakie Japanangka.

A Reading from the Book of Blakie

Blakie strode down the slope, all windmilling arms and blowabout rags, red dust boiling behind and a fleet of flies scudding above. Around his neck was a quartz crystal on a hairstring necklace. His daks were held up with a length of fencing wire, his chest jangled with a bandolier full of filthy knives. A bloody snake's head wobbled out of a coat pocket. In his left hand he held a huge fighting stick.

'Oh no!' I groaned to Lincoln. I'd forgotten about Blakie. 'Hasn't anyone put him out of our misery yet?'

Lincoln clicked his tongue, sighed fleetingly. A sign of disapproval perhaps, though whether of Blakie's arrival or my lack of respect for an elder was unclear.

Growing up on Moonlight we were forever being threatened and regaled with tales of the demons who lurked in the bush at night, monsters with snakes in their hair and crystals in their eyes, fabulous creatures who'd rip your head off if they caught you dreaming in the wrong direction.

These stories were presumably no more than standard Warlpuju fear-mongering, but I thought they'd all come to life at once on that distant winter night when Blakie first wandered into camp.

I remember lying in the swag with Hazel, terrified, as he

stomped from fire to fire and sent a withering blast of invective at the bewildered Warlpuju.

'Fuckin sea comin,' he growled, 'flood water risin, green sea roar, wash away white man, wash away blackfeller white as a ghost inside...'

Blakie's physical presence was bad enough, but infinitely worse were the whispers that followed him.

Blakie was a sorcerer.

Sorcerers out here can cure you or kill you, depending on the mood, and Blakie's mood tended to swing towards the murderous end of the scale.

He was occasionally called upon to save the sick from whatever was possessing them, and they did tend to make speedy recoveries, though my father contended that that was more from fear of their doctor than anything else.

But when the doctor had it in for you, that was it. You might as well give up the ghost, say your good-byes, start the sorry business. He could rip the bones out of your body with a single glance, send his *manti* – his spirit familiar – into your skull and suck the eyes out of their sockets, seduce your woman from the other side of a claypan, turn himself into a whirlwind and hurl you into the clouds.

Blakie's origins were a mystery. Some of the old people said they'd seen him as a boy, chained to a tree out at Kilyubatu, in the desert north of here. The Kilyubatu mob swore that he'd been raised by dingoes. Teddy Bushgate had it on good authority that he'd been thrown, fully formed, out of a volcano. Us kids, except for Hazel, who was strangely immune from the universal terror and seemed almost fascinated by him, called him Mamu: the Demon.

My old man told me once that, as far as he could piece

together the story, some missionary mob had taken the young Blakie to an orphanage in Adelaide, from where he'd absconded into the desert. He emerged years later, blistered, burning and mad as a car-load of camp cooks.

When the Moonlight mob were hunted off the place he stayed behind, of course: if Adelaide couldn't contain him, Bluebush sure as hell couldn't. And when they came back he was still there, roaming across the country, as wild as the whirlwinds that rattled the camp from time to time.

One of which whirlwinds, it appeared, was about to be unleashed.

Bindi pulled over. I had little choice but to do the same.

'Why are we stopping?' I groaned.

'Oh, more better we let him give us an earful now,' Lincoln replied. He'd always been pretty casual about Blakie. Lincoln had been in Darwin working on the wharves when it was destroyed by Cyclone Tracey, and Jack reckoned he'd been pretty casual about that too. 'Otherwise he might get really wild.'

If Blakie wasn't really wild already, I didn't want to be there when he was: he stormed up to the convoy, caterwauling and cat-walking, letting fly with a volley of spittle and spite which didn't diminish even when he got to Lincoln. If anything, it intensified: he halted, roared, dragged the poor old bugger out of his seat and hoisted him into the air. There must have been twenty people there, but such was the awe in which Blakie was held that they just sat and gaped like a load of slaughterhouse cows.

He had a fist pulled back, apparently about to belt Lincoln, when he suddenly stopped, distracted by something.

Me.

He stared at me with those ferocious eyes, and I wanted to shrivel up and disappear. He forgot about Lincoln, dropped him with a thud and moved in close to me. Very close: I could feel his parasites hopping over to check me out. His hair was as black and greasy as a morning-after frypan. There were desiccated grasshopper legs on his lips and dead blowies in his beard. His face was a mess of scabs and scars, his nose looked like the sort of thing you'd scrape off your bull-bar. I got a close look at the inside of his mouth: it was a *concerto grosso* of cold sores, hot breath and black teeth.

'Mechanic daughter?' he grunted, his curiosity evidently piqued. 'Em'ly Tempest?'

If I'd been thrilled when Lincoln remembered me, I felt horrified that Blakie did.

'Just passin through, Blakie,' I assured him. 'Just passin through.'

He gave me a look which made it abundantly clear that if he had anything to do with it I'd keep on passing.

'You bin city?' he asked.

'Been to the city,' I answered, nodding politely.

'Which?'

'Adelaide. And Melbourne,' I added, remembering that he was said to have unpleasant recollections of the City of Churches.

Lincoln, meanwhile, had climbed to his feet, and put a hand on Blakie's shoulder to draw him away from me. Blakie glared at him, yelled something I couldn't understand. The two men flew into a fiery debate – or rather Blakie did, while Lincoln tagged along behind, looking in turn puzzled, sceptical and finally concerned.

My Warlpuju was almost as rusty as Bindi's rifle, and

whenever elders were talking business the language became arcane, but from what I could follow Blakie was issuing some kind of threat. Or was it a warning? With Blakie there wasn't much difference: it's easy to be a prophet of doom when, should the prophesied doom fail to occur, you're crazy enough to make it happen yourself.

Blakie stood there snarling and growling, his great brow buckled, his beard fierce, his nostrils winged, his eyeballs snaking sideways. Something had been stolen. Or speared. But what? *Wartuju juntaka*. A fire bird? And someone was going to pay for it. I had no idea who, but Lincoln certainly wasn't his usual easy-going self.

The argument ended when Blakie suddenly wheeled about and gazed up into the hills from whence he'd come. We followed him with our eyes. Somewhere in the distance I heard a jet plane passing with a high thunder that sounded like an echo of Blakie's tormented mind.

'See-im that?' he growled.

See what? I thought. A plane? Big deal.

He stood for a moment, a wild, solitary figure with a corrugated forehead and a cavernous mouth, hearing what sounds or symbols I couldn't imagine.

Then he strode off in the direction of the camp.

'He's going to be our guest for the night?' I asked nervously.

'*Yuwayi*. Bit of a wild bugger, innit? Still one of our mob, but.'

Weird bloody mob. 'What was that all about, anyway?'

But Lincoln wasn't listening. He stared after the receding maniac, an uncharacteristically troubled look on his face, then turned his gaze up into the ranges.

'Lincoln?' I repeated. 'What was Blakie on about back there?'

'Mmmm? Oh that? Nothin. Just dreamin. Business.'

But he didn't look as though it was nothing, and some of the heaviest shit I'd ever seen – guys cauterised inside because a rock was moved, somebody speared because somebody else had killed the wrong animal – was 'just dreamin'.

The Dreaming – the Jukurrpa – is everything to the Warlpuju: a map, a mythology, a memory bank, a song cycle, but also a code of conduct, out of which you step at your peril.

'Which dreaming, Lincoln?'

'Mmmm?' He looked like I'd just woken him up, like he suddenly remembered he had a guest. He smiled the old compassionate-Buddha smile, patted my shoulder. 'Oh, not your worry, h'Em'ly. You got enough on your plate, comin home after all these years. Me I might head up north tomorrow, take a look round, see what ol Blakie's on about.'

'You want some company?'

'Eh? No, not this time. More safer you stay ere.'

'Safer?'

'Maybe.'

I was curious, but didn't press him. Regrettably, in the light of subsequent events.

He came to me in a dream that night, Blakie. Or a nightmare, a nightmare in which a big, black man, heavily bearded and caterpillar-eyebrowed, was hunting me over an open plain. I was running for my life, summoning up every ounce of energy my body possessed, but it was no use: my legs were growing heavier, my feet were sinking deeper into the drifting sand. When I collapsed, as I'd known I would, he loomed over me, staring, his eyes burning.

Then he crouched down, thrust a knife-like hand into my right side, ripped out a chunk of dripping flesh. He gazed at it malevolently.

A kidney.

I sprang up in horror and clutched the sides of my swag, grimacing. My heart was spitting sparks. Shit, I thought, I hate dreams! Been hating them for years. A kidney. Christ! What was that supposed to mean? Kidneys have got all sorts of magical implications out here: they're the key to the soul, the powerhouse.

I'd parked my swag out on the edges of the single women's camp. Typical, I thought: out on the edges, uncertain of where I fitted in. The handful of old ladies near me were snoring heartily or murmuring in their dreams. I checked the stars: they'd barely shifted. I'd probably only been asleep for an hour or so. Blakie hadn't wasted any time cutting into my nightmares.

People were still moving round the camp. Starlight glowed off the iron roofs. The windmill creaked. A dog barked, another answered, then the whole bloody lot joined in.

Blakie had camped with us for the night. I could see his fire up on Saddlebag Ridge, blinking and flickering and staring down at the camp like an epileptic eye. Looking at it, I felt vulnerable, lonely. A million miles from home.

I put the blanket round my shoulders, went and sat by Lincoln's fire. Stirred the ashes, brewed a billy. Still shaking. After a while Lincoln came out and joined me. He poured the sugar, then poured the tea and handed me a pannikin with a gentle, reassuring hand.

'You worryin for somethin, Nangali?'

'Just a dream, Lincoln. Just a bad dream.'

'Mmmm,' he nodded, running a ruminative hand through his whiskers. 'Bad dreams. You ave em often?'

'Often enough.'

He thought for a while, studied the stars, fiddled with the fire. Then he counselled me, 'Just wait a while, Em'ly. Don't worry. Don't rush. Just listen, look around. It'll happen. You been away too long. Take a little time for the country to remember you.'

I turned my head to look at him. He smiled, patted my knee.

Take a little time for the country to remember you?

You beautiful man, I thought. And curling up at his feet I drifted off into another dream, the antidote, this one. A vignette from one of the sweeter interludes in my life.

I dreamed about Hazel. I was nervous about meeting her, almost afraid, ashamed of the grief I'd given her. But this wasn't the first time she'd enriched my sleep. I dreamed of the time we climbed the tabernacle tree at sunset and sat in its branches, singing along with a choir of birds. And I remembered how, somewhere in that lilting chorus, just for a moment, I'd imagined I was one of them.

Somewhere in the distance a cock crowed. Or a crow cocked. It was hard to tell the difference. Whatever it was it sounded crook.

I opened my eyes and spotted a rooster sitting on a nearby fencepost. I'd seen better-looking specimens on Redfern rotisseries: it was evil-eyed, balding, with dagger-like spurs and a fierce beak, presumably the secret to survival in this dog-infested world. The sun was still out of sight, but a golden windmill radiated up through the eastern sky.

Dreams, I thought to myself. Bloody dreams. I could be bounded in a walnut shell and count myself a king of infinite space were it not that I have bad dreams. Even when they're as sweet as the one I'd just experienced, they're still a painful counterpoint to the reality into which we must awake.

I stretched out in the swag. Dew lay across the canvas, beaded the grass. The cold night gave promise of a clear day. I rolled over and looked into the fire, vaguely surprised that it was still burning. Somebody must have stoked it.

A movement on the other side of the fire caught my eye. A baby, sucking on a smooth red stone and staring at me with eyes like search lights. And, through the haze of the fire, a woman, poking at the ashes with a stick.

It took a second or two to sink in.

The woman was Hazel.

Rough Music

I lay still for a moment, a battery of emotions pounding my brain. Given the circumstances of our last encounter, it was only my father's assurance that Hazel wasn't here that had given me the confidence to come back at all.

'Am I still dreaming?' I croaked.

'Ah sistergirl, if you are I am too.'

Sistergirl? If only it were that simple.

'Do you hate me, Hazel?'

'Don't hate nobody, Em.'

'I never came back.'

She frowned, shrugged. 'I coped.' The rough music hadn't gone from her voice. Her eyes were still as lively as a stream of tea being poured from a billy at sundown.

Everything else seemed to have changed, though. Hazel had been the wispiest kid on the station, but the passing years had moulded her into one of the rugged matriarchs upon whom the community was built. She was tall, strongly built, languid in her movements, brooding in her looks. She had a smooth, round face, thick hair and a trace of China in her eyes, a vestige of the days when the Chinese and the blackfellers had sought solace in each other's company at the bottom of the shitheap.

She was wearing a white cotton dress, beneath which the

contours of her body flowed as smoothly as the country songs they sometimes sing out here.

'We come in at first light,' she said. 'Saw we had a visitor. Knew it was old Emily straightaway.'

'How'd you figure that?'

'Jesus, how many ways you want?' She swept her hands through the air. 'The shape of your swag. The size of your fire. The cut of your motorcar.'

'Didn't have a motorcar last time you saw me.'

She examined my ute. 'Nah, but if you had of, this is what you would've had.'

I nodded at the toddler: 'I hadn't heard you were a mother.'

She looked horrified. 'Neither had I. Jangala got another missus after me.' Around the time I left the station Hazel had been rather precipitately married off to Jimmy Jangala Lively, who was older than her father. He already had one wife at the time. 'You remember Winnie Broome?'

'Vaguely. She was married to Jimmy's brother, wasn't she?'

Hazel nodded. 'This little one hers.'

'Jangala's married to her as well?'

'*Yuwayi.*'

'Three wives?'

She shrugged. 'Sort of. Winnie come live with us when 'er husband pass away.'

'I'm lucky I got outta here when I did.'

'You be one of Jangala's women?' A smile flew across her lips, a thoughtful, appraising smile that told me, more than anything else, how much things had changed. I was a year older than her, and when we were kids I tended to be the leader. Now it almost felt like we'd changed places: she'd stayed put, absorbed the strength of country, while I'd been drifting about like a boat that had slipped its moorings. 'I don't think so.'

We stood up. 'Gimme a look at yer,' she said. She put her hands upon my shoulders, looked me up and down.

'Bout time,' she said.

'Bout time what?'

'Bout time yer come home.'

'Home?' I looked around the camp, then out onto the lonely, windswept plains.

'Well, yer best bet, anyway. Dunno how much longer you woulda lasted down there. Down south. Come say ello to the family.'

We walked over to her camp, Hazel gliding over the rough terrain with the smooth, low-slung gait that's a hallmark of women out this way. Her feet were bare and her soles were cracked, her eyelashes as long and intricate as melaleuca leaves.

Hazel did the introductions. Jimmy Lively was the same skinny-legged old bull-frog I remembered, hopping about the fire in a fetching combination of short pants, dirty white socks and elastic-sided boots. The news of his proliferating wife-pool did give a certain lecherous edge, however, to what I used to think of as the affectionate gleam in his eye.

I spent a couple of hours with Hazel's eccentric little family and by mid-morning I'd pieced together much of their story. Maggie, wife number one, had been hitting the bottle during the Bluebush years, but now that they were back out bush she'd settled down into a chirpy senility. Winnie, the brother's widow, was a dignified, middle-aged woman with whom Hazel had developed a relationship more mother–daughter than wife-to-wife. She was enjoying a merry widowhood, it seemed, and getting a bit on the side from some young *budju* in the single men's camp. She had two other little kids as well as the baby, but nobody bothered pretending that Jangala was the father.

Hazel's main claim to fame was that she had a job, of sorts, as the community health worker. She was at work now, in the casual manner of the bush community. Every so often some miserable bugger would come shuffling up as we were talking, ask for eye-drops or Panadol, which she dispensed from a drug cupboard in the silver caravan. From time to time she'd catch one of the kids, lather them up and scrub the living daylights out of them. She weighed babies, splashed the Betadine around, massacred hordes of head lice, lanced a couple of what their owners described as 'boilers'.

'Where'd you learn all this stuff, Hazel?' I asked her at smoko. We were sharing a cup of tea on the veranda of the caravan. 'Doesn't look like you just picked it up as you went along.'

'Did a few terms at the uni in Alice. Even went to Darwin. Wanted to go on, become a nurse – proper way, you know – but every time I got started I'd be called back to Bluebush for some family problem.'

I nodded. 'Speaking of which, how's Flora?'

A look of concern shot across Hazel's face. Her little sister had been a sweet child, but so innocent and vague you worried for her. I'd been wondering how she would have coped with the horrors of Bluebush, and Hazel's answer didn't surprise me.

'Ah, Flora,' she sighed, shaking her head. 'She was drinkin for a long time. Then, I dunno, she went a little bit *warriya* – crazy. Follow them Christian mob. Nowadays she's livin in the town camp with some whitefeller.'

We were interrupted by Bindi, who came rambling up with a kid under each arm: 'They got ear-ache, these *two-pella*,' he announced. 'Fix em up proper, eh Nunga-rayi?'

She put the cup down, passed him a syringe, showed him how to use it: 'You're a daddy now, Bindi. You gotta learn to do these things.'

'Why sure!' he burbled, enthusiastically injecting a syringe full of warm water into a child's ear. A vile, tiger-coloured compound of wax, pus and dead fly came gushing out. Bindi took one look, rushed out onto the veranda, vomited over the railing and disappeared.

'Ah well,' sighed Hazel, pulling on a pair of gloves and grabbing the child, who wanted to follow his father. 'One step forward…' She cleaned the toddler's ears and sent him on his way with a milk biscuit and a kiss. 'Gotta keep an eye on em, all this dust,' she said as she stood on the steps and watched him go. 'Too easy to burst an eardrum. Still, better'n sittin around Bluebush sniffin petrol.'

A mob of kids followed us while Hazel did her rounds. Two teenage girls seemed particularly drawn to me: Tilly and Cristal, the camp spunk rats, a pair of fifteen-year-old honeys with apple cheeks and silky bodies. They giggled a lot, brought me little gifts and poked around in my bag when they thought I wasn't looking. I suppose I must have seemed almost exotic to them. The girl who'd left the station and seen the world.

Nice to think that somebody was impressed by my less-than-brilliant career.

I spent the rest of the day in the women's company, and for a few hours I resurrected the sweet rhythm of my childhood. We gathered wood, picked nits, washed our clothes in Cissy Whiskey's cute little hand-powered washing machine. The girls and I went hunting with the old ladies, hooking witchetty grubs out of turpentine bushes and roasting them in the ashes of an open fire.

For dessert, I offered the girls the remaining hunk of my dad's 'survival cake' – a power-packed concoction of rye flour, fruit and nuts that he claimed would have kept Burke and Wills going all the way to the south pole. They weren't impressed. '*Phhh…!*' spat Cristal, grimacing. 'It not even made out of a packet!'

Hazel joined us when she could. She had as sharp an eye as any of the old women, scouring the baked earth for signs of life – tracks and cracks, bees, birds, vines – and hacking sugarbag out of a ghost gum with a ferocious axe. Sometimes she'd string along beside me, a tool or weapon of some sort on her shoulders; at other times I'd feel her watching me thoughtfully from a distance.

The camp was full of people, but Lincoln was not among them. He'd disappeared before anybody else was out of bed. 'Somewhere up north' was all anybody would tell me. I assumed he was following up whatever he and Blakie had been arguing about.

Blakie himself came down briefly from his ridge around the middle of the day, his powerful figure clad in a pair of khaki shorts and a layer of grease and ochre. His chest was furrowed with deep cicatrices, his legs were covered with the scabs and scars that are a legacy of the nomadic life.

He took a piece of meat from a fire. Stood there chewing it and staring at me, his nostrils flared, his jaw working. A piece of gristle lingered on his lips for an instant, then swivelled about and disappeared.

I shuddered and went back to the women, but I could feel his eyes burning into my back.

Late afternoon. The day going down in flames. Hazel and I climbed to the top of the Quarter Mile and sat there in silence.

I found myself being absorbed by the scene laid out in front of me: the angular women gliding back from the bore with babies on their hips and buckets in their hands, the veil of turquoise in the sky, the fish-hook moon, the gathering campfires.

And the woman beside me.

She was sitting on her hands, leaning forward, a thin smile on her thick lips, the sunset copper-colouring her cheeks.

She was part of it all: the air, the earth, the community. She belonged.

I wondered whether I'd ever be able to say that about myself.

Tom Waits Meets Tiny Tim

As Hazel and I made our descent from the Quarter Mile a cavernous station wagon came dropping doughnuts down the track, the horde of young blokes on board looking like they'd just invented testosterone. Dust whirled, the chassis groaned, the motor emitted the great unmuffled roar of the outback bomb.

A couple of apprentice cowboys leaned out the window, one of them upside down. They roared, sang, hooted and howled, saluted us with their green cans.

The upside-downer looked familiar.

'That isn't Ronnie Jukutayi, is it?'

'*Yuwayi*,' said Hazel.

He'd been a four-year-old the last time I laid eyes on him. The squinty, weasel-faced toddler had blossomed into a squinty, weasel-faced adult. His head looked like it was welded out of corrugated iron off-cuts.

'And is that Freddy Ah Fong in the back seat?'

She smiled. 'That's him.'

Freddy was Lincoln's half-witted, half-smashed half-brother. He'd never been foreman material, but now he looked like something out of a Mexican horror movie, pouring the contents of a flagon down his throat then waving the bottle at us in an enthusiastic greeting.

'Wild time in the camp tonight?' I asked.

Hazel didn't look too worried. 'They been in the Bluebush boozer,' she explained. 'Don't worry.' She gestured with her lip at the track, where Lincoln's long blue panel van was following them in. 'Any humbug, ol man'll sort em out.'

She wasn't wrong. The hoons were only half way through their first paralytic circumnavigation of the camp when Lincoln pulled over, got out of his car and blasted them into submission with a look that struck like lightning.

They slunk off to the single men's camp with their tailpipe dragging between their back wheels.

But Lincoln, unfortunately, didn't hang around. He seemed troubled by whatever he'd found up north, and went to have it out with Blakie, who was still up on the Saddlebag. Soon afterwards I heard raised voices, and caught a glimpse of Lincoln rising to his feet and throwing his hat onto the ground. Clearly their argument was unresolved.

I tried to get an idea of what they were on about, but the distance was too great for me to learn anything, and I was shortly thereafter distracted by a perturbation among the drinkers. They'd smuggled in fresh supplies – a slab of beer, a bottle of Bundy rum – and with Lincoln busy elsewhere they broke them out.

The noise level rose with the moon. As the night wore on there was a lot of drunken yelling and a lot of drunken singing, the latter about as musical as the former.

I returned to the single women's camp, lit a fire and unrolled my swag. Tried to get some sleep, but sleep was hard to come by in the general uproar. Where's Lincoln when you need him? I thought to myself. I hadn't heard him return from Blakie's camp.

Festivities reached their nadir when somebody began to accompany a roaring chorus of 'Midnight Special' on an electric guitar that must have been tuned by Deafy Jupurulla.

I poked my head out of the swag, studied them by the firelight as another voice entered the fray. It sounded like Tom Waits singing through a cardboard box at the bottom of the dam: rasping, tuneless, truly horrible. Then it began to yodel. Tom Waits meets Tiny Tim.

'That's it!' I spat, dragging my swag out into the bush and rolling it out behind a distant rock.

As I drifted off to sleep I heard Lincoln, obviously a man after my own tastes, roaring at them to shut up. His voice came from the direction of Blakie's camp, up on the ridge. Things settled down after that, though I could hear one of the drunken bastards snoring, even at a hundred metres.

When I awoke the next morning the snoring had turned to snorting, and it was in my ear.

'What...?' I muttered to myself. And what was that unpleasantly familiar smell?

Halitosis. Equine halitosis. The community kept half a dozen horses in a yard over near the mill. Had one of them escaped?

I opened my eyes a little further: there was a horse's head, huge and toothy, six inches from my own and dribbling green slobber onto my neck. It snorted again, nuzzled my cheek and grabbed the blanket with its teeth.

Shit, I thought, this is worse than yesterday's rooster. I twisted around and saw Hazel, high up in the saddle, her skirt hitched, her shapely knees gripping the horse's sides.

'C'mon, sister!' she grinned. 'Out of the sack! We're goin for a ride.' I took a look at the ragged animal swaying in the breeze beside her.

'Is that meant to be a horse?' I groaned. It looked more like a deflated camel. Tufts of hair, or maybe spinifex, sprouted from its hooves. Flies floated around its weeping eyes.

'More or less.'

'I'll take the less. Has it got a name?'

'Kids call her Nightmare.'

'Great. And you expect me to ride her?'

'*Yuwayi!*'

'Shit Hazel,' I whined, 'I haven't sat in a saddle for years.'

'You'll manage.'

And I did, more or less, my knees remembering what the rest of me had forgotten. She'd chosen the horse well: it crept over the countryside slowly and reluctantly, like a road-train in bulldust, while her own little stockhorse danced about and had to be held back.

We rode out to Jukatayi Parti, a waterhole a half-hour's ride to the north, for breakfast. Baked a few johnny cakes, admired the spinifex. Chatted so easily I began to wonder if we weren't beginning to re-establish the intimacy we'd shared as children.

The rest of the camp was only just beginning to stir when we made our way back in.

'You did all right for a *mijiji*,' Hazel teased, giving Nightmare a playful slap on the rump. Which was a mistake, the horse taking this as a signal for the only burst of energy she'd produced all morning.

'Why the fuck did you do that?' I yelped back at her as

Nightmare, living up to her name, pig-rooted viciously and bolted away.

We shot across the camp at a crazy gallop, or rather the horse did. I just shouted, 'Whoa!' and did my best to keep her company. Together we flew over swags and puddles, whipped up rubbish and reared at the startled sleepers. Having exhausted all other possibilities, Nightmare careered off into the scrub at the foot of Blakie's ridge.

I was just about getting the hang of it when a combination of log jump and low branch sent me flying. The moment I was off its back and flat upon my own the horse pulled up. It slunk back apologetically and began to nuzzle my head.

'Bit late now, ya sway-backed old cow,' I growled.

I stood up, gingerly felt my arse. 'Seems to be all there,' I said as Hazel came trotting up into the clearing.

But Hazel wasn't interested in the condition of my arse. She wasn't interested in anything except the scrub behind me. As I looked at her face it was twisted into a hideous vision of strained lips and hollow cheeks. Her jaw dropped, her fingers flew at her hair.

The little patch of scrub felt suddenly dark and danger-ous, its branches enveloping me like a shroud. I followed her gaze and the shock-wave shuddered through me.

The body in the hollow was half hidden by a rotting log, but we knew who it was straightaway. Both of us recognised the long, thin legs, the checked shirt.

'Oh…my *ngampartu*,' she whispered.

Lincoln.

I walked over, knelt down, felt for a pulse I knew I would-n't find. Touched his chin. It was cold and hard, a rocky outcrop overgrown with saltbush. He'd been dead for hours.

The blood from a massive wound in his right side had congealed in the dirt. I looked around me, helpless, overwhelmed.

Christ. What had happened to him? And what was going to happen to the rest of us?

Then Hazel began screaming and the camp went mad.

Sorry Business

All I wanted was out. The further out the better. I urged the horse up Kampatu Hill, then sat looking at the pandemonium below.

Sorry business. Something else I'd erased from the memory banks. The grieving process among the Warlpuju is fierce, prolonged and violent. When someone dies, their belongings are burnt, their tracks wiped out, their name never spoken again.

The Moonlight mob were the most intense I'd ever seen: they were going berserk. The camp had metamorphosed into a riot of grey ghosts and demons. Grief drove through them, churned them, occasionally erupted, like water from a blow-hole. A piercing ululation bounced off the hills and pounded out over the spinifex. The women wept and screamed, threw ash all over their bodies, the men staggered about, cursing and bashing each other and themselves.

I watched, mesmerised, as Ginger Napangkarti dragged a chunk of glass across her own scalp, a jagged web of blood springing in its wake.

Somewhere in the middle of this chaos was Hazel.

After a while I walked the horse down into the centre of the camp, leaned over to pull the radio handset down from its pole mounting and called Emergency Services in

Bluebush. I told them we'd had a murder. The woman at the other end seemed surprised only by the fact that anybody had bothered to call her. Murder was an everyday occurrence around here. She went off air for a moment, then wearily told me the cops were on their way and that she had other calls to attend to.

As I replaced the mike I noticed Blakie perched up on his ridge, cross-legged and gazing down on the scene with the cold indifference of a kite-hawk contemplating a swarm of mice.

'You mad, murderous bastard,' I whispered fiercely.

I turned the horse away.

Heading out to the waterhole I found myself weeping. My own little sorry business. A string of images came rolling across my mind, and, strangely, they were all monochrome and scratchy, like excerpts from the old sixteen-mills we used to watch on the back wall of the Big House. I saw a pair of little girls running barefoot across parched paddocks, laughing and leaping and weaving as a tall man on a big black horse came galloping up behind them, effortlessly scooped them onto the horse's rump, one at a time, and carried them away.

Jesus, I loved that man. And I *knew* him, knew the smell of his sweat, the scrape of his whiskers, the supple leather of his hand.

I thought about how he'd taken me in when I first came to Moonlight. I'd been confused, angry, bitterly grieving for my mother. Lincoln had twigged to me at once, paired me up with Hazel, drawn me into a world strong enough to sustain me until my father gradually emerged from his own despair.

And how had Lincoln drawn me into this world? By stories. Stories and songs. With Lincoln a journey of any description was a rolling dialogue with the country. A track by a waterhole or an unusual rock, a tree shaped like a woman or a circle of stones, the subtlest change in the landscape, any of these things was enough to get him going: he'd tell you the tale of the ancestral beings that had made it, the songs they'd sung, the paths they'd carved in the Dreaming. For a wide-eyed five-year-old he'd made the country come alive.

Now those stories were gone, that sonorous voice forever silenced.

Four hours, Emergency Services had told me, before the cops could get out from Bluebush. I gave them five, then headed back, not up to communicating with anything other than a white, official face. But when I did come crawling back into camp it was more of a red face than a white one that had arrived to oversee the scene of the crime. A big red face on a big red head above a big red body inside a police sergeant's uniform.

A police sergeant whom, on closer inspection, I recognised.

'Tom McGillivray?'

He turned away from where a couple of ambos were loading the body onto a stretcher and looked in my direction, florid eyebrows arcing down suspiciously. There was another jowl or two under the chin, more of a droop in the moustache, but it was the same Tom McGillivray who'd whiled away all those melancholy summer nights drinking my old man's home brew and listening to Charlie Bloody Pride on our front veranda. One of Jack's many mates. He'd been a sergeant then, and he was a sergeant still. The career path for a copper who chose to remain in Bluebush was clearly not a steep one.

I dismounted, hitched the horse to a post, walked towards him. He glared at me.

'Who are you meant to be? Calamity Jane?'

'Looking a bit that way.' I took my hat off, dusted off my cargo pants, shook his hand. 'I'm Emily Tempest.'

The eyebrows shot up. 'Jack's kid?' He peered in at me. 'Shit, so you are. Only you aren't a kid anymore. What the hell are you doin out here, Emily?'

Jesus, I thought. How long have you got? 'Come out a coupla days ago,' I said. 'Wanted to catch up with the mob.'

'Jack always reckoned you'd end up back out here.'

'Who said anything about ending up?'

He shrugged and pushed his hat back, ran a palm across a sweaty brow. What had been a fine head of hair was turning into a fine head of skin. 'Outstanding fuckin day you picked for it.'

I took a look around the camp. The Moonlight mob huddled among the humpies, their distress settling down into a mournful chant. They looked grey, unhealthy, moulding, like an overturned Salvation Army bin at a suburban railway station. Somewhere in the middle of the mob a boomerang was thumping earth. Two kids began fighting. Gladys rushed out, clipped them across the ears, threw them back into the huddle.

A couple of white cops had the young men corralled up against the shed, where they were trying unsuccessfully to get some sense out of them. Ronnie Jukutayi was clearly the chief suspect. With a face like that he'd always be the chief suspect. Freddy Ah Fong sat miserably tearing at a piece of yellow-streaked meat. A third copper was taking photographs of the hollow from which the body had been removed.

'Poor old bloody Lincoln,' McGillivray said. 'Dunno that I've ever seen one quite this bad…'

'Dunno if I have either.'

'We'll have to wait for the PM, but the ambos reckon – well, his neck's broken, for a start. But it looks like one of his kidneys was cut out.'

I felt a surge in the guts. Suddenly it was all too much, the tension and shock of the last two days. I'd thought a few hours out at the waterhole had calmed me down, but this latest revelation sent my equanimity, and the contents of my stomach, flying.

Crouching in the sand, all I could see was a splintered image of Blakie Japanangka, his ferocious eyes and his filthy fucking knives.

A kidney. Any doubts I had about the identity of the killer were resolved now. A kidney meant sorcery, and sorcery meant the madman on the hill.

'Emily,' asked McGillivray, putting a hand on my shoulder, 'you okay?'

'S'pose I am, but… I mean, Jesus…'

'Jesus all right. Or juju. It's crazy.'

I climbed to my feet. 'Have you spoken to Blakie?' I asked him, wiping my lips and spitting a mouthful of muck into the sand.

'Blakie?' He flashed an angry glance at the young men. 'Christ! Why didn't somebody tell me Blakie was here?'

'Maybe they were worried about your well-being. Lincoln

had a bit of a blue with him yesterday, and look what happened to him.'

'Blakie! Knew he'd kill some poor bastard one day. Where is he?'

I nodded up at the ridge. I followed McGillivray's gaze and watched him work out, just as I'd done, that the body could well have crashed into the scrub from its rocky summit. From Blakie's camp.

McGillivray put a hand to his mouth and bellowed at his off-siders: 'Col! Ross! You too, Griffo! Get over here!'

I tagged along behind the four cops as they made their way up the ridge.

As I reached the summit I glanced back at the camp and saw Hazel, in the middle of the crowd of mourners. She turned around and looked right at me. I detected a movement of her head. Maybe she was hunting a fly, maybe it meant something else.

Was she trying to stop me from doing what I was doing? Was she warning me? Or warning me off?

Whatever her intentions, I had no time to alter the course of events. The cops came marching up to Blakie. He was sitting by the fire, as solid as a termite mound, but not as friendly. There was a cold gleam in his eyes: it could have been a reflection of his mood or the crystal into which he was staring. Blakie always had a crystal or two about his person.

McGillivray eased his big butt onto a rock in front of him.

'G'day Blakie. Remember me?'

'Oh yes,' Blakie responded, not raising his head. '*Kurlupatu* Sergeant. Ma-killer-prey. Seen you travellin. Eagle wind.'

'Emily here tells me you had a bit of a blue with…' he paused; '…with that old man Kuminjayi yesterday.'

I was pleased that McGillivray knew enough about Warlpuju beliefs not to say the name of a deceased person – from here on, Lincoln would be referred to as Kuminjayi – but I was sorry he'd included me in his explanation. Blakie turned those terrible eyes in my direction. They were like slits in the side of a burning forty-four. 'Oh, she hungry as a hawk, that *parnparr*. Mebbe dove.'

McGillivray glanced at me, momentarily nonplussed. 'Yeah, well I'm sure she'll fatten up when she gets a bit of that outback tucker into her, but it's Kuminjayi we're talkin about now, mate. You know what's happened to him?'

'Yuwayi. Two-inch mudlark makin six-foot hole.'

Mudlark. One of Lincoln's dreamings.

'Anythin you wanner tell me, Blakie? Bit of an argument, was there? Got out of hand? Be easier if you tell me about it now, rather than in at the station.'

In at the station? Blakie didn't like that idea much. His sideways glance was barely perceptible, but it said more than some people say in a lifetime.

'This country… too many snake. Need fire. Bushfire,' was his cryptic response.

'Right,' said McGillivray. 'So you thought you better sort im out, eh?'

'Oh, fire sort im out itself.'

McGillivray nodded patiently. He'd been in the job so long he may well have acquired some competency in the language of the mad. Psychological illness was rampant among the Indigenous communities of the Centre, services to deal with it stretched at best. Cops were often the front-line troops.

McGillivray's off-siders didn't look so patient. Ross and Col glanced at each other, rolled their eyes. Griffo, a big flabby bloke with a high voice and a shaved head, fiddled restlessly with the cuffs on his belt.

Blakie sat there stolidly, as oblivious to the cops as he was to the flies that crawled around his eyes.

McGillivray scratched at the sand with a stick.

Griffo was the first to break. 'Look mate, we just want a simple answer. There's a dead body down there. We wanner know whether you might be able to tell us anything about it. Like whether you were responsible, for starters.'

McGillivray shot a jagged glance at his constable, but the direct approach did seem to elicit a response.

'Oh yes,' Blakie growled, 'I'm 'sponsible, all right. Very 'sponsible.' As he was speaking he'd been poking at the fire with a greenwood stick. He suddenly pulled it out of the flames, studied the smoking end for a moment, then snapped it in two. With a single thumb.

I studied his hands: they were like a set of Stilson wrenches. It didn't take much imagination to see them wrapped around Lincoln's ancient throat. Nor to see why everybody gave Blakie such a wide berth.

He was the only man I'd ever seen kill a fully grown kangaroo with his bare hands. I must have been ten or eleven at the time. I'd been out hunting with a mob of young blokes when a roo flew out of a declivity in front of us. The dogs gave chase, but they'd only gone twenty metres when Blakie suddenly shot up in the roo's path, threw it to the ground, whipped his knee into its back and broke its neck.

The young men had been falling over themselves to let him have the roo. But right now Griffo wasn't as savvy. He grabbed Blakie by the scruff of the neck and dragged him to his feet. 'Okay mate, I think you'd better come along with...'

McGillivray put a moderating hand upon Griffo, but Blakie already had his own hands upon him: one into the groin and one among the rolls of his neck.

Blakie squeezed and heaved. Griffo gasped. His transition from rugged outback rozzer to guided missile took about half a second, the length of time it took Blakie to pluck him from his feet and send him smashing into his partners. I dived out of the way as one of them came flying in my direction.

Blakie was thirty feet away and accelerating before Bluebush's finest had dragged itself up out of the dirt.

The younger cops did the usual cop things – a lot of yelling and cursing, a lot of pumping arms and pushing legs – but they ended up doubled over, lobster-faced and gasping for air. Griffo looked like he'd be going home in the ambulance.

McGillivray didn't bother. He knew Blakie. He climbed to his feet and stood there glowering, hands on hips, teeth clenched. Angrily watching his prime suspect cruise up into the Jawangu Hills behind the camp.

I Might Try

An hour later I was sitting in the dirt, leaning against a rear tyre and brooding upon the ironies of coming home. As McGillivray had said, an outstanding day I'd picked. I'd arrived just in time to see my utopia torn apart.

A stubble of burnt grass crumbled under my fingers. A low wind hissed through the poverty bushes that lined the road. Spiky leaves rained down from the mulga trees.

McGillivray was standing in the doorway of his troop carrier, barking orders and reports into the radio, drumming on the dash impatiently. His men had been consigned to the foothills where they were searching, doubtless in vain, for signs of their runaway.

He came over to me looking flustered, but then he took a look at my scowl, went back to the vehicle and returned with a cup of coffee.

'Got tea if you'd rather, Em.'

'Coffee's fine, thanks, Tom.' I took a swig. Sweet as a toffee and bitter as cloudy ammonia, but it did the trick. 'Been rustling up the cavalry?'

'Bloody oath. Alice Springs is sending up more men. Trackers comin out from Bluebush. Getting the chopper over from Tennant Creek. Blakie's done it this time.'

'You're not wrong,' I murmured. I was unsure whether he

was referring to Blakie's killing of Lincoln or his humiliating the cops.

'Worst thing is I had him in the slammer a few months ago. If only I could have kept him there, none of this would've happened...'

'What was he in for?'

'Assaulted some ringer he reckoned come too close to his sacred bloody stones. Over at Carbine Creek.'

That sounded like Blakie. The Warlpuju see that every element in the landscape is suffused with religious significance, a significance which Blakie defended vehemently. Crystals were of a particular importance to him. I assumed that something like this was what his blue with Lincoln had been about: a site had been infringed, a taboo broken, and Blakie had seemingly appointed himself judge, jury and executioner.

'Case clear as a bell,' Tom was saying, 'but fuckin Legal Aid managed to get im off.'

'What he needs,' I suggested, 'is a proper psychological assessment.'

'What he needs,' McGillivray responded, 'is a proper psychological boot up the arse and ten years in the slammer.'

McGillivray leaned against the ute and took a huge swig from a water bottle, his Adam's apple going like a jackhammer. When he'd finished he emitted a long, gravelly sigh and crouched down beside me. Beads of water dripped through his moustache and trickled down his chin.

'So Emily,' he said, 'where's that leave you?'

'What do you mean, where's that leave me?'

'I mean, I dunno if it'd be a good idea for you to stay out here right now.'

A brooding silence ensued, and then I muttered, 'I'll stay wherever I bloody want to stay, Tom.'

'Okay, okay,' he said, backing off as he saw my hackles rise. 'I'm sure you will. From what I've heard about you from your old man, you usually do.'

'And just what have you heard from my old man?'

'Jesus, calm down, will ya? I'm not coming the heavy, I'm not poking my nose into your private business. If anything I'm grateful to you for pointing us in the direction of Blakie. I'm speaking as a family friend, not a copper.'

I picked up a freshly fallen twig of bush mint, ripped off a leaf, crushed it in my fingers. Took a breath of its soothing aroma.

'You been away so long,' McGillivray continued, 'I imagine this place kinda loomed in your imagination, like some outback Shangri-La. But it's changed, Em.'

'I'm not a fool, Tom. I've changed too.'

'I remember Moonlight Downs when you were a kid. Sleepy Hollow meets Uncle Tom. Relations were mostly pretty good…'

'I do know that,' I snapped. 'I'm a manifestation of those relations myself.'

He shook his head in frustration. 'Not even listening, are you, Em? Same obstreperous little bugger you always were. Got your counter-punch primed before I've even opened me mouth.'

He stood up, took a step or two away, looking lost for words. Then decided to change tack. If words weren't going to have any effect, he'd throw in a bit of concrete.

'You stop into Bluebush on the way out here, Emily?'

'Bluebush? Christ, no, gimme a break. Refuelled at the

Resurrection Roadhouse and pissed off. I remember Bluebush.'

He nodded at the Warlpuju. They were still huddled outside Lincoln's humpy, weeping and keening.

'You didn't wanner stay there ten minutes – they were there for ten years. I lost count of the number of bodies I dragged out of ditches, drowned in an inch of water. The brains I scraped off windscreens. The early morning knife fights.'

'I have heard a bit about the Bluebush days, Tom. Dad used to give me reports from time to time. I gather that was why Lincoln worked so hard to bring em back out here.'

'And look what's happened to him.'

'Well…'

'What I'm sayin, Emily, is that things have deteriorated. Relationships with the whitefellers have got worse. There was a lot of bitterness over the land claim…'

'I heard somebody burnt the old station house down.' It had happened the week after the land claim court case was decided in the Warlpuju's favour. Nobody was ever charged with arson; there were a lot of Bluebush hoons cruising around the countryside that weekend, a lot of angry station people grumbling about their new neighbours. Half the local population – the white half – were suspects.

'And that was only the start,' McGillivray grunted. 'Sometimes I reckon it'll never end.'

'What'll never end?'

'The violence.' His eyes were half-closed, but in the thin brown slits I could make out the reflection of the trees. He scratched his jowls, stroked his moustache with a massive index finger, gazed into the distance. 'Even among

47

themselves. *Specially* among themselves. Chuck a murder like this into the mix an there's no tellin what'll happen. I just know I'd feel a lot more comfortable if I knew you weren't out here in the thick of it – for your father's sake, if nothing else.'

I found myself touched by his solicitude.

'Look, Tom, I appreciate what you're trying to do. But... well, two buts, really. The first is that I can look after myself...'

He rolled his eyes. 'You think you can...'

'Tom, I've travelled through some of the roughest places in the world, including a few years hanging round the edges of the inner-city Koori scene in Melbourne. If I can survive those I oughta be able to survive whatever Moonlight can throw at me.'

'And your other?'

'My other what?'

'Your other "but"...'

I took a swig of coffee, studied the ground. 'Not quite sure how to put this, Tom, but... I didn't just come back because I wanted to reminisce about the good old days...' My voice trailed off.

He studied me for a moment, glanced up at the hills, where his men were busily wasting their time, then sat down in the dirt beside me.

'Wanner tell me about it, Em?'

He was a big man. Powerful once, overweight now, with a flush in his cheeks and a trickle of sweat dripping down from the inner rim of his hat. But decent, I thought, under that rugged exterior, as decent and sweet as a jar of home-made jam. When I was a kid he used to take me, Hazel and the rest of our little mob out to the waterhole in his police van. I'd often seen him let blokes off with a warning when he could have locked them up, or settle a blue with a stern word.

'I've been away for what, twelve years now, and in all that time I never felt at home. Never knew where I was going.'

'Must admit,' he said, 'your old man was always a little vague about exactly what you were up to.'

'Don't blame him. I was pretty vague myself.'

'I heard you were studying geology. Jack said you were gonna make him rich.'

'Yeah, did a year of geology. Then I got distracted by Chinese, for some reason.'

'Chinese! What brought that on?'

'Started off looking at old maps of the Silk Road in the Earth Sciences Library at Melbourne Uni. Before I knew it I'd spent a couple of years trying to figure them out. Then I enrolled in a law degree, when I got so pissed off with what you mob were doing to us that I thought I could fight fire with fire. Didn't stick at any of them, though.'

'And after uni?'

'After uni I just…' – I shrugged my shoulders – 'floated, I suppose. Worked at whatever came along. Whenever I had enough of a stash together, I headed off overseas. Deck-handed on a yacht across North Africa. Ran a bar in Turkey. Travelled through Rajasthan – on a bloody camel, half the time. Spent six months wandering along the Silk Road itself. I was running so hard it never occurred to me that I was lost. Truth hit me a few weeks ago, back in Melbourne.'

I gave McGillivray the story. I'd been called up for jury duty. The feller in the dock was some fabulous creature –

part lawyer, part farmer – who'd been caught in a bottom-of-the-harbour tax avoidance scheme. As I watched him being sworn in, a thin smirk on his fat face, I was struck by a feeling of déjà vu. We went through the motions, but he got off of course. They always do. My fellow jurors took more note of the cut of his suit than that of his jib, and I wasn't on the ball that day myself. My mind was elsewhere, trying to trace the memory sparked by the defendant.

I remember the night of the court case I slept badly, my sleep lashed by dark dreams. At four in the morning I gave up. Outside there was a soft rain falling: neon lights were buzzing, hoons in crimson muscle cars were thrashing up and down the main drag. I was living in a dingy Northcote flat, working in a Turkish bar, eating a lot of pita bread and chips, drinking a lot of cheap booze. I lit a smoke, switched on the radio, fiddled with the dial and found myself listening to a station from country Victoria. An old Jimmy Little song – *the* old Jimmy Little song – 'Telephone to Glory' came floating through the static.

Suddenly it hit me, the memory that had been nagging at me all day.

It was the only other swearing-in I'd ever witnessed: Lincoln Flinders, giving evidence at one of the early land claim hearings.

'Do you swear to tell the truth?' they asked him.

He thought about it for a moment. 'I might try,' he answered.

Might try. I loved that, especially when I knew that he was talking about his dreaming, about a belief so ingrained in his soul that he quite literally wouldn't have lied about it to save his life.

I pulled on a coat, went for a walk, found myself standing on an empty railway platform watching the first rays of the winter sun struggle for a spot among the carbon monoxide. Rubbish drifted, cats prowled, weeds crept along rusty fences.

'And that,' I said to McGillivray, who'd been sitting patiently while I told the story, 'is when it dawned on me.'

'What dawned on you?'

'The reason I'd so often been drawn to other people's deserts.'

'Which was?'

'That I was running from my own. And I knew if I was ever going to have any peace of mind I had to come back to Moonlight Downs.'

And so it was that I found myself, a few weeks later, sitting in the dirt and baring my soul to a burly outback cop.

'May be that there's nothing for me here either, Tom, but I have to give myself a chance to find that out for myself.'

A ripple of tenderness scudded across his face, then he nodded and grunted: 'Okay, I hear what you're sayin, Em. But I still dunno if you'd be wise to stay here right now. I got a bad feeling about this. A feelin like maybe it isn't over yet.'

He looked around the camp, his brow furrowed, then up into the hills into which Blakie had disappeared. For a moment he looked like Lincoln, troubled by a premonition he didn't understand, and I felt a shiver rattle my backbone. Maybe he was right. Maybe I was being rash. McGillivray had, after all, spent twenty years working among whatever dark forces lurked in these parts, and may well have developed a sixth sense for them. If he was nervous, maybe I should be as well. But what else was I going to do?

'You wouldn't consider staying with your old man for a while?'

'I just come from the Jenny, Tom. I love old Jack, but do I want to spend my time sitting on top of a gold mine in the middle of a salt pan with him and his trained gorillas? I don't think so.'

'You could come with us, back into Bluebush...'

'Bluebush!'

He appeared to be offended by the look of alarm that shot across my face. I was, I supposed, insulting the place he'd chosen to make his home. But Bluebush! What a dump! The sort of town where it's easier to buy a silencer than a decent coffee. When we visited town, I'd never leave my father's side: as a little black kid, you could feel the antagonism radiating out from the whitefellers when you passed them in the street.

And what a mob they were themselves. A bigger collection of dickheads and drop-kicks you'd have to travel a long way to find: boozers, bruisers and substance-abusers, rockjaw Germans and lockjaw Yorkshiremen, grease monkeys and gamblers, meatworkers, meat-heads, missionaries, maniacs, men on the run, men on the dole, men on the Witness Protection Program. Peddlers, pushers, whores and bores, desperadoes of every denomination. You name it, they were there, drawn to the town like flies to a carcass.

'Tom, the only way you could get me to go and live in Bluebush would be if you were to knock me out, handcuff me and throw me into the back of your paddy wagon.'

Blue-Bloody-Bush

Sssskkk@@@###~~rrrxxxttt!

I was floating up from the bottom of a deep blue dream, but the noise ripping in through the open window of my Bluebush apartment sounded like metal on metal, and one of the metals had an ominously familiar crunch to it.

Was this some sort of local initiation ritual: you wake up in the morning to find some bastard's run into your car?

I checked my watch. Ten to six. Urk. The party in the flat opposite mine had kicked off at about the time most parties were winding down, presumably after they'd been chucked out of the pub. Sounded like one of the revellers was going home via my car.

I stumbled to the door, hesitated, then went back and slipped into a sarong. This was Bluebush, after all: if I went out there in my present state, I'd have some ravenous meat-worker devouring me for breakfast.

Bluebush. I still couldn't quite believe I'd been here for over a week now. Settled in, at least to the extent of picking up some underpaid bar-work at the White Dog and the over-priced abode in which I now found myself.

It wasn't McGillivray's admonitions that had brought me here. On the contrary, there was nothing as likely to make me dig my heels in as being told to go. My intention to stay with the community, however, depended upon there being a community with which to stay. At Moonlight Downs there no longer was one.

Before he died Lincoln had voiced his concerns about his people's willingness to remain on Moonlight, and he'd been proven right. Blackfellers often move away from an area when an important person dies, but they don't normally move hundreds of kilometres, which was what the Moonlight mob had done. Whether their motivation was fear, thirst or respect for the dead I wasn't sure, but within a day or two of the funeral the entire community packed up and pissed off.

Hazel and a few of the closer kin were the first to go, disappearing into the desert to complete the mourning rituals. When they'd be back nobody could tell me. Since the death, nobody seemed to be telling me anything.

Then Bindi and a car-load of young men went off to the neighbouring Strangeways station. And finally what little was left of the community simply chucked their gear into the three or four working cars and took the ominous road to town.

I joined them. No way was I up to camping out at Moonlight on my own, not with the Wet on the way and Blakie on the loose. It was only a temporary move, I told myself, a place to stay until something better came along.

From somewhere outside I heard an engine roar, a dog bark and a voice bellow, 'Shuddup, ya mongrel!'

I opened the door and spotted a monstrous four-wheel-drive ute, obligatory Rottweiler on the back, obligatory moron in the front, negotiating its way out of the opposite flat's driveway. From the dent in my own Toyota, I figured the driver belonged to the von Ribbentrop school of negotiation.

Surely he wasn't going to do it again?

'Oi!!'

He did it again, the bastard. Nonchalantly rammed my car out of the way and gunned the motor for a getaway down the drive.

I raced over and thumped his window. The bloke at the wheel gazed at me, a what-have-I-done-wrong look on his raised palms and curled lip.

Oh Christ, I thought, looking into his bloodshot eyes, I'm in Bluebush. This is what you get: head like a weathered gumboot, great wobbly arms covered in great wobbly tatts, face bedecked with something that wouldn't look out of place on a rotten grapefruit. Skinny in places, fat in others. Twenty-five going on fifty. Been taking deportment lessons from the Rottweiler.

'You got a problem?' he rasped. He sounded like he gargled on Handy Andy.

'Yeah! You! You just hit me car! Twice!'

The bloke glanced at the dented fender.

'Your fault,' he declared.

'My fault? Jesus, mate, you got more front than a bloody bulldozer. How is it supposed to be my fault?'

'Yer blockin the exit.'

I waved an arm in the general direction of the driveway. 'There's plenty of room for a car – didn't know you'd be coming along in a fuckin aircraft carrier.'

I was being a little disingenuous here: the block of flats in which I'd made my home was nicknamed Toyota Towers because of its popularity as a base for miners and other workers from out bush. The four wheel drives just about outnumbered the cockroaches.

My neighbour knew it as well. ''T's what ya need out here, lady,' he retorted, 'somethin with a bit of grunt.' He glanced disdainfully at my little ute, then began to drive off.

'Hold it you!' I yelled.

He ignored me, came very close to running over my toes. I thumped his dropsides. The rottie snarled, but it was held back by a chain. I judged I'd be out of range, and I was. Just. I grabbed hold of what looked like the most valuable items within reach – a Kanga jack-hammer and a theodolite – and dragged them onto the ground.

The bloke hit the anchors, jumped out and looked at the gear, his sneer rapidly transmogrifying into a full-blown glare. From the wobble in his beard and the spittle on his lips it appeared that he was getting a little agitato. Looking, in fact, like he was about ready to clobber me. His knuckles had gone white, his nostrils were standing at attention.

I braced myself, prepared to duck, weave or kick him in the nuts. But then he took a closer look at me and changed his mind. When I get fired up I'm like a thorny devil: small but fierce-looking. Not as horny, thank Christ.

Doors in the surrounding flats were creeping open, curtains were being dragged back, bedraggled faces were appearing. The rest of the neighbourhood was crawling out to enjoy the show.

You could read the bubble floating over his head: enough of a shame job belting a woman in public without making a mess of it.

'Look, lady,' he whined, ostentatiously studying his watch. 'I haven't got time for this crap. Got a job to go to.'

He scribbled a number onto a cigarette packet: 'This is Brad, me panel-beater…'

'Got your own panel-beater, have you? You do this sort of thing often?'

He handed me the packet, went towards the cab. 'Tell em Camel sent ya. They'll give yer a discount.'

That gave me a moment's pause. This fuckwit was called Camel? That had to be the worst name I'd heard since Galloping Big Dick died.

He used the pause to make an escape, picking up his gear and jumping back into the driver's seat.

'They'll give *you* a bloody discount, Camel!' I yelled at his tailgate, giving it a farewell thump as it rattled down the drive. 'Don't think I'm paying for this!'

I surveyed the scene around me. The sun had risen, as had the contents of the coloured jocks worn by the blue-singletted gorillas who stood in every other doorway of the courtyard surveying me back. All this early morning excitement was proving a bit much for their delicate sensibilities.

'What are you lot gawking at?' I roared.

They scuttled.

The debris of last night's party – maybe last month's party – bottles and bongs, pizza boxes and porno – lay scattered among the dogshit on Camel's little patch of weedery. The front door of his unit was agape, as was the gob of the bearded, beefy bastard enveloping the couch like a layer of molten mozzarella. Charmingly attired in a blue singlet, yellow Y-fronts and an empty rum bottle, this one was presumably too hungover to go to work.

A bracing aroma, a blend of smoke, sperm and stale beer,

drifted out on the early morning breeze. Lighting for this depressing tableau was provided by a set of fluorescent tubes glowing with that ugly pallor they assume as the day dawns around them, sound by a distant bass guitar and a set of hands unseen making mincemeat out of 'Smoke on the Water'. *Duh duh duuh, duh duh duh-duuh, duh duh duuh, duh-duh.*

I sat on the steps, head in hands, heart sunk. Christ, I thought. Bluebush!

The town had a population of some fifty million: a thousand blacks, a thousand whites, the rest cockroaches. The cockroaches were on the go early this morning, crawling around blinking at the light of day, their dark brown armour glistening in the sun, their feelers flickering. The weedy geranium bush at the doorstep looked as though it had struggled up through a hole in the concrete, taken a quick look around and was heading back down. Even the dogs yelping in the distance were wondering what canine-karma they'd accumulated to end up in this pissant town.

I was wondering the same thing myself. I stood up to admire the view. Still life in a mining town. Well, not that still, actually: the smokestacks at the smelter were pumping it up and pouring it out, as they did, morning, noon and night. The furnaces were blazing away with enough firepower to blind the angels. The battery was rumbling.

Over to the west, the green mountains – of mullock – were simmering and stinking. Further on was a chemical inferno: the retention ponds, with their hissing blue cyanic waters, their evil green banks, their sagging fences, their odd little toxic rainbows leaching out into the desert.

I'd been to the ponds once. Never again. Skull and crossbones country. You could feel the cancer stirring in your cells just looking at it.

Food smells began to waft through the air.

Meatworkers and miners were staggering out to tables all over town and getting down to the serious business of making their selection from the enormous smorgasbord of dead animals and their parts which comprised the Bluebush breakfast: schnitzels and mince, chicken wings, red gum, sausages and cutlets, rib bones, lamb shanks, pigs' heads, bulls' balls – you name it, it was being battered, baked or boiled in oil, chilled, grilled or charred in lard, filleted, fricasseed, skewered, stewed or brewed and demolished by the ravenous men and rough women of Bluebush.

Driven indoors by the radiant depression, I put on some coffee and some Louvin Brothers, made toast, lit a smoke. Charlie and Ira were singing 'When I Stop Dreaming'. Sweet harmonies and sweet aromas filled the room, but did little to ease my mind.

Another mess you've gotten yourself into, girl, I admonished myself. Another fine fucking mess.

When I'd thought about coming back to the Centre, the prospect of being stuck in this dirty dust-hole, this monument to red neckery and black despair, hadn't figured in my calculations.

Like a lot of other people, I'd ended up in Bluebush because I didn't know what else to do.

I found myself idly scratching shapes in some sugar I'd spilt on the kitchen table the night before. Almost of their own accord, it seemed, the shapes formed themselves into letters and the letters turned into a word: 'haze'.

Haze. The word was open to a couple of interpretations,

and between them they might have been bookends to the state of mind in which I found myself. On the one hand, a haze was what I seemed to have been floating along in ever since I first left Moonlight, years before.

On the other hand, something told me that if there was a way out of the fog, if I were ever to find a home, Hazel Flinders would be part of it. If I were ever to get a foothold in this country, it could only be with her assistance.

But would she let me? I'd buggered up her life once before. Would she ever trust me again?

She'd be coming back sooner or later, and I wanted to be there when she did. Not at Moonlight – not yet, at any rate. I wasn't up to Moonlight. The deserted outstation was too much to tackle on my own.

Bluebush was my only option; I'd stay here until I knew what she and I were going to make of each other. She'd said it was about time I came home. Well, we'd see.

I glanced at my watch. Getting on for seven. I'd promised to come in early, help Stan with the twelve o'clock swill, but that still gave me a few hours. I grabbed a book, slipped back under the covers and read myself to sleep. Since Camel's party had kept me awake half the night and the book was entitled *A Delineation of the Precambrian Plateau in North Central Australia with notes on the impinging sedimentary formation* – when I'm trying to understand a locality I like to start from the ground and work my way up – that took about ten seconds.

Party Girl

There were two pubs in town: mine, the White Dog, and the Black Dog, which was even worse. The main danger I faced at the White was the constant barrage of marriage proposals to which I was subjected by the old timers in the front bar. When things got frisky at the Black, you were likely to end up with a billiard cue through the skull.

We were generally frantic at lunch time, but I quite enjoyed it. I'd put on my running shoes and sprint from one end of the bar to the other, trying not to skittle Stan, who'd run the White for twenty years.

After lunch the miners and meatworkers scuttled back to their respective holes and sometimes we'd find time to join the regulars for a quiet drink. There was usually a comforting monotony about the conversation: I'd find myself counselling them against blowing their super on time-share apartments and Russian brides, laughing at their stale jokes and reminding them to take their tablets.

Today, however, was not one of those days. We'd been joined by a rowdy mob of blokes who seemed to have wandered into the wrong establishment and showed no signs of pissing off.

'Be more at home over the road,' Stan grumbled as I made

my tenth trip to the back bar, from where the strangers' conversation was rising into a crescendo.

'Hate to tell you this Stan, but they'd probably be there if they hadn't been banned last night.'

'Jeez,' said Stan, looking seriously offended, 'you mean we're gettin the Black's rejects?'

There were eight or nine of them. Station hands, I picked up over the next half hour, though not the kind of station hands I remembered from my childhood. The men who worked the stations back then were unworldly, shy, often awkward blokes who'd take their hats off when a woman entered the room. Country men.

These guys looked like urban refuse: stone-faced teenage mutants, toothless drifters in John Deere caps, a rat-faced Northern Irishman, a couple of leathery bikies looking for a place to lay low and a shifty, swivel-eyed little Pom who called himself a cook and who'd apparently given the entire stock camp an opportunity to lie low when he poisoned them with a green beef casserole. They were, it emerged, from Carbine Creek, a station north of Bluebush. One of Moonlight's neighbours in fact, though I couldn't recall ever having been there.

I was pulling another beer when I heard the word 'Moonlight'.

I tuned into the conversation.

'... so den the witchdoctor points a bone at em,' squeaked the Irishman, slapping the table, 'and the fuckin wallopers dunno whether to shit or swim!'

A wave of laughter erupted as a bloke with a backyard buzz-cut, prison tatts and tropical sideburns took up the tale. 'They reckon the sarge has called in the army to try and track him down! Choppers and dogs, black-trackers, C-fuckin-I-A, and they still can't find him.'

'Shouldn't be that hard,' yelled one of the drifters. 'All ya gotta do is head for the hills and follow your nose.'

This wasn't the first time I'd heard the Moonlight incident discussed in the bar. One blackfeller's killing another was nothing to get excited about, but the general consensus was that the killer beating up four of Bluebush's finest and making an escape was the best thing that had happened round here since the mayor was caught in flagrante with Benny Birkham, the town's one-man Mardi Gras. But I didn't like the way this conversation was heading. Coming from these guys it sounded unclean.

'All for a runaway coon,' yelped the little Pom.

'Shoulda just handed out more knives and let im finish the job,' interjected a yellow-cap cowboy, his teeth just about falling out onto the table in his excitement. 'Get rid of the lot of em.'

'Wouldn't that make Earl's day?' asked one of the bikies.

I found the jug was overflowing in my hands. I put it on the bar, a red mist falling across my eyes, but I'd only taken a step in their direction when I felt a hand upon my shoulder.

Stan. He was standing there looking at me, his eyebrows raised.

'You reckon they're worth the bother, Emily?'

I glowered at him for a moment. The red mist lifted a little.

I had to hand it to Stan. He was a little old guy with a stoop and a hump and a head that looked like it was being pulled towards his left shoulder by an invisible rubber band, but he knew how to run a pub. Tranquillity seemed to radiate out from him.

'No,' I sighed. 'Don't suppose they are.'

'Why don't you take a break? You been workin yer little arse off. I don't want a compo claim for, what?—RSI of the pullin arm? Go and get a bit of fresh air. Kaz can keep this mob tanked up. Come back at dinner time.'

Ten minutes later I was walking down Hawker's Road when I spotted a dirty police Toyota pulling away from one of the Warlpuju houses. McGillivray was at the wheel, and I flagged him down.

'Top of the afternoon to you, Tom. You do look like a bag of shit.'

He was decked out in crud-encrusted overalls, a filthy cap and topsoil thicker than most of the surrounding desert could boast.

His eyes narrowed. 'You spend a week crawling in and out of snake holes and see what you look like.'

'So,' I said with an innocent smile, 'did you get your man?'

If his eyes had narrowed any further he would have ruptured his eyelids. Not that I could blame him for looking pissed off.

'My man...' Tom growled. 'I'll be amazed if we ever do get im, way Pepper an Archie are doin their job.' He shook his head. 'I been workin with those boys for twenty years. Best trackers this side of the Alice, an I never seen em so arse about. If I didn't know better I'd say they were doing their best to avoid him.' He glanced at the house and grunted. 'Fuck it, I do know better and they were doing their best to avoid him.'

'Not a sign, eh?'

'Oh, we got signs. We got signs comin out our arse. Things disappearin from stations and mining camps, the odd butchered bullock, the odd rifle shot. Trouble is they're always somewhere we aren't. We know he's out there, but Pepper an Arch don't wanner come within a bull's roar o' the bastard.'

'You blame em? Dangerous man, Blakie. Specially for them.'

He started up the ute. 'Anyway, if it's all the same to you, Em – even if it isn't – I'm outta here. There's a hot bath round here somewhere with my name on it.'

'What were you doing here anyway, Tom?' I asked, pointing my chin at the house.

'Just dropped Pepper an Archie off at the family seat.'

A howling chorus erupted from behind the corrugated iron fence. Somebody was singing along with that black-feller classic, the Warumpi Band's 'Fitzroy Crossing'. Somebody else was singing along with something else, or possibly it was the same song, sung in a different key with some of the same words and a melody which occasionally intersected with the original.

'Sounds like the family's having a welcome-home party.'

'Same one they were having when I picked em up a few days ago.' More yells. Laughter as well, but it was that lean, desperate laughter which is only a decibel away from murder. 'In the words of Johnny Cash, the road goes on forever but the party never ends.'

'Robert Earle Keen.'

'What?'

'They're his words. Johnny just sang em.'

65

He frowned, shoved the gearstick into first. 'Whoever said it, he was a wise man. Give yer a lift?'

'Thanks, but don't worry about it. I'm nearly home.'

I'd only taken a few steps before I was sprung by the mob inside the house. A lot of the revellers were ex-Moonlight. They came pouring out the front gate and dragged me inside with an offer I couldn't refuse: warm wine, wet chips and effusive greetings from a score of old friends, half of whom I'd never met before.

The scene inside the house looked like a game of paralytic pass-the-parcel – the parcel in this case being a flagon of Fruity Lexia. When one disappeared another appeared in its place. The party kicked off on the front veranda, surged into the lounge room, trailed into the kitchen, staggered out the back door and collapsed under the saltbush.

I made my way through the crowd. My fellow party animals came in all shapes and sizes, all ages and denominations, the common denominator being thirst.

Gladys Kneebone, whom I'd last seen serving up the *chat du jour*, was cracking jokes and laughing like a cyclone. Slippery Williams was gazing at a television which, like him, wasn't properly tuned in. Jeanie Marble wandered up and wrapped me in a giant bear-hug, then subsided onto the couch and fell asleep.

'Jeanie looks like she's been through the wringer,' I said to Gladys.

'*Yuwayi*, most of the bloody ringers, too.'

There were even a couple of whitefellers among them. Whitefellers, that is, in the Territorian sense of the word, which is to say not blackfellers. One was an olive-skinned young bloke – a copperfeller? – with clean teeth, curly hair and a floral shirt. I didn't catch a name, but from what I could gather from Slippery's toothless introduction the bloke was either a Cuban or a Cubist. The other whitefeller was an old guy with a head like a radioactive strawberry and a name which sounded like 'Jack Derrida'.

'Not the deconstructionist?' I asked Slippery.

'Jack?' came the reply. 'No way. Bit of a pisshead, but he wouldn't hurt nobody.'

Jack's contribution to the discourse, 'Eeeeeaaagheeoo', was about as comprehensible as that of his namesake. He tried, and failed, to shake my hand, but the momentum kept him going as far as the laundry door, from where he was last seen raining death down on the pansies.

I wandered out into the backyard, and eventually found myself among the wallflowers – the old, the infirm, the insane, the Christian – perched around a fire beside the fence. They were a sea of tranquillity amidst a mighty ocean of booze. A billy was boiling. Tongues were clicking, teeth were clacking.

Prominent among the group were Archie and Pepper Kennedy, McGillivray's trackers, two skinny old brothers with patches on their pants and beards growing out of their noses. Archie and Pepper had been born out in the Plenty Desert west of Moonlight. They hadn't seen a white man until they were adults and could, it was said, follow a fish through a flooded river. They were sitting on their swags and sipping at pannikins of tea. Pepper silently handed me a brew as I joined them.

I took a sip, winced, then took another. Suddenly hungry, I pulled out of my pocket a packet of sunflower seeds, the only food I could find, and began to nibble away at its contents.

Pepper looked on with interest.

'What that you eatin there, Nangali?'

'Try some,' I said, offering him the packet. He picked out a handful, put them in his mouth, and immediately spat them out.

'*Man* eat this one?' he asked.

'Woman does,' I told him. 'This woman, anyway. I hear you had a busy week out bush with old Tom.'

''E bin give us bit of a run around the country.'

'And all to no avail.'

'Eh?'

'You didn't find Blakie.'

'Man I can foller. Dunno if that one man.'

'He's a bit of a man.'

'Bit of a man?'

'The arsehole. Why do you reckon he'd do a thing like that?'

Pepper looked away. 'What thing?' he murmured.

Were my senses deceiving me, or did I detect a sudden tension in the air? There were eight or nine people sitting along the fence, and suddenly it seemed as though they were hanging on to our every word.

'Kill that old Kuminjayi.'

Pepper took a sip of his tea, stared at the dirt, then muttered, 'Dunno that 'e did.'

My own pannikin paused mid-air. 'What?' I asked.

'Hard to say what it is bin kill a man.'

'Breaking his neck, ripping his kidney out and chucking him over a cliff will usually do the job.'

'Mebbe Blakie kill im. Mebbe *mamu*.'

Mamu? Devil? Yeah, sure Pepper, I mused. If it was, then

the devil had incarnated in the form of a wandering mad-man with a fighting stick and a bandolier full of rusty knives.

Whatever reply I was about to make was drowned out by a sudden uproar.

It was Lenny Coulter and his mother, Lucy: one moment two inebriated faces in the crowd, the next a couple of screaming maniacs who had to be kept from each other's throats by a pack of party-goers.

What the ante was I had no idea, but Lenny – about eight-een, camouflage pants, fluorescent orange T-shirt – upped it when he screamed at his hangers-on, 'Lemme go an I'll kill 'er, the ol cunt!'

The epithet whipped his mother to new levels of fury. 'Don't you call me cunt, you *come* from my cunt!'

Once would have been bad enough, but her pounding rep-etition of the phrase shocked her restrainers long enough for her to grab a star-picket and begin weighing into anybody in the vicinity of her son. When he retreated in my direction I scrambled over the fence.

By the time I ventured back into the yard Archie and Pepper had pissed off, and I took the opportunity to do the same.

As I wandered along the dusty footpath I found myself thinking about the tracker's comments.

I came to a vacant lot that offered a view of the north-western desert and paused to take it in. The country between the road and the sky was as bleak and empty as a cattleman's gaze. Somewhere out there was Moonlight. Somewhere out there was Hazel. And somewhere out there was Blakie, his brain wandering as crazily as his legs.

Blakie hadn't killed Lincoln? Like hell he hadn't. It wasn't just the fact that he'd assaulted him the day before, or that he'd virtually confessed to the murder. It had to be Blakie because there was simply nobody else in the camp who could have done such a thing.

I ran through the possibilities.

One of the elders? No way. Too old, too weak, too respectful of Lincoln. One of the young men, then? Was the devil involved, the demon drink? I doubted it. Sure, Lincoln had been yelling at them to shut up, but I'd heard them, seen them. They were in party mode that night, not murder mode. What about Freddy Ah Fong? I dismissed the thought as soon as I raised it: he hadn't looked sober enough to throttle a chook, much less his brother.

Could it be payback, then? Indigenous Australia, like tribal cultures from LA to Sicily, is racked by a never-ending cycle of vengeance. When a person dies, when a taboo is broken, when a sacred site is breached, somebody is inevitably held responsible. In the worst cases, the avenger will coat his body in red ochre, sharpen his spears, drag the dreaded emu-feather slippers out of their hiding place and set off on his secret mission of revenge.

Could this be the case here? Could Lincoln have unwittingly been blamed for some distant death or breach of a taboo?

Once again, it didn't seem right. Rough around the edges I might have been, but surely I'd have picked up something. When the red ochre men were on the move it was hard not to know about it. Everybody went to ground, stoked the fires, watched their backs, did a lot of whispering. Kids were hidden away, dogs let loose. There'd been nothing like that going on.

A maniac, it seemed then, was the only logical solution, and a convenient maniac was what we had in the turbulent, rolling-eyeballed Blakie. Everything pointed to the crazy bastard. It had to be him.

Why, then, was I beginning to feel the first little pricks of doubt?

A Ringer's Breakfast

A day later I walked into the yards of the Jalyukurru Aboriginal Resource Centre, the blackfeller organisation for the Bluebush region, and searched for signs of life. There were none. The nearest I could see was an immobile figure I took to be that of Kenny Trigger, the coordinator, stretched out on the office veranda with his battered boots over the railing and a battered hat across his face.

As I crossed the yard a puff of smoke emerged from a hole in the top of the hat. A good sign. He was still alive. Either that or he was conducting a DIY cremation.

'Morning Kenny!' The boots twitched in response. 'How's business?'

The hat rose slowly to reveal a ruddy, half-shaven shambles of a face topped by a mop of gritty hair and buckled by a wry smile.

'Boomin,' he drawled, the cigarette flickering on his upper lip. 'Come to give it another go?'

'*Yuwayi.*'

The Jalyukurru Resource Centre was a demountable office and a corrugated iron workshop on a three-acre block in Bluebush's rough-as-an-emu's-knees industrial estate. It was also the only way of keeping in touch with the bush mob. The remote communities were linked by a network of two-way radios, and Jalyukurru was its base. I'd been here three days in a row now, trying to raise Moonlight, hoping that Hazel would have come back in from the desert.

'Good luck! Albie Green come in from Blue Sunday Bore last night.' Blue Sunday was an outstation west of the Stark River. 'Dropped in to Moonlight on the way. Said it was empty as a surfie's socks.'

'Albie said that?'

He stared at the air for a moment. 'Maybe he didn't use that particular expression, but the meaning was clear enough. Moonlight's fucked. For now, anyway. Nothing there but wind and crows.'

I shrugged, trying to appear more nonchalant about the community than I felt. 'Things come and go.'

'Well this one looks like it's been and gone. Bloody shame, really. Had a lot of promise, Moonlight, but it all hung on the one feller. He was *kirta*, you know, the traditional owner, or one of them. But he cut it in the whitefeller world as well.'

Kenny Trigger cut it pretty well himself, if from the opposite direction. A whitefeller who managed the black outfit with the same elegant inefficiency with which, he explained to me once, Coleridge had managed the finances of his regiment: income into the left pocket, expenses out of the right.

'Kenny,' I complained at the time, 'that doesn't make sense.'

'Neither does *Kubla Khan*,' was his reply.

Kenny Trigger might have looked like a ringer's breakfast, but my father had him figured for the smartest feller in town. For what that was worth when the town was Bluebush. He'd originally come up here with a half-finished doctorate in anthropology lurking in the bottom of his back pack, but whatever academic ambitions he'd once held had, like the doctorate, gradually turned to dust in the face of a relentless Warlpuju lassitude.

Kenny shifted in his seat and bits of paper fell from his lap and hit the deck. They might have been raffle tickets or office memos, they might have been hefty government cheques – Kenny treated them all with the same dedicated lack of interest. Another skill he'd acquired from the Warlpuju.

A few days earlier Kenny had gone to get a bank loan, and he related with relish the bank johnny's bewildered comment on his list of assets – one twenty-year-old jeep: 'Jeez, mate, haven't got much to show for forty-seven years, have ya?'

But he did have another asset, Kenny, one that he couldn't have put on paper: his intimacy with the Warlpuju. He'd spent twenty years among them as a kind of transport officer *cum* drunk-tank coordinator *cum* pocket anthropologist. He spoke the lingo as well as anyone alive and was married to a Warlpuju woman; they knew that when the shit hit the windmill he'd be there with them.

'So who becomes *kirta* now that he's gone?' I asked.

'College of Cardinals is debating it as we speak, but er...' he took a final drag, flicked his butt out over the railing, and covered his ears in anticipation of the barrage, 'Freddy Ah Fong's putting his best foot forward.'

'Freddy? Fuck me dead! We'll have to change the station's name to Moonshine!'

Freddy had only ever been the most peripheral of visitors to the community, and now that they were back in town he was flourishing. He was living in the Drunks' Camp, north of the town boundaries. When I'd bumped into him a couple of days earlier he'd put the hard word on me. He needed sixty-two bucks to get a bus to Alice on a mission of great importance. He had the two; all he needed was the sixty.

The only indication of the kind of natural leadership skills his half-brother had by the barrel was when Freddy scored. I'd spotted him a couple of times trooping off to the park, carton in hand, a little fleet of fellow drinkers lapping at his heels. Freddy and the Dreamers.

'And the buzzards are gathering already,' Kenny added, his eyebrows bunched conspiratorially.

'Buzzards?'

'Freddy's been spotted being chauffeured around town in some distinguished company of late,' he explained. 'They tell me that Massie…'

'Who?'

'You dunno him? Lance Massie?'

'Rings a bell. Who is he?'

'Territory Government's local bagman.'

'Government's got a bagman?'

'Got a District Manager for the Department of Regional Development. Amounts to the same thing. Been here for years. Word is that the little greaseball…'

'Slow down, Kenny. Which little greaseball?'

'Massie, of course.' Of course. Kenny was the only Australian under eighty still in the CPA – the Communist Party, not the accountants – and I could see him salivating at the prospect of a little anti-estab scuttlebutt. 'He's been putting the word round the Anzac Club that there are some great investment opportunities going begging out at Moonlight.'

The Anzac Club was the watering hole of choice for the

squattocracy – the station owners and their toadies – and the town's elite: businessmen, senior public servants, mining executives, brothel owners.

'Invest in what? Wind?'

He shrugged, smiled, flipped his hands and rolled his eyes.

I took a look around. The dominant themes of the Resource Centre were rust, dust and wire. Little willy-willies struggled to get a rise out of the gravel. Mangled motorcars were overflowing out of the workshop. A pair of overalled legs protruded from beneath one of the cars. That'd be Wally King, the mechanic. One of the legs was prosthetic, a testament to his sloppy Occ Health and Safety practices. A hundred citrus trees sat under a shade-cloth in the corner, gloomily contemplating the fate that awaited them when they were planted out on the outstations.

Reggie Cobar shuffled past with his weekly rations: a carton of beer and a carton of corn flakes. Presumably he poured the one onto the other. Reggie was a dilapidated whitefeller who camped in the scrub on the edge of town. I'd thought he looked kind of cute, at first, with his Santa Claus beard and his ribbon of dogs, but the image soured when Kenny told me what he was said to get up to with the dogs. Finding a mate might have been tough in the old days, but it wasn't *that* tough.

I tore myself away from the scenery, rose to go into the radio room, then hesitated. 'Mind telling me something, Kenny? Given your position as an honorary Warlpuju elder and all that.'

'Dunno about the Warlpuju bit. Or the elder, for that matter. The honorary's not far off the mark, given what they pay me. Fire away.'

'What do you know about Lincoln's death?'

He winced, then shook his head and said, 'I know I wish it hadn't happened.'

'Do you know why it did?'

'Christ, who knows why anything happens round here?'

'Or who did it?'

He paused, studied me for a moment. 'What are you getting at, Emily?'

'Yesterday I asked something similar of Pepper Kennedy. Asked him why'd he reckon Blakie'd do a thing like that, and he reckoned he didn't know that Blakie did do it. Said it might have been a *mamu* killed him.'

'Oh yeah,' he replied, rolling his eyes. '*Mamu*, eh? *Mamus* are responsible for everything from an attack of the nits to a dose of the shits. Saves a lot of arguments, having someone to blame. Think of it as hunter-gatherer conflict resolution.'

'You heard Blakie was getting stuck into Lincoln the day before he died?'

'Heard something about it, but not in any detail. Mulga curtain's come down on that one.'

'Any idea why?'

He took a sip from a pannikin of rust-red tea, thought for a while. Face like a well-trod cattle-dog he might have had, Kenny, but he did have rather attractive eyes: they were like drops of dew on a blade of grass.

'Fear's presumably got a lot to do with it,' he said eventually. 'We're talking Blakie, after all. He's one out of the cracker barrel, that feller. No telling what he'll do to you, body or soul. Wouldn't surprise me to hear they were arguing, though. Lincoln was about the only feller round here who'd square up to Blakie without shittin his britches.

Course there's always the possibility that Blakie really didn't kill him.'

'Oh come on,' I said with a conviction I was beginning to wonder about. 'Blakie was ready to kill him the day before…'

'You sure of that?'

'Well, ready to belt him, anyway. Then they have another round at night and Lincoln turns up filleted in the scrub next to his camp. What's it look like?'

He leaned forward, rested his chin on an elbow. 'What were they bluin about?'

'I overheard them, but I couldn't figure it out. My Warlpuju isn't up to scratch. Blakie seemed to think that Lincoln had broken some taboo, maybe violated a site.'

'Yes?' He looked at me, wanting to know more.

'You want to know which one, but that's what I couldn't understand. It sounded like he was accusing Lincoln of having speared something…a *wartuju juntaka*.'

'Fire bird?' He studied the ground for a moment, scraping at his whiskers with a tobacco-stained finger. 'Never heard of no fire bird. I could ask some of the old fellers if you like…'

'I'd appreciate that.'

'But if it is connected with Lincoln's death I dunno that I'll get much more than you did.'

'If you could ask them anyway, I'd be grateful.'

He settled back into the chair, fumbled through his pockets for tobacco. As I opened the office door I heard him singing softly to himself. I was firing up the radio when he called out to me:

'Got it!'

78

'Got what?'

He sang another couple of bars.

'Maybe it wasn't *wartuju juntaka*,' he suggested. 'Maybe it was *wartujutu juntaka* – fire crystal bird…' I came back out and stood in the doorway. 'It's from the Diamond Dove Song Cycle, an epithet for the dove itself. One of Lincoln's dreamings.'

'Hazel's a diamond dove too.'

The Warlpuju regard themselves as the reincarnation of ancestral beings whose sites they have a duty to protect. Hazel's dreaming was a grey, delicate bird with rings around its eyes and flecks of white on its wings. The diamond dove.

Kenny sang another line of the song and a scene from my childhood assembled itself in my memory. Lincoln had just climbed a hill down the southern quarter; Hazel and I were tagging along in his wake. We might have been six or seven years old. As he gave us a leg up onto the rocky outcrop at its summit we startled a bird that had settled there. The three of us stood there in silence and watched it whirr away to the north-west.

'Poor little thing,' I said. 'We frighten it from its home.'

'No, not that one,' Lincoln told me. 'She headin for ome now. Karlujurru, that bird. Diamond dove. Home north of ere. Little bit long way.'

'How can you tell?'

'She Jukurrpa belonga we. Dreamin.'

'Jukurrpa. That means you dream about her, that dove?'

He glanced at Hazel, who smiled at him, then he turned back to me. 'That mean we *are* her. We diamond dove, just like that bird. Spirit way.' He tousled Hazel's scruffy hair. 'Me an this little scallywag ere.'

Twenty years later Kenny Trigger, sitting on this dusty front veranda, expressed a similar concept.

'Hazel?' he responded. 'She'd be more important than ever, now that poor old Lincoln's Kuminjayi.'

Hazel.

I wondered, fleetingly, whether she could have shed any light upon her father's death. She knew more about him and his dreamings than I ever would.

Maybe Kenny Trigger could fill me in.

'This diamond dove,' I asked him. 'Has it got a particular site?'

'Got a stack of them. Comes up along Hollow Creek, cuts across the Del Fuego ranges and disappears out to the north-west.'

'Lincoln was somewhere up north just before he died.'

'Well, if you're talking north o' Moonlight there's – lemme think – Kirripulnyu. Winnijari. Main place is Karlujurru itself, of course.'

'Karlujurru?'

'You know the Tom Bowlers?'

'Of course. Up near the Carbine boundary.'

'That's it. Karlujurru, the Warlpuju call it. It's the dove's main dreaming site.'

The Tom Bowlers were a crazy conglomeration of granite core stones up on the northern borders of Moonlight. If Kenny was right, and he usually was, then this had been the place Lincoln was referring to the day we watched the dove disappear.

'And if Blakie was bawling him out,' Kenny continued, 'that'd make sense as well.'

'How so?'

'Blakie's a self-styled enforcer in things traditional. If you step out of line – and a long, meandering bloody line it is, invisible sometimes, sneaking underground and coming up behind you at other times – he tends to dish out the punishment.'

Suddenly it was all too much. I needed help with this and there was only one person who could give it.

'Don't suppose you've any idea where Hazel's got to, do you Kenny? I can't help but feel she'd shed some light on all this…'

'Hazel? Could be anywhere. When a feller like that passes away, she'd have a lot of obligations. Visit his places, sing his songs. Put his soul to rest. She's a proper bush girl, that one. Even when the rest of them were in town, her and her little mob'd spend half their time out bush, roamin across country. I'd be careful talkin to her about it, though… Never know what you're going to stir up. She's been through enough.'

I scratched my head, nodded. Clearly there was nothing I could do but wait. Given what Kenny Trigger had just told me, it did seem fair enough to regard Blakie as the prime suspect. There'd been a breach, real or imagined, of some tribal law, perhaps something to do with Karlujurru, and Lincoln had been killed in retribution. Why wasn't I satisfied?

I went into the radio room and picked up the mike. 'Victor Sierra Nine Delta Bravo Jalyukurru to Moonlight Downs. Do you read me? Over.'

Nothing.

I repeated the call half a dozen times, without response. I could just about see my voice crackling out of the static and floating over the deserted camp.

I gave it another ten minutes, then Kenny came in.

'I've got to shut up shop now,' he said. 'If you want to keep trying, you can lock the door after you.'

I studied the radio for a moment, silent except for the white noise. Not something I wanted to listen to sitting here on my own.

'Thanks, Kenny, don't worry about it. I'll try again tomorrow.'

I picked up my hat and followed him out the door.

I took the short cut home, wandering through the back alleyways. I like alleyways, and I like perving into people's backyards: they're the window to a community's soul. In Bluebush's case, the soul was one of broken bottles, blasted grass, peeling paint and massive padlocks.

I was approaching my own place when a barrage of barks came slamming out of the yard behind mine, closely followed by a slavering, sabre-toothed German shepherd bent on ripping my head off. There was a cyclone wire fence between the dog and its dreams, but the second or two before I realised that were interesting.

'Fuckin dogs!' I gasped, my heart pounding. And fuckin Bluebush too, for that matter, since the two were pretty well inseparable. Whitefellers were forever whinging about the coon dogs, but their own dogs were much more dangerous. The worst you could expect from a camp dog was scabies, but if one of the town dogs got stuck into you you'd be lucky to get away with all your limbs attached. The streets of Bluebush were not for casual strolling. In this town a front yard wasn't taken seriously unless it had some canine killer baying for blood at the gate. Leather-studded pig-dogs, black-snouted shepherds, Rhodesian ridgebacks, Rottweilers,

Dobermen, Doberwomen, bitzers and bitches and brindles of every description were hiding behind every gatepost, ready to launch themselves like incubi from somewhere deep within their owners' twisted psyches.

I went into my own place, still shaking, and poured myself a stiff drink – to my regret, since the drink was milk and its stiffness was a consequence of Bluebush's restricted range of secondhand fridges. I put on a Lucinda Williams CD and flopped onto the couch. Lucinda was singing 'Sweet Old World' and, just for a while, I tried to pretend it was.

Motor Jack

The next morning I awoke, once more, to the sound of Camel's roaring four wheel drive. Got you now, I said to myself. I leaped out of bed, stomped out the front door and down the path. Out of the corner of my eye I noticed a swag on the front lawn, a hunched figure stirring inside it.

The drunken buggers are even camping on my lawn now, I thought in passing. I'll send that one packing as soon as I've sorted this other bastard out.

Camel had a couple of rotties on board this morning, big, hungry-looking buggers, their teeth like rows of bottled milk, their paws scrabbling over the metal tray.

So engrossed was he in his ten-point turn that he didn't see me until I reached in, turned the motor off and yanked the keys out of the ignition.

'Morning again, Camel!'

His eyes shifted in my direction, slowly and sluggishly. 'The fuck you think yer doin?'

I took a moment to answer, distracted by the lump on my lawn. A head emerged from the swag, a head with which, I was pleased to realise, I was intimately acquainted. The bloke took a look around, saw Camel and me in our morning conversation, climbed to his bare feet and began padding across the gravel with the hunched, tentative gait of a polar bear on hot rocks.

'Same as usual,' I said, turning my attention back to Camel. 'Trying to talk turkey.'

'Aw fuck off…'

The man from the front lawn made his way round to the other side of the car. He leaned forward, ropy arms on the window ledge, stomach taut, stubbies tight, blue singlet falling open onto a vast expanse of hard, hairy chest.

Built like a bull-bar the bloke might have been, but it was the bright blue eyes that held you – the bright blue eyes, at least, that held Camel. He put his head in through the open window and carolled, 'G'day!' He glanced up at me and smiled. 'Mornin, Emily.'

'Morning, Jack.'

'Everything under control here?'

'More or less.'

The dogs snarled. Jack looked at them and frowned. 'Whadder you boys whingin about?' he growled, and patted the nearest, tickled an ear. They sat back down, tongues lolling. He'd always had a way with animals.

Camel managed to tear himself away from this terrifying spectacle for long enough to ask, 'Who's this cunt?'

'This cunt's me father, Camel. Jack, Camel. Camel, Jack Tempest. Sometimes known as Motor Jack.'

'Nice to meet you, Camel,' said Jack. He extended a hand, but Camel was hanging onto the wheel like it was a barrel and the ship was going down. 'You the lad ran into Emily's ute?'

Not much escaped Jack's eye: he'd taken in the dent in my car, the location of the driveways, the look on my face and the keys in my hand at a single glance.

'This is the lad,' I told him.

He took a look at my dented fender. 'About eight hundred bucks' worth, I'd say.' Then he turned his attention to the inside of Camel's vehicle. 'Nice sound system ya got there, mate. Retractable, is it?' He put a huge thumb on the dash, wedged his fingers under the bracket and ripped the stereo out in a single, smooth movement. 'More or less.' Camel spluttered like an overheated cattle truck.

'Whadderye reckon, Emmy?' Jack enquired, holding the equipment up for my perusal. 'Worth eight hundred bucks?'

'No, but if it'll help Camel lie straighter in bed at night…'

Jack straightened up, cheerfully slapped the dropsides. 'Righto, buddy! Ya can piss off now!'

'Thanks Camel,' I said as I gave him back his keys. 'I needed a new stereo. I'm touched.'

'*You're* touched?' he snarled, then gunned it down the driveway. The rotties gave Jack a happy parting bark.

He stood and watched the Toyota go, feet apart, arms akimbo, big grin brightening up his face. 'Ah, Emily Tempest… the trouble you get me into!'

'Trouble? You enjoyed that more than I did. Besides, he's a miner. Eight hundred bucks! They earn that much by smoko.'

Jack looked at me in bewilderment. '*I'm* a miner. I lose that much by smoko.'

'When did you arrive?'

'Two in the morning. Didn't want to disturb you.'

'You should have. Come in and I'll knock up a big hairy breakfast.'

A minute later I was at the kitchen bench, whistling cheerfully and battering a steak into submission. Jack loomed up beside me, occupying the kitchen like a bullock in a burrow.

'Nice place ya got here, girlie,' he said, looking the flat over.

'Fuckin ace. And I wish you wouldn't call me girlie, Jack. I'm twenty-six years old.'

'You'll always be my girlie, girlie. But I'm serious. I like it. I mean, it's kinda compact, sure, but it's… appropriate, you know. Like you.'

I lowered an eyebrow at him. 'Like me? Oh thanks. You mean I'm overpriced, falling apart and riddled with vermin?'

But I was quietly smiling. Appropriate? Probably as heart-felt an expression of affection as I was ever likely to get out of the old bastard.

Soon afterwards I dropped the steak onto a plate in front of him, followed it up with a pair of eggs on toast. He pulled an ancient fob watch out of his pocket, put it on the table, began to hoe noisily into his breakfast.

'Timing yourself eat, are you?' I asked.

'New diet I read about,' he replied. 'Doesn't matter *what* you eat, long as you cut down the amount of time you spend eatin it.'

For a moment I thought he was serious, but then he grinned and said, 'Nah, got a lotta things to do. Just passin through, I'm afraid. Thought I'd pop in and see how you're getting on.'

He didn't look like he was in any particular hurry, though. As he ate, he flicked through one of the books I'd left on the table. The book was *Gouging the Witwatersrand*, a seventy-year-old history of the discovery of the legendary South African reef, the author a mining engineer by the name of Kresty Wagner.

'Still hangin on to these old things?' he asked.

'Sentimental value, Jack.' The book was an old friend. I'd lugged it around with me for years. It haunted me, that book, with its black and white photographs of blacks and whites. The book was a paean to imperialism, of course, but it said more than it meant to: its pith-helmeted heroes were invariably accompanied by a group of blacks slaving away in the background, smashing rocks, pushing trolleys.

Jack, inevitably, took a more practical view.

'Resourceful buggers, those old timers,' he said. 'Look at the Spanish windlass. And the way they got the dolly rigged; they're using a bucket, a rope and a couple of saplings to do a job we'd import a million dollars' worth of German machinery for.'

He flicked through the book for a few minutes longer, then mumbled, 'Can't stay long, honey,' through a mouthful of masticated Brahman. 'Gotta see a man about a map, then I'm back out the Jenny as soon as I can pick up a hydraulic hose for the excavator.'

But his eyes strayed back to the watch, and I knew his mind was on things other than hoses and excavators.

'I ever tell you the story behind this watch?' he asked casually.

'No, but I think you're about to.'

I knew the signs: the drifting eyes, the distant, rocky smile. Motor Jack marshalling his narrative forces. I've heard so much bullshit under the rubric of 'bush yarn' over the years that when I hear the term I tend to reach for the crowbar. But when Jack tells a story the stiffs sit up and pay attention.

'Isn't it the one Tim Buchanan left you?'

'Yeah, it's that, but for me it'll always be more Lincoln than Tim.'

'How so?'

'Lincoln and me, one time, we took a mob of cattle across to The Isa, and Tim asks us to pick up this watch e's had in the jeweller's. Bit of a family heirloom, you know. Anyway, we got an hour or two to spare, so Lincoln pulls it out an says in a way I don't like the sound of, "I've always wondered how one o' these things works. Now might be a good time to find out."

'"An just how do you propose to do that?" I ask im.

'"Why, take a look inside, o' course."

'Well I'd have hit the fuckin roof if there'd a been a roof to fuckin hit. "Lincoln," I says, "you touch one screw of that thing an we'll both be fucked. Tim'll feed us to the dogs."

'But Lincoln just flashes that old trademark smile and before you know it he's got the thing in pieces on the swag. Needless to say this is too much for me to bear, so I creep off to the pub. When I come back a couple of hours later Lincoln's got the truck loaded an he's leanin against the bull-bar, studyin the clouds, cool as an ice cube.

'"Okay mate," I growl, "where is it?"

'"Where's what?"

'"Where's Tim's fuckin watch," I bellow, "that you had in a hundred pieces a couple of hours ago?"

'So he pulls it out of his pocket an fuck me dead if it isn't runnin smooth as a banker's pants! Six months later I hear Tim sayin if the rest of us worked as well as that watch, he'd make a quid out o' the place yet.'

Jack eased himself back, stretched out his arms, gazed thoughtfully out into the strip of desert between the bitumen and the sky.

'Still can't believe he isn't out there, the old goat.'

Lincoln and Jack had known each other for thirty years, been mates in a way blackfellers and whitefellers weren't meant to be mates back then. I came up behind him and put an arm around his shoulders.

'He probably is still out there somewhere, Jack.'

He sat there for a minute or two, then gave voice to the question that had been lurking under the surface of our conversation: 'So what do you reckon happened to him, Em?'

'Blakie happened to him.'

'You sure of that?'

'Jesus. Not you too.'

'Me too what?'

'Joining the ranks of the doubting Thomases.'

'Just like to be sure.'

'I like to be sure myself. I asked Pepper Kennedy the other day. Reckoned it mighta been a *mamu* killed him.'

'Devil? Well, he wasn't wrong there. Trouble is, which one? Devils out there are thicker on the ground than termite mounds. There's big hairy ones and little slithery ones, there's black ones, white ones, there's goat-bearded ones and feather-footed ones. There's roaring mad ones and there's shithouse rat ones that'll pour you a drink and knife you in the back without you even noticing.'

I smiled, went back to the bench, gathered together the wherewithal for a pot of tea. As usual, a conversation with my father was turning into a maze of left-field images and non sequiturs, and I needed a drink myself. We talked and drank and laughed at each other's stories until we were interrupted by a knock on the door.

'Don't tell me Camel's come to get his sound system back,' I said.

Jack glanced at the watch. 'No, that'll be for me,' he said, climbing to his feet.

'I didn't know you were receiving visitors.'

'Told you, I come to see a man about a map.'

'I thought you were speaking figuratively. Like when you say you gotta see a man about a dog.'

He looked puzzled. 'Far as I know, Emmy, I never said nothing about no dog.' Metaphorical speech never was one of Jack's strong points; life in a mining camp didn't do much to encourage it.

Jack's visitor was a tall, solidly built bloke with fading blond hair and a rust-coloured moustache, maybe in his early forties, carrying a PVC map canister. He was wearing a khaki work shirt, safety boots and a pair of jeans with a big brass buckle. Jack introduced him to me as Bernie Sweet. The name meant nothing to me. I had him figured as just another bit of flotsam that had washed up on the Bluebush shore until Jack prompted me.

'You remember Bernie, don't you Em? He was working Pigeon Ridge when I had that claim over at the Golden Fleece.'

I rolled my eyes. 'I remember the Golden Fleece: more fleece than gold.' I took a closer look at my visitor. 'Have to excuse me, Bernie; all you blokes looked alike to me back then. Bunch of big apes covered in oil and sweat.' He didn't look much like an ape now, I had to admit. Bit of a hunk, actually.

He smiled, raised his hands. 'It's okay, I've had a shower since then.'

It wasn't until he opened his mouth that I recognised him. It was his voice: its smooth, deep tone, unusually mellifluous for this part of the world, and the touch of an accent. German, perhaps, or Dutch? No. South African, that was it. Nothing remarkable about that; the mining industry out here was a little United Nations.

I remembered a bit more about him as we chatted. He'd first come here as a young engineer working for one of the multinationals, but had left not long afterwards to do his own thing. The Territory had taken a toll, though: the first time I met him he came across as charming, confident, ruggedly good looking. Full of veiled references to lost reefs and bluster about what he was going to do with his fortune when he had it.

From the look of him now, he was still waiting. The voice was still there, but it was subdued. He had blistered knuckles, a slightly ragged edge to his moustache and a glimmer of steel showing through his safety boots.

'So how long are you in town for, Emily?'

'Haven't quite decided yet, Bernie. Not long, I hope.'

'And then it's back down south, I suppose?'

'Not quite sure about that either. I was hoping to spend some time out at Moonlight Downs.'

I caught a flash of concern in the corner of his eyes. 'But there's no one out there! Are you sure it's safe?'

'You're well informed.'

'The whole town's talking about it. I don't know that I'd want to stay out at Moonlight Downs,' Bernie went on, 'not with some madman on the loose.'

'Bloody oath!' interjected my father.

'Okay, okay…' I mumbled, holding up my hands in self-defence. The whole world, it appeared, was conspiring to keep me away from Moonlight. 'I'm old enough to make up my own mind. Can I offer you a coffee, Bernie? How about a freshly ground Jamaica Blue?'

'Hey!' Jack interjected. 'You didn't offer me one of those.'

'Thought you were a tea man, Jack.'

'Might have been once, but you've gotta move with the times.'

When they sat at the table I noticed Bernie glance at the old mining book.

'Check out the pictures,' I told him. 'Might see someone you know.'

He opened it up and examined the inside cover. '1928!' he grinned. 'Just how old do you think I am?'

'Anyway, mate,' said my father, pulling a battered notebook out of his bag, 'maybe we better get down to business.'

Bernie opened the canister and unrolled a folio of fluorescent charts I recognised as magnetic intensity surveys. Jack put on his glasses, leaned forward and studied them.

'So what are we lookin at?' he asked, the conspiratorial curl in his voice telling me that there was something slightly under-the-table about the transaction. Not that there was anything unusual in that: the mining industry knew about insider trading long before the stock-broking one did.

'Two linear magnetic highs, trending 346 magnetic north, Jack,' Bernie answered.

'What's the orientation?'

'Both dipping north-easterly.'

'And the strike length?'

'Fifty to a hundred metres.'

Jack ran his thumb along a grid line, then paused. 'So the outcrop I was telling you about'd be... roughly here?'

I soon found myself lost in the more compelling events in

the kitchen sink. I liked prospecting better in the old days, when it was just a matter of me and Jack bashing rocks.

They took a break when I delivered the coffee.

'So, where are you working now, Bern?' I asked.

'Oh, just a small show. The Impala, we call it.'

'Keeping up the African connection?'

He shrugged. 'I suppose so. There are three or four of us working it. Out in the desert, west of here.'

He was pointedly vague about exactly where out in the desert, and I knew better than to press him. They were all vague about the specifics, worried that somebody would jump them.

'Finding anything?'

'Not much.' They all said that as well. 'Bit of gold. Copper. Scheelite. Galena. Keeping us off the dole, but not much more.' He smiled, raised his cup. 'We live in hope, though.'

Bernie finished his coffee and left soon afterwards, and Jack filled me in on what the two of them had been up to. He'd struck a promising site out west of the Warren Ranges and wanted a look at it from the air. When you wanted a cut-price aerial perspective on things round here, Bernie Sweet was your man. He'd picked up – i.e. flogged – the maps a few years ago, while working for an aerial geoscience company, and made a bit of beer money hawking them to needy prospectors.

'Anyway, Emmy,' Jack said, rising to his feet and poking around among the books and papers for his hat, 'I better be on my way myself.'

'Where'd you park?'

'Out the back.'

'Bloody nasty dog out there. Watch it.'

'I'll do that.'

He took a load of gear out to the car.

By the time I joined him, he had the Alsatian licking his hand, frolicking around and barking in its excitement.

'See you soon, darling,' he said as he climbed aboard his four wheel drive.

'You talking to me or the dog?'

'Take your pick.'

The Alsatian farewelled Jack with a besotted yap, and I thought I'd take the opportunity to open up a dialogue.

'Hey, boy!' I said, patting my leg.

The boy went berserk, charged at the fence, barking ferociously and spraying me with saliva.

Jack grinned and began to drive away.

'Fucking Bluebush!' I yelled after him. 'Even the dogs are racist.'

All in the Game

I took a seat in the front row of the ten-tier stand among a sea of familiar faces with an excited, festive air about them. Bluebush's outdoor basketball stadium was distinguished by its cracking asphalt, anaemic floodlights and Con Panopoulos's fast food van, at which you could buy anything from a souvlaki to a pirated DVD.

The absence of any other entertainment for hundreds of kilometres in any direction ensured a sell-out crowd at every game. Tonight's epic was between the Panthers, the local blackfeller team, and the Schooners, something the police had cobbled together as a PR exercise. As such, the Schooners were an abject failure: they were hulking, big-footed bastards for the most part, a head taller than their opponents but nowhere near as skilful. More eloquent with their elbows than their hands.

Through my Moonlight connections I was getting to know the town mob, and they'd turned out in force for what was a rare opportunity to get one back at the cops.

Kristy and Linda Callaghan came back from the van with their arms loaded.

'What's for dinner?' I asked.

'F'n Cs.'

'Scuse me?'

'Fish,' enunciated Kristy, 'And chips.' She grinned as Linda slapped an arm around my shoulders and a tomato-saucy chip into my mouth.

Freddy Ah Fong was dancing around in front of the crowd, urging them on, putting a hand to his ear whenever the roar wasn't loud enough. They tried to get a Mexican wave happening, but it rapidly degenerated into an uncoordinated mess of flying objects: paper, mainly, but also hats, shoes, the occasional child. Gladys Kneebone threw a loaded thick-shake.

On the other side of the court, Kenny Trigger spotted me and raised his stubby in a cheerful greeting. I went over and sat beside him.

'Evening, Kenny. Come here often?'

'To the basketball?' He rubbed his chin. 'Well, I thought about popping down to the Concert Hall to catch a performance by the Bluebush Symphony Orchestra. Or there's a production of *Die Rosenkavalier* on at the Bluebush Opera House that's been well reviewed…'

A lusty roar from the crowd told us that the Panthers had scored yet again. One of the Schooners dismally brought the ball back down, and as he passed by us I recognised him: Rex Griffiths, the victim of Blakie's ball-tearing getaway out at Moonlight Downs.

I'd seen a bit of Griffo since moving into town, and I'd heard even more of him. Down at Toyota Towers the balmy evening air was regularly rent by the sound of music blasting out from one of the neighbouring apartments. Even worse than the hours and the volume was the occupant's taste, which ranged from Rodney Rude to Rodney Rude. I'd been about to call the cops on him once, then I discovered that he was the cops. Griffo. Tonight he looked like a walking experiment in the Second Law of Thermodynamics: he was falling apart, with particles of water flying off him at every angle. Either he'd just hosed himself down or he had an unbelievable sweat problem.

As Griffo approached the top of the circle, one of the Panthers – a skinny, good-looking boy in bare feet and a sloppy singlet – stole the ball, charged at a solid wall of Schooners and somehow appeared on its far side, then flew down the court and slam-dunked with an acrobatic leap through the air.

The boy jogged back past us and winked at Kenny.

'Athletic lad,' I commented.

'Takes after his old man.'

'Who's that?'

'Me. He's my oldest boy. Jar.'

'*Jar?*'

'Couldn't keep his nose out of the jam when he was a kid.'

The half-time whistle blew. I was rolling myself a smoke when a toddler came crawling out of the crowd, bumped into my leg, examined it with interest and began to ascend it. I gave him a helping hand, and he clambered into my lap and fixed me with a puzzled stare.

Hell, I thought, taking in the chubby cheeks, bulging eyes and blond hair. Bloody ugly baby.

The toddler's appearance seemed even more remarkable in the light of the young woman who came cruising along to retrieve him. She was as beautiful as the child was ugly: long legs, honey-coloured eyes, a body to die for and a blue dress that looked like it had been poured onto her and left to dry. Her skin was as shimmery and black as a crow's throat.

She gathered up her baby, then stopped, crouched down and stared at me, open-mouthed.

'Em'ly Tempest,' she said at last, and a sweet, vacant smile floated across her face. Kenny looked on with interest, obviously wondering if I was going to recognise her. It was the smile – or its vacancy – that finally slotted her for me.

'Flora!' I exclaimed. Hazel's little sister. She'd been a cute, slightly dippy nine-year-old the last time I laid eyes on her. Now she'd turned into an outback Naomi Campbell.

'*Yuwayi*,' she answered.

'So how the hell you goin?' I gave her a hug, made room for her on the bench.

'I'm goin fine.'

'What have you been up to?'

'Oh, just livin. Livin and lookin around. I got a lot of eyes.'

'You're not wrong there,' I said, although I wasn't sure what she meant. 'And you're a mummy now, are you?'

'*Yuwayi*,' she smiled. 'This little Jampin my one.'

The little Jampin, on cue, began grizzling, groped for a breast, then launched himself into a tantrum when it wasn't forthcoming. Flora placidly reached into her bra, pulled out a tobacco tin and extracted from it a handful of boiled lollies. He snatched them from her hand and toddled off.

'People bin tellin me old Em'ly Tempest back in town,' she said to me. 'Come home to the star country.'

'The star country?'

'You see em?' she asked, shifting her eyes to the heavens.

I followed her gaze. 'The stars? Yes, I suppose so. They seem to be up there in their…usual place.'

Kenny looked at me and raised an eyebrow.

'But can you see what they *doin*?' Flora persisted. She sniffed, focused on the sky. Her gorgeous mouth fell open. 'There's a little wind. You look closely you can see em blowin about among the tracks, like a lantern.'

'Tracks? What tracks?'

'The birds. They leave a trail through the air.' She nodded to herself, then added, 'Not everyone can see it.'

I remembered Hazel saying that these days Flora was a 'little bit crazy'. She'd always been slow-witted; now, it appeared, her wits had come to a crashing halt.

'Where are you living, Flora?'

'Westside Camp. Hard place, that one. Songs all broken, window full of screams... but we get by, my little boy an me.'

'You didn't go back out to Moonlight with the rest of the mob.'

She paused, shifted her gaze to the north. 'Moonlight?' she shook her head, sadly. 'I been there sometimes, but too much work in town. Important job, growin up this little boy. He gonna be important man one day.'

'Could well be. He certainly knows what he wants.'

She stood up. 'Better see what he's up to. Good to have you back, Emily.'

She took my hand, gave it a gentle squeeze, and was distracted by the whistle that signalled the resumption of hostilities out on the court. She watched the game for another minute or two, but when she turned around and looked at me her eyes were completely devoid of recognition.

Go Brother!

Flora blinked, shook her head and wandered back to the side of the court, where she was joined by a middle-aged whitefeller.

'So that's Flora,' I said to Kenny.

'That's Flora.'

'How long's she been like that?'

'Hit the booze hard when she was still a kid. Got the DTs, then she got Jesus. Dunno which did more damage.'

'Who's the bloke?'

'Les Crawley.'

I took a closer look at him: blue singlet, scrubby dark hair, every-which-way teeth. 'That where the baby gets his good looks?'

'Nah. Creepy's been done for attempted break and entry of half the swags in town, but he isn't responsible for little Jampin. He's only been in town a year or so. Shacked up with Flora a few months ago.'

'So who *is* the father? Whitefeller, I presume, and a bloody ugly one.'

'Nobody seems to know.' He leaned forward, cracked his knuckles and smiled darkly. 'Pretty upmarket specimen, if you want my opinion.'

'Oh?'

'As you might have noticed, getting a straight word out of Flora's not that easy, but after the birth she was wandering around telling everyone that when the little feller got a bit older he was going to get a – what was it again? – "a golden chariot with eyes like fire".'

'Sounds almost biblical. Don't tell me there's been another bible-basher over the back fence.' During my younger days we'd had a rash of randy priests and pastors at whose hands the expression 'missionary position' took on a whole new meaning.

'No, don't think so. Things have gone quiet on that front in recent years. All we've got now are the Little Sisters of the Poor and a couple of middle-aged Inland Mission ladies who're more interested in each other than anybody else. The way it looks to me, you've got some toff…'

'Why a toff?' I pointed an accusatory finger at him. 'This wouldn't be your left-wing bias rearing its lovely head?'

'Bias? Me?' He threw his head back and laughed. 'Jesus, Emily, life's going to be interesting with you around. No, I'm going for the silvertail because whoever it was, he tried to keep it quiet. Back alley job. Your tin-tails – riff-raff like Les – couldn't care who knows about what they get up to. No, some bugger's knocked her up, then fed her a line about giving the kid something – a motorcar, I suppose, if she'll keep quiet about it. God knows, there's no shortage of candidates – place is full of whitefellers who'd get all hot and sweaty over a good-lookin lass like that.'

I let it slide. Not much I could do about it, and such liaisons had been going on for generations. I returned my attention to the basketball, where things were hotting up. The second half looked like being even more fiery than the first; little skirmishes broke out behind the play, and the referee struggled to keep a lid on things.

The circuit-breaker came from an unexpected source. A dusty four wheel drive rolled up and a young bloke climbed out of the cab and spent a few minutes checking out the game. He was wearing what would have looked like a police uniform – khaki shorts and shirt – were it not for the addition of a little red beanie. When yet another skirmish broke out, he wandered over and spoke to the Schooners bench, pulled on a purple singlet and joined the game. The boost to the coppers' fortunes was immediate. It didn't come from his speed – when he dribbled the ball he seemed to go wandering down the court with all the urgency of a cow coming home at sunset. Nor did it come from his height – no more than average. But he did have a knack of quietly appearing in the right spot when the ball was coming down, and casually lobbing baskets from the three-point line.

Even more important than his contribution to the scorecard, though, was his contribution to the atmosphere. Whenever Jar performed one of his magic steals, the newcomer would throw up his hands in mock despair and watch with wry pleasure as the boy flew down the court. When his own long bombs landed he seemed surprised, and it was only the fact that they landed as often as they did that made you realise there was more class than arse about them.

His team-mates sparked up when he joined them, but what really surprised me was that the crowd seemed to appreciate him almost as much as their own players; Freddy acknowledged his plays with a roaring 'Go brother!' and the Callaghan sisters looked like they were positively tonguing for him.

'Bloke seems popular,' I said to Kenny, 'for a cop.'

'Jojo? Aye, they appreciate a character when they see one, this mob. But he's not a cop.'

I took a closer look at the insignia on his vehicle. Parks and Wildlife Commission.

A sudden scream from the crowd distracted us. Flora's little Jampin had wandered out onto the court and was standing there, wobbling on his feet and watching in fascination as the crush of players bore down upon him. The men attempted a scrambled halt, but it wasn't going to be quick enough.

Moments before the stampede struck, the bloke in the red beanie, who until then had been loping along behind the pack, somehow appeared at its front. He scooped Jampin up and cradled him in his arms as the flying squad fell in a heap around them.

Kenny whistled. 'That was close.'

The game finished soon afterwards, but the cheers were drowned out by a heavy crane truck that came rumbling in through the front gate. It had the words *Jalyukurru Resource Centre* emblazoned on the door.

'Bloody hell,' muttered Kenny as two young blackfellers in blue singlets and baseball caps climbed down from the cab and sheepishly made their way to where we sat.

'Who's this?' I asked.

'Clive James.'

'The writer?'

'The water works team.' He called out to the two men as they approached. 'Why'd you bring the truck, fellers? Taxi didn't arrive on time?'

'I'm Clive,' said the feller in the red cap, ignoring Kenny and accepting my proffered hand.

'And I'm…' said Yellow Cap.

'Let me guess. James?'

'*Yuwayi*. How'd you know?'

'Boys have been down Kupulyu, checking out the new long-drop dunnies,' said Kenny. 'We just put em in a few weeks ago – Tuesday I get a call from Johnny Friday telling me they're blocked. Told him they don't get blocked – they're just a hole in the ground.' He turned to James. 'What was in them?'

'Everythin,' said Clive. 'Bottles, cans, kangaroo bones, car parts. Mob out there been usin em as a rubbish hole. One of em even had an old pram stuffed down it.'

A voice from over my shoulder cut into the conversation: 'Did you check for a baby?'

I looked around. The speaker was the latecoming Schooner, the feller with the red beanie. What was it they'd called him? Jojo. He was standing at a bench near ours, towelling his torso – and, I couldn't help but notice, a pleasant torso it was – mulga brown, muscular, with a smattering of chest hair and the fluidity of movement that seems to speak more of the bush than the gym.

'Jojo!' exclaimed Clive. 'When'd you get back in?'

'Half-time.'

'You musta put the foot down.'

'Wasn't driving a semi-trailer, mate. And Kenny,' he added, 'don't go knocking Clive and James for being late – they've been working their arses off.'

'We had to dig new holes,' explained Clive. 'Move the toilets. Jojo give us a hand. Drove the backhoe.'

'Very multi-skilled,' I said. 'Was that parks or wildlife?'

'Wildlife,' he grinned. 'Definitely.' He dragged a singlet

down his chest and walked over to join us, still drying his hair.

'Jojo,' Kenny said with unusual formality, 'like you to meet Emily Tempest.'

'Not Motor Jack's daughter?' His face lit up: he was dark eyed, dark haired, with a day or two's beard and lines around his eyes that suggested either a lot of sun or a lot of laughter. 'Heard there was a daughter somewhere, but I never believed she wasn't another one of his tall tales.'

'Dunno if I ever quite believed it myself.'

'Jojo Kelly,' he said, shaking my hand.

'Jojo? What sort of a name is that?'

'Wasn't my idea – blame my mother.'

'She stuttered?'

'She was a Beatles fan.'

'Jojo was a man who thought he was a woman!'

'*Loner*,' he said sternly.

The water works team were looking restless. 'We better take the truck round to the yard, Kenny,' said Clive.

'*Yuwayi*,' added James. 'We wanner get back in time to see the fight.'

Clive frowned, and Jojo looked up with interest.

'Do they issue a timetable for that sort of thing around here?' I asked.

'Just about,' said James. 'Last night, Billy Winter got beaten up by a couple of meatworkers out back of the Black Dog. Tonight he's bringin his brothers back for a rematch.'

Jojo frowned. 'Danny be there too?'

'*Yuwayi*.'

'Shit. Danny's supposed to be going out bush with me tomorrow. Better go and fish him out.'

'Better hurry,' said James. 'There they go now.' A huge

yellow panel van came cruising low and loud down the street outside the sports ground, headed towards the centre of town.

Jojo followed the car with his eyes. 'See you guys later,' he said. 'Nice to meet you, Emily.' He shambled off towards his car, feet bare, hands in pockets, a towel draped over his shoulder. As I watched he gave a little hip-swerve and shuffle, as if there was a tune playing in his head and he just couldn't resist the beat.

'Jesus Kenny, don't tell me he's really going down to the Black to stick his beak into a fight,' I said as Jojo hopped into the cab, snapping his fingers. 'He seemed like such a nice boy.'

'Yeah,' Kenny drawled. He threw me a speculative glance. 'He did, didn't he?'

A Dirty Green Cardigan
Caught in the Windbreak

The next afternoon I went back down to the Jalyukurru Resource Centre for the usual bemusing conversation with Kenny Trigger and the usual depressing conversation with the ether in my attempts to raise Moonlight Downs on the radio.

I was climbing despondently to my feet when a single word came whispering back through the static.

'Emily…?'

I sat back down, my heart galloping. The voice was Hazel's.

'Victor Sierra Nine Delta Bravo Jalyukurru to Moonlight Downs. That you, Hazel? Over.'

'*Yuwayi*,' she replied. 'Over,' she added, belatedly remembering her radio etiquette.

'Oh Hazel,' I cried, ignoring the etiquette myself, 'it's so good to hear you. Are you okay?'

'Oh, you know…' I could picture her standing beside the radio, her shoulders shrugging. 'It's wintertime…'

'So who have you got there with you? When'd you get back to camp?'

'We come in last night. Just me an the family here now. Others have gone on into Bluebush.'

'You got a workin motorcar?'

'We had one.'

'Had?'

'Only got as far as the camp. Jangala got it up on blocks already.'

'Hazel, I'm dying to see you. When can I come?'

I lost her reply in a wave of static, then my heart lifted as she repeated it. 'How bout now?'

'Can't come right now, Haze. Gimme a bit of time to get me shit together. Tomorrow morning okay?'

'Lookin forward to tomorrow, Emmy.'

'So am I, Hazel.'

I spent the rest of the day in a state of restless anticipation, picking up supplies and loading the ute, but when I reached Moonlight Downs the next morning the heavy-duty desolation of the place smacked me in the face. I pulled up at a deserted humpy and took in the signs and symptoms of its sudden abandonment: the blistered frypan on the dead fire, the armless doll, the dirty green cardigan caught in the windbreak. Little mounds of grey sand were piling up against the walls.

Worst of all was the wind itself, a restless, unsettling spirit which skittered through the camp and lifted the odd willy-willy of rubbish into the air. Tumbleweeds rolled and spinifex crept. The desert, it appeared, was reclaiming its own.

And Hazel looked like collateral damage.

The delight she'd shown at the sound of my voice on the radio had evaporated now that she'd taken in the wreckage of her community. I walked over to where she sat by the fire, alone.

'Hey sister!' she said, smiling wanly into my eyes.

I crouched low, touched the back of her hand. Her own eyes were all that was left of the old rough beauty: they were like pools of water in a blasted quarry. For the rest, she was all battered passion and fatigue. Her hair had been hacked off, streaks of ash ran across her face and down her neck.

'Hey sister,' I answered with all the cheer I could muster. 'How are you going?'

She shrugged, glanced at the camp. 'You know… pluggin away. Lonely out here with everybody buggered off.'

'Give em time, Haze. They'll be back – long as there's someone here to show the way.'

I leaned forward, took her hands in mine. 'Hazel, I haven't had a chance to say this yet, but I did want to tell you how sorry I am for your loss.' This was the first time I'd been alone with her since the chaos that followed her father's death.

'I know that, Em. It's your loss too.'

She turned away, studied the ground, looked as if she'd aged ten years. It was grief. You could feel it. You could almost touch it. Not just for her old man, but for her community, her mob. Without them she was only half alive. I had a sudden vision of her as the last of her people, a lonely misfit prowling out on the edge of the powder country while the rest of the mob were living it up in town.

When we were kids I'd sometimes found myself wondering whether Hazel didn't feel some kind of affinity with Blakie. She'd run, screaming and giggling like the rest of us, when he hove into view, but I'd catch her glancing back at him with a delicious fascination in her eyes.

Looking at her now I could see how much the two of them had in common: they were both visionaries, both travellers in the world of dreams. The difference was that Hazel's was a more generous vision, something she tried to communicate to others; she wanted to go places, sure, but she wanted to bring her people with her. Blakie's, on the other hand… well, I'd seen what Blakie's could do.

But even Hazel's vision was of little use when there was nobody to share it, when the people to whom it should have meant the most were getting their dreams from a TV or a green can.

I slung an arm across her shoulders. Don't worry, I wanted to tell her, and maybe did in some obscure way. It isn't your fault. It isn't just you and it isn't just here: I've seen it everywhere from China to Africa: the whole world's moving into town.

I thought about the fifteen-year-old Hazel I'd left behind: quirky, eclectic, eccentric, but when something was important to her, as tough as a drop forge.

She wasn't going anywhere, and I loved her for it. Buffeted by the wind and drained by the loneliness she might have been, but she was staying put. She was her father's daughter.

'How long can you stay?' she asked me.

'Just a day or two. I've got to be back at work tomorrow night. I'll be able to come out for a longer stay in a week or so.'

A dog appeared, then another, then a pack of them, loping in from the scrub. Jimmy Lively and Maggie weren't far behind them, marching back into camp in a cloud of dust and flies and dropping a porcupine onto the fire. Winnie came out of the shack with her kids and Hazel brightened up. All of a sudden the atmosphere didn't seem so oppressive.

The old bloke's eyes lit up like blown coal when he spotted the supplies I'd brought out – biscuits and apples, tinameat, white flour, golden syrup, milk powder – and he spent a feverish minute or two poking his way through the cardboard boxes.

'Aaiiiyy, my little Nangali,' he crowed at me, hawking and spitting and sticking his big wet schnoz into a packet of Drum tobacco, 'you too good to this ol feller!'

'I figured you been living on goannas and bush bananas so long you'd appreciate a bit of real tucker.'

'You better look out, h'Emily,' chortled Maggie. 'Allus room for nother missus in the family.'

'Aaagh!' I yelped, glaring and shaking my fingers at him in a sign of the cross, 'don't start trying to rope me into the harem, ya poddy-dodgin old bugger!'

I don't know whether or not Jimmy knew what a harem was, but he sure as hell knew about poddy-dodging – the rustling of young, unbranded stock – and he just about pissed himself laughing.

'Ah, come on, h'Em'ly,' he wheezed, slapping a knee, 'you little bit long in the tooth for poddy now!'

'Fuck off! I'm twenty-six. How old are you?'

This stumped him. He stared into the air for a moment, tilted his head, scratched his whiskers and said, 'Mmmm, might be somethin…'

'Oh something!' I growled, but I was beginning to see how Hazel had managed to remain a member of this eccentric outfit for so many years.

We sat by the fire, Jimmy and I chiacking each other while Maggie cooked up the grub – or grubs, witchetty for the most part. Others I wished were. Hazel was carving a wooden snake, and I noticed several other craft pieces around the shack: a wire-burnt coolamon, a quartz crystal on a length of string and a wind-chime dangling from the veranda. The latter, on closer inspection, turned out to be more sculpture than wind-chime, a ring of banded stones suspended from a crystal and held together with a length of string.

Weird, I thought. But typical Hazel. It brought to mind some of the objects she'd used to decorate her space when we were kids: feathers, fossils and thunder eggs, insects suspended in gum, globs of honey and blobs of spinifex wax. Once she brought in a bush potato which was a perfect replica of an erect dick, complete with balls, and we watched in fascination over the next few days as detumescence set in.

I was sitting by the fire chatting with Hazel and Maggie and chewing on a porcupine bone when I heard a motor approaching. Something big and beefy. A red F100 came rumbling down the track. It pulled up at the shack and something else big and beefy climbed out of the driver's seat.

'Hurl Mars,' Maggie whispered, suddenly uncomfortable. She scuttled into the shack.

Hurl Mars?

Mars Attacks

Whatever it was, it was dressed, surprisingly, in black. From the tip of the toe to the top of the broad-brimmed hat. It looked like Johnny Cash heading for a funeral – possibly his own.

Our visitor looked about distastefully, sniffed the air.

'H'owner for Carbine,' Jimmy explained.

Ah yes. Earl Marsh, from the neighbouring Carbine Creek Station. Although I hadn't met him yet, I had met some of his employees in the White Dog, and I knew him by reputation.

Carbine was one of the oldest properties in the region, but Marsh himself was something of a ring-in, having snuck in from Queensland a few years before. Jack had told me a bit about him. The whitefeller station owners hated land claims, and Marsh had been one of the biggest noises in his opposition to the Moonlight one. He'd done more than shoot off his mouth: he'd hunted Aboriginal Lands Council anthropologists off his property with a shotgun, bulldozed sacred sites, initiated a press campaign to show that those he termed the 'real owners' – a couple of old blackfellers who worked for him – weren't interested in getting the land back.

From the look of him now – dark shades on a red, blistered face, a mess of tatts on his forearms, a black cigar and a massive, buckle-smothering gut – he hadn't come to offer his condolences for our recent loss. He rumbled up and towered over us. He had squat legs, broad shoulders and the ubiquitous elastic-sided riding boots. He would have killed any horse he tried to sit on, but that was not so unusual for your latter-day stockman, who was more likely to be mounted on a thoroughbred four wheel drive than a horse.

'Hello, old man,' he barked, us women apparently invisible.

'Good afternoon, Mr Mars,' chirped Jimmy.

'We got a problem,' Marsh announced, pleasantries out of the way. He had a voice like Darth Vader's big brother. Quite a feat, considering that he spoke without moving his jaw. The Territory, I reflected, must be a hell of a place for lip-readers.

'Them bloody mongrels of yours,' he continued, nodding at Jimmy's pack of canine lassitude. 'They been attackin me cattle.'

It's his neck, I decided. That's what makes this guy such a weird-looking dude. He hasn't got one: his head just erupts out of his shoulders, like an enormous blood blister.

Jimmy scratched his pants in contemplation, sucked through sparse black teeth. 'Aaaiiyy,' he murmured. 'Reckon they must be quiet dog.' He waved an arm at the dogs by way of explanation, but he was looking worried. You had to sympathise with Jimmy when it came to dogs: the poor old bastard was down to his last half a dozen.

'I seen the evidence, old man,' the visitor insisted. 'Seen the evidence with my own eyes. You people, you let your animals run wild. Wild!' he repeated, warming to his theme. 'I just come down from the North Block. Three separate attacks, there's been. Poddies, mainly. Half a dozen savaged, rest of em spooked as hell.'

'North Block, eh…?' Jimmy crooned sympathetically.

'Can't say I didn't warn you,' Marsh growled. 'What we got here is a situation which needs, like… resolution.' He glanced at the rifle mounted in the cabin of his F100.

'Bullshit!' I interjected. 'What we got here is a situation which needs, like, clarification.' Dogs had been shot round here before, and I didn't feel like watching it happen again. I climbed to my feet and pointed a porcupine leg at the dogs. 'Look at them, for Christ's sake! Cattle? They'd have trouble attacking a mixoed rabbit.'

The dogs played their part beautifully, huddling in the distance like a flock of new-mown sheep. All except for old Leather, the attack dog, who couldn't help himself and was curling an upper lip in a manner most un-sheeplike.

Marsh swivelled his shades in my direction. After a long interval the words 'Who're you?' forced their way through his clenched teeth.

'I'm your worst nightmare, Mr Marsh.'

'My what?'

'A Moonlight woman with a law degree.'

He looked like the long-drop dunny in the men's camp had just been shoved up his left nostril.

'Lawyer, eh?' His shook his head, then said it again, his lips skirting round the word as if it were something dredged out of the aforementioned dunny.

I almost smiled. The only thing they hate more than blackfellers out here is lawyers. The prospect of a black lawyer must have been causing a meltdown somewhere in among the neurons. And it wasn't that far from the truth;

one of my non-degrees was in law, and I figured I should be able to get a Lands Council lawyer to back up whatever bullshit I improvised now.

'Who you workin for?' he asked warily.

'I'm working for Moonlight, and what do you mean "North Block"? If you're talking north of Carbine we never go out there, and if you're talking north of Moonlight, it's not your land.'

Hazel put a hand on mine and mouthed the words, 'Emily, hush!'

Marsh studied me for a moment, then turned to Jimmy Lively. 'Old man, I thought we had an agreement. Who is this nosey little bitch?'

An agreement?

Jimmy, never much of a fighter unless his opponent was edible, scuffed the ground uncomfortably. 'You remember that ol mechanic longa Moonlight, back in Tim Buchanan time? Motor Jack? This h'Emily, daughter for im now.'

Marsh sniffed the air. 'Never heard of im, nor his daughter.'

Must have been before you got through the rabbit fence, as Jack used to say about these Queensland interlopers. I spat a bit of porcupine gristle onto the ground, licked my fingers. 'So what's this agreement?'

'What?'

'You said you had an agreement.'

'I told old Jungle Jim ere when I come across him down the Mosquito last week, I got a signed agreement with the owner to run cattle on the North Quarter.'

'Owner?' Christ, I was thinking, with a sinking feeling in my chest and Kenny Trigger's scuttlebutt surfacing in my memory, this bloke doesn't fuck about. Was he part of the distinguished company who'd been chauffeuring Freddy Ah Fong round town? 'What owner?'

'Wait ere,' he rumbled.

He lurched back to the F100, then returned with a grubby document which, on closer inspection, turned out to be a ninety-nine-year lease on the north quarter of Moonlight Downs.

At the bottom of the page, under the heading 'Moonlight Downs: Owner' and over a date reading August 4th, was a great wobbly X and the words 'Freddy Ah Fong: His Mark'. The initial letters of the latter two words were heavily capitalised in an attempt to give the paper a bit of a legal finish.

Hazel read it as I did, and looked puzzled. Jimmy didn't seem too perturbed; he just sat there, nodding politely and chewing his tobacco. Not that this surprised me; for one thing, about the only thing on the paper he could read was Freddy's X. For another, you could have told Jimmy his arse was on fire and he would have continued to sit there nodding politely and chewing his tobacco. He was a nodding and chewing sort of guy.

I wasn't in such an accommodating mood. 'Enjoy your paddock while you can, Mister Mars.'

'Marsh!'

'Mr Marsh. You don't seriously expect this bullshit to stand up in court, do you? You think you're dealing with a pack of fucking savages? The ownership of Moonlight Downs is vested in a trust, of which Freddy is merely a member – a senior member, maybe, but anything as significant as this needs to be ratified by the entire membership. Adequate compensation needs to be paid, terms and conditions agreed upon. Next time you see me, Mr Marsh, I'll be packing an injunction. In the meantime, I'd suggest you get packing yourself.'

'I got an agreement…'

I gave him back his folder. 'What you've got, Mr Marsh, is an X on a piece of paper.' I sat back down, gathered together the wherewithal for a smoke, fidgeted in my pockets for a light. 'You'll be hearing from us.'

He gave me a long, slow stare.

'What'd you say your name was?'

'Emily Tempest.'

He folded his arms, squared his legs, not talking. Not with his mouth, at any rate, but his Ray-bans suddenly looked like ray-guns. He swung his overgrown head round and stormed back to the F100. I noticed Winnie's kids looking out through the hessian door, bug-eyed and slack-jawed.

As Marsh opened the car door old Leather, seeing his chance, galloped out and bit him on his broad behind.

The Carbine man didn't miss a beat. As he heaved his carcass into the cabin he swung down, swiftly and accurately, with the tyre lever that had materialised in his big right fist. We could hear the skull crack from twenty feet away. The animal collapsed in a heap of teeth and skin.

The kids shot back into the shack.

'That's one less to worry about,' Marsh grunted. He drove off without a backward glance.

We sat there chewing his dust, all of us a little shell-shocked. Maggie appeared, looking about as sprightly as the dog.

Eventually Jimmy shuffled over to the dead animal, put a

hand on its neck and gave it a last massage. 'Ah shit!' he crooned mournfully, 'me best fuckin dog.'

Hazel nestled into my side, looking for comfort. She hadn't said much, but when she put her hand in mine I could feel the pulse racing. We watched as Jangala pottered around for a shovel, picked up Leather and carried him into the scrub.

'Emmy?' she said.

'Uh-huh?' I answered, vaguely, my mind on other things.

'Can we get outta here for a while?'

I looked at her. 'Where do you want to go?'

'Maybe out the old gaolhouse?'

Which did surprise me, so much so that I was momentarily distracted from the question that had been bobbing around my head from the moment I spotted Marsh's dodgy contract.

Which was, what had inspired him to get it signed the day before Lincoln died?

In the Gaolhouse Now

As I drove through the late-afternoon scrub I spent much of my time weaving around termite mounds and fallen logs, but overall the track was in much better nick than I'd expected it to be.

'Bit easier than the first time we come out here, Haze?'

'*Yuwayi.*'

She was sitting beside me, still carving her little snake, but tense, I could tell. I caught a glimpse of her face in the mirror, and saw moisture in her eyes.

I gave her hand a squeeze, and she smiled briefly.

As we cruised through the mulga the sense of anticipation awoke old memories. A scene came rolling across my mind like something out of an old movie, the kind of film somebody should make about the Territory – full of subtle encounters and tender close-ups – but which only ever seem to emerge from other people's deserts.

How old had I been, the first time we came across the gaol? Thirteen? Maybe fourteen. Early on in the year of my disgrace. I'd been out riding with Hazel. We'd scrounged a couple of stock horses off Jack, and were laughing and galloping through the scrub, as was our wont. We were about an hour's ride north of the homestead. I remember I pulled up to watch her race past: she rode beautifully, rode as if she were floating over the saddle, a talent she'd inherited from her father. We were from different worlds, Hazel and I – hers black and mine a sort of… off-white, but the borders of each had long dissolved and we lived our lives in the middle. She was my best friend, my first love.

The horse shied, and as I twisted in the saddle I spotted something through the trees at the foot of a nearby hill.

A tin roof.

'Hang on, Hazel!' I yelled. 'What's that?'

She pulled up, gasping – not from fatigue, though we'd been riding for hours, but from exhilaration. She looked back at me, wild-eyed and wet with sweat, the tip of her tongue flashing through crooked teeth.

'What's what?'

But she followed my line of sight and looked wary.

'Kantalkuyu,' she said cautiously. 'Ol police station. Fore kurlupatu move away to Jupiter Well.'

It's no coincidence that the Warlpuju word for cop also means 'cheeky', which, in Aboriginal English, is to say 'brutal'. An oblique comment upon the force's policing practices in the early days. Some of the later ones too.

I pulled my horse round. 'Gonna give it a geek?'

Her voice became smoky, her brow as rippled as the earth over which we were riding. 'We don't go there, Em. Dangerous place nearby. Man's place. Woman not allowed.'

'Oh.' I knew what that meant. But… 'Just close, though, right? Not actually *there*, eh Haze? C'mon, I really wanner look at it. Old cop shop, what else is there like that round here? We could just go for a quick squizz…'

I began to move away, but she pulled me up. 'Aaiiiyy…

Just roundabout the building then. No more. Up in the hills behind, there's a place. Mebbe cave. Janapularti. Stay away from there. Okay?'

'Okay.' I began to move off, but she wouldn't let me go. She grabbed hold of my reins and frowned at me.

'More than okay, Emily. I know you, you gotta promise!'

'Yes Hazel.' I looked her in the eyes. 'Cave in the hills. Janapularti. We won't go there, I promise.'

I cantered off, and she followed – reluctantly at first, but by the time we reached the ant-bed building she was beside me, as curious as I was. We reined in our horses, dismounted and stood in front of the building. There was a dirty great padlock on the front door and bars on the windows, but round the back, where the roof had lifted slightly, the crumbling masonry gave us an easy entrance.

We crawled through the wall and entered a dingy room shot through with bolts of light. One of them hit a calendar on the opposite wall: 1942.

That explained the station's hasty abandonment. Able-bodied men had other things on their mind that year. Debris from its former life was scattered about the building: charred utensils in the fireplace, green bottles, a broken table, a hand-made broom.

We made our way into an adjoining room, this one fitted out with black steel bars: the cell. I touched a metal bunk, then felt an importunate hand upon my sleeve.

'Emily, look!' Her eyes were wide open.

Up against the opposite wall, half-submerged in shadow and dirt, was a six-foot-high bookcase.

Full of books.

I ran a hand across the leather spines, deciphered a few

titles. 'Robinson Crusoe,' I read. 'Poetical Works of Tennyson. Persuasion... The Ruby-something of Omar someone... Kenilworth. Lavengro.'

The names meant nothing to us. And yet...

We'd grown up on writing, Hazel and I. Our friendship had been suckled on the written word. She'd been five or so when Jack taught us to read: he said that having her company was the only way he could rope me into staying still for long enough. Once we had the basics, we devoured every scrap of writing on the place: newspapers and magazines, mail-order catalogues, missionary texts, *National Geographics*, Jack's geology books, the sepia-coloured Australiana he read from time to time, a battered Henry Lawson. We enjoyed them all: they were like radio signals from a distant planet.

But the collection in front of us was something else. We both felt it.

They were the planet itself.

I pulled out a fat red volume and blew away the dust. The book was worn, torn, water-marked, mottled with wasps' nests and spider webs – but readable. We sat on a bunk by the window, shoulder to shoulder, hip to hip, arms around each other's waists, and read from where it fell open:

> ...*You have seen Sunshine and rain at once: her smiles and*
> > *tears*
> *Were like a better way: those happy smilets,*
> *That play'd on her ripe lip, seem'd not to know*
> *What guests were in her eyes; which parted thence,*
> *As pearls from diamonds dropp'd.*

Hazel and I looked at each other, astounded. I didn't know what she made of it, but to me it seemed that the words floated up from the page and hovered in the air, before breaking up and drifting away in a trail of golden particles.

The little ant-bed gaolhouse was our hideaway that summer, our enchanted cubby-house, our garden of words, our refuge from the rain-battered or sun-blasted afternoons.

They were troubled times on Moonlight Downs. Tim Buchanan was in the Alice Springs Hospital, from which he would emerge only for his own funeral. The banks, who Jack reckoned had put him there, were looking to recover what they were owed. A succession of hard-nosed bastards came poking round the station, measuring rust and dust, going through the chaotic books, looking at us like buyers at a slave auction. It wasn't that long ago that a station's niggers were listed as assets, like so many head of cattle or miles of fencing.

None of this touched Hazel and me. Not at first, anyway, so immersed were we in our discovery. We dusted and scrubbed the place furiously, decked it out with flowers, crystals and improvised furniture, struck up an acquaintance with the only other occupant, a bush rat named Jajju.

And we read the bookcase from top to crumbling bottom.

Exactly where the library had come from we never did discover – presumably it was the legacy of some eccentric constable or bookish missionary, left there when the station was abandoned in the forties.

It was an odd, eclectic assortment. Many of the books were impenetrably outdated: long-winded stories about sermonising soldiers and war-like priests, Rotarian morality tales and Edwardian romances in which blokes with names like Horace and Headingley ripped their ladies' bodices in the manner of a Sicilian mail-sorter opening a suspicious envelope. But upon those crumbling shelves we found what I later realised was most of the great poetry and prose of the English language – Milton, Marlowe, Shakespeare, Austen, Tennyson – as well as a set of beautifully illustrated geological texts and old mining manuals. It was here that I came across my *Gouging the Witwatersrand*.

Hazel and I would lie on a swag, bodies entwined, sometimes reading from the same book, sharing discoveries, fragments, following tracks and trails. Our styles were different. I was always more fluent than she was, and read things from beginning to end. Hazel's approach was more visceral: often I would read to her out loud, and she'd latch onto images and phrases, roll them around her mouth, delighting in their colour and texture.

'*Bring me my bow of burning gold,*' she'd say, her eyes full of wonder.

'*At the round earth's imagined corners…*

'*His flashing eyes, his floating hair!*'

I was shaken out of my reverie when the Toyota rounded a bend and scattered a mob of kangaroos. Hazel looked up as the biggest of them made a scrabbling escape via the bonnet. The mulga thickened; splinters and wheels of light spun through the branches that scraped against the windscreen.

She was still quietly working away at the wooden snake. I glanced at the carving and did a double take: its head bore a distinct resemblance to that of Earl Marsh.

I shouldn't have been surprised: Hazel had always had a

gift that way. As a kid she was rarely without a pencil or piece of charcoal. Many was the time I'd seen her capture the kinetic energy of a galloping horse or a bushfire on the horizon with a few deft strokes on a piece of wood.

Perhaps it was the carving in her hands, perhaps it was our proximity to our little hideaway, but Hazel seemed to be regaining something of her equilibrium. As we drove into the gaolhouse clearing she studied the snake for a moment, looked into its eyes – then threw it out the window.

A Devil, a Dove, an Avalanche

The police station seemed more or less as I remembered it, which was another surprise. Given the general disintegration that was happening everywhere else in our lives, I'd expected it to be white-ant shit and silt by now. The veranda was looking a bit wonky, but the red earth walls were still standing, the tin roof was more or less intact. They built them to last in those days. I even spotted a bush rat scuttling for cover as we went in.

'Surely that isn't Jajju?'

Hazel smiled. 'His family.'

She lit a lantern.

Signs of recent occupation appeared in the sphere of yellow light: a swag on the floor, cooking equipment on the hearth, pannikins and billies, paint pots, pint pots. The décor was all Hazel: feathers and flowers, bottles, eggs, a row of rocks and fossils on the window ledge.

And, surprisingly, paintings. Some on the sides of packing boxes, some on sheets of metal or paper.

It took a moment or two for that to sink in, but when it did, it hit me like a bird of prey.

'Jesus, Hazel, these are yours?'

'*Yuwayi.*'

'I've never seen anything like them.'

And I hadn't. Especially the ones on paper: there were eight or nine of them, tacked onto pieces of wood and leaning against a wall. I took a closer look and saw that she'd painted over – or into – a set of old maps. Geological maps, magnetometer surveys, your standard one to two-fifty thous. God knows where she'd found them, but the result was an evocation of country that somehow captured the sense of the word from both an Aboriginal and a European perspective.

I picked up the painting closest to me: it was an intricately patterned pool of black and white feathers and wings in a fringe of silver. There was something almost Chinese about it.

'This is gorgeous. What's it about?' I asked her.

'Mudlark dreamin.'

'And the purple one?' A simpler design, this: swathes of indigo and crimson through a field of mauve.

'That Laughing Boy story. You remember?'

'Vaguely. And what about the one next to it?'

'Zebra finch.' A galaxy of grasses – windmill, woollybutt, kerosene – with a flash of lightning through its axis.

What I took to be the work in progress was parked on the seat of a chair in the centre of the room, simmering in the last rays of the sun that levelled through the skylight. It was one of the maps, tacked onto a slab of wood. I picked it up and examined it. The painting was earth-coloured, ochre washed, with wings and wheels and white flowers. But shot with the odd bolt of blue-grey, like the blurred image of a diving bird.

I ran my eyes down the right-hand side, where the legend of the original map was a poem in itself:

Whippet Sandstone
Red Hills Granite
Greenstone
Greywacke
Porphyry
Tuff
Micaceous Quartzite

Under the legend were some scribbled additions: 'anorthositic norite, dunite, limonite'. I liked the way Hazel had left the hand-written notes uncovered. They conjured up an image of some grizzled gouger in stubbies and steel-caps, a dirty pencil in his fat fingers, scratching his hopes and observations onto the map. God knows how many times I'd seen my father doing exactly that.

So deftly had the arrows been incorporated into Hazel's design that they looked like the tracks of some ancestral being.

'This is so amazing, Hazel. What is it?'

She came up beside me, her bare feet padding over cool stone.

'Don't you recognise it?'

'Should I?'

'Diamond dove,' she whispered.

Diamond dove. Again. The dreaming and its multitudinous manifestations – people and places, creatures, songs – was beginning to emerge as the motif of my return to Moonlight.

That was when it struck me: the connection between these paintings. 'My god,' I said. 'This is a series. You're painting…'

She nodded. 'A portrait of my father,' she said softly.

I hugged her. 'No wonder they're so beautiful,' I whispered, but, even as I said it, I was wondering what the story depicted in the painting had to do with the argument between Lincoln and Blakie, and how it was connected to his murder. I was curious, but unsure of how to broach the topic without resurrecting painful memories.

I chose instead to probe around the edges. 'Diamond dove... Which site have you painted? I know it's got a few of them.'

'Main one,' she explained. 'Where it travels out through Karlujurru. You remember the story?'

'Remind me.' Sometimes it seemed that every puddle of a creek or crack in the ground had a tale to tell. I'd heard dozens of them from Lincoln. This one, I remembered, was something about the creation of the Tom Bowlers.

'The one about the av'lanche.'

'The avalanche?'

'*Yuwayi.* That *kupulumamu* – you know? white devil – was attackin her out near Jalyukurru Hill.' She ran a finger across the painting, tracing one of the blue bolts. 'That dove, she flew up and round so fast she made a whirlwind, bring down the mountain, kill the devil with a landslide. You can see it here, the broken bones...'

She touched what looked like crushed spinifex, embedded in thick, green paint.

'The blood...' A blot of ochre. 'The fallen rock...' The brush strokes here seemed to have been mixed with crushed crystal.

I stood back and studied the painting. I could make out neither devil, dove nor avalanche, but there were all sorts of other things going on, a cross-hatching of tradition and change.

'It's a really unusual painting,' I said.

'Unusual?'

'Alive. Makes you feel like you're moving across the country yourself, you know? Like looking at a 3-D film.'

'Never seen a 3-D film.'

'Or watching the old ladies dancing at sunset; the way the light moves through the dust around their feet. I didn't even know you could paint, Haze. Where did you learn?'

'Lady teacher come up from Papunya, year or two ago.' Papunya, a sprawling community north-west of Alice Springs. The birthplace of the contemporary desert art movement. 'Give us a few brushes, taught us how to use em. I been muckin around on me own since then.'

'Mucking around?' She'd been doing a lot more than that.

'I mainly work out here,' she said, glancing around the room. 'The peace, helps me see what I'm doin.'

I put the painting back against the chair, then glanced out the window. The copperburr bushes were a fiery filigree of seeds and leaves, the wiregrass was shedding scintillas of light.

So absorbed had I been in the paintings that I hadn't thought to ask the obvious question.

'Hazel – the books, what happened to them?'

'I was wonderin when you'd ask. They're there...' She nodded at the fireplace. 'What's left of em.'

On the mantelpiece lay three great ledgers with marbled covers and gold embossing, the kind used by station book-keepers in the days of elegant hand-writing and Kalamazoo accounting.

'That's them?'

'Have a look.'

I pulled one down. Inside it, pressed like a flower, lay a sheet of tea-coloured, heavily creased paper on which I could make out a line of verse:

When I consider how my light is spent ere half my days in this dark world and wide

As I leafed my way through the pages familiar fragments and phrases emerged, like stars coming out of twilight:

Methought I saw my late espoused saint...
Why this is Hell, nor am I out of it

There were dozens of them, usually a whole page but sometimes half a page, sometimes a tattered fragment, all of them carefully placed between the thick sheets of the old ledger.

'What happened?'

'You ever meet that Brick Sivvier, took over the station from Tim Buchanan?'

'Saw him from a distance. Not enough of a distance, from what I can recall of old Prick.'

She grinned. 'Think him or 'is boys just turfed em out back. Place been used as a storage shed. Ringers used to camp out here, mighta read em, mighta smoked em, I dunno. Lot of em must have got washed away in the wet. I scouted around when we first come out here, coupla years ago. Found em in odd places. Fished a few out of the rocks over the waterhole.'

I spent a minute or two leafing through the ledgers. There wasn't much of our library left, but what had survived was fascinating in a strange, palimpsest sort of way, a collision of images and colour. As I turned the pages I felt like a swallow darting through a cathedral.

I put the ledger back, went across to the window and touched the rocks on its ledge. Some I knew at a glance: I was Jack Tempest's daughter, after all. In our house we read rocks the way city kids read cereal boxes. I recognised galena, phenocrysts of augite embedded in a chromite matrix, two crystals of hornblende, intergrown and rimming, gorgeous, criss-crossing sheets and books of phlogopite.

Others didn't yield their identities so easily. I picked one up and studied it, intrigued. I'd never seen anything quite like it. It was a hexagonal crystal, three centimetres long, with beautiful, tin-white terraces of growth and reflective cleavage planes. I was trying to work out what it was when I caught in its vitreous crystal surface a distorted image of Hazel coming up behind me.

'This where you been staying?' I asked her, putting the crystal down.

'Sometimes.' Her voice was a low, sumptuous growl. 'When I want a getaway. Just like we used to. Do a bit of paintin, maybe, a bit of thinkin.'

'What do you think about?' I asked, sensing that in bringing me here she'd taken an important step back towards the intimacy we once shared.

'Oh, things that have gone. Things that'll never go. You, sometimes...' she added with a poignancy that cut like a butterfly knife: both ways.

I put a hand to her cheek. 'I'm sorry I left you, Haze. Sorry I never came back.'

She studied me for a moment, smiled uncomfortably, then turned away, picked up some of the kindling that was lying on the hearth and put it in the fireplace.

'Emmy,' she looked up and said. 'Let's go for a swim?'

'You're full of surprises today.'

'Down the rock-hole.'

'I didn't think you meant in the trees, but isn't it getting a bit chilly?'

'More better. We'll make a fire.'

Which we did, the kindling crackling up at the first match.

I brought in the coffeepot, put it on the fire. We stepped out the back door.

The sun had disappeared, but the bush was suffused with a salmon afterglow. We set off walking, then she walloped me on the arse and broke into a wild laugh and a wilder sprint. We bounced over the rocks like a couple of dingo pups, tearing off our clothing and a little of the gloom that had been enveloping us these last few weeks.

Hazel reached the rock-hole first and dived in. I held back, watching her lissom body arc and slip through rings of black water. She reappeared, spray flying from her hair, breasts floating among flowers and gum leaves.

'Whadderye waitin for?' she laughed. She had a wonderfully wicked laugh, Hazel, a laugh that had been all too scarce of late. Her eyes were as darkly shimmering as the water. I hit the pool feet first, just about landed on top of her.

'Emily Tempest, ya little bitch!' she screamed when she eventually struggled to the surface.

I wrestled her under, and for twenty minutes we horsed around like the kids we'd been the last time we did anything like this.

Later we sat on the bank, naked, watched the moon rise, listened to the night life emerge. Mopokes hooted and crickets called. Small things rooted and shuffled about the undergrowth; a kangaroo mouse poked its nose out of a tuft of grass, took a look around, its black eyes glowing. It scratched its nose and disappeared. Suddenly Hazel cocked her head, listening. She lifted her chin and uttered a trilling 'pooor-pa, poor-papa' sound. A moment later there came an answering call.

'Come and have a look at a sister,' she whispered, and I followed her for some forty feet through the mulga. She poor-papa-ed again, signalled me to stop, then crept forward alone. When I caught up with her she was crouching alongside a tiny platform of twigs and grass stems in the fork of a bush. On it I could make out a bird, the moonlight reflecting off its diamond-flecked wings. It gazed up at Hazel with no apparent fear.

She glanced at me, put a finger to her lips, then rejoined her conversation with the bird in the soft whisper-singing I'd sometimes heard her using in childhood.

I leaned back, looked at her silverblue, moonlit face and shoulders, moved by the beauty of the sight: one diamond dove talking to another.

'Brrrr...' she suddenly shivered, clutching her elbows.

'Getting a bit that way, isn't it? Let's go back.'

We pulled on the odd article of clothing – a dress here, a cardigan there – and made our way back to the building, our hands joined.

The fire was blazing and the room was filled with the smell of my Jamaica Blue. I broke out the chocolate and we lay in front of the fire, wrapped in a blanket, drinking and eating and watching shadows run around the walls.

I closed my eyes, contented, nestled against her stomach.

Once, years before, I'd been out bush with Lincoln and the mob. It was a stiff winter's night, and I was caught unprepared: not enough clothes or dogs, my knees knocking, my legs laced with ice. Lincoln, personally oblivious to weather, must have heard me shivering. He threw on another blanket but it didn't help. Then he dug up a shovelful of hot coals and buried it under my swag.

'Ere ya go, li'l Nangali,' he whispered. 'That'll warm ya.'

Warm me? My god, it suffused me, it seeped into my bones in ways I'd never felt before. And hadn't felt in all the years away from Moonlight.

Until now.

Taboo

I awoke at dawn feeling strangely uncomfortable, chilled. Hazel was lying with her back to me, perfectly still, but there was none of the peace of sleep about her. I touched her shoulder, and she rolled over and looked at me. She was holding an owl feather to her chest, and it was wet with tears. I touched her cheek.

'What is it, Hazel?' I whispered.

No reply.

'Are you crying for your father?'

'Maybe. Maybe for you too. Everything so tangled up – just like it was when you went away. You stir everything up so much, Emily. Things are just beginning to work out for us here, then you come back and it's crazy again.'

I didn't know what to say, except that I'd been asking similar questions of myself.

She lifted herself onto one arm, looked down at me. 'That painting,' she said, nodding at the one on the chair. 'Remember the story I told you?'

'The diamond dove and the white devil?'

'You're in that painting too, Em. Trouble is I can't figure out where. Dunno if you're the devil or the dove.'

I lay there for a while, saying nothing, then climbed out of the swag, went and sat on the back step.

This was where it had happened. Somewhere in the swirling colours of the dawn I saw myself again, saw a fourteen-year-old slip of a girl in a yellow dress walking along the track down by the waterhole, her arms folded, her eyes glowing with wonder at what the world was doing.

It was afternoon then, a crackling, ozone-laced afternoon. Lightning cleaved the western sky; batteries of rain hammered the distant hill-tops. The ranges were disappearing under a swivelling grey veil, but it wasn't here yet: golden beams lowered in through the thunderclouds and turned the trees into a kaleidoscope of green and yellow. Wind stirred, creatures were scuttling for cover, but to me it seemed that an unaccountable stillness slowly arose and enveloped me.

Hazel was nowhere to be seen. We'd been doing a bit of muckabout hunting and had separated, trying to track a wallaby. She was probably back at the gaolhouse by now. I stopped, stood there listening, waiting for what I didn't know, hardly daring to breathe.

And then, somewhere in that roaring silence, I heard it: music, a strange, ethereal melody that seemed to shake the very leaves in the trees. I looked around, alert, an ominous curiosity looming up inside me. The music was coming from the west, from the direction of the cave hill. From the men's place.

My heart told me to piss off as quickly as I could, to get back to the gaol, find Hazel, ride home. But I was of an age where I was beginning to listen as much to my head as to my heart, and I felt as if there was a massive rope around my waist, dragging me in.

I hesitated, then turned around, crouched low and headed for the cave.

It was getting on for dark by the time I got there, and I made my way nervously through the bush. As I drew closer to the hills the music seemed to swivel around and come from another direction. I followed, but it shifted again, and I became disoriented: the song was a circle whose centre was everywhere at once.

I began to back away, but the music changed tempo and key and took on a new intensity, a screaming-in-your skull quality, a vicious rhythm that threatened to tear the top off my head.

Panic and bile reared in my throat. I ran, cascading through the melaleuca, my bare feet flying over rough ground, until at some point I slipped on a root and slammed into the earth. Fire and darkness jarred in my mind, a rush of images roaring through. Snakes hissed, scorpions twisted; the wind screamed and a shadowy figure seemed to rise out of the earth, firing a volley of crystals into my brain. I lay huddled on the ground, my ears covered, my eyes clenched, a chasm of dread opening before me. I was on the point of falling when a hand touched my shoulder.

Hazel.

This all occurred many years ago. Since then I've travelled the world, been to some desperate places, seen a lot of good and a lot of evil; but Hazel following me into that place remains the most courageous thing I've ever seen.

'Emily,' she mouthed, her face stretched with fear, 'what are you *doin*? We gotta get outta here! Come on!' She dragged me to my feet and we ran, white-eyed and tear-arsed like there was a howling tornado at our backs. She held onto my hand; kept holding it as I stumbled through the spinifex. Held on still as I tripped one last time and fell, a wave coming over me, gathering me up and sweeping me out into the merciful night.

When I came to, it was to the accompaniment of a slow, bouncing pain in my temple, the slap and jangle of leather and metal, the smell of horse sweat. I raised my head. The ground swivelled for a moment, then flew up at me, but before I could fall too far I felt a steadying hand on my shoulder. I dragged myself upright, rubbed my eyes, realised I was draped across a horse's withers.

I turned around, found myself looking at a familiar, reassuring face.

'Lincoln?' I rasped.

His expression was a fearful mask of sorrow and resignation.

'Lincoln, what's going on?'

'What goin on?' he said, wearily shaking his head. 'Old Emily bin muckin up, like always.'

I noticed Hazel on her own horse, moving along behind us. She was grim faced, silent, staring into the distance.

I heard a dog bark and my own house appeared before me. Lincoln walked the horse up to the veranda, where my father was standing with his hands on his hips and a scowl on his face.

The horse drew to a halt. I made to jump down, but before I could do so Lincoln put a hand on my shoulder:

'Nangali...'

I turned around, looked up at him, lowered my eyes: 'I'm sorry Lincoln.'

'Sorry no matter. Just listen to me, one time. You always lookin for somethin. Lookin ahead, long way. That's okay, might be you learn a lot of thing, but sometime you gotta slow down, listen to them ol people. Take a look inside yourself. Understand?'

'Understand,' I nodded, shame-faced.

I climbed down, went into the house, where my father's anger seemed almost a relief after Lincoln's disappointment. He calmed down soon enough, though, made us both a cup of tea and joined me at the kitchen table.

'What are we going to do with you, Em?'

'What do you mean?'

'Jesus, Em, you stuck your nose into a men's sacred site. There's people out there who think you should be dead.'

'Fuck.'

'That won't happen, of course – not with Lincoln and me around, but you're not to go anywhere near the camp. Not if you want to stay in one piece.'

And that was when he laid it on me: he thought I should leave the station. Straightaway.

Still rattled by my own stupidity, I sat there in a stony silence as he outlined his reasoning and his plans. He told me he'd been worrying for years about my lack of formal education, about what he called my 'wasted talent'. Said I was fourteen now, that the crunch years were looming, and that if I was ever going to make anything of myself it was time to get started. He had a sister in Adelaide who'd offered to take me in, and the Aboriginal Scholarships Program would cover most of the costs.

'And it's not just you,' he said, frowning. 'Right now I'm worried about the whole box and dice.'

'Which box and dice?'

'All of us here. The community. Sivvier's bringing in more and more of his own people.' Brick Sivvier had taken over the property a few weeks before. 'The other day I had some shifty git come sniffin around the workshop like he owned it. Went down to the Big House to talk to Brick about it, and he looked down his nose at me as if I was some kind of cockroach. And he's talking about the blackfellers like they're not even there. Thing is, Em, I dunno if any of us are gonna be here much longer.'

My initial reaction was anger: Moonlight Downs was all the home I knew, and I was buggered if I was going to see us kicked off it. But as the day wore on and I mooned around the house, other ideas began to rise to the surface. I'd never been further south than Alice Springs. I'd always thought of 'Down South', the city, as some kind of mechanical monster looming across the other side of the desert, something that chewed you up and spat you out.

But if there was danger in those crowded streets, there was, as well, a certain allure. The city was the place where things happened, where the decisions and the money were made, where fashions and ideas were fomented.

And there was something else. As I grew older I was feeling more and more hemmed in by the restrictions and narrow-mindedness of the community, more torn between the black and white aspects of my heritage. The incident at the cave was the crowning shame of a series of indiscretions: I'd been arguing with the elders, asking too many questions, talking back, chatting up boys of the wrong skin.

Could I see myself spending the rest of my life in this dump? No way.

The wide, white world was beckoning. I knew I'd have to tackle it some day; given the mess in which I found myself, maybe now was the time.

That night, after Jack had gone to sleep, I snuck out of my bedroom window, ran down to the camp, hid in the darkness and spied upon Hazel and her family. Eventually the others drifted off to bed and she was left alone by the fire, brooding over a pannikin of tea. The depression seemed to radiate out from her, and I cursed the bloody-mindedness – my own – that had brought her to this pass. I crept in close, flicked a pebble at her back.

'Hazel!' I called softly.

She looked around, spotted me in the darkness and frowned, but sidled over to where I lay. 'What you doin here?' she whispered.

'Had to talk to you.'

'Don't let anybody see you, Emily. You should go back home now.'

'What's going to happen to you, Hazel?'

A brief silence ensued, then she said, 'They're marryin me off.'

'What! Who to?'

'You know that Jangala, Jimmy Lively, over Kirrinyu?'

'Shit. He's older than your father. And he's already got a wife.'

She shrugged.

'Hazel,' I said, 'I'm goin away…'

'Where away?'

'Down south.'

'Alice?'

'Adelaide.'

'Adelaide!'

'Got no choice, Hazel, but I'll be back, I promise.' I squeezed her hand.

A voice called out from the shack. 'Hazel!'

'Comin,' she responded, then looked back at me and whispered, 'Oh Emily, why you gotta break every rule in the book? Can't you at least read the bloody thing first?'

I didn't know what to say. She kissed me, fiercely, then went to join her little sister in the swag.

'Goodnight, Hazel,' I heard her father call, and then his voice dropped a decibel or two: 'And goodnight to you too, Emily Tempest.'

I sat there in the darkness for another ten minutes, an ineffable weariness stealing over me. 'I'll be back,' I mouthed to the sleeping camp.

The next day Jack drove me into Bluebush, where I spent the day getting ready to go down south. That evening Jack put a call through to Brick Sivvier and was told that he needn't come back to work, his services were no longer required. Neither of us was surprised, though we put a different spin on it. To Jack it was the incentive he needed to get to work on a promising mining lease out at Jennifer Creek. To me it seemed part of the punishment for my transgression. And when we found out, soon afterwards, that the Warlpuju had been given the arse as well, the proximity of the events was not lost on me.

Our last day was their last day. Jack and I drove out to pick up our gear and we met them on the road to Bluebush. The picture is still there, mig-welded into my memory: the line of cars, the women weeping, the kids gawking, the men ash-faced. Hazel was nowhere to be seen.

Twelve years on I'd grown up, acquired an education and travelled the world. But still, apparently, I'd failed to redeem myself in the eyes of the person whose acceptance I wanted most.

I heard the door of the gaol rasp and she came out and joined me. We sat there in silence, until I rolled a smoke and offered one to her.

'Shit, Em,' she said, 'you trying to corrupt me? I'm supposed to be the health worker, you know?'

'Not exactly a huge crowd for you to set an example for, is there?'

She rubbed my knee, put an arm around my shoulder. 'If only you hadn't stayed away so long, Em, maybe it wouldn't have been so difficult. Why didn't you come back earlier?'

'Lots of reasons, Haze. I was afraid, for one. And I suppose I wanted to see the world, break out of the shithole in which I imagined I'd been raised. Same as most kids.'

Hazel snorted. 'Most kids don't have to kick the door down to get out of the house. Emily Tempest...who ever knew what to make of you?' She grinned, shook her head. 'Tempest? Christ, you was a little bloody cyclone, with your mouth full of questions and your fists full of answers, your spinifex kisses and your wild white ways.'

She rose to her feet, slapped me across the shoulder. 'Come on, you crazy bugger, we're not gonna sort anythin out sittin here. Let's head back in; they'll be wondering where we got to. Go now and we'll be home for breakfast.'

Investigations

Twenty minutes later we were cruising along the track, Ry Cooder ripping into 'Get Rhythm' on the tape deck, Hazel tapping time and grinning like a wet gecko.

'Nice music,' she said.

'Great riff,' I agreed. 'I'll try to get back out in a few days.'

'You gotta go back in to Bluebush right away?'

'I'm supposed to be at work this arvo. Better go, unless you got enough money to keep me in the style to which I'm accustomed.'

'I got a couple o' bucks.'

'That's about the style I'm accustomed to.'

'But Jangala got a nine hundred dollar book-up at the store.'

'Nine hundred bucks? Shit! We're in the red. How'd they let him get that high?'

'His friendly smile?'

'His cunning-as-a-one-eyed-camel smile. Remember the time he managed to con those tourists into towing him all the way to Katherine?'

'Plenty o' people get towed round here.'

'Yeah, but usually in a car that's broken down. That one didn't even have a motor.'

'Oh, that time.'

We drove on for a while, then I said, 'I'll only stay in Bluebush long enough to get a bit of a stash together, then come and spend some time out here.'

She put a hand on mine. 'Long as you don't wreck the place.'

'I'll probably be more trouble than I'm worth, but I'd like to help get the community going again.'

'Wouldn't we all?'

When we reached the camp none of the others seemed particularly concerned about us: evidently they were used to Hazel and her wandering ways. She pottered around with her horse gear for a while, played a game of scratch-basketball with the kids, then began to gather together the wherewithal for a meal.

'You got time for a feed?' she asked.

'Sure. Don't have to be at work until five.'

I wasn't planning to go in straightaway anyway. I wanted to make a closer inspection of the patch of mulga in which Lincoln had been murdered, and Hazel's preoccupation with the meal gave me the chance.

I'd been reluctant to visit the site in her company. Death in any form brings up a vast array of taboos among the Warlpuju; the death of a loved one magnifies those taboos enormously.

So while Hazel pounded a damper and cooked up a stew I went over and stood on the edge of the scrub. The crime scene had been accorded the full extent of the detailed scrutiny warranted by yet another dead blackfeller: roughly zip. Whatever perfunctory investigations the cops had been carrying out had been disrupted by the appearance, and dramatic disappearance, of the prime suspect.

I got onto my hands and knees and wondered if I could do any better.

Nope, I decided a few minutes later. I can't.

I don't know what I'd expected to find. Fingerprints, maybe? There were fingerprints there, or what must have been fingerprints before the wind and the weather got to them. Fingerprints by the square metre. Entire hand prints in fact, not to mention foot prints, knee prints, nose prints, even a set of teeth, all of them mementos of the mayhem that had erupted on this site a few weeks earlier.

But what did they tell me? Bugger all. A lot of people had been doing bizarre things to each other, trying to assuage their grief.

I already knew that.

Okay then, if my eyes weren't going to be much use, how about my brain?

Hungry as a hawk. Who'd described me that way recently? Shit. Blakie. Maybe it was time I started satisfying that hunger with a few well-placed questions.

About motive, for one. Why would anyone want to kill Lincoln? Why would they have chosen that particular method? And this particular place?

The last question seemed a logical place to start, given that I was on location, as it were. Why here?

The site's proximity to Blakie's camp had led the cops – and me – to assume that he was responsible, but did it have any other attributes? It was isolated, for one, close to the single men's camp but far enough away to be beyond the noses and ears of the dogs. And, by local standards, the scrub was thick. The ideal spot for an ambush.

I took a few short steps into the mulga, then a few long

ones, and ended up at the foot of a low rise. When I climbed it I found myself surprisingly close to the main road.

I stood for a minute or two, lost in the mottled landscape of my own thoughts.

Why here?

The answer emerged from the topography.

An outsider.

If you were an outsider wanting to kill someone in the camp, this would be the logical spot. You could sneak in, conceal yourself, wait for your target to wander by and be gone before anybody knew about it.

Violent death was as common as snotty noses in the blackfeller camps. Anyone investigating would automatically figure it as an inside job. The mutilation, with its intimations of sorcery, would have strengthened the supposition.

Somewhere up ahead, through the knotted branches, I spotted movement in the air. A black hawk hovered, radiating violence. What did it have its eye on? I took a step forward and saw a flock of zebra finches moving through the grass, eating seeds. The hawk glided down, landed less than a metre from them, waited as if it had all the time in the world – which it did. The finches froze; even I froze, although the blood was rushing in me. The hawk sprang with a casual, hopping movement, seized a finch, killed it with a blow to the brain. The survivors scattered like the blast from a shotgun.

Zebra finch: one of Lincoln's dreamings.

It was the sight of that sudden attack that put into words the half-baked speculation that had been floating around all morning in the half-baked custard of my brain.

The words, of course, were 'Earl Marsh'.

Did our sensitive new-age neighbour have the same approach to blackfellers who were a pain in the arse as he had to dogs which bit him on the arse? He'd fought the land claim tooth and nail: had he decided to fight the claimants similarly? He didn't look like he had the brains to blow his nose, much less set up the murder as an inside job. But, until I knew him better, how could I tell what he was capable of?

He had a motive of sorts: his anger over the land claim, the return of a horde of unwanted neighbours, the trouble with the dogs. He had the means: I could well imagine those massive slab-hands wrapping themselves around Lincoln's neck.

And, more than anything else, he had that dodgy lease, conveniently 'signed' the day before Lincoln died.

Convenient? Shit, it was more than that. Not exactly a smoking gun, but getting there. A spent shell, perhaps; something which could be tied to a gun. If I could find any evidence of the bastard's being here I'd take my suspicions to McGillivray.

I made my way through the silver leafwork and the spindly branches, slowly and deliberately, my eyes scouring the earth.

From time to time I crouched down, studied the sand, searching for anything out of place. The main occupants of this little patch of scrub were ants: white-ants, honey-ants, mulga ants, meat-ants, slow-moving moneybox ants. They scurried across its surface in furious formations, snapped their mandibles, built their turrets and towers. If there was a success story in this country, they were it. They'd be here, moiling away, when the rest of us were grains of sand in the desert of time.

Around them the subtle panoply of desert life wended its way: centipedes and butcher-birds, barking spiders, sunrays, the prickly little fruits we call teddy-bear's arseholes, dried-out paddy-melons.

But nothing extraneous did I find, nothing to suggest that a big ugly whitefeller had blundered this way before me.

I reached the road and gazed at it bleakly. Six inches of drifting bulldust, a mess of ridges and ruts and furrows crissing and crossing and cutting into one another as far in as the wind-rows. What would that maze tell me? Sweet FA.

Or would it? As I turned to leave, I noticed a break in the wind-row, a few feet from where I stood. A narrow indentation. I crouched low, studied it. A few feet further on was something similar. The sand around them went against the grain of the prevailing ripples. Tyre tracks, perhaps? Smoothed over? I paced them out. Couple of metres apart, a bit more. Wide enough for an F100? Possibly. Had somebody parked here? Could well be.

Were there any other signs of an intruder? I cut a wider arc out from the tyre tracks and found what I'd missed the first time: boot prints, taking a circuitous, northerly route to the hollow. The prints were faded, caved-in, weather-worn, but the further you got from the hollow the more visible they became, as though someone had made a hurried attempt to cover them up.

I stood up, stretched, tried to imagine the scenario. The darkness, the stealth, that ruddy face gleaming in the Moonlight.

I shuddered.

I heard my name floating on the wind. Hazel's beautiful, high-pitched warble. I was glad to go: the little copse was giving me the creeps. I made my way back through the mulga, pausing only for a glance at the red-earth hollow in which we'd found the body.

I walked past it, then stopped.

Red earth?

Not entirely. A flash of iridescence gleamed through the dirt.

I swept it aside to uncover a spray of tiny blue pebbles.

Blue

Not pebbles, I decided as I rolled them between finger and thumb. More like shards, little splinters of hewn rock, rounded and smooth on one side, rough-split on the other. What were they? Opal? No, they were too angular, almost metallic. One of the sulphides, perhaps? Chalcopyrite? Labradorite? Maybe.

Where could they have come from?

I sifted through the surrounding earth, and scouted a wider area, but could find nothing resembling them, no outcrop from which they might have been chipped.

What did they tell me, these little stones? Not much. They reinforced the possibility of an outsider, perhaps, but would do no more, not unless I could somehow link them to Marsh. The ground on which I'd found them had had fifty hysterical mourners stampeding over it.

And they weren't just mourners: they were nomads, wanderers. Even these days, they tended to spend a lot of time on the move, both by foot and by car. Anybody from the camp could have picked up a few fragments of non-indigenous rock in their travels and unwittingly brought them here in a trouser cuff or a boot sole. The cops could have brought them. Or the paramedics.

I could have brought them here myself.

With such thoughts rolling around my head and the stones rolling around my pocket, I made my way back to the shack.

Hazel was sitting by the fire, grinning and flipping a damper on her nimble fingers.

It was beautiful. We slopped on a layer of golden syrup, ripped it apart and ate it, sipped some tea, passed a pleasant hour in each other's company. I checked my watch: time for me to go. Jimmy and Maggie had loaded my ute with supplies and gifts for the refugees in town: bush potatoes, conkerberries, a trussed-up goanna I hoped nobody was expecting me to put out of its misery.

Hazel stood in the doorway to say goodbye, a blanket about her shoulders, cheeks glowing.

'I'll try to get into town,' she said. 'Come and see you.'

'You do that,' I said. I reached out and feathered the back of her hand. 'I'll put a candle in the window.'

'A candle? Hang on, I got somethin better'n that.'

She ducked inside and came out a moment later with a wind-chime, a replica of the one hanging from her veranda.

'A present,' she smiled, putting it in the back of my ute. 'Hang it on your front porch.'

She planted a kiss on my cheek. 'Thanks for comin, Em,' she whispered. 'We'll work it out.'

As our heads parted I opened my eyes. Hazel's own eyes were as lustrous as the mineral in the wind-chime dangling over her shoulder.

Eh?

I took another look, soft-focused. Pulled the stones out of my pocket, compared them with the flashes of blue in the upper section of the wind-chime.

They were the same.

'Hazel, the stone in your wind-chime, where'd you get it?'

'Oh, people…' I felt a sudden tension, a tightening of her fingers in my hand. 'People bring it in. From out bush.'

'Which people? And from where out bush? It might be important. There wasn't any sign of it last time I was here.'

She hesitated, let go of me, tugged at an ear-lobe, chewed her lower lip. And then it clicked. God knows, it had taken me long enough.

Blakie.

Minerals. Crystals. Rocks. Fossils. Stones of every lustre and colour and composition. They were a magnet for him, they were his trademark, his signature-tune, his call-sign. How often had I seen him and his bloody rocks: he'd talk to them, sing to them, polish them, he'd sit for hours gazing into their depths. He knew their lattices and refractions, their stories and symmetries, their hidden intelligence. Anything out of the ordinary and he'd be onto it. Like me, really. He and I had that much in common.

It all tallied: the reports of pilfering from mining camps, the crystals on her window ledge, the wind-chime. And yes, even the old mining maps she'd transformed into works of art.

'He's been here, hasn't he Hazel? Blakie.'

She shuffled awkwardly.

'Sweet Jesus. How could you? You've been sheltering him.'

She turned away, stared at the ground, ran a hand through her hair. Looked uncomfortable.

Bloody uncomfortable. Much more so than she'd look if shelter was all she had to hide. I felt an icy hand clutch my heart. The owl feather in her swag.

I grabbed her by the sleeve, glared at her in a rush of rage and jealousy. I'd often suspected that she had a soft spot for Blakie, but it had never occurred to me it could be *that* soft spot. 'How could you?'

She pulled away. 'Emily, you don't understand...'

'Oh, I understand all right. You've been screwing him!'

'No, you don't understand. He's like a child, that *warriya*, but...'

'He's a bloody psychopath, that *warriya*!' I roared. 'He'd kill you as casually as he'd pick his nose. Probably eat you as casually, too.'

'I mean that sometimes he does things an he doesn't know what he's doin. Says he can hear spirits...'

'He hears voices! It's called crazy, Hazel. Schizophrenia, paranoia, I don't bloody know, I'm not a shrink, but what I do know is that he's as twisted as a bloody dishrag!'

'...but I'm sure he wouldn't have killed my old man.'

'How could you know that? And even if he didn't kill him it doesn't mean you gotta fuck him!'

'The old people are talking.' She nodded out at the northern plains. 'There's troublin signs: sickness, bad dreams. Couple of weeks ago, they reckon there was an earthquake up in the hills.'

'They've been giving us that bullshit all our lives.'

'That's why everyone was so quick to head back to town. They're afraid.'

'They just wanted to go back to the pub!'

'They're sayin there's a *mamu* out there...'

'There's a fuckin *mamu* all right, and he's in your bed!'

'And why are you so worried about who's in my bed?'

'I thought we...'

'We? What do you mean "we"!' Suddenly she'd had enough of my badgering, and somewhere, deep down, I couldn't blame her. She took a step backwards, stomped her foot, fixed me with a furious glare. 'All *you* ever did was stir up a lot o' trouble and leave me to wear it. Tried to tell you last night – thought we mighta been getting somewhere. But no, nothing's changed, old Emily's gotta keep goin like a bull at a gate. You roll up after all these years and everything goes wrong: my father killed, the community torn apart.'

I took a moment to unravel the implications of what she was saying. 'Jesus! You're not suggesting *I* had anything to do with him finishin up, are you?'

'Don't imagine you strangled him, no. You'd have trouble reaching his neck, for starters. But who knows what you stirred up? You might not even know yourself.' She swept a hand out in the general direction of the desert, fixed her gaze on me. 'There's things out there give you a nightmare to even think about.'

'But sleeping with Blakie...'

'So he shares my swag from time to time! So what?' she glared. 'Who I sleep with is none of your business. He's still one of our mob.'

Right. And I wasn't. The anger shot up in me like the sparks from a farrier's hammer. 'One of your mob?' I spat back at her. 'Last person I heard describe Blakie that way was your old man.' I pulled the stones out of my pocket, shoved them into her face. 'You don't reckon he killed him? Well, next time he pops in for a cuppa and a fuck you might ask him what these were doing on the ground next to your father's throttled body!'

That stopped her dead. Stopped me dead too, the guilt bobbing up through a whirlwind of anger and jealousy.

She stared at the stones, shifted her gaze to the mulga, then back to the wind-chime. 'You found these…?'

'Yes,' I snarled, then wheeled around, stormed back to the ute, jumped into the seat and threw her into gear.

Christ, I thought, I'd never understand Hazel or her mob. Whenever I thought I was getting anywhere the ground would shift beneath me. Had the city changed me, or had I always been a crazy outsider and just too stupid to notice?

I hit the road, flat chat, furious. My last glimpse of Hazel was a red blur in the rear-view mirror.

Only when I missed the turn-off and skidded into a fish-tail did I slow down.

As the fury subsided it made room for questions.

Blakie had been sleeping with Hazel. What did that mean? Did it make it more likely that he'd murdered her father, or less likely? Could he have killed him to get him out of the way? Lincoln was a bit more relaxed about Blakie than everybody else, but I doubt whether he'd have wanted him for a son-in-law. Their argument about the diamond dove. Was it about the place, the dreaming – or the person?

But then my thoughts returned to Marsh, he of the dodgy deals and the pit-bull personality.

The madman or the cattleman? I didn't know what to think, but if Hazel thought I was responsible, I'd bloody well prove her wrong. And the only way I could do that was to find out who was.

Shoot!

As soon as I got back to town I phoned the Aboriginal Lands Council in Alice Springs. I was put through to a field officer named Miller, to whom I made my complaint about Marsh and his trespassing cattle. He promised to look into the matter and get back to me.

My next port of call was the police station, where I tried, without success, to speak to Tom McGillivray. His day off, they told me, but I knew where he lived so I decided to go and hassle him at home.

As I was walking back to the car I heard a rough voice behind me.

'Emily?'

I turned around. A shapely, big-haired blonde in a tight red dress and silver sandals was standing there staring at me, a young girl bouncing around beside her.

'It is, isn't it? Emily frickin Tempest?'

'Candy?' I asked, peering at her.

'Course it's bloody Candy! Haven't changed that much, have I?'

'Only for the better, Candy.' I gave her an enthusiastic hug.

Candy Wilson, in addition to being one of my oldest friends, was that rarest of the rare, a white Territorian who'd actually been born there and emerged with her faculties intact. Her father was head stockman out at Edge River for most of my childhood. After an initial demarcation dispute at the Edge River Races one year, she and I had ended up as good, if sporadic, mates.

She had turned out a bit of a rough diamond though, if the rough diamond drilled into her left nostril was anything to go by. She had, as well, an array of fat rings on her fingers and a fierce little scorpion tattooed above her right breast. Fair enough, I decided. From what I'd seen of Bluebush, cultivating a rough edge was one way to survive. Cultivating a cactus hedge was another. She was looking pretty good, albeit in a slinky, slightly harried way that whispered 'single mum'.

'So, Emily,' she was saying, 'what on earth are you doing back here?'

'What are *you* doing here, more to the point. I thought you'd be long gone, woman of the world like yourself.'

'Woman of the world! Huh! I was pregnant a year after you left.'

'Didn't have me to keep you on the straight and narrow.'

'You! Fat lot of straight and narrow you would have kept me on! Remember that rough-rider boy I sprung you with at the rodeo?'

'Should've stuck with him: there's been too many smooth riders since him. And what about you? Is there a Candy Man?' I asked.

'Don't get me started, bitch!' she laughed. 'The men of Bluebush! Jeez, I oughta write a book about the bastards.'

The little girl at her side began jiggling around and dragging at her mother's sleeve. 'Mum, you promised me an ice-cream.'

Her mother frowned. 'Don't push it, Teisha love. Say hello to Emily Tempest. Em's one of my oldest friends. You ever heard me talk about her?'

'No.'

'You will. Look Em,' she said to me, 'can't stay; gotta sort this one out. Where are you living?'

'Toyota Towers.'

She tore the top off a cigarette pack, scribbled a phone number on it and handed it to me. 'Give us a call.'

When they'd gone I drove out to McGillivray's place. His property, as I'm sure he would have preferred to hear it described, ten acres of spinifex and wind and a red-brick hacienda at the posh end of town. Posh in the sense that you could take a walk there without getting raped or scabies.

I found the man himself in the yard out back, a big bay stallion stamping and snorting furiously as he struggled to restrain it with a twitch. He gave the stick another twist and the beast stood still, but its massive shoulders were radiating rage. He stroked its mane, whispered into a quivering ear. Like a lot of other blokes on the fringes of the cattle country, McGillivray was a bit of a cowboy manqué.

'Tom…'

He glanced at me, nodded curtly, then got back to the business at hand, his own hands busy with a wad of twisted horse nose.

'Sorry to interrupt.'

'Yer can make up for it by stickin some of this…' tossing me a bottle of gentian violet, 'onto what's left of the poor bugger's eye.'

From what I could see there was bugger all left of the poor bugger's eye: the good eye spat fire as I scraped pus out of the gruesome wound that was all I could find of the other and coated it with purple paint.

'What's happened here?' I asked, momentarily mesmerised by the stream of pus and blood that trickled down the horse's head.

'Infection. Started out as a grass seed in the eye. Vet took it out a couple of weeks ago.'

'The seed?'

'The eye.'

'Urk…'

'Thought we'd got rid of the infection, but it keeps coming back. All this fuckin dust and heat…' He waved a despairing arm at the adjoining red-dirt paddock.

When we were finished we watched the horse go pounding out into the paddock. It swerved to avoid a stump it hadn't seen until the last moment, then careered off into the rest of the mob, scattering them like billiard balls. McGillivray shook his head. 'Gonna have to put a bullet into that poor bugger one of these days, but I can't bring meself. Had him fifteen years. Give it a bit longer – maybe it'll clear up.'

The horse pushed its way up to a clump of lucerne hay, misjudged it and stumbled, then angrily flicked back its head, looking for somewhere to lay the blame.

'Maybe,' McGillivray said sadly.

We adjourned to the back porch. McGillivray pulled a beer out of an old fridge by the door and tossed it into my lap.

'Okay, Emily, shoot!'

'You're a cynical bastard, Tom. What makes you think I'd need anything other than the pleasure of your company to bring me out here?'

'Yer old man, for one. I seen that look in his eye when he thinks he's onto a buster.' He licked the foam from his mo with a big, ugly tongue, then added, 'And from the look of you, you reckon it's Lasseter's lost reef. This's about Lincoln, I suppose?'

I nodded, then gave it to him both barrels. Blakie and Marsh. Everything I had. It wasn't much, but it was too much for his delicate equilibrium.

'Jesus, Emily!' he interjected when I got to the Earl Marsh bit. He even rolled his eyes – for Tom, after twenty years among undemonstrative Territorians, the equivalent of an hysterical fit. 'You *tryin* to dip me into it or what? I mean, Blakie we can handle…'

'You've done a great job so far.'

'Okay, okay, so you can't get decent help these days, but we'll get im in the end. By waitin if nothin else. But you're askin me to interview Earl *Marsh*? About a dead black-feller?' He looked like he'd just spotted a quartet of hooded horsemen cantering up the drive. 'You must've forgotten how things work out here. When Marsh bought Carbine he joined the gods! One call in the wrong direction from that particular quarter and I'm bookin rabbits out on the Gunbarrel Highway.'

'Somebody's gotta check out the tracks. Somebody's gotta find out what inspired him to sign up Freddy the day before Lincoln died. He have ESP or what? Just think of it as one of the perks of the job, Tom: all that fresh air, travel, you might even score a bit of free meat.'

'Fuck the free meat – it's dead meat I'm seein, an it's got my brand on it.' I gave him my coldest stare, the one Jack referred to as the Refrigerator. He wiped the sweat off his brow, chewed his inner lip, seemed to tear a sizeable strip from it. 'Oh all right, Emily, all right, course I'll look into it. But, shit, it'd be a lot less complicated if you could prove to me that Blakie did it.'

One of Tom's kids – a six-year-old girl who looked so much like her old man that I thought I saw a big red Dennis Lillee moustache on her lip – came out and delivered a plate of *lebkuchen*, courtesy of his German wife. Like her husband, she'd spotted me for work at first glance and was keeping well out of the way.

I took a biscuit, bit a chunk off, then glanced down at the splinters of blue stone I'd just shown him.

'Blakie probably did do it, Tom. I just want to be sure. Tell you what – I'll make a deal.'

'Reckon I need another beer before I'm ready to do a deal with you, Emily.' He glanced at my stubby. 'How's yours goin'?'

I picked it up and showed him. 'Slowly.'

He went across to the fridge, pulled out another bottle, came back and settled into his chair. 'Okay,' he said warily, 'let's have it. This… deal.'

'You investigate Marsh…'

'And you?'

'Gonna do what my father's been telling me to do for years.'

'What's that?' He flipped the ring and took a swig.

'Get me a man.'

His eyes grew dark and narrow. 'And which man would that be?'

'Blakie,' I answered, then ducked as a mouthful of beer came spraying in my direction.

The Jindikuyu Waterhole

I nestled down among the rocks – two massive slabs of iron-stone on the spur of a sandstone plateau – and prepared myself for another day's hunting. I lay on my stomach, adjusted my binoculars, swept them across the valley below. What my little hideaway lacked in comfort it just about made up for in vantage. From its massed battlements I could spot anything that moved within a wide circumference of the Jindikuyu Waterhole. Without, I hoped, being spotted myself: the last thing I wanted the mad bastard to know was that I was after him.

Jindikuyu, five hundred metres below, was a lonely water-hole at the base of a valley in the hills to the south of Moonlight.

By noon the main disadvantage of my observation post had become apparent. It was exposed to the sun. When I got up that morning I'd dressed lightly – T-shirt, shorts, boots – for what looked like a warm day, but now I regretted it. I pulled the blanket over me, but it still seemed like an oven in there. The gravel that had slipped inside my singlet was turning to mud between my breasts. My elbows looked like shrivelled waterholes, my armpits smelt like onions. The water-bottle I'd brought with me had long been emptied, and I was reluctant to make the long haul back to the car in case he came while I was away.

I peeled the last of my oranges, sucked the juice out of it, ate the flesh, picked at the pith and thought about McGillivray's doubts about the wisdom of my undertaking. I was beginning to share those doubts. This was my fourth waterhole, and all I had to show for my efforts so far was a muddy stomach and mild conjunctivitis.

McGillivray had had more than doubts, of course. When I told him what I was planning to do, he hit the roof and told me I was sailing close to a charge of interfering with the course of justice.

I came anyway. I was sailing close to all sorts of things, the least of which was a criminal conviction. Round here criminal convictions are like sorry scars and body mutilation – a rite of passage. Everybody who's anybody's got one.

Blakie had to be out there somewhere, and I was going to find out where.

One thing I'd always known about him was that, for all his crazy peregrinations, he tended to have a bolthole. Or a series of boltholes, carefully concealed havens among which he circulated and within which he stored the trophies and emblems of his eccentricity: his bottles and bones, his feathers, coins and coloured stones.

Jack and I had stumbled across one of his camps once, while we were out prospecting. It was in a little hollow in the hills above the Mosquito Creek Waterhole. We'd known whose it was at a glance: the translucent skins stretched between branches, the ochre stones and crystals, the reek of green meat. Unfortunately Blakie had come back at the wrong moment and sent us on our way with a volley of spittle and imprecations, but the memory lingered.

The Mosquito had been my first stake-out, of course, but in two days of careful observation I hadn't seen a thing. When I did finally screw up my courage and check out the campsite, I found a family of mulga snakes that looked like they'd been settled there for generations.

If the Mosquito Creek hadn't given me Blakie, however, it had given me an idea of how to find him. Water, that was the key. Blakie might be able to sleep with his rocks, but he couldn't drink them. There were only half a dozen permanent water supplies within striking distance of the Moonlight camp. If I staked them out, one by one, sooner or later I was bound to come across him.

Looked like it was going to be later, I decided by late in the afternoon of the Jindikuyu stake-out. It had been a long hot day. Blakie must have thought so too: clearly he wasn't going to show.

My thoughts turned to Hazel. As they tended to do. I'd fucked things up there all right. As I tended to do.

Blakie and Hazel. I still couldn't believe it. Blakie and a pus-eyed dog would have been a lop-sided enough item – in favour of the dog – but Blakie and my beautiful Hazel? How could she?

I rolled onto my back, closed my eyes, let my mind drift down corridors of filtered light. What would she be doing now? Pottering round the camp, carrying water, cooking. Painting, perhaps. Thinking about me? Christ, who could say? Probably not.

I stirred myself, sat up, took a look around. The only movement to be seen was a shimmer in the air and the odd meandering bullock.

Knock-off time. I'd had enough. McGillivray was right: this was crazy.

Two parrots appeared, scudding through the air like small green boats, rising and falling and forging their way forward: heading for the waterhole. I decided to do the same, get a drink before making the long haul back to the car. I picked up a water-bottle, clambered over the rocks and made my way down to the hole.

I was twenty metres west of the water when a sudden perturbation in the shrubbery made me look up in alarm.

A bullock came clattering out of the umbrella bushes. I sighed with relief: just another thirsty nomad. It stood there staring, tentative-eyed, wing-ribbed, tongue like a dried-out porcupine, then decided I wasn't a threat and moved forward.

Know how you feel, feller, I thought as I watched its great grey body go panting up to the water's edge. Don't worry about me: there's enough for both of us.

I took a step forward, then stopped in horror as a monster exploded out of the waterhole.

It was mud-swathed, water-whirling, huge and hairy, presumably human, with a roar in its throat and an axe in its hands. The bullock's terrified bellow was cut off by a terrible, arcing blow which finished up half way through its skull.

I stood there, rooted in more ways than one.

Where the fuck had Blakie come from? How had he got here without my seeing him? This wasn't the way I'd planned it.

I dropped onto my stomach and hid behind a boulder.

Had he seen me?

Maybe not. I heard him squelching through the mud, heard the carcass being ripped, hacked and cracked, all to the accompaniment of a sonic cocktail of every imaginable bovine fluid.

If I was the next item on the menu he was taking his time getting to me.

Half an hour later I smelt smoke, heard the sound of wood being smashed. I poked my nose round the side of the rock. He was sitting with his back to me, a fire at his feet, a mess of bloody beast beyond. Soon there came the smell of roasting meat. Rib bones. Sizzling offal. Later a set of crocodilian jaws crunching, a pair of fat lips slurping like the suction pump on a slaughterhouse floor.

He began to sing, his big, bull-frog bass hammering out into the night.

Another hour and the singing turned to snoring.

I gave him thirty minutes, then inched my way back up the hill, my heart hitting the mouth-tops every time a rock rolled or a branch broke.

When I finally made the lookout, I was tempted to do a runner, so shaken was I by the closeness of the encounter. But no, I resolved, I'd set out to do a job, and I was determined to see it through. I put a blanket round my shoulders, leaned against a rock. I tried to stay awake, but sleep crept up on me in a subtle flood. The stars were still high in the sky when the cold awoke me. I studied the waterhole: Blakie's fire could be seen dimly glowing at water's edge.

When it grew light enough I was alarmed to see that his blanket was empty. I instinctively glanced behind me, visions of that terrible slaughter-axe racing through my mind, but there was nothing there. Blakie came back into the camp below soon afterwards, a snake draped across his shoulders.

I kept the glasses on him, watched him go about his morning activities. He ate, sang, laid his stones out on the ground and studied them. One time he stopped for a shit under a wirewood tree. So clear was my view that I saw his attendant flies disappear, then return, evidently deciding that Blakie was a better prospect than a free-range turd.

Finally he filled a water-bottle, threw a slab of meat and an armful of bones into an improvised back pack – a blanket twisted around his shoulders – then set off, striding down the valley with the slow, relentless gait of a post-prandial goanna.

I followed. He headed west, keeping to the flats and foothills, for which I was grateful. It made it easier for me to keep to the ridges. From time to time, when I had to cut across a gully or skirt an incline, I'd lose him. But whenever I got back to the heights he reappeared.

I had a moment of concern when he reached the blacksoil plains. It would have been impossible for me to tail him out across those bare, cracking tablelands without being seen, but he swung north, rounded the cape and headed up into Koolya Gorge. For the next twenty minutes I more or less retraced my steps as he worked his way up the gorge.

I lost him in a stand of desert oaks at the bottom of Pangulu Hill, and was surprised when he reappeared a minute later, making his way up its cliffs.

Now I'm fucked, I thought. I'll never be able to follow him up there.

But he'd only climbed for four or five metres when he disappeared.

'What the hell…!' I said out loud.

I studied the spot where I'd last seen him. A clump of hoya vines clung to the rocks there. I focused on the vines, trying to work out what had happened to him.

Soon afterwards his head appeared; he peered up and down the valley, then vanished. There was a cave of some sort in there.

I sat back, allowed myself a brief smile.

I'd found the bugger's hideout.

Taking Blakie

'Emily, Emily, Emily…' He didn't so much enunciate as exhale. Slowly and sadly, like a tyre coming out of a patch of tea-tree scrub.

'Tom, Tom, Tom… What's troubling you?'

'All these complications…'

'Complications! What a worrywart you are. I'm doing your job for you.'

McGillivray gave me a long, sceptical gaze, then returned his attention to the road. I was in the passenger seat of his Toyota, and we were twenty minutes away from the Jindikuyu turn-off.

After my encounter with Blakie, I'd driven straight into Bluebush and told the cops that I knew where he was hiding. Tom hadn't looked too convinced, but he had little choice but to follow up my lead.

'Cleaning up your crime rate,' I went on, waving my arms about. 'How many other regions have got loose murderers roaming around them? Unsolved homicides? Escaped maniacs?'

'We haven't even managed to track down your last suspect yet.'

'Hurl Mars? Not avoiding him, are you?'

'He's a hard man to catch. Sent a constable out to talk to him, but he's been over at the stock sales in Mount Isa. Before that he was in Canberra. On business.'

'Canberra! What sort of business?'

'He's becoming a big cheese in the Cattlemen's Assoc- iation, your Mr Marsh.'

'Hope they showed him how to use a knife and fork.'

'His missus tells me he's back now, but he's out the stock camp. Doesn't know the meaning of a returned call. If we haven't heard from him by the time I get back from this wild goose chase, I'll go and track him down meself.'

'Maybe the wild goose'll solve the mystery for us.'

'Blakie?' he frowned. 'Maybe.' His maybe sounded as big as his beer gut. 'You sure you'll be able to find this place again?'

'Pretty sure.'

'Normally I would have asked Pepper an Arch, but they don't want to go anywhere near Blakie. Tried to get the ranger to come along – he knows the country as well as any whitefeller, but his office told me he was out bush.'

I had a few doubts of my own, not the least of them about the quality of Tom's support staff. I glanced back at the second police Toyota behind us: the A-Team. There were five of them, and I couldn't help but notice the lingering, malicious attention they'd paid to their equipment – cuffs, clubs, guns, sprays, even a net – when we were loading up. Griffo was there, of course, as were the other two who'd come off the worse for the wear after their last encounter with Blakie. Payback was clearly as much an incentive for them as was any desire to enforce the law.

Tom must have detected my concerns. 'Don't worry about

the boys' – he jerked a thumb at the car behind us – 'they've all done their cross-cultural communication course.'

I looked back in time to see the cross-cultural communicator in the driver's seat open his window, limber his lips and let fly with a glob of spit, much of which ended up on his colleagues in the back.

We parked the cars a couple of kilometres away from the cave, and I led the party up into the southern side of the gorge. We reached my vantage point opposite Pangulu Hill just before it became too dark to see what we were doing. There was a bit of sporadic grumbling from the troops when Tom wouldn't allow them a fire, but they did have thermoses of coffee – rummed-up coffee, from the smell of it – hamburgers in foil and thick government swags. They were doing a damn sight better than I had last time I was here, chasing Blakie on a breakfast of orange pith and adrenalin.

McGillivray shook me awake before dawn, and I led him up to the ridge, both of us stumbling about in the dark while his team remained in their swags. 'Won't be needing em just yet,' he explained. We stretched out alongside each other, concealed among a row of scrubby emu bushes that rimmed the ridge, until it grew light enough to see.

'Okay,' I told him. 'It's on the opposite cliff. Fix your glasses on a point about half way between the gneiss and the mica schist.'

'The nice and what?'

'Reddish rock on the left, yellow one on the right. Little patch of greenery there. Hoya vine.'

He studied it, took the glasses away, squinted, rubbed his eyes, then tried again.

'Got it,' he said at last.

'Some sort of cave in there,' I explained.

'Hmmmm…' came the rather dubious response. 'I see.'

'So what do we do now?'

'We wait.'

'How long?'

'Till we're sure he's at home. Already tried taking him in the open once. Don't want to make that mistake again. We're only gonna get one chance. We go sniffin around down there he'll know for sure.'

He nestled down among the shrubbery, and we made a bit of desultory conversation. The talk turned to my early years: the front veranda, the home brew, the old man.

Tom had the scarifying task of informing my father of my mother's death. It was how they first met. Tom was a constable then, officer-in-charge of the Borroloola Police Station. Alice had been travelling with some of our country-women in the back of a utility which rolled out on the highway. She'd been thrown and crushed.

It wasn't until months afterwards that Jack realised how considerate Tom had been about the whole ghastly business, how seriously he took the role of a small-town cop: he'd brought us into town from the station where Jack was working, helped arrange the funeral and dropped in, from time to time, during the miserable months that followed.

Jack got the job on Moonlight soon afterwards. When Tom McGillivray turned up a few years later, promoted to sergeant and transferred to Bluebush, the acquaintanceship developed into a friendship.

It may have been the fact that he'd had to deliver bad news to my old man once before that made him suddenly wary:

'When we go in, Em, you stay here, right? Like we agreed? I'll leave you with a radio so you can listen in, but no more heroics.'

I glanced at his team of sleeping uglies. 'Don't worry, I wouldn't want to put them under any pressure. Right now, though, I've got other pressures on my mind. Or my bladder.'

'Uh. Right. You go and kill a tree, I'll keep an eye out for Blakie.'

I dropped down from the ridge, made my way back down the faceted slopes until I came to the only tree in sight – a heavily canopied bloodwood that had somehow managed to survive and prosper in this stark environment.

I hitched my dress up and squatted low, then surrendered myself to the eternal pleasures of an early-morning piss in a lovely, lonely landscape.

'Ahem…'

The cough came from directly above.

I sprang to my feet, whipped my undies up and my dress down, took a step backwards, lost my footing, stumbled, recovered and looked up.

For a moment I could discern nothing but the thick foliage of the tree, then I spotted a pair of boots on a branch in its upper reaches. The boots were attached to a pair of bare, bronzed legs. I tried to place him but the bugger was wearing khaki clothing which seemed to disappear among the greenery. It wasn't until I spotted a red beanie higher up the tree that I realised who it was.

'Jojo Kelly!'

His head popped out of a thicket of leaves. 'Morning, Emily.'

'What the fuck are you doing up there? Aside from perving at my bum?'

'Looking for you, actually.'

'Well you found me.'

'I meant youse – plural. If you're with Tom McGillivray. Got some garbled message saying he wanted a hand.'

'Well you found us plural. Now get down from that bloody tree so I can make a citizen's arrest.'

'Hang on.'

A minute or two passed. 'Look,' I said, exasperated and jiggling, 'are you coming down? I'd like to finish my piss in peace.'

'Go right ahead, don't mind me. What's for breakfast?'

'A bollocking from McGillivray, I hope. He's up on that ridge, by the way.'

'I know. I spotted him just before you made your grand entrance.'

I gave him another thirty seconds. A lot of leaf-rustling took place, but there was no sign of his descent.

'Hello!' I called.

'Hmmm?'

'What are you actually doing up there?'

'It's a nice tree. Why shouldn't I be up it? Besides, there's a hive.' I noticed a few bees sidling in from the grasslands below. 'We can have honey in our tea.'

'We're not here for a fucking picnic,' I grumbled at him as I climbed back up the slope, annoyed, and yet, at the same time, grudgingly amused and curious to know what he was up to.

The police camp, by the time I got back to it, was a hive of another kind: the cops were up and about and moving around as though they meant business. They were checking their watches and guns, adjusting their body armour, uncoiling ropes and nodding at McGillivray as he rattled off a string of orders.

'What's happened?' I asked.

McGillivray looked at me with an unusually appreciative eye. 'I owe you one, Emily. He's there all right.'

'You saw him? Blakie?'

'Just now. Poked his big ugly mug out through the vines, took a look around and went back inside. He won't get away this time.'

'Good. Go get him! Your mate's here, by the way.'

He paused, gazed at me blankly.

'The ranger.'

'Jojo? He's here?' The men looked at each other, momentarily taken aback. McGillivray studied the slope I'd just climbed. 'Where is he?'

'Up a tree, last I saw him.'

He rolled his eyes. 'That'd be right. Whatever, we don't need him now. Half a dozen of us ought to be enough to do the job.' He gave me a hand-held radio, then drew his men together for a final briefing. 'Righto, you lot, now listen up. We don't know whether he's armed or not: he didn't have a gun on him last time we saw him, but that doesn't mean a thing. He could have an arsenal in there for all we know, so don't take any chances.'

They moved out in what was obviously a carefully pre-pared manoeuvre, and, to my surprise, they actually seemed to know what they were doing.

Four of them moved out to opposite sides of the rock face and began to make a steady ascent, while the two others –

one of them McGillivray – zig-zagged across the valley floor and up through the desert oaks at the base of Pangulu Hill. I could eavesdrop on their whispered conversations by means of the radio.

I lay among the bushes and watched, so absorbed by their manoeuvring that I didn't hear Jojo until he came up and stood behind me.

'What's going on?' he asked.

'They're about to grab Blakie Japanangka.'

'Ah. That explains it.'

The four men on the hill had assembled directly above the cave by now: two of them prepared to make a descent, the others wedged themselves into support positions on the ridge.

I nodded at the cliff. 'There's a cave in there.'

'I see.'

'His hideout.'

'Hideout?'

I looked up at him and frowned. 'Yes, and if you can't do anything other than repeat everything I say, perhaps you could at least stay out of sight; you'll ruin the surprise.'

'Oh, I doubt that,' he said.

Then he popped over the edge of the ridge and began to descend the slope in a casual, sideways lope, his big feet ploughing long furrows into the dirt and raising clouds of dust.

'What are you doing?' I called out, jumping up and suddenly finding myself tumbling down beside him.

'Love those entrances, don't you?' he asked as he helped me to my feet.

I spat the sand out of my mouth and looked up to see

McGillivray waving at us to get out of sight. Jojo reacted as if the wave was a greeting, gave a cheerful reply and resumed his descent; I had little choice but to do the same. By the time we reached the valley floor, McGillivray was just about purple. The radio crackled in my hands. 'Emily! Jojo!' he hissed. 'Get out of sight or I'll bloody well throttle the pair of you!'

Jojo had the message by now. 'Righto, righto, if you insist,' he murmured, then we sat with our backs against one of the sandstone blocks scattered across the valley floor. He immediately seemed to lose interest in the imminent arrest, his attention caught by a sand shrimp slowly working its way beneath the dirt and leaving a tiny furrow in its wake. He picked at it with a blade of grass, then reared back in feigned horror when it rose out of the dirt.

He looked at me and asked, 'How did they know he was here, by the way?'

'I followed him.'

'Ah. I see.'

The two coppers on the rock face were directly above the cave by now. I looked around from our boulder in time to see them pause, brace themselves, nod at each other, then hurl themselves in.

A long silence ensued, during which Jojo climbed to his feet, clambered up our rock and sat there watching, interested at last.

Griffo's voice finally came crackling over the radio. 'It's empty, Sarge!'

I didn't need the radio to hear McGillivray's reply. 'Wadderye mean it's empty? He's there. I just saw him!'

'Well he isn't here now.'

'How deep is the cave?'

'Hard to say. Looks deep.'

'Have you checked it out thoroughly?'

'Pretty well.'

'Check it out bloody well. He must be in there somewhere.'

Another anguished silence ensued.

Jojo dropped down from the rock and began walking towards the scene. I followed, slightly worried about the reception I'd get, but McGillivray only had eyes for the activities on the cliff.

The silence was shattered by an echoing gun shot, a strangled oath and the sight of two cops emerging from the cave at full tilt. They made for the ropes, but one of them missed and fell to the ground, his fall broken by the vines and trees below.

By the time we reached him, he was kneeling on the ground, face down, big arse pointing skywards. It was Griffo, battered, bruised and clutching his head as if it were about to fall off.

'You right there, mate?' asked Kelly.

'Centipedes!' muttered Griffo, a dazed look on his face as he climbed to his feet.

Jojo looked surprised for the first time since I'd met him. 'You shot a *centipede*?'

'I thought it was a snake, it was that big. Spider webs in the back of the cave were crawling with em. Walked into em. Jesus, I hate centipedes. Oh fuck!' – he ripped his helmet off, his face transformed into a quivering mass of shivers and shudders and gaping holes – 'there's another one!'

A wicked black arthropod, its little legs flickering like strobe lights, came spiralling out of the helmet and landed on the rocks, then scuttled away.

He raised his gun, but Jojo put a hand on his arm. 'Okay, Tiger, I don't think it's gonna do any harm now. Have you been bitten?'

'Just once, I reckon. On my neck.'

I considered suggesting a tourniquet, but Jojo, frowning at me as if he read my mind, pulled a handful of leaves out of a pouch on his belt, crushed them and rubbed the resulting oily liquid into the bite. 'Try this,' he said.

McGillivray came up and stood over us, the now-familiar look of exasperation clouding his face.

'Do us a favour, Jojo; go and have a look in that cave for me, will you?'

'You think there's any point?'

'No, but if you do happen to come across Blakie, would you mind asking him if he'll let us arrest him?'

Jojo shimmied up the cliff and entered the cave. Less than a minute later he was on his way back down.

'Empty, Tom.'

'Is there a fire escape or something? I just saw him in there.'

'Nothing that I could see.'

'So what are we going to do now?' I asked McGillivray.

'Dunno about you,' he said wearily, checking his watch and casting a cold eye upon the surrounding hills, 'but I'm thinking about that all-day breakfast at the Resurrection Roadhouse.'

While he assembled his troops, Jojo made his way to a low outcrop, stood there looking down at the jutting rocks and tessellated pavements of the valley floor. I came up beside him.

'Any sign of him?'

'Only the ones he wants us to see.'

'Why do I suspect you're not surprised by this shemozzle?'

He made no response, but put a hand into his shirt pocket and drew from it a small brown feather.

'Very nice,' I said. 'Where'd you find it?'

'Up the bloodwood.'

'Feather up a tree. Unusual.'

'It is.' He passed it to me. 'Take a closer look.'

'Owl, I'd say.'

'Anything else?'

'Looks like it's seen better days. Comes from a ragged old owl.'

'Comes from a ragged old something. Do you see those tiny smudges at the top?'

'A ragged old owl with questionable hygiene?'

'It's ochre. Smell it.

'Goanna fat,' he said when I had done so. 'Touch of spinifex rosin at the base of the quill, too.'

'What are you getting at?'

'The bloodwood. I wasn't the only one up it last night.'

I paused, stared at him. 'Jesus. What was he doing up there?'

'Same as me, I'd imagine.'

'Watching me have my morning piddle?'

'I don't know what you got up to before I arrived, but he was watching the lot of you, for sure. It's the best vantage point.'

'How the hell did he know we were even here?'

'How many ways do you want? He could have seen your tracks. I did.'

'We arrived just on nightfall.'

'Or heard your cars.'

'We parked a couple of kilometres away.'

'Still a million possibilities: you could have spooked a bat, silenced a cricket. A hopping mouse could have told him, for all I know. This part of the world, it's like an orchestra to Blakie and he's – well, he wouldn't think of himself as the conductor, but perhaps he's on first violin. And if there's a piccolo off pitch or a timpani out of time, he'll hear it.'

I sat there for a few minutes, staring off into the distance, thinking about what he'd said and wondering about the sense of what I was doing. I remembered Lincoln's words to me. 'Take a little while till the country gets to know you.' Was there an undercurrent of something similar in Jojo's voice?

As my thoughts drifted, I found my eyes meandering across the rock face opposite, the one we'd just descended. It was fretted and fringed with hieroglyphs and scribbled shadows, a calligraphy of little dips and folds and charcoal figures. One of which suddenly looked like a face: a dark, furrowed visage topped with matted hair and a purple headband.

I blinked, and it disappeared.

A Cup of Tea at the Godsfather

The day after my return from this ignominious shambles I got a call from the Lands Council in Alice. A lawyer by the name of Charles Harmes. He wanted to talk to me about Earl Marsh and his dodgy lease, and asked if we could meet the next afternoon.

'No worries. How about the Godsfather?'

'The *Gods*father?'

'The café at the northern end of the main street. Sign on the front says "The Godfather's", but we're more into Jesus than Brando round here.'

'Sounds like an offer I can't refuse. Will you be free all afternoon? I'll explain when we get there.'

The Godfather's was Bluebush's attempt at inner-city café society chic. For years it had been a greasy takeaway, notorious for its camelburgers and dead white chips. The current owner, Helmut Apfelbaum, had slapped on a coat of paint and arranged a few striped umbrellas artfully out the front, but he hadn't got around to the back yet. The itinerants he employed to peel the spuds would sit out on the back steps, smoking and yarning and chucking the skins into the long grass that had sprung up around the overflowing septic tank.

Despite the flagrant abuse of health regulations, the coffee wasn't bad – Helmut ground his own – and the conversation was a cut above what you got at the White Dog. The town's intelligentsia, teachers and nurses, tended to hang out there on a Friday afternoon and soak up the ambience. Much of which, if the wind was blowing the wrong way, came from the aforementioned tank.

Today the café was full of tourists and Charles stood out like a poodle in a pack of camp dogs. Lawyers with a social conscience inevitably have a haggard, hangdog look about them, and Charles was as hangdog as I'd seen. He was in his mid-thirties, wearing crisp jeans and a blue checked shirt. He had a receding hairline, a receding chin and, by the look of the creases in his jeans, a receding personality. The only thing that wasn't receding was his nose, an immense proboscis of a hue that suggested it had sat through too many outdoor land-claim hearings.

'I haven't eaten,' he said when the introductions were out of the way. 'What do you recommend?'

I studied the blackboard menu. Marinated buffalo steaks. Crocodile skewers. Wild boar sausages. Helmut was going all gourmet.

'A cup of tea. Weak black is probably your safest option.'

'I prefer it white.'

'Don't say I didn't warn you.'

To his credit he didn't, when, minutes later, he poured his milk from its cute little silver jug and watched in dismay as it came tumbling out in yellow chunks.

'Helmut!' I yelled.

The owner came shuffling wearily over, a tea-towel on his shoulder, hair sprouting from every possible orifice. He'd had a long day. A long life, if it came to that, as had the milk.

'Helmut, look at our bloody milk!'

He peered, sniffed, winced, then shuffled to the kitchen and back without a word of apology, without a word of any description except for a complaint about the waitress. 'She must haf used last week's supply by mistake,' he grumbled as he placed a fresh jug on the table. 'Dese girls! Do you haf any idea vot it's like trying to get staff out here?'

'You could try selecting them by some criteria other than the size of their breasts.'

I'd only been coming here for a few weeks, but that was long enough to observe that Helmut's employees tended to be Swedish backpackers who aroused memories of his Bavarian youth and lasted about as long as the first failed seduction.

'Perhaps the first thing I should do,' said Charles, after a restorative sip of his Earl Grey, 'is thank you for bringing the matter to our attention. It does appear that Mr Marsh is engaging in behaviour which could only be described as egregious, and possibly illegal.'

'Like murder?'

Charles blinked. 'I beg your pardon?'

'Nothing.' I knew I was going to have to go it alone on that one; the Land Council Legal Department's brief went a long way, but not as far as homicide. 'You've looked at the lease?'

'I don't know that I would dignify it with that name, and in point of fact, no, we haven't. Which is, in itself I might add, sufficient reason for it to be regarded as lacking in any legal standing whatsoever.'

'*Que?*'

'Article 7.6 of the title deed states that for any agreement on the land use to be legitimate it needs to be confirmed by both a two-thirds majority of the owners and their legal representatives. To whit, ourselves.'

'So you'll go out there and tell him to piss off?'

'Quite. Or we will.'

I was raising the cup to my lips, but the last comment made me pause, mid-air. 'I dunno that I like the sound of that "we".'

'I held a meeting yesterday with the traditional owners.'

'You managed to round them up?'

'We found sufficient numbers to make a quorum here, in the Bluebush Town Camp.'

'Including Freddy Ah Fong?'

'Freddy was there, but his contribution to the discussion was... minimal.'

'You mean he was pissed?'

'Possibly. He does seem to have been struck by a certain... amnesia...'

'That'd be guilt.'

'...over his negotiations with Mr Marsh. Be that as it may, the owners have authorised the Lands Council to demand Mr Marsh remove his stock forthwith or face the consequences. We've sent a field officer out to investigate and, as you said, there are upwards of a thousand head of cattle contentedly grazing upon Moonlight pasture.'

'So where do I come into it?'

'When I suggested that it would be usual practice for a representative of the community to accompany us when such a demand is presented, what might best be described as a rather profound silence settled over the group...'

'Ah. The breach into which Kuminjayi would normally step.'

'At which point someone suggested you.'

'I'm not a traditional owner. My mob come from up the Gulf country.'

'They do seem to regard you as a member of the community.'

'I'm touched.'

'It was you who drew the matter to our attention. And it was you who, from all reports, was not afraid to... beard the lion, so to speak. All in all, it would seem that you'd be an appropriate representative.'

'Does Marsh know you're coming?'

'Well, not as such, no. If he knew the reason for our trip I doubt whether he'd sit around waiting for us. But I'm pretty sure he's there. I put in a call to the homestead and spoke to someone I presume was his wife. She said he'd be back today.'

'Today?' I checked my watch. Two-thirty. Charles leaned forward, looked a little wary. Here comes the crunch, I thought.

'I've got a plane waiting out at the airstrip,' he explained. 'We could be out there and back before sunset...'

I sipped my tea, my mind busily weighing up the pros and cons of Charles' suggestion. The main con, the prospect of Marsh slaughtering me on the spot, would presumably be reduced by the fact that I was packing a lawyer. A real one, this time.

What were the pros? A chance to sink the elastic-sided slipper into Marsh, see a bit of new country from the air and, most important of all, carry out a bit of extra-curricular sniffing. Maybe shed some light onto the circumstances of Lincoln's death.

'So you'll come?' Charles asked.

I smiled darkly. 'Lemme at im.'

The plane was a single-engine Piper Warrior, the pilot a gangly farm boy named Jason who looked like he would have been more at home at the handlebars of a BMX than the controls of an aeroplane. I studied him warily: he had the shades and the cap, the flak jacket and the gum, but did he have the flying skills to get us there in one piece? My doubts diminished when I observed the supple ease with which he handled the take-off and the hour's flight to Carbine Creek, but they came rushing back with the landing.

We were still some distance from the station runway when our engine spluttered and fell silent. Our boy-pilot yelled, 'Oh my God!' and jerked the throttle back and forth. No response. 'Have to bring her in downwind!'

Christ, I thought, is this how I'm going to end up? As a pile of avgas-scented ashes on Marsh's doorstep?

I was sitting in the front seat, and watched in heart-thumping horror as the wind gathered momentum and the earth flew up at us. I closed my eyes and a string of images appeared: my father, for one, then Hazel, and finally, ever so fleetingly, my poor dear mother.

I opened my eyes to see the runway rushing into view. 'Not gonna make it!' Jason screamed. We thumped down in rough pasture a hundred metres short of the runway, hit a rock, jerked skywards, bucked about by some killer wave, levelled out and made another touchdown.

The plane shuddered to a halt. The three of us sat there, motionless, stunned. Jason's fingernails had embedded themselves in the yoke. Charles looked like he'd swallowed his briefcase.

'Nice piece of work, Jason,' I said, my voice quavering. 'If it's all the same to you, I think I'll drive next time.'

Jason climbed out, stretched his back and made a dubious inspection of the undercarriage.

'Wheel's gonna need replacing,' he gasped.

'Thought we were, too, for a moment there. Got a spare one, have you Jason?'

'No way I'll be able to fix that out here.' He kicked the battered strut, massaged his forearms. 'What a fucking mess.'

'Quite,' commented Charles, adjusting his Adam's apple. 'And it's about to get a lot messier.'

He nodded at a shed adjoining the homestead, maybe a kilometre away, from which a familiar red F100 was emerging, slow and ominous.

Carbine Creek

We stood there watching the big utility home in on us.

As it pulled up we were all relieved to see that the driver was not Marsh, but an old timer who chose to remain nameless, and looked like a sun-dried Fidel Castro. He studied us for a time and then asked, 'Youse'd be the lawyers?'

Charles and I glanced at each other. Had there been a breach of security? It was possible. The station owners were little emperors out here, with tentacles stretching in every direction. Somebody – the charter company, air traffic control – must have tipped Marsh off that the Lands Council was on the way.

Charles replied that yes, we were the lawyers, or he was, and introduced me as 'Ms Tempest, my associate'. Fidel said nothing, but took a plug of tobacco out of his mouth and put it behind his ear, scratching his skinny arse as he looked me up and down.

I looked him up and down right back, wondering as I did so whether his curiosity was motivated by my gender or my ethnicity. Or by his lively and enquiring mind.

While we were standing around swapping silences with the Cuban lookalike, Jason got on the radio, raised air traffic control and told them we were stranded. Charles and I glanced ruefully at each other when Bluebush eventually said they'd get a rescue party out there by mid-morning.

'Tomorrow!' muttered Charles. 'We'll be lucky to survive that long, once Marsh finds out why we're here.'

We piled aboard the F100 and headed for the station. 'So Mr Marsh is expecting us?' Charles asked.

Our driver's response was incomprehensible, but the cigarette on his upper lip wobbled in a way that seemed to suggest the affirmative.

Fidel wasn't offering much in the way of a commentary. He didn't need to. The station spoke for itself: manicured lawns, gravelled walkways, wide verandas, wicker chairs. A classic outback homestead. Marsh was doing all right for himself. The Big House was constructed of mottled sandstone and nestled among a small forest of poinciana and casuarinas. To the east was an orchard of oranges and lemons, figs, paw paws, mangoes. To the west was a collection of outbuildings, including workshops, a meat house and the single men's quarters.

If our driver was a master of taciturnity, the woman waiting for us at the front gate was his polar opposite.

'Good afternoon,' she enunciated, all gushes and smiles. 'Welcome to Carbine Creek. So lovely to meet you. I'm Nancy Marsh. You must be the lawyers?'

Jesus, I was thinking, this is Marsh's wife?

She was tall, dark-haired, somewhere out in the no-man's land between buxom and fat, dressed in a red floral dress and a pink straw hat. I put her in her late thirties, maybe ten years younger than her brute of a husband. And she was a *Pom*: the accent was north-of-England riff-raff, with an overcoat of aspirational squire's lady. Judging by the colour of her skin, she must have a chronic antipathy to sunshine, particularly given the size of the portions in which it came out here.

If I'd been asked to imagine a Mrs Marsh, I'd have pictured something scrawny and put upon, with skin cancers the size of cockroaches and a mouth full of fencing nails. Maybe dressed in footy shorts and steel-capped boots. What on earth was this displaced English rose doing out here with Cro-Magnon man? She didn't look like she'd been kidnapped.

'Indeed,' responded Charles, automatically ratcheting up into legal mode. 'Charles Harmes, and my associate, Ms Tempest. Emily. And our pilot, Jason… er, Jason.'

'I'm sorry, Earl isn't here just now,' she smiled. 'He's been held up, in the South Paddock. Water problems…'

'Nothing serious, I hope.'

'Or personal,' I couldn't help but put in.

She looked at me, momentarily perplexed, then explained, 'Par for the course round here, I'm afraid. Water table's getting lower every year. I didn't think he was expecting you this early. Come in and make yourselves comfy. I'll get Alyssia to put the kettle on.'

Ten minutes later we were ensconced in the lounge room and Mrs Marsh and a teenage girl introduced as 'Alyssia, the governess' were busily stuffing into us a sumptuous afternoon tea – scones with jam and cream, lamingtons, home-made biscuits, sponge cakes, the works. I'd assumed Earl Marsh's generous gut came from the all-the-beef-you-can-eat deal that was the basis of every station menu. By the time I'd fought off Mrs Marsh – Nance, she insisted – and her third slab of chocolate sponge, I was thinking about it in a new light.

During the course of the conversation I picked up a little

of her personal history: she'd come from the English mill town of Preston ten years before, somehow ending up as a governess on a property in Queensland. It was there that she'd met and fallen for the irresistible Earl. They'd been on Carbine for five years now.

Nance looked aghast when we told her about our hazardous landing, cooed sympathetically, confirmed that we didn't have any broken bones and shuffled us off to the guest-house – a comfortable, two-roomed bungalow with a wide veranda and green-striped awnings, spotlessly clean, with polished wooden floors and lancewood railings – for 'a nice lie down'.

While Charles and Jason were revelling in the good life on the deck chairs I took the opportunity to have a look around. I thought I might try to talk to some of the station hands and see what I could pick up about relations between Carbine and Moonlight. I poked my nose into a few sheds, but the only hand I came across was the withered revolutionary who'd driven us in from the plane. He was in the workshop, where he was crankily cannibalising a clapped-out grader.

I tried the perennial opening gambits – cattle prices, roads, rodeos and rain – but his responses were little more than grunts, until I mentioned that my father had been a mechanic on Moonlight Downs. He muttered something like 'more dogs than cattle' – his comment, I presumed, on the fact that it was now in the hands of the blacks.

I gave up and returned to the bungalow, where Charles and Jason were sipping at their drinks and marvelling at our reception. Nance had been and gone, leaving iced water, towels, even toothbrushes and combs.

'Still can't work it out,' said Jason, gazing at his toothbrush in wonder. 'Normally when I bring you Lands Council mob out to the stations, they set the dogs onto us.'

'Don't get too comfortable,' I warned. 'The boss isn't home yet. Probably got the dogs on the ute.'

'Exactly what I was thinking,' said Charles. 'There may be a case of mistaken identity happening here.'

'We'll find out soon enough,' said the pilot, taking a long draught of beer and settling deeper into his chair. 'Nance said dinner's at six. If it's anything like afternoon tea I can't wait.'

At the appointed hour the three of us came in the back door of the homestead. Nance looked up from the stove, an apron over her dress, flour on her hands. She ushered us in, sat us down in the lounge room, plied us with drinks, passed round the nuts and olives. Alyssia was setting the table in the adjoining dining room.

'Earl's back,' said Nance. 'He's in his office. Maybe you could let him know dinner's ready, Emily? It's just down the corridor there, on your right.'

This'll be interesting, I thought as I followed her directions and came to a spacious, wood-panelled room looking out onto the poincianas.

The room contained all the accoutrements and paraphernalia of your modern station office: paper-strewn desk, computer workstation, filing cabinets, bookshelves, gold-framed photos of sour-faced, hefty beasts and one sour-faced, hefty owner.

Marsh looked like he was just out of the shower: barefooted and freshly scrubbed, skin glowing, dressed in a singlet and shorts, relaxing in an armchair, grinning and gazing in rapt attention at a television. I was almost embarrassed to see that I'd sprung the poor bastard watching a Wiggles video. It took me a second or two to notice the small girl, about two or three years of age, perched upon his knee.

The girl turned around and gazed at me with the most angelic expression I'd ever seen, an intriguing amalgam of surprise, curiosity and delight. Indeed, everything about the child was angelic: the aureole of dark ringlets around her alabaster face, the full lips, the perfect teeth and the wide blue eyes.

Amazing, I thought. How could Earl and Nance have produced something like this? God must have taken every skerrick of potential beauty their genes possessed and refined it into this single exquisite creation.

The spell couldn't last, and it didn't. Earl noticed the girl looking away from the box, followed her gaze, and the grin faded. If the girl did have anything of the angel in her she needed it now, as Marsh leapt to his feet, a look of disbelief sweeping across his face. This was the first time I'd seen him without shades: his eyes were the same bright, puzzled blue as his daughter's.

The girl hit the floor, but the angel stood her in good stead: she rolled with the fall, rolled again, then looked up at me, still smiling. 'More?'

'Sure,' I answered.

She did another roll, then grinned.

'Deadly!' I said. 'Good afternoon, Mr Marsh.'

It was taking the station owner a second or two to get his thoroughly smacked gob working. Finally he pointed a fat finger at me and spluttered, 'You!'

'Me…'

'What are you *doing* here?'

'Nance sent me to tell you dinner was ready.'

He continued to gape, his mouth full of silent questions and his eyes swivelling around the room as if he expected the answers to come in through the window. He started to march past me, paused, went back and scooped the child off the floor, then headed for the kitchen. She gave a little wave as she jogged past.

'Nance!'

As he passed through the lounge room he presumably came across Charles and Jason. 'Jesus!' I heard him exclaim, 'they've overrun the place!'

When he reached the kitchen I heard snatches of heated conversation.

'But Earl, you told me to expect the lawyers…'

'Fuck, Nance…'

'*Earl*…' a low, dangerous note resonated in her voice, a note which told me there was an unsuspected steel blade inside that flowery red sheath and that one of the causes in which it was brandished was decent language.

After a moment's silence he tried another tack. 'These aren't *my* lawyers, hon, they're the *blackfellers*' lawyers…'

'Earl, you know my opinion on this matter. I couldn't care less if they're the devil's dentists. Right now, they are our guests; they've had a nasty experience and I've invited…'

The door was closed, the conversation reduced to muffled undertones.

I cast a quick eye round the office. What was I looking for? I had no idea: anything that would give me any insight into Marsh and his dealings with Moonlight. I knew he was pissed off about the land claim; had something tipped him over the edge?

I had a quick rummage through the papers on his desk:

statements and accounts, reports from stock agents, pamphlets about forthcoming shows and field days. Marsh even had an out-tray.

I riffled through it. He was as terse with the word processor as he was with the mouth, but there was a surprising order to the paperwork. Nothing there was more than a few days old, which suggested that the filing cabinet against the wall could be a useful source of information.

Once again, things there were in surprisingly good order. 'Moonlight Downs' had its own folder, and it was chock-a-block, with everything arranged in neat, chronological order. From the cursory glance that was all I had at my disposal, most of the stuff in it looked old, written in the heat of the land claim process. As I knew, Marsh had been heavily involved, playing the aggrieved neighbour card for all it was worth: he'd written numerous letters, reports and statements objecting to the claim, both to the court and to the press, as well as to other locals who believed they were in the same boat. Each of his contributions was carefully dated and filed. He even had a copy of the judge's final report, heavily underscored and highlighted, the margins riddled with angry comments.

At the other end of the corridor I heard the kitchen door open. A momentary silence ensued, then I picked up the sound of Marsh introducing himself to my companions in a manner that could almost be called civil. To Charles I heard him say: 'We got business to discuss, but maybe it'd be better if we left it till the mornin…'

I heard Charles politely concurring, then Marsh went quiet. Looking around for me? How long did I have left? Not long.

I flipped through the folder until I came to the more recent stuff. There was surprisingly little of it; evidently he'd quietened down when the land was handed over. Had he accepted it and moved on, or had the anger sunk into his inner being and begun to rot, like the metal splinter that disappears into the body, festers and throbs, and then one day bursts forth in a shower of pus?

I detected the sound of heavy bare feet padding down the hallway. One last letter came to hand. The letterhead was 'Department of Regional Development', the 'Re:' was Moonlight Downs, the date a couple of weeks before Lincoln's death. It was signed 'Lance Massie, Regional Manager'.

Lance Massie. I remembered the name. How had Kenny Trigger described this bloke? As the right-wing Territory Government's bagman. I quickly scanned the contents: it seemed to be offering to help Marsh in his negotiations with Moonlight, but so deep was the bureaucratic bullshit in which the writing was mired that it wasn't immediately obvious what the negotiations were about. The hand-written PS at the bottom of the page caught my attention: 'We'll work with you on this one Earl, but your main obstacle is going to be, as ever, Lincoln bloody Flinders. Stay strong and true! Lance.'

The footsteps were almost upon me. I closed the cabinet, slipped back into the armchair, sensed him in the doorway. I stared at the screen, nervously cracking my fingers and wondering how much he'd seen.

The Secret Ingredient

Marsh snorted, and I looked around.

'Just catching up on my Wiggles, Mr Marsh.'

He shifted from one bare foot to another, his blue eyes sweeping the room, his face frozen in its customary scarlet scowl. Had he seen me at the filing cabinet? Was he trying to decide which limb to tear off first?

'Dinner's ready,' was all he said, then he added, 'but I'm not. Just gonna put some clothes on.'

He turned on his heels and walked away.

I closed my eyes, sighed with relief, then joined the others in the dining room.

As we were sitting down at the table there came a heavy footfall from the direction of the veranda and a knock on the front door. Alyssia went out to investigate, and came back with yet another pilot and legal team. The real ones, this time, Greg and Neville. A couple of disgruntled, balding company types in dusty white shirts and Akubra hats who looked pissed off that they'd had to walk in from the airstrip.

Marsh was almost apologetic. 'I told the mechanic to bring yez in, but' – with an accusatory glance in my direction – 'he prob'ly thought he already had. Anyhow...' the smile on his face was like a flower struggling to survive on a rocky desert outcrop, 'yer just in time for a feed.'

There followed one of the stranger evenings of my life. A more heterogeneous dinner party one would be hard pressed to find: black and white, left and right, women and men, young and old, educated and un, New and First Australian, but we struggled to find a common ground, as you do.

The leaven in the mix was the Marshs' daughter – Amelia, as she turned out to be – who sat in her high chair regaling us with tales of her imaginary friends. The isolation of the outback was obviously proving a rich breeding ground for her imagination. Her closest acquaintance was a little creature called Treebark, who had green hair and parents named Slugger and Duania, Slugger being the mother. An oblique comment, perhaps, upon relationships within her own family and the cause of an arched brow and the shadow of a smile from Marsh.

Amelia seemed to take a particular shine to me, and between courses dragged me out into the yard to meet her chooks, Eyesore – because it had a sore eye – and Bottlesharp, because its feathers were the colour of broken glass. Treebark, she assured me, was watching us from the ghost gums down by the creek. She also introduced me to a talking calf named Bruce. When I asked what Bruce could say, she had words with the calf, which did indeed respond, making a noise which Amelia translated as: 'I want to go to the ocean on a train.'

The real surprise of the evening, though, was Marsh himself. Whatever the reason – his wife's old-world notion of hospitality, the kicking-in of the Bundy rum to which he liberally treated himself, maybe the mollifying presence of the Beautiful Girl – his anger slowly faded, his spirits rose and he began to open up. Indeed, in his own bearish manner, he was the life of the party, the monolith around which the natives were expected to dance.

He sat at the head of the table, glass in hand, elbow on the table, leaning forward and fixing various members of the party with his powerful blue stare, badgering us with questions, then cutting off our replies with his own opinions, most of which were carefully calculated to offend somebody in the room. He launched scathing attacks on lawyers to the pilots, pilots to the lawyers, and blackfellers to all and sundry, always making sure that the lawyers, pilots and black woman in the room heard every word.

At different times throughout the evening I heard him arguing land rights with Charles, debating the interconnectedness of market and drought cycles with his own lawyers, grumbling about the effects of heli-mustering on cattle condition with the pilots. He related a rambling story about some emu, a station pet, which apparently thought it was a cattle-dog. He was full of bullshit about min-min lights, prairie oysters, bush aphrodisiacs and pointed bones, the last with a malicious eye in my direction.

The one group who were apparently immune from criticism was Pommy migrants. Nance bustled around, making sure we were all fed and watered, but keeping a quiet eye upon her man. Once or twice, when he looked like he was about to stray beyond the bounds of propriety, she'd flash a warning signal, but more often she was encouraging, obviously familiar with the performance.

When Neville, one of the lawyers, showed signs of a cold, Nance said something to Marsh about his bush remedy. I smiled to myself. These guys always have a bush remedy.

Minutes later I was watching Neville miserably contemplating a concoction made up of lemon concentrate, chilli pepper, Worcestershire sauce and 'the mystery ingredient'. There's always a mystery ingredient, too. From the look on the lawyer's face when he drained the glass, it might have been sump oil.

From scattered fragments of the conversation I learnt a little about Marsh's personal history, and, again, it wasn't what I'd imagined. As owner of the station, of course, he was the Enemy – blokes like him had been riding roughshod over my mob for centuries – but he wasn't to the Big House born. Far from being sensitive about his past, he seemed to revel in it. His old man had been a drover and a drunkard over Winton way, his mother, when she wasn't on the road or up to her elbows in babies, a cleaner in the local pub. Indeed, his background was not that different from my own. The main difference, of course, was in the colour of our respective mothers, but even there I found myself reflecting that the black and white trash often had more in common than either of us would want to admit.

I felt the similarity more strongly than ever when Marsh stuck an old Slim Dusty record on the stereo. Charles' upper lip curled; he looked more like a Nick Cave man. Fat chance, I thought. If Nick Cave had wandered into a gathering like this they'd have trussed him, stuffed him and eaten him for the main course. Nance was presumably responsible for the Celine Dion CDs on the bottom shelf. The company lawyers' concept of country looked like it didn't stray too far from Shania Twain.

When 'Leave Him out There in the Long Yard' came on, Charles was discussing a recent High Court appeal with

Greg and I saw him roll his eyes and mouth the word 'monotonous'. Marsh was busily swapping fishing stories with the pilots, but I saw from the light that flared in his eyes that he'd noticed the comment as well.

'Monotonous?' he boomed. 'Whadderye expect? He's singin about the bush!'

He took a noisy swig of rum, and then, when he had everybody's attention, repeated 'Monotonous!' in such a way as to leave you in no doubt that, limited though Slim's vocal and narrative range might have seemed, there were as many permutations and possibilities within its parameters as there were in the bush itself.

Marsh turned out to be something of an expert on the subject of old Slim. He glared at me suspiciously when I expressed my admiration, but when he saw that my interest was genuine, he took me through his collection. It was a treasure trove: over sixty albums, many of them seventy-eights, some of them signed. He'd met the Great Man – not just at some stage-door signature-fest, but out bush, on the road. The first time he was a bung-eyed kid in his father's droving camp when Slim dropped by in his famous home-made caravan.

'You take all these,' he said, waving a hand out over the collection, 'add em up and whadderye got? Ya got a story. Our story,' he said with added emphasis, though I had my doubts as to whether or not he was including me in the 'our'.

Fair enough, I thought to myself as I was lying in bed that night, but the description inevitably reminded me of Lincoln Flinders. He was another story man, but that didn't stop some bastard killing him.

Nothing I'd learnt about Marsh in the last few hours had

swayed me from the suspicion that he might well have been that bastard.

Indeed, what I'd learnt about him probably increased the likelihood of his being the killer. I knew him and his ilk: they tended to take the law into their own hands, strike first. It was a brutal, semi-civilised world out there, and Marsh was born and bred into it. They treated the blackfellers worse than they treated their dogs, and I'd already seen how he treated dogs.

I lay there, listening to the sounds of the night: distant generator humming, cicadas whirring away in the poin-cianas, the occasional night-bird calling: boobooks, nightjars. Something that sounded like a seagull, though God help it if it was.

What was wrong with my scenario? I was drifting off to sleep when it struck me: it wasn't the violence – he'd be more than capable of it if anybody got in his way, and from the glimpse I'd had of the letter from Lance Massie, Lincoln had clearly done that. My problem was the subterfuge: the knife in the night, the attempt to pass the death off as a ritual killing. That was what didn't seem in keeping with what I'd seen of the man. If it was, then he was an even more cunning bastard than I could ever have imagined. It was still possible, of course; but it didn't feel right.

The meeting the next morning proved to be something of an anti-climax. We gathered together in the station office, everybody embarrassed by our intimacy of the night before except Marsh, who seemed impervious to such feelings.

The whole thing was carried out with much greater restraint than would normally have been the case. Charles presented Marsh with a court order to remove his stock from the North Quarter, Marsh responded in kind: he had a letter, drafted by his lawyers, which demanded compensation for damaged fencing, gates and roads, and an offer to withdraw the claim in return for a formal lease of the same section of land. Charles replied, as everyone present had known that he would, by saying that such a request would have to go to the traditional owners, but that, until then, the court order would need to be obeyed. Marsh didn't look too happy, but nor did he look surprised.

Twenty minutes after the meeting finished, our back-up plane arrived and we headed for Bluebush.

When I got back to town I tracked down McGillivray, found him in his office, told him that Marsh was back home, and that if he wanted to look into Marsh's connection with Moonlight, he could do worse than begin with Lance Massie.

He pinched the bridge of his nose, closed his eyes then looked up at me resignedly. 'Lemme get this straight. You not only want me to investigate Earl Marsh, prominent land owner and growing cheese in the Territory Cattlemen's Association. You want me to include in that investigation the local manager of the Department of Regional Development?'

'That's about it,' I said, not without some sympathy.

He sighed, leaned forward, head on palms, ran his fat fingers through what was left of his hair and muttered something he'd been muttering a lot lately.

'Emily, Emily, Emily…'

The Captain of the World

I left McGillivray to his despair and raced down to the White Dog, just in time to begin my shift. I came home at sundown, washed-out and exhausted. Between mad sorcerers, crashing planes and blustering cattlemen, it had been a hell of a week.

And it wasn't over yet. I'd only been in the shower for twenty minutes when I was disturbed by a mighty thump on the front door and a roaring rendition of my name.

Jack was back in town.

I stepped out of the shower, threw a towel around my hair and a robe around my body, opened the door.

'Hi, Jack.'

'Hijack! That's about what a bloke's gotta do to see his own family these days. I've been standing here for ten minutes.'

'Sorry, Dad. You wouldn't believe the week I've had. Come in.'

He began to gather up the pile of rubbish he'd left by the door: as well as the usual monstrous swag, he had an overnight bag, a tin of rock samples, a carton of beer and a box full of fresh food.

'Never did master the art of travelling light, did you, Jack?'

'Figured it was my turn to make dinner,' he explained

with a devilish grin, putting the food on the kitchen table. 'Look after my little girl.'

'Mmmm. I could handle that. What's on the menu?'

'Irish stew.'

'Sounds good.' I settled back on the couch as he poured himself a beer and began bustling about the kitchen. 'Maybe you could put a little less whisky and a few more vegies in it than you used to.'

'Don't worry,' he said in his usual self-assured manner. 'I know how to move with the times.' He reached into the box and I glimpsed a little white Gladbag out of the corner of my eye.

I sat up. 'Cocaine?' I asked.

'Tofu,' he grinned.

'You're going to put tofu in an Irish stew?'

'Had this hippy come and work for me last year. He put it in everything. Got quite partial to it. Good for the figure,' he added, ruefully patting his stomach.

'I think I'd rather stick to the peas and potatoes; I'd even prefer parsnip to tofu.'

He looked a little offended. 'But I thought you'd like it – all those hairy-legged women you been hanging round with in Melbourne.'

'They weren't that hairy, Jack, and they weren't all women. But don't worry, I'm sure it'll be delicious.'

'What about this then?' He pulled a brand-new blender out of the box. 'Banana smoothies for breakfast?'

'God, that hippy really taught you a thing or two.'

An hour later we were weighing into the stew. 'You haven't lost your touch,' I assured him. 'Tofu notwithstanding. So how long are you in town for?'

'Not long. Heading out for Green Swamp first thing in the morning.'

'Sounds exciting.' Green Swamp was a leprous roadhouse a hundred and eighty k's out west: its distinguishing features were the largest collection of beer coasters in the southern hemisphere, a wall full of fading photographs in which tits, bums and billiard cues were heavily represented and Barney Kipper, who for twenty years had maintained the region's phone lines from his own stool in the bar. 'What's on out there?'

'Funeral, actually.'

'Oh. Sorry. Maybe not so exciting.'

'Well, kind of a wake, truth be known.'

'Oh yeah? Piss-up, you mean. Re-insert the exciting. Who's the lucky man?'

'You ever meet old Snowy Truscott?'

'Not that I can recall.'

'Drilled a few holes for me out the Burnt Shirt. Come from over Winton way, but he'd been workin round here for years. Nice bloke. Died a few weeks ago, but we're only getting together now. I'm heading out with some of the fellers in the morning. Play kicks off at eleven.'

'Play?'

'Cricket. Green Swamp versus the World. I'm captain of the World.'

'You're having a game of cricket for his funeral?'

'Wake.'

'Still seems a strange way to say goodbye to someone.'

'Why? Very fond of his cricket, Snowy was. Figured we might make it an ongoing thing: the Snowy Truscott Memorial Cup. Went the way he would've wanted to, old Snow.'

'Killed by a bouncer?'

'Rolled his truck.'

'Way to go…'

But Jack wasn't altogether present himself; while we were eating I sensed that he had something else on his mind. 'Emily,' he began when we were sitting out on the back porch with a cup of tea. 'There's something I want to talk to you about.'

'Had the feeling there might be.'

He studied me for a moment, locked onto me with those blue magnets.

'Tom McGillivray's told me about your little escapades.'

Ah.

'It's one of the reasons I come in,' he continued. 'Told him I'd kick his arse from here to Sunday if he so much as let you into the same *desert* as Blakie again. Or Marsh, for that matter. They're as bad as each other, those two.'

'Not exactly up to Tom, Jack. I'm a big girl now.'

'You watch it, Emmy. Specially Blakie. Marsh I haven't had much to do with, but I've seen Blakie in action. Seen him rip a feller apart for lookin at him the wrong way. For *lookin* like somebody who looked at him the wrong way. You're playing with fire there, girl. Black fire. Watch it.'

'Usually do, Jack.'

He frowned, but let the ambiguity hang in the air.

'I miss Lincoln as much as anyone, Em,' he continued, 'and there's nothing I'd rather see than his killer brought to justice. But not if it's going to cost me my daughter.'

'I haven't taken too many risks so far, Jack.'

'Crashing planes and chasing Blakie around the bush on your own isn't taking risks?'

'Well, there was those…'

He put his big hand on mine. 'You're all I've got, darlin. I'm not telling you how to live your life – I know you better than that. I'm just asking you to…think of me, I suppose. Be careful.'

I looked out over the yard, thought about my mother. His grief when she died. 'Righto, Jack,' I nodded. 'I'll be careful.'

He was up early the next morning, humming away to himself in the kitchen while I was still in bed. By the time I surfaced his swag was rolled up and stashed near the couch, along with his numerous boxes and bags. He'd made us a big breakfast – porridge, toast and banana smoothies – but we didn't have time to make much of an impression on it before we were interrupted by a horn from outside.

Jack took a look out through the curtains, then checked his watch.

'Bugger me, they're here early.'

'Who is?'

'Couple of my blokes, plus a few others who wanted to come along and say goodbye to Snowy. Sorry, darlin, I better get going.'

He gathered up his gear in one almighty load and headed for the door as cautiously as a docking oil tanker.

'You right there, Dad?' I asked from the breakfast table.

'Righter than summer rain!' came the cheery reply from somewhere inside the pile. 'It's all a matter of balance, girlie. Balance! You could move a fuckin mountain if you had it properly balanced.'

He opened the door and edged his way out. Seconds later there came a terrible crash and a burst of unadulterated outback invective that would have had a socio-linguist scrambling for the microphone.

'What was that about balance?' I hollered.

I went outside. Jack was sitting amidst the wreckage, rubbing his pate and glaring at Hazel's wind-chime. One of the blokes from the car was coming over to give him a hand as well. As he drew closer, I saw that it was Bernie Sweet, the miner who'd sold Jack the maps.

Jack rose to his feet, slowly and awkwardly.

'Emily! Why the fuck have you got a lump o' fuckin' – Jack paused, then took a closer look – 'what *have* you got a fuckin lump of hangin off your front door, anyway?'

'Actually, I was going to ask you about that. What do you reckon it is?'

He took it down, pulled a lens out of his shirt pocket and raised it to his eye. 'Brown stuff's... hmmm, yep, one of the peridotites. Olivine, probably. Pretty lively, but... darker'n what you normally get round here.' He licked it. 'More sugary, too.'

'It's sweet?'

'Grainy.'

'And the beautiful blue?'

He turned it over, raised his eyebrows as a spectrum of colour rippled across its cleavage planes. 'Not quite sure. What do you reckon, Bernie?'

He passed it over to Sweet, who gave it a cursory glance, frowned and gave it back. 'Not quite sure myself.'

'If I had to make a stab at it,' said Jack, 'I'd say labradorite.'

'Thought it might have been,' I said. 'Seen anything like it before?'

He thought for a while. 'Round here? Can't say I have. Found some years ago, over near Winton.'

'Worth anything?'

'Find yourself a bigger bit and you might be able to knock up a pretty necklace. But no, not really. Gets in the way of the gold. You still haven't told me what it's doin danglin in your doorway.'

'It's a wind-chime, Jack.'

He rattled the stones, put a hand to his ear, listened in mock rapture as they clunked together.

'Scuse my ignorance, Emmy, but I'd a thought a wind-chime was meant to, aah... *chime*?'

'It's a present from Hazel.'

Sweet grinned at Jack and asked, 'Who's Hazel?'

'Friend of mine from Moonlight Downs.' I turned to Jack, who was loading himself up again. 'And its chime is more for the eye than for the ear.'

Jack didn't look convinced. I don't know that I was myself. Five minutes later they were heading out for Green Swamp.

The Sandhill Gong Woz Her

I came home that afternoon to find the neighbours standing in little clusters out on the footpath, talking at each other in an animatedly un-Territorian manner and gesticulating at their apartments. There were about twenty of them, most of them blokes, none of them happy.

I got out of the car, wondering whether this was a party I should be crashing.

Two of those at the back of the crowd turned around and gave me the evil eye: Ernie Ratzavic – Ratsarse to his friends – and his drinking buddy, the globular Slim Timms, who dressed like an extra in a Clint Eastwood movie but was in fact manager of the town laundromat.

I walked over, curiosity outweighing my instinctive caution.

'Evening fellers,' I said. 'What's going on? Bit of neighbourhood bonding?'

Aside from a little shared sneer, they ignored me and returned their attention to Rex Griffiths, who seemed to be in charge of the proceedings.

Rex was in mufti, or as close to mufti as your off-duty Bluebush copper could get – in his case this meant stubbies, thongs and a T-shirt with the slogan 'Great Aussie Bloke' – but he was still playing the cop. He had the tongue and the notebook out, the pen in the hand, the frown on the fore-head, and was assiduously scribbling notes as the crowd called out to him.

'Then there was my set of Micro Trend Diamond Steel knives,' growled Ernie.

'And a slab of beer,' Slim put in hopefully.

'CD player,' said Hardy Stein.

'A meat axe,' spat some swivel-eyed blue singlet who looked as mad as one.

'Shit,' said Griffo, 'what did they have, a road train? How many of em were there?'

'And a money jar,' said Charlie Cleland. 'Must have had forty bucks in it.'

'Forty bucks!' retorted his flatmate, Mal Hanson. 'You wouldn't have forty bucks in the bank!'

Charlie looked offended. 'The money jar is my bank. What about the chainsaw? I had a Stihl chainsaw, perfect workin order.'

'Perfect fuckin workin order my arse,' muttered Mal. 'You left it out the Blue Moon months ago.'

During a momentary lull in the proceedings Ernie pointed in my direction. 'Why don't we ask our little black lady if she knows anything about it?'

I raised my hands, palms upwards, tried to make myself a smaller target. 'Will somebody tell me what's going on?'

'We've had a break-in,' Griffiths responded. 'Lot of break-ins. Half the flats have had their back doors reefed open. They would have done the other half if Bones here hadn't been asleep on the couch when they tried his place.'

Bones, named either for his occupation as a meatworker or his skeletal physique, gave his audience a modest wave of acknowledgment and a flash of yellow teeth that may have been intended as a smile.

'Bunch of coon kids,' he said. 'Give em a hell of a fright.'

'Bones'd give Freddy Krueger a hell of a fright,' somebody threw in, but I wasn't hanging around. I stomped over to my own place and unlocked the front door.

Sure enough, the back door had been forced open, the flat ransacked. The saving grace was that there hadn't been much worth stealing. As far as I could tell, all I'd lost was a couple of beers from the fridge, a bit of cash from the bedside table and a CD by my favourite ragged-arsed black-feller band, the Warumpis. My books, I was grateful to see, were untouched; books were never a hot item on the Bluebush black market.

I went back outside and reported my losses to Griffiths.

'So what are you going to do about it?' pressed one of the mob.

Griffiths didn't look comfortable. 'Mate. There's what, six, seven hundred black kids in this town. You expect me to round em all up and shake em down?'

'Hey!' yelled Bones, looking like he'd just risen out of a grave, 'there's one of em now!'

I followed his outstretched finger and saw Lenny Coulter strolling towards us from the bush end of the court, his eyes half closed, his mouth moving. He was wearing low-rider jeans, a Bombers baseball cap and a discman. Scratchy rap music hissed out of his headphones.

'Oi!' called Griffo, advancing towards him. 'You!'

Lenny seemed oblivious to the threat until he opened his eyes and saw a mountain of Bluebush constabulary rumbling towards him, upon which he did what any other camp kid would have done: turned on his heels and ran. Griffo gave chase, but he was no match for Lenny, who moved with an astonishing speed considering the pants. He wove his way around the pack, cleared a fence, galloped down the yards and headed for the highway.

Several younger members of the mob tried to cut him off but he spotted the move and changed direction. One eye on his back, he hared off on a course which, I realised with horror, led straight into the path of the four wheel drive that had just come cruising round the corner.

The driver was fortunately on the ball. The vehicle slammed to a halt centimetres from the fleeing Lenny, who grasped the bull-bar, gave a brief wave of acknowledgment, then disappeared into the bush across the road.

The driver emerged from the cabin. Another cop, I thought. Then I spotted the red beanie.

'Hang on, fellers,' Jojo said as the mob reached him. 'What's going on?'

'Little fucker just broke into our houses,' gasped Bones.

'Lenny?' Jojo glanced into the bush. 'Not his usual style.'

'Him and his mates. Flogged everythin they could lay their hands on.'

I joined them. 'We don't know that it was Lenny at all,' I said. 'I think he might have just chosen the wrong moment to take a short-cut through the court.'

'Emily Tempest! Don't tell me they hit you too?'

'Afraid so.'

'Surprised they had the nerve. Let's have a look.'

As he parked his car, Griffo muttered something about the CIB and drove off. The rest of the crowd slowly dispersed.

Jojo and I walked back into the court. I led him into my flat, showed him the broken door, told him what was missing.

'Oh no, not the Warumpis! Which one?'

'*Big Name No Blankets*.'

'Oh man, the classic.'

He went out into the little piece of scorched earth that passed for a yard, crouched on his haunches, then leaned forward and made a close examination of the dirt. He glanced at my own feet, then looked back at the scuff-marks on the ground. He scratched the surface, scooped up a tiny amount of sand between thumb and forefinger, studied it, let it drift away. He walked in the direction of the back fence, slowly and carefully, his brow crumpled, his eyes never leaving the ground. He stood on a railing and looked out into the alley.

I watched with interest.

'What do you reckon?' I asked when he came back.

'Half a dozen of em,' he replied with a surprising confidence. 'Eleven, maybe twelve years old. Two in bare feet, two in trainers, one in thongs, another in scruffy boots. One's wearing a white sweatshirt, another's in a green baseball cap and a moth-eaten red singlet. Biggest boy's got a limp. Little feller's got a runny nose and a bung eye.'

I almost fell off the porch. 'That's the most amazing piece of tracking I've ever seen. You got all that from just looking around the yard?'

'More or less.'

'That's better than Pepper and Arch could have done.'

He smiled modestly. 'Dunno if I'd go that far.'

'I mean, I can see how you could work out their footwear,

limps and whatnot, but how the hell do you know about the bung eyes and baseball caps?'

'Trade secret,' he said as he headed for the back door. 'But you might want to have a look at the alley.'

I walked out through the gate. The neighbour's Alsatian put on its usual performance, but I was getting used to it. There was a message sprayed onto the back fence in bright red paint and letters two foot high: SANDHILL GONG WOZ HER.

'Russell Kutuju and his cousins,' Jojo called from inside the flat. 'Known to everybody in town as the Sandhill Gang. I saw them sneaking back into camp five minutes ago.'

While I scouted around for something to throw at him, he made his way to the front door. 'Love to stay and enjoy your hospitality, Ms Tempest, but I better go and have a word with them before they get rid of the loot. Back in an hour or so.'

I followed him out onto the veranda, watched as he got into his Toyota and drove away.

I went inside and showered. Found myself scanning the meagre contents of my wardrobe, feeling suddenly skittish. Pulled myself up. Knock it off, I said to myself. You're acting like a girl, and a bloody white girl at that. I brought myself back down to earth by knocking up a batch of scones.

An hour later the Landcruiser came rattling back up the drive. Jojo emerged from the cabin, went round and began speaking to the occupants, many of whom immediately jumped into their vehicles and disappeared. By the time he'd made it to the fourth flat most of the neighbourhood had assembled on the lawn.

'A few of you already know,' he called out, 'but to save

wear and tear on the tonsils, I'll tell you *en masse*. The cops have recovered a number of items which they believe were stolen this afternoon. If you make your way down to the police station, you'll be able to claim what's yours…'

Most of them were gone before he finished the sentence.

I was sitting on the veranda, watching with amusement.

'Hey, Jojo!'

He ambled over towards me.

'Emily.'

'Who's on the desk down at the station? He's going to need the wisdom of Solomon to sort that lot out.'

'Rex was there a few minutes ago.'

'Bloody hell.'

His smile faded. 'You wouldn't be taking the piss out of our thin khaki line, would you?'

'Pretty fat fuckin thin line in his case. Oh well, I don't suppose there'll be much competition for my Warumpis.'

'Shouldn't be any,' he said, reaching into his pocket, pulling out a CD and dropping it into my lap.

'*Big Name No Blankets*! How the hell did you manage that?'

'I know those boys. Wasn't that long ago I was leading a similar sort of life myself. Limited number of places you could hide a stash like that between here and the camp. Took me about five minutes to find it. Big beefwood on the edge of the mulga, west of the camp.'

'Well, thanks very much. I suppose the least I could do is offer you a beer. And I would if the boys hadn't flogged it all. How about a cup of tea?'

'Won't say no.'

'And a scone?'

'Now you're talking.'

'Pull up a slab of concrete.'

I went inside and loaded up the tea-tray. When I came back out he was sitting down, his back against a post, his legs fully stretched, his eyes closed. He casually waved away a blowie which settled on his knee, then opened his eyes.

'Strewth,' he exclaimed when he spotted the scones. 'You didn't tell me they were fresh out of the oven.' He took a bite, followed up with a swig of tea. 'Mmmm. Have to see if I can get you burgled more often.'

'So did you catch the culprits?'

'Not my job. But I did have a word with Ditch Williams. You know him?'

'Know the name.'

'He's their uncle; asked me to take em out to Kupulyu Creek. Figures a spell out bush'll do em good.'

Kupulyu Creek. I'd heard of it. Like Moonlight, a fledgling community, a little band of people struggling to escape time's gravitational pull. Kantiji country, a few hours to the south-east.

I settled back into the wickerwork chair, pulled my feet up underneath. A minute or two drifted by as we quietly worked our way through the scones.

'So who are you, Jojo?'

He raised a brow. 'Who am I?'

'You seem so at home around here. You can spot a witch-doctor in the dark. You listen to the Warumpis. You know where the townboys stash the loot. But you didn't grow up round here.'

'How can you tell?'

'You're – what, twenty-seven, twenty-eight? I'd have come

across you. But you do sound local: got that parched-out Territorian drawl, the sun-dried eyes.'

'I first come up to the Centre when I was eight years old. Me and me mum.'

'Just the two of you? Like me and Jack.'

'I suppose so. Grace was an arts coordinator on various communities out from Alice. Yuendumu. Ernabella. Spent a year living out of a swag on the outstations west of Papunya. She had a rather… how would you put it?… chaotic idea of parenting. Long as she had a paint brush in her hands, she didn't notice what I was up to. I spent more time running around the bush with a mob of little mates than I did in the classroom. Then we moved in to Alice, only there running wild meant something different. Something a lot more dangerous.'

'So how come you didn't end up in some gutter?'

'I spent plenty of time in gutters, actually. Or I would have if they'd had gutters where I was lying.'

'Yeah, but you're not still there. What happened?'

'Shit, you are a pushy little thing, aren't you?' He stared off into the scrub across the road, ran his fingers through the sand and said, 'I suppose the bush is what happened.'

I waited.

'When I was eighteen,' he continued, 'I picked up a casual job delivering stores out to the stations. Spent a couple of days marooned by a flooded river and found myself thinking about what I'd left behind when we came to Alice. You know. The colours, the kids, the waterholes. Thought how much I missed them.'

He paused, but the silence between us was a comfortable one.

'So you ended up a ranger.'

'Buggered if I could think of any other job was going to let me loose out bush. One of the blokes stuck by the river with me was Tom McGillivray. He took me under his wing; helped me get into Parks and Wildlife. I've been working round here ever since.'

We sat there quietly drinking our tea, then he went on, 'You grew up at Moonlight Downs, didn't you, Emily?'

'Mainly.'

'Well, you know what I'm talking about, then. Bit of a riot, wasn't it?'

I closed my eyes, tilted my head back, enjoyed the last lingering rays of the sun and thought about the wild, aimless days of my childhood. I pictured Hazel and me running along a dry creek bed, no clothes, no cares, hair streaming. Coming across a pool and diving in. Bobbing up, laughing so hard we just about drowned.

My body felt lithe and alive; maybe it was the sun, maybe it was the memories. When I opened my eyes, he was gazing at me, a bemused smile on his face. 'Yeah,' I smiled. 'Most of the time.'

Soon afterwards he hauled himself to his feet. 'Suppose I'd better go and earn my pay,' he said, then an idea seemed to ripple across his face. 'Chances are I'll be heading out to Kupulyu first thing in the morning. Want to come along?'

I gave the invitation a moment's consideration. 'Interesting to see what the community's like.'

'Be a good thing, having a woman along. You could do the cooking.'

He made it off the veranda, but not before I'd knocked his

beanie off with the nulla-nulla I kept by the door for such eventualities.

'Pick you up at seven?' he called from his car.

'Unless I get a better offer.'

That Cake – It Flew!

Jojo rolled up early the next morning, gave a quick beep on the horn. I grabbed my pack and headed for the door.

Sprawled across the back seat was the collection of hats, hoods and attitude known as the Sandhill Gang. A long grey streak of a dog, a cross between a whippet and a pony, lay stretched out on the floor.

'Let's go,' I said to Jojo. 'Neighbours get a look at us, there'll be a lynch mob.'

He did a casual u-ie in the driveway and headed south.

The boys sat there in stony silence. The only member of the gang to show any animation was the dog, which stirred itself, climbed up and peered over my shoulder, looking for a feed. It had huge teeth, terrible breath, a great grey tongue and a set of balls that bounced around like coconuts in a tropical breeze.

'Dog's called Rollo,' said Jojo.

'I can see why.'

'Boys persuaded me to bring him along.'

'He's looking hungry.'

'So am I. Hey, Russell!' The boy closest to the window looked up. 'Have a look in the bag at your feet.'

The boy reached down, rummaged through the bag, came

up with a bag of toasted sandwiches wrapped in foil. Ham and tomato. A trace of life gleamed in his eyes.

'Dig a little deeper, there's a thermos.'

By the time we'd finished breakfast, the hats and the hoods were still in place, but the attitude was breaking down. One of the boys opened a coat and revealed a puppy he'd somehow been concealing, and it proceeded to play havoc with Rollo. The boys and I sussed out each other's names and countries, ran through the people and places we had in common. They were Russell and his brother Red, their cousins, Willy, Ring and Wildboy.

'What the hell were you boys doing,' I said when I thought it was safe to do so, 'breaking into people's houses like that?'

'Sorry Em'ly,' said Russell, a sheepish smile on his mouth, the puppy cradled in his arms. 'We did'n know you bin livin there.'

'Shouldn't matter who's living there,' Jojo growled. 'You boys'll be men soon. Bout time you started acting that way.'

By the time we reached the Hawk's Well Waterhole, they were really sparking up. They were coming into their own country: they scrutinised every rock and tree, whispered and tugged each other's shirts at every watercourse or hill.

Jojo drove slowly. Not long before we reached the Kupulyu turn-off he cast an anxious glance at the western sky. Purple clouds floated across the horizon, trailing rain.

'We driving into that?' I asked.

'Hopefully not. You know what it's like out here – floods one end of town, drought at the other. We've come this far, don't want to turn back now. If we do run into trouble it'll be near Kupulyu. Plenty of people around to give us a hand.'

The road was heavy with the recent rain but manageable,

and in twenty minutes we drove into the Kupulyu community: a dozen Colorbond houses, a similar number of
humpies, a health centre, a store and, some five hundred
metres to the south, a school.

An old man in a grey singlet and a blue stockman's hat
was sitting on a spring bed in front of one of the houses.
When Jojo emerged he smiled, came over and shook his
hand. Jojo introduced him to us as Johnny Friday, leader of
the community and driver of the tractor parked alongside
the house. Johnny said they were expecting the boys, and
suggested we take them straight over to the school, where
the kids had prepared a welcome.

Jojo looked suspiciously at the road between the community and the school, which appeared to have been the focus
of the downpour.

'What's that road like, Johnny?' he enquired. 'Good
road?'

'Oh, my word, yes, very good road, that one.'

'You're sure?'

'Oh yes, very sure.'

We got a hundred metres down the track before sinking to
our axles in a quagmire of black glue.

We piled out, walked back to where Johnny was waiting,
watching us.

'Got bogged, Johnny.'

'Mmmm, I see,' he replied, nodding sagely. He considered
our predicament for a moment, then added, 'Mmmm... I
bin get bog, that same place, just this morning.'

Jojo and I glanced at each other.

'Can I borrow your tractor?'

'No worries, mate.'

The school, when we were eventually towed into it, consisted of a large, silver classroom, a teacher's van, a gaudy plastic playground, an orchard and a few acres of red dirt with goal posts at either end.

A solid, bearded bloke with a florid face and a navy windcheater was standing on the veranda of the van. In his arms was a Black Forest cake slightly smaller than one of the tractor's tyres.

'G'day, Con,' said Jojo.

'Jojo.' He looked out to where Johnny Friday was rolling the tackle back up into the winch. 'Where would we be without Johnny and his tractor?'

'Probably hoeing into that cake. Morning tea, I hope?'

'Kids have been baking all day.' He placed the cake on a table, came down and shook my hand. 'Con Christou.'

'Emily Tempest.'

He frowned slightly. 'Tempest?'

'It's okay – I don't bite.'

'From Moonlight Downs?'

'Among other places. You know Moonlight?'

'Made a few trips out there. Heard your name on the bush telegraph. That old Kuminjayi had been badgering the Department for a new school, and I was slotted to be the first teacher.' I frowned, felt as though a shadow had just passed over the day. 'Tragic, the way it all turned out.'

'It's not over yet,' I replied.

Con introduced himself to the Sandhill boys, teamed them up with their Kupulyu counterparts, grabbed a football and thumped it out onto the oval. 'Okay fellers, go and sort out your pecking order,' he yelled. 'Cake time in ten minutes.'

The boys went haring off in pursuit, with Rollo bringing up the rear.

We walked up onto the veranda of the van. 'Come inside,' said Con. 'You'll want to freshen up. Siena! Macey!' He indicated the cake. 'Nobody's to touch this until we get back, okay?' Two stringy girls nodded compliantly, and we followed the teacher inside.

'Bathroom's over there,' he said.

Jojo washed his hands, then muttered, 'Better go out and keep an eye on that cake.'

As he swung the door open, Con looked out onto the veranda. A look of horror shot across his face.

'Aaagh!!!' he bellowed. 'You little bastards!'

I followed his gaze

There was a riot going on around the wretched cake. The Sandhill Gang were in the thick of it, of course, shovelling great handfuls into their mouths, chucking cherries into the air and catching them with their teeth, but the Kupulyu mob weren't far behind.

A couple of boys were smacking each other with creamy fists, and Siena and Macey were hungrily licking their fingers. Toddlers were being thrust aside, although one determined little boy was making ferocious sorties up at the cake from under the table. Even Rollo looked like he'd scored.

The Kupulyu teacher pushed past Jojo, burst through the crowd, picked up the plate, stared at the shattered remnants in dismay.

'Have the fucking lot then!' he roared, and sent it spinning out through the air.

The kids stood there, gawping and gaping, wide-eyed, as

the plate whizzed over them. Crumbs and globs drifted down and landed on their heads. There was a stunned silence until the plate landed with a piercing twang on the other side of the yard.

A little girl in a long blue dress was standing in the yard. Her enormous eyes retraced the path of the missile. Her jaw hung down.

'That cake,' she said at last. 'It flew!'

Into the silence burst a tiny, half-choked splutter. Jojo. Then he began to laugh, a rollicking burst of pure delight that pealed across the yard like a set of bells.

The Kupulyu teacher glared for a moment but the contagion caught, and in seconds the schoolyard was full of kids and adults rolling around in the mud clutching their sides and slapping each other's backs.

They were still giggling about it when Jojo and I left for Bluebush later that afternoon. The kids ran along beside us, whistling and hooting, slapping the sides of the vehicle, swinging off the gate.

'That cake!' they called after us. 'It flew!'

At the Hawk's Well

Kupulyu disappeared in the rear-view mirror and we hit the main drag. Headed north, up into the fading embers of the day. Cool air drifted in the open window. I settled back, put my legs up on the seat, nestled my head against the blanket, content to be quiet. My eyes were half closed, but from time to time I found them drifting across to the man at the wheel.

Tiny drops of rainwater clung to the corners of his brow, to the whiskers on his jaw. The habitual smile hung about the corners of his mouth, the outward expression of what I'd come to think of as his natural state of mind: amused, surprised, at ease with the revolutions of the world.

His fist – hard, scarred, dappled in black mud – moved down to the gearstick, and I found myself imagining it slipping over onto my thigh.

The shadows lengthened. The termite mounds on the passing plains looked like an invading army; kamikazi birds swooped among our wheels.

Coming up to the Hawk's Well Waterhole, Jojo stretched his shoulders, twisted his neck, ruefully rubbed a knee.

'Any permanent damage?' I asked him.

'Don't think so, but jeez, they can move, those kids.' We'd spent the last hour at Kupulyu playing barefoot football, but only one of us had had the sense to retire before getting hurt.

'I'd help with the driving, but I imagine your department's got rules against that sort of thing. Want a break for a while?'

'Just what I was about to suggest. How about Hawk's Well?'

'Sure.'

'Been there before?'

'Heaps. I love Hawk's Well. Dad and I used to stop there for a cup of tea whenever we were down this way.'

'I could boil a billy now, if you like.'

'Yeah, all right.'

When we reached the turn-off he pulled over and edged the vehicle down the overgrown track that led to the water-hole. Tussocks of ribbon grass brushed along the under-carriage of the vehicle.

'Mmmm,' he shivered, flexing his back and wriggling his shoulders. 'Tickles.'

He parked on a shallow rise overlooking the water. Took an axe from the cabin and walked away. He had a smooth, easy gait, his boots kicking through the spinifex, crunching over loose stones.

The Toyota clicked and creaked, unwinding. I got out of the cabin and did the same, then sat on a rock overlooking the waterhole. Light shot away from the sandstone, hummed in the plants: grevilleas and sedges, burr daisies, rock ferns. A lonely fig tree struggled for a foothold on the cliffs.

Birds darted and called: honeyeaters and wood swallows, kingfishers, finches. A pair of rock pigeons took off in noisy flaps, glided across the water, alighted upon a shelf.

I remembered a comment my father made once, as we sat

here years before: 'Make it all worthwhile, don't you reckon, places like this? It's as if they take all the energy out of a hundred square miles of rough desert and force it through a single fuse.'

The only human sound to be heard was from Jojo, the crunch of his boots on a branch, the soft thunk of iron on wood. He was three metres away, his back to me as he worked.

He turned around, grinned, the hovering sun burnishing his face. 'Gonna have a fire, might as well make it a decent one,' he said as he walked towards me, his arms full of branches, his beanie dusted with leaves and pollen. He dropped the wood, cleared a patch of grass.

As he crouched low to put the sticks in place, his shirt rucked up over the top of his shorts to reveal a finger's-breadth of flesh, the lower stretches of his arcing spine.

I watched him for a moment or two, the breath rushing across my throat.

'Jojo.'

'Eh?' He looked up.

I took a couple of steps towards him, put my hand on his beanie, pushed my fingers under its rim, ran a hand through his wiry hair. Lifted my top and drew his head towards my bare belly, let it nestle there for a moment. 'The fire. Don't know that I need one right now.' I took his hand, moved it up under my skirt.

He stood up, smiling into my eyes. 'Must admit, I was kind of wondering myself.'

'About the fire?'

'About you. Us.' He stroked the inside of my thigh, brushed lightly against the tender flesh further up. 'This.'

I rubbed my cheek against his jaw. It was pleasantly sweet and rough-whiskered. 'While since I felt one of those,' I said, moving against his fingers.

I pulled him in close and kissed him hard, felt his tongue dance in response. 'While since I felt one of those, too.' I slipped my hand inside his hard yakkas. 'Not to mention...'

'Don't say it,' he whispered, and drew my body into the fold of his arms. Ran a hand down my spine, massaging it with fingers that felt as smooth and strong as the limbs of a ghost gum. Cupped my arse, lifted me off my feet and kissed my throat, slow kisses that seemed to ripple through my body.

A low moan escaped from my throat and I pulled my head back. Caught my breath, took a look around.

'Dunno if this is such a good idea.'

'Shit,' he gasped. 'Now you tell me.'

'Not what I meant.'

I freed myself from his embrace, went back to the vehicle and grabbed my red blanket. Came back and threw it over the stones and the porcupine grass. 'Now,' I said, grappling with his buttons, 'it's a good idea. Bloody great idea, in fact.'

We lay down, eased each other out of our clothes, then eased each other out of our brains.

The next morning we loaded the Cruiser and headed back down the track. Even when we hit the highway Jojo drove slowly, with one arm on the wheel and the other around my shoulders. I kicked my shoes off, nestled up close to him, enjoyed the warmth of his body, the solid strength of his ribs.

'You gonna give me back my hat?' he asked.

'No.'

'But it's part of my uniform.'

'Bullshit. And besides, it matches my blanket.'

'You gonna take your hand out of my pants?'

'You really want me to?'

'Well, no, but I don't know what Freddy Whittle'll think about it.'

'Who?'

'Bloke who's driving the truck that's about to overtake us.'

I looked up as a huge Kenworth came roaring up alongside us. A burly character in a towelling hat gave us a wave and a blast of the horn as he accelerated away.

'Oh well,' said Jojo, 'that would've made his day.'

We drove for another minute or two, Paul Kelly on the tape deck. *Nukkinya*. A lovely song about another black chick and her feller in the morning sun.

'You gonna be my girl?' asked Jojo.

'I'm gonna be your something.'

'What's that supposed to mean?'

'Let's wait and see. No other… complications?'

'Complications?'

'Attachments.'

He thought for a moment. 'Just Annie.'

I frowned. 'Who's Annie?'

He patted the steering wheel. 'We're riding in her.'

'That's all right. Car I can handle.'

As we approached the town boundaries, he asked me, 'Your place or mine?'

'You've seen mine. Is yours any better?'

'It's pretty rough.'

It was gorgeous – an open shack made from mulga poles and sandstone, with central posts of rough-dressed desert oak. The house was on a ten-acre bush block on the outskirts of town: it had an earth floor, an open fire, a solar shower and a big spring bed which looked like it could do with some company. Over the next few hours we made lunch, made love, and made it to our respective jobs with moments to spare.

Looking Down the Barrel

That afternoon set the pattern for the next couple of days, which we spent enthusiastically slipping in and out of each other's beds and bodies. On the morning of the third day, however, Jojo was due to go out bush. We spent the night in at my place.

I woke up at first light, heard him pottering around the room.

'Do you have to go?' I asked him.

'It's my job.'

'When'll you be back?'

'Few days.'

'Can I get in touch with you?'

'I'll try to give you a call. If you need to get me you can try the Emergency Services frequency.'

He came and sat on the edge of the bed. 'How long you got?' I asked.

'Half an hour.'

'Just time for breakfast.'

'What's for breakfast?'

'Don't worry, you'll like it,' I grinned, dragging him back to bed.

Forty minutes later he was running out the front door, a piece of burnt toast in one hand, a pair of boots in the other.

I turned over, settled down into a pleasantly post-coital sleep, and was still there a few hours later when the phone rang.

'Hello,' I said, or tried to say, but whoever was on the other end of the line probably didn't hear much more than a discombobulated groan.

'Emily?'

'Tom?'

'Just calling to say good-bye.'

'Shit!' I woke up in a rush. 'Not the Gunbarrel Highway?'

'Worse. Darwin. Staff Development Course, they're calling it. Re-education Camp, more like it.' Tom had done a stint in Vietnam. 'Re-educate me not to fuck with the cattle kings.'

'You interviewed Marsh?'

'Yeah, and your man Massie, too, who read me the riot act and told me that whatever dealings his department had with Carbine Creek were "commercial-in-confidence" and of no bearing whatsoever upon any murder. By the time I got back from Carbine there was a message telling me to get me miserable arse up to Darwin, post haste.'

'Which of them was responsible?'

'Both of em, I imagine. Proper gang bang.'

'What about Marsh? Did you get anything out of him?'

'I got everything out of him except his breakfast. He's in the clear.'

Shit. That only left Blakie, and how the hell was I going to catch him? But then McGillivray went on, 'Far as I can tell. Which probably isn't far enough for you, but there's a limit to how far you can stick your bib in round here without getting it bit off.'

'What'd he have to say for himself?'

'It wasn't so much what he had to say as what his men had to say. When I went out there Marsh was in the stock camp, cutting and branding bulls. With half a dozen blokes who swore he was doing the same thing the day Lincoln died.'

'That's it?'

'That's what?'

'I mean they would, wouldn't they?'

'Would what?'

'Say that. He's their boss, Tom. They're hardly going to say he was out doing a spot of recreational strangling. Besides which, we're talking Carbine cowboys, right? IQ lower than a bull's balls?'

'These bulls didn't have any balls. Not by the time Marsh was finished with em. I was lucky I did myself.'

I wasn't going to let him off that easily.

'I'd still find it hard to believe your Carbine stockman could remember what he was doing five minutes ago, much less five weeks ago. I've *met* those boys, Tom. Seen em in the bar. Flotsam from the shallow end of the gene pool if ever I saw it.'

He was a step ahead of me.

'Emily, Lincoln was killed the day after the Edge River Races. And they remember it because they were pissed off with Earl Marsh for dragging em outer their swags before dawn when all they wanted to do was curl up and die.'

'Well, if they were so pissed how do they know what he was up to while they were asleep?'

His reply was a positive bark.

'Oh Jesus, give it a rest, will you, Emily! You already got me in enough shit. Marsh was camping with a mob of blokes, and one of em would have heard him drive away, and they couldn't all be bullshittin me. Just give it a bloody rest! If you want a fishing expedition go to the Gulf – you got nothing on the man except you don't like him. Right now I don't like him much myself, but being an arsehole isn't a hanging offence round here. If it was, the trees'd be full of arseholes.'

'Wish you hadn't put it like that, Tom. Not at this hour of the morning.'

'It's eleven o'clock,' he said suspiciously. 'What have you been up to?'

'Minding my own business.'

'That'll be the day,' he responded. 'And by the way, the Edge River connection explains Freddy Ah Fong as well.'

'Freddy Ah Fong?' I repeated slowly. I was having trouble tearing myself away from the horrible image of a bunch of arseholes hanging from the trees.

'This contract. I agree, it isn't worth a gecko's goolies. Except in so far as it pisses you lot off.'

'Well it does that all right.'

'Which is what it was intended to do,' Tom explained patiently. 'Marsh is chairman of the race committee and he was in the process of having Freddy thrown off the property for being in his usual state of smashed as a bottle, when Lance Massie tells him the feller he's maulin is part-owner for Moonlight Downs.' Massie again, I thought. This cat's got its paws all over the cage. 'Marsh didn't get to where he is by being a man to let a chance go by: half an hour later he's got Freddy's piss in his pocket and his X on a piece of paper. Says he just wanted a bit of extra feed for the Dry. But my take on it is that he was trying to cause a bit of family friction, you know? Stirrin the possum. It's the way things work out there, part of the general… cut and thrust. Dunno if you could call it ethical, but you couldn't call it criminal neither.'

'Depends on who's being cut and what's being thrust. What about the foot prints and tyre marks at the camp?'

There was a pause from Tom's end of the line, a pause which told me I'd hit a tender point. 'Not enough left of the foot prints to tie em to anything. Too old. Too worn. Could have been made by anybody.'

'And the tyre tracks…?'

'I took a techie with me to check em out. Might have been a car parked there. Probably was. About the right time, too. But there wasn't enough to make a positive ID, nothing to tie to a particular vehicle.'

'I could see that for myself, but at least you could measure the wheel span. Get an idea of what was parked there.'

'Yeah, we measured the wheel span, but if they are tyre tracks, which I'm not saying they are, they could have come from any one of half a dozen different makes and models – which I'm not saying they did.'

I drummed the bedside table, waiting for him to finish.

'Well?' I prompted him, when it became apparent that he thought he had.

'Well what?'

'The half a dozen different makes and models. Was one of them an F100?'

'Jeez, you never give up, do you?'

'Somebody killed a friend of mine, Tom. If that red-nosed bloody redneck had anything to do with it I want to know.'

'Emily, the bloke's got a half a dozen witnesses who put him fifty k's away at the time of the killing.'

'Tom, getting answers out of you is like trying to pull teeth. Out of a chook.'

'Okay, okay.' I heard him take a deep breath. I could just about hear his eyes rolling. 'Yes, Emily, the tyre marks could have come from an F100.'

'So what now?'

'Whadderye mean "what now?"? I get dressed up and go to Darwin for a dressing down, and you go back to mopping vomit, or whatever it is you do down at the Dog. There's nothing in it, Emily. You're pissing in the wind. And by the way…'

'Yes?'

'I wouldn't go near Marsh for a while if I were you. Not just now. He's bloody ropeable. By the time I caught up with him he'd already spoken to Massie. Seems to think you might have been poking around his office. While you were his house guest, perhaps?'

'Fuck him.'

'Thank you for that, Emily. I'll bear your constructive attitude in mind when I'm getting strips torn off me by the Commissioner.'

I wasn't satisfied, but I could see I wasn't going to get anything more out of the wallopers, not until I put a bit more flesh onto the bones of the body of evidence.

'I truly am sorry about Darwin, Tom. Anything I can do for you?'

'You could try keeping yer nose outer police business.'

'Goes without saying, Tom.'

Goes without doing, too, I thought as I hung up the phone.

Dropping the Rods

I got out of bed, did an hour of yoga – the legacy of a six-month stint in a shared house in Fitzroy – then undid whatever good I'd done with a continental breakfast: a coffee and a smoke.

I sat out on the porch, staring at the bottom of the cup and feeling guilty.

While I'd been cavorting around the countryside with my new feller, I'd allowed myself to be distracted – as I'd done so often in my life. Lincoln had never shown me anything other than unconditional love and friendship, and I'd forgotten about him; he was one of the most decent human beings I'd ever encountered, and I'd let some bastard break his neck and done nothing about it.

Nor could I shake the feeling that I was in a peculiarly unique position to discover the truth: I had a foot in both camps, so to speak. For much of my life, that had been a disadvantage: I felt like a white woman in the black world, and a black woman in the white one. Now, perhaps, I had the opportunity to use my knowledge of both worlds, inadequate though it might be, to do something decent. And I had one other vital qualification: I cared. Others cared for him too, of course: Hazel and the rest of his family, for starters, but the whitefeller world was one that would be forever foreign to them.

I flicked the dregs of my coffee out into the grass and climbed to my feet, a renewed determination to do at least one decent thing in my life – to find out who'd killed him – smouldering in my breast.

What to do? Ideas skimmed through my head like the flock of ducks I startled once when I was out hunting at the Bullet Holes. And my problem now was the same as I faced then: which one to pick?

Blakie was still my number one contender. Although, after the debacle of my last attempted arrest, I was just about ready to put him down as an act of God. When he was out there, on his own country, he was virtually untouchable.

I wondered how much of my determination to track down Blakie was due to sheer jealousy. And how did things stand between Hazel and me anyway? Maybe it was time one of us attempted a reconciliation.

But Marsh's big black hat was still in the ring, whatever McGillivray reckoned. I had a stack of unanswered questions about the Carbine manager and his dealings with Moonlight Downs. Not the least of which was, given that he'd had McGillivray carpeted for asking a few simple questions, what did he have to hide?

But how to get at the bastard? I needed facts, information, proof. And to get them I needed an entrée into that surly, self-satisfied world of hats and cattle.

What were my options? Go sniffing around the station? I'd tried that once, and what had I achieved? Bugger all.

Maybe I could tackle some of the bit players. But who

were the bit players? Fidel, the old mechanic? Pull the other one. The other Carbine station hands? Forget it.

What else was on offer? Fencing contractors? Stock inspectors? The local roads blokes? What the hell would any of them know about Marsh and his malefactions? Unless they'd been involved in them, in which case poking my nose in could be a risky business.

My trouble was that I didn't have any status. I wasn't a bookie or a bouncer, I wasn't a cop. I couldn't go round putting the squeeze on people. I was just a member of the public.

Okay, so where was the logical place for a member of the public to begin? With the servants, of course. The public servants. One public servant in particular. What could be more straightforward than that?

Almost anything; I wasn't that naïve. But Lance Massie's name had been breaking out all over the place of late. And if I did pay him a visit, even if he was in cahoots with Marsh, at least he wasn't likely to strangle me in the office. Even Northern Territory public servants didn't do that.

Lance Massie. How had Kenny described him? The Territory Government's bagman. Area Manager for the Department of Regional Development.

What the hell was 'regional development', anyway? It sounded like something that could cover a lot of dirty underwear, especially when it was being worn by the Territory Government. The only things developing in the Bluebush region were melanomas and salt pans.

The mine that had been the town's raison d'être for forty years was down to the dregs. Small businesses were folding. Saturday morning was auction time: you'd see some poor mournful bastard huddled against the back fence while a hundred hungry bargain-hunters rummaged through the detritus of his life. Even out at the meatworks things were looking lean.

Maybe Massie wanted a few runs on the board. If there was anything untoward going on between Moonlight and Marsh – or any of the neighbours – something told me he'd be up to his Territory Government tie-pin in it.

But how was I going to get anything out of him? He knew who I was, for a start. Presumably Marsh had told him something about me, but how much? Did he even know what I looked like? And why did I find myself treading round the name so warily? I'd never even seen the guy, much less had any dealings with him. Or had I? The name had sounded familiar when Kenny first mentioned it to me. Unpleasantly familiar. Where had I come across it before?

I put on a Slim Dusty tape, parked myself out on the front porch, painted my toenails purple and watched Bluebush go about its morning ablutions. Didn't do that for long. Bluebush going about its morning ablutions was not a pretty sight, and the sounds were even worse: Griffo sounded like he was washing out his nostrils with a fire hose.

I went back in and sat at the kitchen table, humming along with Slim, who was yodelling his way through 'When the Rain Tumbles Down in July'. The classic early recording. He'd worn his Y-fronts tight in those days.

Lance Massie. He was something out of the old days as well, I was sure of it. The old Moonlight days. Something to do with my old man, perhaps? Lance bloody Massie. I rolled the name round my mouth, hit it with different accents and associations. It refused to give up its secrets, but the smell wouldn't go away.

I glanced at the books on the table: *Gouging the Witwatersrand* had worked its way to the top of the pile, as it tended to do. I studied a fading photograph: a line of chaps in long white socks and pith helmets standing around a hole in the ground; in the background, the poor bastards who'd dug it. The Bushveld, circa 1928. It reminded me of some of the primitive early shows my old man and I had worked.

My father. Why did he keep bobbing up whenever I thought of Massie? Was he the connection?

Another unpleasant feeling arose from somewhere south of my stomach, worked its way up to my head and down to my fingers. They – the fingers – trembled as they dialled Jack's satellite phone. I'd had a sudden insight into where I might have met the bastard.

'Dad, a quick question…' I could hear heavy machinery roaring away in the background.

'Better make it a very quick one, Emmy. I'm perched on top of a thirty foot tower with a wrench in one hand and a hundred yards of drill rod in the other.'

'What are you holding the phone with?'

'You wouldn't want to know. Shoot.'

'Remember when Brick threw us off Moonlight?'

'Careful…'

'The government feller involved, don't suppose he had a name?'

'Aw…jeez, Emily!'

'What's wrong?'

'You just made me drop the fuckin rods! Why'd you have to go and remind me of that jumped-up little piece of shit? Sure he had a name. Still got one. See him sneakin round the traps in his lemon-scented limo. Sir Lancelot bloody Massie.'

'Thanks, Dad.'

Thanks a lot, I brooded as I hung up the phone. Public servant or not, I could scratch Lance Massie from my list of helpful resources. He and the Tempests had a history.

I'd only seen the man once. Once was enough. He'd been sitting out on the veranda of the Moonlight Homestead, Akubra hat jammed onto one end of him, RM Williams boots onto the other, cigar in between. Trying to out-cowboy the cowboy sitting next to him. The cowboy, Brick Sivvier, was a pig of the first order, to be sure, but at least his porcinity wasn't an affectation. Throwing us off the station came natural to him. It was a Queensland thing: he was just cleaning out the deadwood.

Massie was something else. Even at fourteen, and with a single glance at my disposal, I'd been able to see that. He was a sleek, slippery individual, a walking Hall of Mirrors. If he'd ever had a self, it had long since disappeared under a dozen different layers and accretions. He was an imperson-ation of an impersonation, a natural-born apparatchik who'd slithered out of the womb and sniffed to see which way the wind was blowing. If, by some miracle, Kenny Trigger's revolution ever did come about, Massie would be the one strutting about in the Mao jacket and the Stalinesque moustache.

I replayed the veranda scene in my mind.

Jack had come to pick up his termination pay, and discov-ered that the Warlpuju were being terminated as well. We'd met them on the road to Bluebush, and Lincoln had given us the story. Sivvier had told them to pack up and piss off, and he'd followed his words with actions: he'd bulldozed the humpies, shot the dogs, shut the store, hunted the nurses, clobbered a few fellers who got in his way. When the shiny-pants government feller arrived Lincoln had complained, sought some kind of official redress, only to have Massie tell them it was a matter of private property, nothing to do with him. Indeed, should they continue to trespass, Sivvier would have every right to call in the cops.

Now the blokes responsible were relaxing on the veranda in front of us. Jack gave them a cheerful wave. 'That's Sir Lancelot,' he muttered, 'the little government greaser.' Sivvier maintained his usual Easter Island demeanour – whoever christened him 'Brick' knew what they were about – but Massie responded with a brief, starchy wave. The sort of thing the Queen trots out for the tour of Botswana.

When we went round to the pay office, Jack spotted Sivvier's Range Rover and a flash government four wheel drive parked under the magnificent banyan tree. Five minutes and a nifty bit of winch-work later we were on our way, Jack extending another salute to the blokes on the veranda.

When Massie and Sivvier returned to the carpark, they found their vehicles dangling like a pair of fluffy dice, twenty foot up the tree.

Tom McGillivray told us that a warrant for Jack's arrest had come out from the highest levels, but that the lowest levels – he and his colleagues – were so busy pissing themselves laughing they couldn't figure out what they were supposed to be charging him with. Word was that Massie had been gunning for Jack ever since, his only restraint being the fact that any move he made was sure to revive memories of an event he'd rather have forgotten.

Lance Massie. Not likely to be particularly co-operative when he heard my name on the phone.

But what if he heard somebody else's?

A Bit of a Local Legend

'Massie!'

The voice coming down the phone sounded as if it had been having Man of the World lessons from Julio Iglesias: it was beautifully modulated, mellow and forceful. And phoney as hell. This was my man all right.

'Mr Massie? My name's Caroline Crowe. I don't think we've met, but I've heard a lot about you. I'm with the *Territory Digest*.'

'Caroline!' I could feel him pulling in his paunch and sharpening his tie. The *Digest* was the Territory Government's big-budget, taxpayer-funded PR rag. When it called, the faithful answered. 'Of course, I've seen your work. How can I help you?'

'We're doing a cover story on investment opportunities in the Territory, and I was wondering whether you'd have an hour or two to fill me in on developments in the Bluebush Region. From what I hear you're a bit of a local legend.'

'Well, thank you.'

'I'll be coming up through Bluebush around two this afternoon. Is that too short notice?'

'Of course not.' I could hear a set of chops being vigorously licked. 'It'll be a pleasure. I'm slotting you into my diary as we speak.'

'Great! Ciao!'

'Ciao!'

I spent the rest of the morning packing myself into the tight little yellow silk number that was the closest thing to killer bee I'd been able to pick up at the op-shop. I applied liberal helpings of mascara and lipstick, cleaned off the stray clumps with a cotton ball and blow-waved my hair until it was nearly straight. I grabbed my new pharmacy sunnies, a pair of big-framed Versace knock-offs that I hoped would prevent his recognising me if he ever spotted me in my usual ragged-arsed blackfeller outfit. And at one-thirty I climbed aboard a pair of stilettos and headed for the door.

I thought it was all for nothing, though, when I wobbled into Massie's monument to reflective glass and external plumbing and found my old mate Candy Wilson parked at the receptionist's desk.

'Can I help you?' she intoned, then gawped and gasped, 'Emily! Is that you under there?'

I just about fell off my shoes but I didn't have time for explanations. There was a goggle-eyed git in tight pants and a purple shirt bouncing out of the office behind her. I shot her a desperate look, then looked at him and smiled. 'Mr Massie? Caroline Crowe.'

'Please,' he smiled, gliding past the befuddled Candy and out across the floor like something out of Disney on Ice, 'call me Lance.'

'Nice of you to make yourself available at such short notice, Lance.'

'My pleasure,' he beamed, wrapping his hand around my own and his eyes around my chest. 'We're always happy to co-operate with the *Digest*.'

Massie was just as I remembered him, only more so. Thinner on top but with a nasty little mo for compensation. The bursting shirt and nasal capillaries suggested that happy hour had broken out and taken over the whole week. That explained why he was still in Bluebush, where your better-class alcoholic could just about go unnoticed. He was wearing a sign around his neck which said: 'ROTARY, GOLF CLUB, PRAWN COCKTAILS IN A SILVER DISH'. Well, he wasn't. The closest golf course was five hundred kilometres away. But he might as well have been.

He was in his late forties, dripping with Thai silk, Italian jewellery, Spanish leather and Outback sleaze. Did he always dress like this, or had he nipped out for a grease and oil change when he heard that the *Digest* was coming?

He looked me in the shades. I'm not a tall person. Neither was he: Massie by name but not by nature.

'Please,' he crooned. 'Come in. Candy!' A snap, this; evidently he was unimpressed with the way she was struggling to wipe the gawk off her gob. 'Coffee, please!' He turned back to me and smiled salaciously. 'Or can I tempt you with something a little stronger?'

Candy twisted her nose at his back and poked her tongue out.

I gave him my goofiest smile and assured him that coffee would be fine. The anti-boss vibes radiating from Candy suggested that she wasn't about to rat me out. As he waltzed me into the office, I slipped her a wink. She responded with a 'Be careful!' grimace.

Massie's inner sanctum was a rococo variation on the theme which dominated the rest of the building: outback-crypto-fascist, a veneer of public-service rectitude over-laying a profound crassness that expressed itself in singing fish, flashing mirrors, golf trophies, a bronzed bull's scrotum and a bar that wouldn't have been out of place in a Gold Coast brothel.

The bookshelves were strictly motivational: *Chicken Soup for the Soul*, *Sun Tzu and the Art of Business*, *The Seven Habits of Highly Effective People*, *Awaken the Giant Within*. The gold-framed MBA on the wall looked like a mail-order job from the University of Las Vegas.

By the time Candy arrived with the coffee, Massie and I were getting along famously. I was playing it smooth and cool, he was playing it as fast and loose as his pants would let him. He leaned forward, put his chin on his fingers and fixed me with a piercing stare.

'So how long have you been with the *Digest*?'

'Not long; just a few months.'

'And before that?'

'Canberra. Aboriginal Liaison Unit with Mining and Resources.'

'Uh, Canberra!' he said dismissively. 'I was offered a rather senior position down there recently...'

'Oh?'

'No names, no pack drill. Turned it down, of course. Once the Outback gets into your blood,' he sighed, 'you're never quite the same.'

His only awkward moment came when I told him the angle I wanted to take in the story.

'You're looking at *Aboriginal* enterprise?' he gasped, just about falling out of the papa-bear chair.

'The suggestion's come down from Doug's office,' I replied,

dropping the Chief Minister's name in the spirit of that famed Territorian informality.

'Doug's office...' he repeated sadly, his man-of-the-world tones drizzling into the woodwork.

'Yes. They're concerned that there's been too much negative publicity about the impact of land claims upon development – so much so that it's scaring off potential investors. The new approach is to put a positive spin on the situation, publicise some of the more successful examples of co-operation between black owners and white partners.'

While Massie was busy looking aghast, I glanced out through the open door, where Candy was still sending me strange signals.

'This could be a little less... straightforward than I'd anticipated,' he intoned, bending his brow and vigorously checking out the contents of his left ear with a little finger. 'Perhaps if you could fill me in on what you've covered so far?'

'Well, the major mines – Ranger, Gove. The Granites. Kakadu, of course. Uluru... They're all on Aboriginal land.'

Massie sat there looking more and more deflated as the list went on. His paunch began to reassert itself, his moustache drooped. What examples of thrusting Indigenous enterprise did he have to compete with Uluru and Kakadu? The couple of moth-eaten blackfellers they dragged out of the pub to put on a show out at the Rodeo River dude ranch? Captain Racket's Silver Billy Tea Tours?

'Perhaps in the Bluebush region,' I suggested sympathetically, 'we could concentrate more on potential than on up-and-running projects?'

'Hmmm,' he replied, nodding sagely but unable to keep

the relief from bubbling up at the corners of his mouth. Potential? I could almost see him thinking. Just my line. Wind me up and watch me go. He looked like he'd been feeding off 'potential' for twenty years. 'That would be a sensible move. Some really exciting opportunities opening up in this region. And, loath as I am to... blow my own trumpet, this office' – he swept a grandiose arm around the room, lowered his voice and his eyebrows – 'has been a driving force behind them all.'

I spent the next few minutes scribbling into my notebook while he got his mouth into gear and dragged a dozen projects in from the outer limits of the Never-Never. The Heartache River Nickel Project, the Wonder Gully Gold Mine, the Black Snake Tourist Park. They were all cutting edge, they were all imminent, they were all the results of his own hard work, they were all awaiting a final component, viz. nickel, gold or tourists, and they'd be off like a fleet of rockets.

He gave me prospectuses, surveys and impact statements, he gave me shiny brochures and pamphlets. As evidence of his blackfeller bona fides, he gave me a guided tour of the little collection of artefacts on the sideboard: boomerangs and beads, coolamons, clapsticks and a dot painting.

'And this,' he said as he picked up a red chalcedony knife at the end of the sideboard, 'is the centrepiece of our little collection. It was given to me by a dear friend, the chief of one of the local tribes.'

'What is it?'

'It's the weapon a kadaicha man would have used to' – he gave a wicked smile, leaning so far forward that I copped a blast of whisky breath, and inscribed a curve through the air between us – 'slice you open.'

'Oh my goodness!' I gasped in mock horror, clutching my hands to my chest.

When we were back in our seats, I leaned back, crossed my legs, glanced at my notebook and asked, 'And I've been told there are some interesting initiatives at… let me see, now – Moonlight Downs? Something to do with one of its neighbours?'

His smile froze, stuck like a bull in a bog. 'Moonlight Downs?'

'Ye-e-es.' I flicked back to a previous page. 'An Aboriginal cattle enterprise. Among other things.'

He leaned forward, flashed his lightly browned teeth. 'Caroline – do you mind if I call you Caroline?'

'My friends call me Caro.'

'Caro?' he beamed, his eyelids fluttering. 'Moonlight Downs is at a rather… delicate stage right now. I wonder if we might discuss it over a drink, perhaps? At the Blue Lagoon?' He glanced at his watch. 'They do a martini which is simply' – he actually kissed his fingertips – 'superb.'

I considered his proposal, my fear of discovery being rapidly overhauled by an intimation that with a bit of booze in him this bloke would be rabbiting on like a Kakadu bus driver. Probably hoping to be rabbiting on in other ways as well, but we'd cross that bridge when we came to it.

'Why not?' I said.

As we walked out through reception, Candy was staring at her computer and desperately pounding away at the keyboard.

'Candy,' he said, 'Ms Crowe and I are popping down to the club for a short break.'

'Right,' she said, not looking up.

'Back in half an hour.'

'Right.' She continued to hammer the keys.

'Or so.'

'Good.'

Massie looked at her for a moment, slightly puzzled, then guided me through the door, but we'd only gotten as far as the carpark when a great boozy bellow stopped us in our tracks.

'Hey, boss!'

Freddy Ah Fong was standing across the road, swaying like the last pickled onion in the jar, a broad beam illuminating his soggy face. He began to travel in our direction. I put on my glasses and kept my back to him, praying that he wouldn't recognise me.

'Christ!' Massie muttered. 'The Great Black Hope… just ignore him.'

But thirst had given Freddy wings. He was moving faster than we could ignore.

Massie drew a keyring from his pocket and pressed the remote. A magnificent metallic gold Range Rover fitted out with every imaginable extra – alloy wheels and winch, tinted windows, ladders and racks and rows of halogen driving lights – flashed back at him.

'Hey! Boss!' called Freddy again.

He was almost upon us when Massie said, 'Excuse me for a moment, Caro. Occupational hazard.'

He turned to face Freddy, a grimace on his flushed face. The conversation I couldn't catch, but I did spot a tenner appear and disappear. Massie was slipping the wallet back into his clingwrap daks when Freddy, mission accomplished and boozer looming, yelled a cheery farewell: 'Thanks, boss!' Then he slipped me a great, slobbering wink. 'An you watch out for this feller, h'Emily, e's a randy little bugger! Like a bit of black velvet.'

Massie stopped, his shoulders suddenly hunched, his cheeks red, his eyes swivelling suspiciously. He turned around and asked, 'What did you just say, Freddy?'

I discovered a sudden itch behind my right ear, and began to back away, very slowly, to where my own car was parked.

'Why nuthin, boss,' rasped Freddy, picking up that there'd been a sea change and that it might have had something to do with him. 'Just a little joke between me and the missus ere. Why I never even knowed you know 'er.'

'You know her yourself, Freddy?'

'Why h'Emily? Sure!' He relaxed, grinned. 'She all doo-dahed up right now, but I'd know that little girl anywhere. Daughter for ol Motor Jack!'

'Motor Jack? Jack Tempest?'

'*Yuwayi!*'

'This is his daughter?'

'*Yuwayi,*' Freddy beamed. 'Just about growed 'er up meself.'

I was retreating more directly now, but I couldn't let that one pass. 'Bullshit, Freddy! Only thing you ever growed up was a beer gut!'

Massie turned around, glared at me, his face flushing from bright red to deep purple. He was nearly as black as Freddy when he snapped, 'Candy!' She'd followed us out and was standing in the doorway. His brow buckled, the tendons in his neck leapt out. 'If Miss Tempest enters these premises again, I want you to call the police and tell them we've got a trespasser.'

I took off my shoes, walked back to my car, my feet breathing sighs of relief. As I drove away, I glanced back at Massie: he was standing beside his overblown motorcar, his fat face fuming, his fists clenched.

And as I looked at him, another face rose to the surface of my memory: a toddler's face, this one. A toddler who'd ascended my leg at a basketball game and turned on a similar exhibition when his mother wouldn't give him a boiled lolly.

The Director's Cut

I was lying on the couch that night, licking a Paddle-pop and my wounds, when the telephone rang and a husky voice came down the wire.

'Hi, Emily.'

'Candy! Well I fucked that one up good and proper, didn't I?'

'Yeah, I'd skip the Mata Hari bit if I were you. That's what I was trying to warn you about: Massie knew you were back in town. We had Earl Marsh in here grumbling about you just the other day. It was fuckin Emily Tempest this an fuckin Emily Tempest that.'

'Bastard doesn't talk like that when his wife's around. I have heard I'm not Earl's favourite person; now I suppose I'll have to add Massie to the list. Needless to say, you didn't fess up to knowing me?'

'I value my job more than that. You had little Arseholes fooled for a while with the Country Party tart thing, but even he can put two and two together if you give him a calculator and hit him on the head with it.'

''Specially if he's got Freddy Ah Fong on the team.'

'Ah, Freddy…' she sighed. 'He's a bit of a regular round here.'

'What are you doing working there, Candy?'

'Well, it's a job, honey. And in case you haven't noticed, there aren't that many round here that don't leave you over-exposed to the sun or the sack. More to the point, though, what the hell are you up to?'

I considered my options for a moment or two, then settled back on the couch, rearranged the cushions and gave her the director's cut. An old friend in whom I could confide was something I'd been sorely missing of late, particularly in light of my troubled relationship with Hazel.

'Well, why didn't you just ask me?' she exclaimed when I finished. 'I had a lot of time for old Lincoln.'

'Candy, I didn't even know you were working there.'

'So you really think Marsh could be involved in Lincoln's death?'

'I don't know, but I'm sure as hell trying to find out.'

'He and Massie are thick as a meatworker's dick...'

'Why Ms Wilson!'

'...but I'd be surprised if they were up to anything you could call illegal. Massie's quite a stickler for the rules, actually.'

'We're talking murder here, Candy. I imagine it tends to operate by a different set of rules.'

'Maybe. You still at Toyota Towers?'

'Yep. Number 6.'

'Gimme a day or two. I'll see what I can rustle up.'

Late the next afternoon she appeared on my doorstep with a wary expression on her face and a fat envelope in her hand. I invited her in, offered her a beer.

'Just the one,' she replied as she settled onto the sofa. 'Gotta get Teisha's fish fingers on. Anyway, more than me job's worth getting sprung with the likes of you.' She tapped the package. 'Especially if anybody saw me giving you this.'

'What is it?' I asked.

'Everything I could find in the department's records that had anything to do with Moonlight Downs. When you're finished with it, destroy it, okay? Every page.'

'No worries, Candy.' I gave her a hug. 'I don't know how to repay you.'

'You've already repaid me, Em.' Her eyes gleamed. 'Life was never boring with you around.'

As I got the drinks and flopped down on a chair opposite her, we chatted and filled in the gaps in our respective resumes: her father was managing a station out at Saddler's Well, she'd had half a dozen different fellers, none of whom had had the sense to stay around. Like me, Candy had done time down south – Sydney, in her case – and never fitted in. She'd been back in Bluebush for a couple of years, and had begun working as a receptionist for the Department of Regional Development a year ago.

While we talked, I was scouting around for a chance to put the question that was on my mind, but it wasn't until she raised the topic of her employer that I saw an opening.

'Candy, do you mind if I ask you a rather… delicate question?'

'Delicate? Emily, you wouldn't know the meaning of the word.'

'What can you tell me about your boss's sex life?'

She raised her eyebrows. 'See what I mean?' She tilted her head back, took a swig of her drink. 'Okay: Massie's sex life. Two things come to mind straightaway. One, there's not as much of it as he'd like there to be, and two, I'm not part of it. Thank Christ.'

'Do you remember Flora?'

Candy said nothing, but looked suddenly discomfited.

'Hazel's little sister,' I prompted her.

'Yeah, I remember Flora. Never know if she remembers me, though.'

'She wouldn't perchance be part of it, would she? His sex life, I mean.'

Candy cradled her face in her hands, made a long, involved study of her glass.

'You're looking particularly thoughtful there, Candy.'

'It's like this, Emily. From what I can gather, Massie'd fuck a dog chained to a tree, or try to. Whether he had it off with Flora, I've got no idea. Her little boy is, what, one or two years old? Whatever happened was before my time. But, er…'

'Ye-es?'

'Well… you aren't the first person to raise that possibility.'

'Who was the other one?'

She paused, drained her glass and looked at me. 'Lincoln,' she said at last.

'What!'

'Couple of weeks before he died.'

I leaned forward. 'Tell me more.'

'It was one of the stranger meetings I've seen in my time there. Couldn't exactly call it a meeting, I suppose: more of a whistle-stop encounter. Lincoln wandered in, un-announced, wanted to speak to Massie. Wasn't accusing him of anything; just had a rather unusual request.'

'Which was?'

'He'd seen one of those heavy-duty prams, four wheel drive jobs. Apparently Flora's living rough in one of the camps... he wanted to know if Massie would buy her one, that was all. Said – this made as much sense as everything else in the discussion – said he'd give Marsh the water if he bought her the pram.'

'What water?'

'Buggered if I know.'

'How did Massie react?'

'In his usual high-powered, senior executive manner: died in the arse.'

'I can well imagine. Changes colour quicker than a chameleon, your boss.'

'Lincoln didn't even get past the front desk, actually. Massie looked at him like he was a raving maniac, suddenly remembered a meeting he had to attend and hit the road running.'

'What did Lincoln do?'

'You know Lincoln: he was his usual even-tempered self. Just shook his head, said to say hello to my old man for him and wandered out.'

We sat there in silence as the implications of what I'd just been told ran around my head.

'What are you going to do now?' Candy asked.

'I know what I'd like to do: get drunk, stoned, rooted and as far away from this mess as possible. But I don't suppose any of those things are likely to happen. Look, Candy, why don't you leave it with me for now? You've got a lot more to lose than I have – a job, for starters. I'll have a look through this stuff.' I patted the paperwork. 'See if I can make any sense out of it. In the meantime, keep your eyes open; let me know if you spot anything. I'll call you in a day or two.'

'Okay. If you're happy with that, so am I. Must admit, it'd be a disaster for me to lose my job right now – they're like the Mafia, this mob. Get em off-side and you end up at the bottom of the billabong in concrete gumboots.'

She stood up and I gave her a farewell kiss.

'We'll catch up when I'm not odour of the month.'

'I'd like that.'

When she'd gone, I ripped the envelope open and examined its contents: a folder full of photocopied documents and computer printouts. I looked at the first page: a letter from Massie to his masters in Darwin. The 'Re' was 'Moonlight Downs'.

There were a lot more: letters, memos, planning applications, mineral exploration leases, business plans.

Candy had been busy. So, by the look of things, had Lance Massie.

Sun Tzu Out of Chicken Soup by The Seven Habits of Highly Effective People

An hour later I shoved the folder into my backpack and headed down to the boozer. I pulled up at the corner, uncertain of where to go. Tonight felt more like a Black Dog night. I needed something rugged to wash Massie out of my system.

It wasn't his evil deeds that were troubling me as much as his evil prose. The motivational gurus on his bookshelves had trickled down into his computer and you couldn't read a line without bumping into a core value, a hypervision or a mission statement. His Collected Works had more windows of opportunity than a Hamburg whorehouse, more cutting edges than a combine harvester, more benchmarks than a drunk's forehead. For a bloke who'd spent twenty years with his snout in the public trough, Massie had an amazing grasp of the language of private enterprise. His conceptualisation ranged from blue sky to black hole, his strategies from eagle to seagull. He dared to dream, and when he'd done dreaming it was time to walk the talk and churn white water.

All of this, I reflected, from some pathetic fuck shuffling taxpayers' money around a quarter of a million square kilometres of spinifex?

I ordered a glass of the Black's black-market bourbon, repelled a couple of drunken boarders and took my wad of papers out to a quiet corner of the beer garden.

Okay, I decided. Somewhere in this lexical septic tank there must be some hard information. I pulled out a notebook and scrolled through the folder. Whenever I came across an actual fact – a date, a location, a person, a meeting held, a deal done – I jotted it down. Out of those disparate bits and pieces a pattern – if such a thing existed – must surely emerge. At the very least, I hoped to find some speck of an insight into what was going on at Moonlight Downs.

I worked rapidly and in half an hour I'd finished.

I took a swig of the bourbon and studied my notes. What did they tell me?

Not much, but that may have just been the bourbon, which had a kick like a one-armed bouncer.

The main function of the Department of Regional Development in regard to Moonlight Downs, it appeared, was to milk the land claim for all it was worth. This meant recruiting to the cause every disgruntled neighbour with a ground axe or a disjointed nose, every local entrepreneur who could dream up some detrimental effect of the land going back to the blacks. There was, it appeared, the possibility of Commonwealth Government compensation for lost earnings.

Massie's operation had the feel of an office assembly-line; there'd been a lot of cutting and pasting, a lot of inserting names and dates, but it was all more or less to the same end: squeezing the teats of the Canberra cash-cow. That was regional development, Territory-style. That was your rugged, outback individual: these days the Akubra was off the head and in the outstretched hand.

Tour operators, miners, roadhouses, retailers, they were all there, looking for a cut. Mick Czaplinski, for example, the proprietor of Micky's Menswear, had done his bit for the cause, his call for compensation based on a loss of income due to the disappearance of your well-accoutred white stockman. That was about the general level of argument.

While the department was thus busily raising scrounging to an art form, it was also sounding out and revving up potential investors who thought they might be able to make a quid out of doing business with Moonlight Downs. Here they were being encouraged to avail themselves of the Commonwealth Government's Regional Business Initiatives Scheme. I was astonished to realise that these were often the same people. Mick Czaplinski, for example, was seeking a government grant for what sounded like an on-line version of the old hawker's van he had trundled around the bush twenty years ago.

I added them up. Jesus! Flogging a dead horse they might have been, but there was no shortage of jockeys ready to jump aboard. More than forty local businesses – storekeepers and miners, fencers, contractors, stock agents, neighbouring stations – had registered a commercial interest in the Moonlight Downs Land Claim. I hadn't known there were that many local businesses.

I ran my eyes down the list, searching for anything that could be in any way relevant to Lincoln's death:

Gillcutter and Co. Harkness and Sons. North Siding

Pty Ltd. Winch, West and Chambers. Impala Productions. Annie Downs. Sundowner Transport Industries. Barber and Partners.

On it went. Some I knew by name, others by reputation. Sam Barber was a local roads contractor-cum-thief whom Jack had seen, years before, spluttering his innocence as the cops dug up a load of stolen equipment from his yard. Sundowner Transport Industries: that'd be Freddy Whittle and his old Kenworth. Annie Downs was Mallee o'Toole's threadbare station out on the Stark River. Winch, West and Chambers sounded like a top-drawer law firm, but was, in fact, a trio of old reprobates who'd been struggling for years to get their backblocks horse abattoirs out of the red and had thus far done little more than feed themselves and their dogs.

The rest looked like the usual outback assortment, the hopeful and the hopeless, the parasitic and the paralytic, the mired fly-by-nights and the failed fortune-hunters who wake up one morning somewhere out in the browner parts of this big brown land and realise they've been stuck in a shit-hole like Bluebush for twenty years.

For each registration of interest there'd been a meeting, and for each meeting Massie had efficiently noted everyone involved. The half-dozen references to Carbine were accompanied by the words Marsh, E. In May, I noted with interest, Marsh had brought a friend: Wiezbicki, O.

Wiezbicki, O.? Wiezbicki, O....

What sort of a name was that? Wiezbicki, O. Sounded like a new super-breakfast. But once again, it rang bells.

Wiezbicki, O. Where had I heard the name before? Had

Marsh come packing a lawyer? Or was it a station employee, one of the dickheads I'd come across at the pub? Maybe somebody I knew from the old days?

I went back to the original document, and only then did I notice what I'd missed the first time: also present at the meeting had been one Flinders, L.

I looked up, my head spinning. What the hell had the four of them been meeting about?

I needed a breather. I rose to my feet, stretched my back, walked into the main bar. Stilsons, the alcoholic labrador after whom the pub was named, was sleeping it off under a pool table. Meg, the alcoholic cook who named it, was sleeping it off at the kitchen bench. She stirred herself, rattled the cutlery, found a chopper and began slamming away at a slab of meat. What day was it? Thursday. That'd be the Vienna schnitzel special. Or the dreaded Hungarian goulash/chocolate pudding double, which sounded better but tasted like both courses had been cooked simultaneously in the same dish.

The Black Dog's kitchen hours tended towards the haphazard – generally they lasted about as long as Meg did – but the food was popular. The diners were lined up along the bar, and a gruesome spectacle they made. I was surprised how many of them I knew. Unfaithful bastards; I'd thought they were regulars at my own establishment, but they must have been spreading their favours around. Old Bob the Dog, who looked like a bearded egg, was furiously shovelling in the spag bol. Tommy Russell, sitting next to him, had taken off his glasses; presumably you needed windscreen wipers when you were sitting in the vicinity of Bob and a bowl of spaghetti. Andrea Bolt had stuffed herself into something chiffon and was glaring at her battered flake as if it were a personal enemy.

Even my Toyota Towers neighbours were represented: I spotted Camel, hunched up against a window, yapping into his mobile phone and pointedly ignoring me.

I bought a stubby, and as I returned to my seat paused at the side gate to take in the scenic wonders of the Bluebush night. You name it – gravelly waste lots, broken bottles, bullet-riddled forty-fours, acres of acned bitumen bathed in a pale fluorescent wash – Bluebush had it.

I went back down to my table, took a long swig of the beer and a longer swig of the Massie. It was like wading through fresh vomit, something I'd been doing too much of lately.

Any of the documents, with the right sort of massage and manipulation, could possibly give me a hint as to what was going on out at Moonlight, but that massage and manipulation was beyond me. I felt as if I'd found the key, but lost the door.

I plodded on for another half an hour, but nothing emerged, neither clue nor insight nor indication of what, if anything, was going on at Moonlight Downs. Marsh and Lincoln had met at least once, in the company of Massie and this mysterious Wiezbicki, but what they were discussing I had no idea. In the end I threw the package into my backpack and headed home, frustrated, weary, not a little pissed off.

I took the alleyway home. The Alsatian was strangely silent – must have been his day off – but when I reached my back entrance I got a surprise of another kind.

There was a light burning in the living room.

Had I left it on? No way. Maybe it was time I got a dog myself.

I flung the gate open, ran up the path and opened the door. I wasn't the first person to do so tonight: the newly replaced lock had been ripped off. I stood in the doorway, aghast.

The Sandhill Gang had returned: they'd left their calling card sprayed across the kitchen wall in letters three foot high.

And this time they'd completely trashed the place.

The Boys are Back in Town

'Blue-bloody-bush!' I muttered for about the hundredth time that month.

I roamed through the apartment, my fury mounting as I totted up the damage.

Their first port of call had been the fridge, which they'd hit like a herd of cattle attacking a waterhole. What they couldn't eat or steal, they'd sprayed around the room. A jar of mayonnaise was the only thing still standing.

My faithful old cassette player? Tape spaghetti. The dunny? Blocked, of course: the camp kids only had to look at a piece of plumbing equipment for it to suffer immediate and irreparable seizure. My books? In the dunny, a good proportion of them. A couple of old favourites – including *Gouging the Witwatersrand*, dammit! – seemed to be missing. Christ, I thought, literate vandals! Maybe the raid was part of an adult education outreach program. The money tin? I didn't bother looking. They'd flogged the wind-chime from the veranda, the crystal from the window, the barometer from the wall. They'd even flogged my new blender.

'My blender!' I moaned. 'You little bastards!' Banana smoothies were the only thing that had kept me going of late.

For a moment I thought 'Massie', out to get his papers back. But that would be absurd. You're getting paranoid, girl, I told myself. No way was this his style. With the amount of unaccountable Commonwealth funds floating around the Territory, he'd employ some black-skivvied assassin with a silenced automatic and a Harvey-Keitel grimace if he wanted revenge.

I collapsed onto the couch. Felt lonely. Wanted Jojo. Spotted the phone beside it and decided to ring the cops.

As luck would have it, an unpleasantly familiar voice announced that I'd reached the Bluebush police station.

'Emily Tempest here, Griffo.'

'Emily. How are you this evening?'

'Shithouse. Have you heard from Jojo Kelly?'

'No, where's he gone?'

'Out bush for work, Ngampaji way. Don't suppose you could get a message through to him, could you?'

'I could try.'

'Tell him his Kupulyu Creek solution to the juvenile delinquency problem is a load of crap.'

'Er, he'll know what that means?'

'It means the Sandhill Gang are back in town.'

'What!'

'I'm looking at the damage as we speak.'

'Have they hit the other flats?'

I took a look out the window: fluorescent lights were blazing, alcohol-fuelled conversations were roaring, Black Sabbath and Lee Kernaghan were serenading each other from opposite ends of the court. 'Doesn't look like it.'

'Phew. That's a relief.'

'Thanks for caring, Griffo.'

'No worries. Are you going to report it?'

'Is there any point?'

'Probably not. I'll pass the message on to Jojo if I can.'

I spent a hectic hour cleaning up the mess, and by the time I was finished the flat was more or less back to normal. My head was taking a little longer. I stripped off, had a shower, made a pot of tea, pulled on a pair of old army britches and stretched out on the back porch.

Count your blessings, I counselled myself. Count your bloody blessings. There were half a dozen gangs in the town camps. Lucky it wasn't the petrol boys – they would have eaten the walls. I even had a bit of tucker left. Well, some biscuits anyway, a packet I found in the back of the cupboard. Milk arrowroots. Good job, too; I suddenly found myself famished from my exertions.

I was salivating over the first one, jaws agape, when something twigged. Milk arrowroots – that was it. That was the connection, the hook, the key, that was the thought that had been bobbing around like an unsinkable turd in the toilet of my subconscious all night.

There was an old bloke who lived out on the Stark River, east of Moonlight. An old bloke everyone round here referred to as Bickie. He was a winemaker, of all things. As a kid I'd figured the nickname came from the giant milk arrowroots he was forever munching as he marched around his vineyards, but Jack once told me it was an abbreviation of his real name. Something Polish and ending in 'bicki'.

Wiezbicki. Oskar Wiezbicki.

A picture appeared in my head: a wizened little white-feller, pale-faced, smooth-skinned, with scrawny legs and big boots, thin lips and a massive hat. But gentle. And clever:

they'd hung shit on him for trying to grow grapes out there, but he'd confounded them all. His label, Rotenstok, was said to survive more on curiosity than oenological value, but I'd spotted it at roadhouses and pubs all over the region. He'd started out small and ended up... well, still small from what I could gather. But alive, which was more than could be said for a lot of the blokes who'd been hanging it on him.

One person who'd never shared the general scepticism about Bickie was Jack, and for a very good reason.

Bickie was a water diviner.

He was always the first person the stations round here turned to when they were looking for water, before they brought in the hydrologists and drillers. Jack had used him for a couple of the early mines, and they'd become mates, after a fashion. Jack reckoned Bickie could smell water the way a mozzie can smell blood.

Bickie it'd be, for sure, this Wiezbicki, O. So what was he doing at a meeting between Marsh, Massie and Lincoln? I couldn't imagine the four of them sitting around discussing next year's vintage. Come to think of it, had the meeting taken place in Bluebush at all? Maybe Massie had gone to them; there was nothing in the files to indicate the venue. Massie had always enjoyed mixing it with the locals – the better class of locals, anyway – on their home turf. I remembered my first sight of him, sitting next to Brick Sivvier, hoping a little bit of Brick would rub off.

What was Bickie doing getting round in the company of guys like these?

I finished my tea and my biscuit. Felt a bush trip coming on, like the first flush of spring.

About time, too, I decided. Bluebush was getting me

down, and my little bit of it stank of White King and black vandalism. I went to bed, huddled against a pillow, felt a wave of sleep stealing over me.

The jagged hum of Bluebush's night machinery gradually softened into the whirr of wings. I found myself floating over a moonlit plain, wind lilting among silver feathers, the watercourses awash with a music soft as rain. In the hills below I could hear dingoes yapping and howling.

I opened my eyes, troubled by something I couldn't put my finger on. Something suggested by the dingoes.

The dog over the back fence. Why hadn't it barked?

Could the Sandhill Gang have somehow silenced it? That seemed unlikely; I thought about the way they treated their own dogs, cuddling and kissing them, smuggling them out bush.

The implications of this question were just beginning to make their way through my head when I detected a faint, scraping noise from the back door. I looked up in alarm. Russell and the boys coming back for more?

The door creaked on its hinges, ever so slightly. A slight rise in the level of the noise from outside. A footfall. A rustle of clothing. What might have been a stifled intake of breath.

Then a long, malevolent silence.

I lay still, strained my eyes, but could make out nothing in the darkness. Until I spotted a blur of movement in the kitchen. I slipped out from between the sheets, slithered onto the floor.

The intruder entered my room on cats' feet and a holy terror swarmed through my heart.

I lay there, listening intensely as the steps drew closer,

then paused. Another couple of steps, then a sudden, furious blow hammered the bed. I heard a sharp snarl of exasperation as he felt the pillow where my head should have been, then a narrow beam of light swept the room. He began to make his way around the bed. I held my breath, did my best to still my heart. He reached the end of the bed, moved round to my side. I braced my body against the wall, prepared to launch myself at him.

Suddenly the room swivelled and swirled and a blast of light shot across the wall. Somewhere outside a heavy motor revved and roared, then stopped. I heard a car door slam.

I looked up in time to catch a glimpse of a shadowy figure haring out through the back door, and heard the crash of a fist on the front one. A fist followed by a familiar voice.

'Emily!'

Jojo.

I scrambled to my feet, rushed to the door and flung it open, threw myself into his arms so ferociously I almost bowled him over.

'Shit, that's an enthusiastic...' he said, then caught a glimpse of my face in the half-light. 'What the hell's going on?'

'Somebody broke into my place.'

'I heard.'

'No, not that. Just now. While I was asleep. You scared him off.'

He bolted into the apartment and out the back door, which was wide open. He pulled the torch from his belt, followed its beam to the back fence.

I came and stood out on the porch; felt suddenly chilled, found myself shaking uncontrollably.

'Jojo!'

'Yep?' came his voice from the alleyway.

'Come back.'

His head popped up over the fence. 'I want to have a look around; he may still be in the vicinity.'

'Don't do that. Please. Just stay with me.'

He came back frowning, studied me for a moment, drew me into his arms. 'You're trembling.'

'This is nothing compared to what I was like a minute ago.'

He held me tight, and his whispered reassurances and the rasp of his whiskers on the top of my head slowly soothed me.

'You didn't get a look at him?'

'Just a glimpse as he ran out the door. It was all too dark and fast.'

He let go of me for a moment, pulled out his torch and ran it across the ground nearby.

'Is that yours?' he asked. He was looking at my nulla-nulla lying in the dirt.

'You ought to know – you're the last person I belted with it.'

'Wasn't it by the front door?'

'It was, but the whole place is topsy-turvy after tonight's goings-on.'

'Don't touch it,' he said. 'I'll get the cops to come and check the place over.'

'Do you have to do that?'

He frowned. 'I don't like the way this feels.'

'It gets worse. There's a dog.'

'Where?'

'Over the back fence, normally. Tonight there wasn't.'

He went out into the alley, shone his torch through the chain mesh, then hoisted himself over the gate. I saw him bend over a prostrate shape close to the house, then knock on the back door. An old bloke came limping out, all splutters and snarls, joined Jojo at the dog's side. Jojo's explanation must have been succinct: a few seconds later the owner was revving up his car. Jojo gently lifted the dog inside and laid it across the back seat. When the owner had belted off down the driveway he came back and joined me.

'Still alive?' I asked him.

'Only just. Gone to the vet.'

'What happened to it?'

'Doped.'

'Shit.' I looked up and down the alleyway. 'What's going on, Jojo?'

'That's what I was going to ask you.'

'Why did you come?'

'To see you.'

'At three in the morning?'

'Got a strange message from Griffo. Said you'd had another visit from the Sandhill Gang.' We were walking back up the path by now. I clutched his arm.

'I did.'

'No you didn't. I spoke to Con just this afternoon; boys are all still out at Kupulyu, doing well.'

We stopped, looked at each other and I felt a tremor run down my spine. 'I think I'd like to get out of here for a while.'

'Out of the house?'

'Out of Bluebush.'

'You should go and talk to the cops.'

'Bare my soul in front of Griffo and his mates? I don't think so.' I squeezed his hand. 'Can't we just go out to your place?'

He considered this for a moment. 'Okay, but let me get the cops to scout around the neighbourhood, just in case your visitor's still on the prowl.'

While Jojo was on the phone, I gathered together a few things, threw them into a bag, and we drove out to the shack. He entered the building ahead of me, lit a lantern, boiled a billy.

I lay down on the big spring bed. He brought me a cup of tea, rested it on the bedside table, slipped in beside me. I rested my head on his chest, looked down at our bodies bathed in blue moonlight. The aromas of the bush – nectar and mint, coolibah – drifting in through the open walls slowly calmed me down.

'Thanks for tonight, Jojo.'

'You don't have to thank me, Emily.'

I buried my face in his neck. 'You're the calm after the storm,' I whispered.

'After the tempest, you mean. And I don't know that it's over. What have you been up to?'

'Just the usual. Poking my nose in.'

'How unlike you. Poor old Tom told me about your shenanigans. He thought you were crazy.'

'What do you think?'

He lay there for a moment or two, his dark eyes gazing out into the stars as they rolled through the trees. A gentle breeze drifted over us and the lantern guttered. 'I suspect you come from a different galaxy than the rest of us. You'll find what you're looking for – long as you don't get yourself killed in the process. Wouldn't want to try and stop you, though.'

'Good, because I've got another suspect to throw into the mix.'

'Oh?'

'Lance Massie.'

'I see. Starting at the top and working your way down, are you?'

'I think he might've fathered Flora's child. Lincoln thought so too.'

'Okay. Could well be. What's that got to do with his murder?'

'God knows, but don't you think it'd be reasonable to try and find out if they're linked?'

He climbed out of bed, threw a piece of wood on the fire, turned out the lantern and closed the door. His shutting-down rituals. He came back and sat in a chair next to the bed, put his feet up alongside me.

'Emily,' he began, 'you're not going to like this, but I have to say it anyway. I understand what you're trying to do, but I think you need a rest. That look in your eyes tonight – you were totally freaked out. You're not going to get anywhere like that. Why don't you leave it with me for a while? I'll ask a few questions.'

'Maybe…'

'You need a break. And I've got the ideal getaway for you.'

'Is this where you tell me I've won the five-star holiday at Byron Bay?'

'Even better. Moonlight Downs.'

'Moonlight!' I raised myself up onto an elbow. 'Don't

know if they want to know about me out at Moonlight right now.'

'I bumped into Winnie and the kids on the road today; they were hitching a ride back into town with the Jalyukurru water works team.'

'Clive James?'

'That's right. It's just Hazel and the old folks out there right now, and Winnie kind of hinted that Hazel's starting to pine for you.'

'Hazel pining for me? That'll be the day.'

But I was pleased; I'd been pining for her as well. It was, I had to admit, the reason I'd hung her wind-chime out on my veranda. The trip also offered an opportunity to combine pleasure with business: I'd drop in and visit a little Polish winemaker while I was in the neighbourhood, see what he had to say about his meeting with Marsh and Massie.

'So what do you reckon?' he asked.

'I reckon,' I paused, reached out, drew him into the bed, slipped him out of his shirt, found his left nipple with my teeth and finished the sentence with a flurry of nibbles and kisses that covered the length and breadth of his body, 'that – we – might not be – seeing – each other – for a while – so we might as well – enjoy ourselves – while we can.'

A Canopy of Leaves and Light

The next morning he drove me back to the flat. I rolled up my swag and threw it into my ute, grabbed my hat and bag, gave him a kiss. He stood by his car, arms folded, and watched me as I drove away.

'See you in a few days, Jojo,' I called back at him. I picked up a few supplies at the store, then headed out onto the northern highway.

It was late morning when I pulled into Bickie's – into Bickie's what? I wondered, looking at it. Too upmarket to be called a camp, but hardly a station. His oasis, perhaps. Twenty acres of trellises and green light, a stone house set alongside the powder-dry Stark River bed. The corrugated-iron shed between the house and the vineyard was presumably where Bickie made his wine.

For the moment I had the place to myself, and I took the opportunity for a bit of a poke around. If Rotenstok had a theme it was water: the name, I recalled, meant 'red river' in some dialect of Polish. A nostalgic gesture once, perhaps, but there was water now a-plenty. A bronze fountain studded with blue glass gushed among water pipes and windmills, a man-made stream trickled through rock pools and green plants. Even the shack looked like it had grown out of an upturned water tank.

A little to the east, close to the river and under a tree, was a grave with a single word chiselled into the headstone: Alicja. Another of Jack's stories came floating up from the past. The tale of an immigrant couple, newly arrived and lost in the desert, of the young wife who'd done a perish and the husband who'd refused to abandon her.

And who'd built, I realised, a kind of outback Taj Mahal.

I heard the sound of an approaching vehicle, and watched as a white Falcon ute came trundling in from the vines. The driver looked at me briefly, then climbed out and stretched his back.

He didn't look much older. Then again, nobody could have looked much older. He'd shrunk, though. Either that or he was wearing a bigger hat.

The only other change was a huge pair of sunglasses: they made him look like an albino blowie. Presumably the sun was troubling his ageing Polish eyes.

'Hello, Bickie,' I said as he came walking towards me with a load of hoses and tools in his arms. He nodded, dumped them at the shed, climbed out of his glasses and studied me, a finger curled round his chin. There wasn't much of him, but what there was was crackling with an energy that suggested he'd be powering on until the day he dropped.

Recognition dawned slowly, but dawn it did – more than it would have done had our positions been reversed. 'But you'll have to give me a Christian name…'

'Emily.'

'Tempest,' he nodded, his voice as deep and cracked as the ravine that split the hills above us. He looked promisingly pleased to see me.

'Hell of a memory you've got there, Bickie. Reckon I was about ten when you last laid eyes on me.'

'Ach… but it's the eyes I don't forget. Such intensity. I remember you sitting on the back of your father's motorcar, watching like a little bush rat as I felt for water. And did I not see you afterwards, with a length of wire in your own hands?'

'Never found anything, though.'

'Perhaps you found things more elusive than water. You've grown up as small and beautiful as your father is big and ugly.'

'He sends his regards to you too.' Which wasn't that far from the truth. I'd given Jack a call from the Resurrection Roadhouse, got a few directions, made sure Bickie was still alive and picking.

Twenty minutes later we were relaxing on the veranda, a glass of rough red in the hand, a slab of cheese and a loaf of rye bread on the table. The Dry was coming to a close, the sun was gathering strength, but here, under this tranquil canopy of leaves and green light, all was coolth. I'd given him the bowdlerised version of my life since Moonlight, he'd given me the biography of his vineyard.

'So, Emily,' he said, stretching out what there was of his skinny little legs to stretch, 'much as I hate to sound like Jesus at the wedding – what's it to be? Water or wine?'

I looked at him blankly.

'Most people come here for one or the other,' he elaborated. 'To what do I owe the pleasure of your visit?'

I held my glass up to the light, studied the refracted images that came swimming through its curves. I didn't actually go for wine that much. To my uneducated palate it tasted like Deep Heat, but the artistry that had gone into its making somehow inspired trust in the artist.

'It's information I'm after, Bickie.'

He raised his eyebrows. 'Information?'

'Little while ago, you did some work for Earl Marsh.'

The eyebrows stayed aloft.

'Manager of Carbine,' I prompted him.

'Ye-es. I know who he is. He came out here with his friend. The government man. Mr…'

'Massie. And you met Lincoln Flinders as well?'

He hesitated. 'Ye-es, we did.'

'Would you mind telling me what the meeting was about, Bickie?'

He'd pulled out a pipe, a beautiful briar, many times repaired. He fired it up, his cheeks full of wind and his eyes full of questions. The first of which was a cautious 'Why do you wish to know?'

I stood up and leaned against the railing. A mottled shadow shot across the open ground. I looked up as a flock of budgies came swerving in, tilted, wheeled and disappeared. Drawn to the water. I rolled a smoke, gazed up into the scarlet hills that brooded over us like an imminent storm. Who else had I seen gazing up into those hills of late?

Lincoln, of course, the day we ran into Blakie. Who was still out there somewhere. I thought of him moving over those stony slopes, his nostrils flared, his eyes full of god-knows-what. Blakie the barking mad. Was I barking up the wrong tree myself?

I told Bickie about my suspicions, told him how I'd hunted Blakie and hassled Marsh, and explained that I was keen to find out what he knew about any business, legal or otherwise, that might have been going on between the two stations.

Bickie listened quietly, nodding from time to time, asking for the occasional point of clarification, contemplating the contents of his glass.

'Mmmm… Lincoln, Lincoln…' he said softly when I finished. 'So you honestly think there could be a connection between Earl Marsh and his murder?'

'I don't know, Bickie. But if there is I'll find it.'

He studied me for a moment. 'Yes,' he nodded, 'I think you will.' He hacked off a chunk of bread, added a sliver of cheese and chewed them thoughtfully. 'I hope – for my own sake, if nothing else – that you are wrong. I would hate to think that I had contributed in any way…'

His voice trailed off into a reflective silence.

'Did you know Lincoln well?' I asked him.

'Yes, quite well, I would say. We had many dealings over the years. Perhaps a friendship of sorts. He was one of nature's gentlemen. Not that Mr Marsh thought so: Mr Marsh is not, I fear, a gentleman of any description. There is, however, a certain… directness about the man. Frankly I would be surprised if he had done such a thing. The violence I could imagine, under certain circumstances, but the… treachery? The attempt, you are suggesting, to disguise it as a traditional killing? It does seem out of character.'

'I must admit, I've had the same reservations myself. So what was your meeting about?'

'Water, Emily,' he sighed. 'Like everything else in this country.'

'Underground water?'

'Of course. Carbine Creek, for all of its history and traditions, and its apparently rich pasture, is even worse off in that regard than most of its neighbours. Mr Marsh's main aquifer will not last another ten years. He needs water badly. And I am confident that I found it for him, although I could not be certain of its quality until the drilling has taken place.'

'Where'd you find it?'

'Therein lay the problem. That was the reason Mr Massie offered his services. I believe he considers himself something of an expert in the field of Aboriginal affairs. Mr Marsh brought him out here to… negotiate.'

'With Lincoln?'

'Yes.'

Christ, I thought, given that pair's history, that suggested either an astonishing amount of ignorance on the part of Marsh or an astonishing amount of big-noting on that of the Little White Hope. Surely he realised Lincoln wouldn't have had any time for the bastard who'd colluded in his people's eviction from the station?

'Where'd you find the water, Bickie?'

'Close to the northern boundary. In considerable quantity, I'm sure. Though of what quality I could not say.'

'Close? You mean on the Moonlight side?'

'You must understand, Emily, the community was still struggling to establish itself. Particularly in the north. I doubt whether anyone other than Lincoln or Marsh had been out there for years.' He sighed, trouble biting at his eyes. 'Yes, the water was on Moonlight Downs. They planned to head on down to the camp, arrange a more formal meeting, but Lincoln came upon us unexpectedly.'

'Let me guess. Marsh asked Lincoln if he could drill?'

'Had he done so there would, I'm sure, have been no

problem. But Mr Marsh is – how do you say it? – a man of the old school. He didn't ask – he told. Massie was even worse: he acted as if the deal was already done.'

'Yeah, I can imagine that. And I can imagine Lincoln's response.'

'He told them to go away. But not in those words. I suspected he was enjoying getting a little of his own back after so many years of the boot being on the whiteman's foot.'

If nothing else, I had at least learned the meaning of Lincoln's remark to Massie about swapping a pram for water; I bet he'd enjoyed that as well.

'What was Marsh's state of mind while this was going on?'

'Ah, Emily,' he said, shaking his head, 'topology I can sometimes read. Men's minds, especially those of Outback Man, I cannot. Suffice to say that he was far from happy. I'm sure that with time, and a little diplomacy, the situation could have been resolved to the satisfaction of all. But time, alas, Lincoln did not have. Nor diplomacy, for that matter. The next thing I heard he was dead. Killed, it was said, by Blakie Japanangka.'

'Do you know Blakie, too?'

He shrugged his narrow shoulders. 'Does anyone know Blakie?'

I let the response settle for a moment. 'And that's it?'

'As far as I know, yes. Mr Marsh and Mr Massie dropped me back here and paid for my services. I have not seen either of them since.'

'You don't know whether or not Marsh actually drilled?'

Bickie shrugged again. 'I'm sorry. I've no idea. I could, perhaps, find out. I know all of the drillers around here.'

'I'd appreciate that.'

I finished my cheese, slipped the wine down into a rose bush. I was ready to roll. Bickie stood out on his veranda and watched me leave, thoughtfully scratching his chin.

As I got out to shut the gate he called out, 'Emily!'

'Bickie?'

'What I said before about you and water.'

'The divining?'

'You should try it again. You may be ready for it now.'

A Knockabout Geology

The road from the Stark River ran close to the north track, and I decided to make a diversion and see for myself the parcel of land around which Marsh's schemes, whatever they were, apparently revolved.

An hour's drive brought me to Jalyukurru Hill, the nearest thing to a vantage point in the northern quarter. I'd never set foot on it before. I grabbed my field glasses and spent twenty minutes grunting my way to the summit.

Once there I wedged myself between two massive slabs of stone, then relaxed, leaned back, let the sun wash over my face.

I took a swig from my water bottle, chewed a bit of jerky, then did what I automatically do when I encounter a patch of new country: studied the rock formations, subconsciously endeavouring to slot them into the geological map that's forever flowing through my mind.

Given a Wantiya mother, a knockabout miner father and a Warlpuju foster mob, it wasn't exactly surprising that I often thought of geological formations as having lives of their own. I imagined them as enormous creatures, crawling through time, interacting with one another, forever changing, forever being changed. Sometimes, lying on a slab of quartz in the afternoon sun, I could feel a pulse that mightn't have been my own.

The west was a folded scarp of red granite and yellow sandstone under an iron-coloured duricrust. Two dark peaks, known locally as the Brothers Grim, towered over the slopes. The rock face there was irregular, rugged, pitted with fissures and frets and lightning scars, streaked with veins of hematite and limonite. Nothing unusual in any of that.

Eastwards, more of the same. The ubiquitous granite, a warped sandstone wall, the odd beetling overhang, a coating of kaolin over the lower slopes. Some interesting shapes and formations but, geologically speaking, par for the course.

Below me was another site in which I had more than a passing interest: the dozen or so acres of bizarrely shaped and weathered granite boulders that whitefellers called the Tom Bowlers and which Hazel knew as her dreaming site. Karlujurru. Diamond Dove. From this angle it looked like a ruined city. Some of the massive corestones seemed to be floating on air, so delicately were they balanced upon each other's backs.

Absorbed in the long-range perspective, I almost forgot about the close-up: the outcrop under my arse. Jalyukurru itself. Jack had cast a prospector's eye over it years before, only to be stopped in his tracks by a minatory glance from Lincoln. I wondered, fleetingly, whether they'd mind my being here, whether I was breaking some taboo.

The boulder upon which I sat was rough and grey, and, given that it was mottled with dents and cavities, surprisingly comfortable. I ran a hand over its fractured face. Hackly and jagged, the texture flaky, almost greasy, with a vitreous lustre. Anorthosite, I decided, with xenoliths of dunite. The coarse-grained gabbro jutting out at the base was something else, possibly norite.

Anorthosite. Dunite. Norite. Was there a pattern there? Something told me there was. Hadn't I seen something similar of late? Possibly, but I couldn't remember where. Hazel's wind-chime? No, the interesting bit there was labradorite, or so Jack had reckoned, and he was usually right.

I put the rocks in my pocket and made a mental note to follow them up with Jack next time I saw him.

I turned my attention to the country below. From the heights of Jalyukurru it assumed a different perspective. A dream perspective, perhaps, the echo of an inland sea. I felt like I was hovering over a red and yellow canvas painted by an old woman with sandy-blighted eyes. The wind guttered, the heat shimmered. Light shot away from an infinity of minerals. A brown hawk clawed air, floated over plains and pasture, went eye to eye with me.

I raised my binoculars and scanned the horizon. A few cattle mooched about. Marsh's, presumably. Bastard was taking his time responding to the court order. Why did that not surprise me? It was poor country this. Relentless, treeless, the wiregrass sporadic and as tough as tungsten, the gibbers the colour of arterial blood. Bare enough to flog a flea, as Lincoln would have said.

Worth killing for? Shit, who could say? Especially if it had water. In Bluebush I'd seen fellers come close to killing each other over a carton of chips. Had Marsh, already enraged over the land claim, been tipped over the edge when Lincoln told him to sod off?

I picked up the boundary fence with the glasses, followed

it along until I came to a gate, on the other side of which lay the waving Mitchell grass plains of Carbine Creek. The transformation here was dramatic. Rich pasture, to be sure, but for how much longer? Strange to think that the station, one of the oldest in the Territory, was becoming a marginal prospect because of its dwindling water supply. How many other properties were going the same way? How much of our future were we slowly devouring?

I followed the fence a little further to the south, then paused, came back and had a closer look at the gate. There was something unusual about it. I studied it carefully, wondering what it was that had snagged my subconscious. It wasn't until I put the glasses down that I realised what it was: the set of wheel tracks ploughing through it. They were much deeper and wider than what you normally saw round here.

I raised the glasses again.

Marsh's F100? Too deep. Cattle truck? Too wide. This was something really big.

What the hell was that big out here? A road train? No, the country was too rough.

A drilling rig, that's what it would be. They could go just about anywhere these days. Earl Marsh, I knew, was looking for water. Had he already drilled? I followed the tracks. They came towards me, up into the lower slopes of Jalyukurru. I lost them for a moment on the outskirts of Karlujurru – you could lose an army in those crazy acres of scattered granite – but then I found them again. And something else. Beside the track was a metal cylinder, rising a foot or two out of the ground.

A capped borehole.

There'd been a drilling rig here all right, and it had drilled on the outskirts of Karlujurru. Depending on the angle, the hole could well have bored right into the site itself. Lincoln would never have agreed to that. Not here. They didn't come much holier than Karlujurru.

Marsh, I thought, you cheeky bastard. Lincoln barely in his grave and already you're drilling into his heartland. Or did you drill beforehand? Was this what Lincoln had found the day he died? Was this why he died? Did he spring you drilling for water? Did the two of you have another argument over it? Did you follow him home and murder him in the night?

I rolled a smoke, took a long, slow drag, thought about the significance of what I'd seen. Whether I was any closer to finding out who'd killed Lincoln.

Not particularly, I decided. Both of my main contenders were still shuffling round the ring. If the aquifer was accessible and deep, Marsh could have killed him to facilitate his rip-off over the water rights.

The trouble was that the drilling could just as easily have been a motive for Blakie. A hole punched through the heart of Karlujurru. Even if Lincoln hadn't known about it when it happened, he still bore ultimate responsibility for the sanctity of the site. He was *kirta*, the owner. In Blakie's merciless system of justice that could well have meant he had to pay the price for its desecration. I thought about the butchered body, the missing kidney, the intricacies of responsibility and atonement among the Warlpuju.

But was I getting ahead of myself? I didn't even know for sure whether or not Marsh had actually drilled here. What was it Bickie had said? He'd found water close to the boundary. This hole was three or four kilometres in. Not what you'd call close. Had Bickie's water been too salty? Were there other drill sites, closer to the fence? Maybe Marsh had been doing some exploratory drilling. I scrutinised the country. There were no more holes that I could see. A lot of the country round here was criss-crossed with old tracks and trails, pock-marked with mines, dams and other desecrations committed before blackfellers had any say in the matter. Could this be one of them? I needed to take a closer look.

I considered my options, thought about climbing down.

No. It was tough, and risky. Steep in parts, loose in others. And getting back up would be even worse. This was no country to be out alone in with a broken leg. I'd have to go the long way round.

I climbed back down to where I'd parked, still chewing over what I'd seen. It would take me a good hour to get around to Karlujurru. I'd have to head up through the Mater Christi Jump-up, and it was a hell of a tough road for my little Hilux. Should I risk it now, or come back better equipped?

The moment I broke out of the scrub I regretted the fact that, absorbed by the view in front of me, I hadn't paid more attention to what was going on behind me.

The big red F100 parked in front of my ute was the least of my worries. The two blokes sitting inside – their fiery faces and John Deere hats marking them as the kind of runaway urban trash who'd overrun the Territory in my absence – weren't such a worry either.

The worry was what was standing next to my car, its arms crossed, its feet squared, its glasses glowing.

Earl Marsh.

Black Hole

We stood there for a moment, sizing each other up.

He reminded me of a lump of weathered granite, all scarlet and black faceted, the sunlight glimmering off his blistered skin, the buckle on his enormous girth-strap gleaming. The most compelling aspects of the man were the five-gallon hat, the ten-gallon hands and the small, worried-looking woman reflected in his shades.

'Mr Marsh!' I began. 'You're looking particularly...' I stumbled around for the right adjective, then settled on the glasses, 'reflective today.'

'You set me up,' he barked.

Small talk, I was beginning to realise, would never be one of the Marsh strong points. 'On a pedestal?'

His nostrils quivered. 'You set your fuckin PC hounds onto me.'

Tom McGillivray PC? Police constable once, presumably; but hardly politically correct. 'I had some concerns which I reported to the relevant authorities.'

'Well, the relevant fuckin authority is cooling its heels in Darwin, from what I hear.'

'That was an impressive piece of political lobbying – congratulations – but it doesn't answer the question, does it?'

'Which is what?' He loomed over me like a loose boulder

in avalanche country. 'Whether I killed some bloody black-feller?'

'Well, some bugger did.'

'That's no reason to go spreading bullshit round about me.'

'I didn't spread any bullshit about anyone. I simply asked a few questions.'

'Questions! You enter my home under false pretences, accept my hospitality and then go sniffing round to see what kind of crap you can dig up. I've had half the Anzac Club ribbing me about it all week…'

'I didn't enter your home under any pretences, and, frankly, I don't think you can blame me for being curious. Doesn't it strike even you as a little convenient that Lincoln is murdered the day after you do a dodgy deal with his drunken brother to take over half his country?'

I noticed a flicker of movement behind the shades, then he muttered, 'Them's the breaks.'

As long as Lincoln's neck wasn't another, I thought, but thankfully didn't say. If a verbal stoush was all I had to worry about, I could have gone the full ten rounds, but I didn't like the situation: lonely road, lone woman, the possibility of a slanging match escalating into something more serious.

I glanced at Marsh's red-faced henchmen. If he was granite, they were termite mound: equally red, but friable, pock-marked and a pain in the arse if you ran into one. The nearer of the two squinted back at me with a twisted grimace. His mate was worse: big nose, weak chin, thick lips. Barbra Streisand on steroids. And half shaven, the pair of them. Why couldn't the blokes out here make up their minds whether to shave or not?

No, I didn't like the situation at all.

But – fuck it! – somebody had killed Lincoln. If this bloke had had anything to do with it, if he knew anything which could provide me with any insight into the murder, I wanted to know about it. This was as good an opportunity as I was likely to get.

The trouble with Marsh, though – the trouble with a lot of these outback meatheads – was that he was such a black hole. I'd been wondering what it would be like to go head to head with him. It was high time I found out.

I took a deep breath.

'Mr Marsh, look, I want to say something to you: I know I'm not one of your… set, okay? I'm not a cattle king and I'm not some big-shot public servant, and I'm not even white, but I'll tell you something else I'm not.' I faced him full on, stared at about where his eyes ought to be. 'I'm not going to go away. I'm not going to stop asking questions until I get some answers, and I'm not going to stop asking about you until I'm convinced that you had nothing to do with Lincoln's death, and frankly, right now, I'm not convinced.'

He stood there, stock still, glowering, then glanced at the Dynamic Duo in the truck. Was this the bit where they began breaking necks? But no, he put a finger to his chin, grappled with a thought. The effort made him look like a gorilla examining a gyroscope. Finally he spoke.

'What makes you think I had anything to do with it?'

'You haven't exactly been a model of reconciliation.'

'Eh?' he grunted.

'You've been a royal pain in the Moonlight mob's collective arse, Mr Marsh. Hijacking their land, killing their dogs, generally scaring the shit out of what little's left of the community. You blame me for suspecting you might have taken your opposition to the next level?'

Another long silence ensued, and then, to my surprise, he held out his hands.

'Look at these,' he said.

'Very impressive,' I answered. And I had to admit, they were – callused, corn-fed, rough as buffalo hide. 'Done a lot of miles. Why are you showing them to me?'

'The point is that what I got,' nodding in the direction of Carbine Creek, 'I worked for. I earned. I was ridin a horse before I could walk. You know a bit about my background: I come from that to ownin one of the most famous properties in the Territory.'

He leaned in close. I could have compared his dentistry with Blakie's if he'd ever opened his mouth when he talked. 'An there's nothin gives me the irrits more'n seein a bunch of useless layabouts pickin up what oughta be prime property without pullin a finger outer their – what'd you call it? – collective arse. Nothin!'

I was willing to skip mentioning the Warlpuju's long-term land management – sixty thousand years of it, at last count – in the interests of my own short-term survival, but there was one anomaly glaring out of his argument that I couldn't let go by. 'I can't see that there's a huge amount of work in getting Freddy Ah Fong to sign the place over to you.'

He chewed his lip, then grunted, 'That was more by way of creating a buffer zone than anythin else. There's a lotta blackfeller stations round the Territory. They got a reputation, believe me. When you got a neighbour won't put in – I'm talkin disease control, noxious weeds, gates, dogs – you need a bit of room. To manoeuvre, like. Bit of breathin space.'

It was more cant than Kant, but, by local standards, Marsh was sounding almost reasonable. So reasonable, in fact, that before I knew what I was doing I found myself seeing how far I could go. Seeing how far I could push the envelope, as his little mate Massie would have put it.

'If I had a neighbour that bad I might be tempted to get rid of him.'

He ripped the envelope to bits and threw it into my face. 'You still tryin to pin this fuckin thing on me!' he snapped impatiently. 'I'm not the only neighbour, you know. There's the roadhouse, there's three other stations, pack of pissant mines, an a stack of bloody blackfellers, one of who's mad as a cut fuckin death adder.'

'Maybe, but you had a motive. I don't know that any of them did.'

Sometimes I say things I wish I hadn't, but I can't help myself. It's in the genes, my big mouth. My only regret was that my old man's big right hook wasn't in the genes as well. Marsh took off his shades and studied me, his eyes like cracks in a slab of blistered liver. 'Motive?' he growled suspiciously.

'Water,' I said softly.

'Water?'

'Water.'

'Water!' he bellowed. 'You think I killed the pig-headed old cunt for some *water*?'

I'd hit it now; water was obviously the tender point in the Marsh psyche. 'Well, why did you kill him?'

'I bloody well haven't killed anyone! Yet!' he added ominously. 'And what the hell has this got to do with water?'

'I know you need it. And I think you might have found it when you drilled on Moonlight.'

'Whadderye mean I drilled on Moonlight?'

'I've seen the borehole.'

'Lady, you wouldn't know a borehole from a bum hole!'

I would have responded in the same intemperate manner, but the crash of his fist upon the bonnet of my car which had accompanied the last outburst brought me to my senses.

One of Marsh's henchmen – the one with the squint – was climbing down from the cabin, his nose twitching, his over-bite bared. He looked like a cross between a hamster and a pig dog. He glanced at his mate with an expression I found hard to read but hoped wasn't saying, 'Here we go again, get the shovels ready.'

Whatever their intentions might have been, they were interrupted by the sound of another vehicle coming down the track. Blackfeller outfit, from the broken-down sound of things. Bindi, I saw gratefully, as his crudbucket-of-the-month came limping round the bend with a mob of women and kids on board. His mother-in-law, Minnie Driver, was sitting on the back, waving a skinny claw and grinning like a bearded dragon. She even had the beard.

Bindi's automotive standards had hit rock bottom: his front axle was a mulga branch, his petrol cap a pair of undies. A jerrycan on the roof was feeding petrol into his fuel pump.

'Everythin all right, Emily?' Bindi enquired as he rattled to a halt beside us.

'Everything's great, Bindi.' Especially now that you're here. 'What are you mob up to?'

'Oh, we's headin for town. Strangeways give us the arse. Too many family, manager reckon.'

The Strangeways manager probably had a point. If the car had had rafters they would have been hanging off them. The more the merrier right now, as far as I was concerned.

'You wanner come along?' he offered, glancing at the Carbine entourage and reading the situation beautifully.

Marsh was reading it as well, and retreated to his car with a glance that was laced with dog-bait.

'Not just now, thanks mate.'

I watched Marsh as he pushed his off-sider away from the wheel and roared off. Terrible temper that man had. At least there weren't any dogs around for him to kill this time.

I didn't feel up to checking out the mystery bore right now. It'd keep. After the traumas of the past twenty minutes all I wanted was a bit of company.

'Did you call into Moonlight on the way, Bindi?'

'We bin camp there last night.'

'Hazel there?'

'Yep.'

Bindi rounded up his mob – some of the old ladies had taken the opportunity for a spot of hunting, a couple of kids had to be dragged down from a tree – and rattled off down the track. I was about to do the same when I noticed movement at the foot of the bushes behind the wind-row. I took a closer look and spotted a carcass disintegrating in the scrub. A bullock. Long dead, from the smell, or lack thereof.

The bag of bovine bones was bad enough, but what was infinitely worse was the fat black snake crawling out of its rotted arse. Deaf-adder. The reptile gazed up at me bleakly, its eyes as cold as a winter dawn, its fangs flickering. Sun-dried shit on wicked scales.

I shuddered, climbed into my car and drove away, fast. But not fast enough to escape the shiver that rattled my back-bone and the sudden intuition that somewhere, somehow, something bad was going down.

Rust

I'd spent a lot of time soaking up bleak vistas of late, but Moonlight took the damper.

They don't come much bleaker than this, I thought as I gazed out over the camp from the relative luxury of the ute. The windscreen was like a magnifying glass, concentrating the sun's rays on the tinder of my unease. Bits of rusty tin rattled and flapped in the wind. Rust was seeping into the soul of the community: the turpentine bushes and blade grass, the scorched scoria, the wire that held the humpies together, the shredded wheels, the wind itself. They were infused, all, with a kind of rust-coloured clarity.

Where was everybody?

I climbed out, called a cautious greeting.

No answer. Not that I'd expected one. If they'd been here they would have come out and greeted me when I drove in. And yet Jangala's car was parked near the shack.

It was the silence that struck me most. Even the radio, perched on its totem pole in the middle of the camp, had gone quiet. Normally it was rabbiting away non-stop, as people from communities all over the region chatted to each other on the Jalyukurru frequency. The only sounds to be heard right now were the rattle of loose tin, the whisper of wind and the squawk of kite-hawks.

Kite-hawks?

There was a flock of them flapping around the campfire, picking at... Picking at what?

I scattered them with a rock. They hopped into the air, pissed off, and settled a few metres away, scowling out from under their dark hoods as I came to check out their lunch.

It was a goanna: three foot long, as fat as a fencer's forearm and nearly as burnt. The sense of foreboding tightened its grip on my chest. What on earth would have made the Moonlight mob leave a prize like this for the scavengers?

Cutting across to Hazel's camp I went past the radio, and decided to put in a quick call to base, in case she'd left a message.

I picked up the mike, but it came away in my hand, the dead leads flopping against my arm. I went to stick them back, but the back plate had been smashed in.

Jesus, I thought, this is seriously weird. Where the fuck is everybody? Has there been an accident? I began to walk towards their shack, and as I drew closer I heard a noise – the creak of metal springs, then a grunt, then another grunt – from within.

I stopped.

Who was shagging who?

Whoever it was and whatever they were up to, they'd made a bloody mess. The shack looked like it had been hit by a whirlwind. Canvases upended on the veranda, paint pots and bottles scattered about, lengths of string – the remains of a wind-chime – blew across the dirt.

'Hello!' I yelled.

No answer.

'Hazel?'

Silence.

I paused in the doorway, my shadow dancing on hessian. Then, with metaphorical kite-hawks tearing at my own heart, I stepped inside.

A gloomy tableau slowly assembled itself in the semi-darkness: dirty cups and saucepans on the bench, a slab of grey meat on the table, an old spring bed. Huge flies crashed against the ceiling.

I could smell the fear, and it wasn't all my own.

'Hello?' I whispered, more in an effort to calm myself than in any hope of getting an answer.

A flurry of wind blew the hessian a little further to one side, a beam of light cut across the murk. Landed squarely upon a pair of eyes, staring up from the bed. Bright, possum eyes. Dead eyes. And an open mouth, the teeth a row of riddled fence posts, the tongue blue.

Jimmy Lively.

A movement in the darkness on the far side of the bed caught my attention. Something black and shaggy arose from the upper body. What the fuck was that? For one horrible moment I thought it was a rat, chewing at Jangala's neck.

Another movement and it revealed itself as the shock of hair on top of a wild, hairy head. I would have preferred the rat.

'Jesus!' I exclaimed. But it wasn't Jesus.

It was Blakie.

He took a hand away from Jangala's neck and put it across his eyes, peering up into the dazzling light from the doorway. His knuckles were smeared with blood.

He emitted a low, crackling growl and climbed to his feet,

came towards me, his eyes full of squirrelly things I couldn't read. And had no intention of staying around to spell out. It looked like he'd just finished throttling Jangala, exactly the same as he'd done to Lincoln, and was eyeing off his next victim.

I threw the table at him and crashed out through the flimsy back wall.

Which was a mistake, for two reasons. The first was that it led me to stumble over another body. Maggie's, this one, looking even deader than her husband. The right side of her head was smashed in, a pool of blood coagulating in the dust. Blakie's carved fighting-stick lay alongside the body. A picture of his blood-stained knuckles flashed before me. At least the poor old girl's eyes were closed.

The second reason was that it put Blakie between me and my car.

Which could well be the fatal mistake, I realised as he came lurching out at me like a nesting crocodile.

I set off running, into the scrub.

Blakie lurched into a rambling pursuit.

My misspent youth hadn't given me much, but it had taught me how to run, and I felt pretty sure I could outpace the middle-aged maniac on my tail. I'd shake him off, circle back round to the car.

Yet another mistake, I concluded soon afterwards, as my wild sprint withered to a canter and then collapsed into a desperate, lung-burning scramble.

I thought about the last time I'd seen Blakie, loping up into the hills with a posse of fit young coppers eating his dust. No way was I going to outrun this bastard.

He took it easy for a while, not in any apparent rush to get in there and wring my neck. But, as the years in which my main form of exercise had been rolling smokes and striking matches kicked in, he began to gain ground.

My mouth felt like it had been mud-rendered, my lungs were raked by fire, my guts wanted to give up both the ghost and the goulash I'd had for breakfast. The crash of branches in my face mingled with the crash of blood through my veins. Strange pains began cutting through my ribcage. Thin red scrawls flicked across my forearms. My heart was all pumped up and going like a pub drummer on top-drawer speed.

I lost him for a while in the thick scrub round the Purrapuru Waterhole. Lost myself too. But when I burst out onto the main track he was there waiting for me. Close enough for me to see the Jack Nicholson gleam in his eyes. Close enough to smell his raw, predatory breath.

I wheeled around and set off in the opposite direction, westwards. At least I was on what passed for a public road round these parts. An occasional station or mining vehicle passed this way. But I was flailing hopelessly and fading fast.

Christ! I thought, if what was spiralling through my brain could be called thought, what have I done? What was it my father had told me about playing with black fire? What had McGillivray told me about interfering in police business? Okay, okay, I conceded, I'd let this be a lesson to me. All this time I'd been trying to pin the crime onto somebody else, when the real killer was the first and most obvious candidate.

I lost my footing, skidded in the gravel. As I knelt in the dirt I heard something up ahead. Something miraculous, man-made, mechanical.

A motor.

Salvation? I staggered round a bend and there it was, in the middle of the road: a white Hino twin-cab. Just a few hundred metres away.

But leaving me to my fate, I realised in despair as it took off. I yelled feebly, waved my arms. Yes! The vehicle stopped. They'd seen me. No, they hadn't! A bloke on the back of the truck jumped down and began to examine the ground.

Shit! He waved his mates forward and climbed aboard. They began to move off. The bastards! I gave a yell so pathetic I could hardly hear it myself. The truck crept slowly forward.

Blakie didn't look too happy at the prospect of my getting away. '*Warlukunjumana*!' he yelled. Come here!

Sure Blakie, no worries.

His face gave new shades of meaning to the word 'ugly' as he leapt at me, but all he got was a handful of shirt. The adrenalin rush that followed gave me a velocity I didn't know I had and carried me all the way to the tow bar.

'Help...' I gasped. The bloke on the back of the truck – skinny and dark, with five o'clock spikes and the eyes of a byzantine Christ – turned round and stared at me in disbelief.

Not that I could blame him, I figured, catching a glimpse of myself in the chrome: denim skirt ripped and ragged, scratches and blood all over the shop, streaks of sweat and dirt, shreds of clothing on muddy breasts.

But he thumped the roof, and I blessed what I took to be his little Mediterranean heart.

'Hey, Bernie!' he yelled, not taking his eyes off me in case I vanished back into the desert, 'pull up!'

The vehicle drew to a halt. The bloke on the back continued to stare. 'You right there, lady?'

Am I right? I bloody well am now that you're here. I could have just about leapt in and rooted him on the spot. I sank to my knees, heaving for breath, but kept a tight grip on the tray. They weren't going anywhere without me.

I glanced back down the track. Blakie stood there agitated and scowling, his nostrils flared, his mouth a mess of snarls and desert dentistry. The prospect of tackling a truck-load of burly miners – there were four of them, and the tray was full of hard hats and hammers, hydraulic hoses, crowbars – was enough to make even him think twice. Presumably they were making their way to town from one of the mines out west.

The driver's window rolled down and a head appeared: fortyish, fair-haired, covered in dust but vaguely familiar.

'Madam?' he asked. 'Do you need help?'

'Help?' I gasped, climbing to my feet. 'You dunno the half of it! Just gemme the fuck outta here!'

They looked shocked. Shit, I thought, just what I need. Prim miners.

'Good God,' exclaimed the driver. 'It's Jack Tempest's daughter.'

It took me a second or two to place him, so scattered were my wits: Bernie Sweet, the miner who'd come to call upon my father. Yet again, Dad and his mates were saving my bacon.

I sucked all the air I could suck, then spat out a scattered explanation: 'There's been a killing. Two killings. Blackfeller camp back there. Bloke who did it... bloody madman, on my tail...'

Bernie looked up and back.

So did I.

315

The track was empty.

'Madman, you say?' he asked, clearly suspicious that the neighbourhood maniac was kneeling in front of him. The dirty back window was rolled down and a head like a hairy gumboot appeared, stared at me: 'If we are gonna give 'er a lift, Sweetie, watch out for your fuckin radio – she'll flog it if it isn't bolted down.'

Camel.

I glanced up into his bloodshot eyes and tried to smile. Even Camel looked like a knight in hairy armour to me right now. 'Look, Camel, I suggest we forget about any little differences we might have had in the past. There's a killer close behind me and there's no telling what he'll do.'

Which there wasn't. At least he couldn't say I hadn't warned him. No sooner had the words left my mouth than something long and lethal came whooshing out of the bushes on the other side of the truck.

The skinny feller on the back gasped, cursed, clutched his chest and looked at the inch of wet wood in his fingers in astonishment. Not that that particular inch was the problem – it had already done its damage. It was the twelve inches still in his body that was killing him.

In the wake of the spear came the madman himself, laying into the poor bastards like a bull with a bullet up its arse. He ripped the back door open with an almighty roar and plucked poor Camel from his perch as easily as he would have plucked a blowie from his beard. Then he speared him into the side of the truck. Head first.

Blakie hit the front passenger door before Camel had hit the deck, ripping it open – just about ripping it off its hinges – with a ferocity that stunned the bloke sitting there, but not

Bernie Sweet, who used the intervening seconds to seize a rifle from the rack behind him.

Blakie grabbed the startled passenger by the beard and dragged him out, began stomping his head into the dirt. Kept stomping his head into the dirt until Bernie levelled the rifle, pulled the trigger and blew a great red hole into his corrugated chest.

I was looking into Blakie's eyes just as he was hit, and such was the fury I saw there that I knew a few grams of lead wouldn't hold him, knew he'd just keep going, insane and unstoppable, until he killed the lot of us.

But he didn't.

He flew up and back, arms and legs going every which way, and landed on the wind-row. He did raise his head for a moment, his eyes burning with high-octane hatred, his green teeth twisted into a ferocious grimace.

Then he dropped back down. Lay still.

The silence reverberated as powerfully as the chaos that had preceded it. Somewhere in the treetops a crow called, a long, falling sigh. A dying sigh. Bernie climbed out, cast a measured glance at the body, checked for a pulse. Didn't find one. Looked up at me.

'That your madman, Emily?'

He turned back to where his shafted off-sider lay gasping against the sides of the truck.

'Jesus!' I heard him exclaim. 'Tony!' Then he got to work.

This is one cool bastard, I thought, as I watched him try to save his mate. Must come from running a show out bush. I looked on with growing admiration as he moved into para-medic mode: grabbing a first-aid kit, applying a pressure bandage, attempting a bit of messy CPR.

I stirred myself and did what I could to help, but it was no use.

'Lost him,' he murmured a few minutes later, shaking his head, glancing at Blakie's body and cursing. 'Fucking thing's gone through his heart.'

I sat on the step, my own heart pierced by a raft of black emotions. Dejection, shock, dismay. And not a touch of guilt. What a mess, I brooded. What an A-grade fucking disaster. And I got the poor bastards into it.

'What was his name?' I asked.

'What?' asked Bernie, looking up at me.

'Your mate. I didn't even know his name.'

'Tony,' Bernie murmured darkly. 'Tony D'loia.'

'He have any family?'

'Family?' For a moment he looked as though he didn't know the meaning of the word, then he shook his head. 'None that I know of. Just us, I suppose. We were partners. Poor bugger – all he was looking forward to was a quiet drink in the beer garden.'

'You're heading in for Bluebush?'

'We were. Fellers have been working hard for weeks.'

I went over and put a hand on his shoulder. 'I can't tell you how bad I feel about all this, Bernie. If I'd known I was bringing this maniac down on top of you…'

He glanced at me, then looked away, shaking his head. 'Wasn't your fault…'

What was left of his outfit had picked itself up out of the bulldust and staggered in to join us by now. First came Camel, gradually unscrambling his brains after his encounter with Blakie. Then Mal, the front passenger and, I realised, his occasional flatmate. Last time I'd seen the bloke he'd been decorating the couch. On closer inspection he looked like a lot of other miners I'd met over the years: head like a dead leatherjacket above a shapeless bulk; gruff, morose, baggy-bearded and blue singleted.

'Christ,' rasped Camel, staring at his murdered workmate. 'Tony. Is he…?'

Bernie nodded.

Camel glared malevolently at the outstretched Blakie, whose resident flies had begun to resettle after their recent disturbance.

'Black bastard!' he spat. I didn't feel like arguing the point, bit of a black bastard though I might have been myself.

Either Mal wasn't as close to the dead man or he wasn't the demonstrative type. Whatever the reason, he didn't have much to say. He settled against the bull-bar and glowered out into the bush, alone with whatever was oozing through his brain.

For myself, I didn't care what any of them did or thought. They'd saved my life. At the cost of one of their own. And Bernie Sweet, clearly the head honcho, couldn't have been more solicitous: he plied me with water and coffee, settled me under a tree, threw a rug across my legs.

'You sure you're okay, Emily?' he enquired, looking over my battered body with an air of deep concern. 'You've had a hell of a shock.'

'Bit shook up, but I'm fine, thanks. Just amazed to be still in the land of the living.'

'And you reckon he's killed someone else back in the camp?'

'Another couple, looked like. But I wasn't hanging around for the post-mortem. And there's a woman missing.'

'We'll get you back to town as soon as possible. You ought to see a doctor. But what about this missing woman?'

'Her name's Hazel. I reckon I know where she'll be – if she's still alive.'

He glanced at his battered workmates, then said, 'Give me a few minutes to sort things out, then we'll see what we can do to help. There's nothing more we can do here.' It was a generous offer, given the circumstances.

He went back to the truck and fired up a short-wave under the dash. I sat in the shade of a whitewood tree, leaned my back against its rough bark and nursed my coffee. Normally I would have found it vile: a murky conglomeration of UHT, sugar and bore water. Right now it was the most beautiful thing I'd ever tasted. Every sip savoured of salvation. Heaven in a pannikin. Alive alive-o.

I settled back, closed my eyes and breathed deeply. Suddenly exhausted and content to let this competent dude run things. Not my usual modus operandi, but what I'd been through in the last hour would have been enough to make George Orwell turn things over to big brother for a bit.

Then I thought, *Hazel*.

My peace of mind shattered like a thunder-egg in a fire. Where the hell was she? I scratched the sand with a stick, drew circles and arrows, found myself beginning to shake with fear. Had she gotten away, or was her broken body lying somewhere in the scrub?

What on earth – or out of hell – had possessed Blakie? For a moment I told myself that maybe their absurd affair would be her salvation. Maybe the fact that they slept together would have stayed his hand, inclined him towards mercy?

Christ, I was fooling myself and I knew it. He'd gone right

over the edge. From what I'd seen of his rampage today, he'd have killed her as casually as he'd have knocked a goanna on the head.

I pulled myself up.

No, until I knew that she was dead, until I touched her cold body with my own hands, she was still alive. Still out there somewhere.

I'm forever making wagers with myself, and I made one now. If she was alive we'd be okay. The lot of us – me, Hazel, what was left of the Moonlight mob. We'd work our way out of these horrors and we'd flourish. If she wasn't…

No. I shook my head. It was too awful to contemplate.

I'd never felt so dependent on anybody in my life.

Bernie came back, squatted beside me. I found his presence – not just his bulk but his burly self-confidence, his fluidity, his ease of command – immeasurably reassuring. With him around, at least we had a chance. 'Police are on their way, but it'll be a few hours. I told them we're heading out to find this friend of yours. She may be injured.'

'From what I've seen today that's not very likely. Blakie doesn't injure, he slaughters. But thanks.'

'My God, you don't have to thank me. If we don't look out for each other out here, who else will?' I smiled gratefully. 'Where do you think she'd be?'

'Place we used to hang out as kids,' I told him. 'Especially when there was trouble.'

'So where is it, this hideaway?' he asked.

'Maybe fifteen, twenty k's to the north. An old police station.'

'Police station?' He gave me a peculiar look, then smiled. 'I don't suppose there's any old policemen out there?'

'Think they're long gone.'

I could see myself getting to like this bloke. So calm in a pressure-cooker situation, so measured, and yet thoughtful. Capable of humour, even, at a time like this.

'Camel's going to stay back here, with the… with the bodies. He'll wait for the police. Frankly, he's still a little too shaken up to be of much use. What did you say your friend's name was?'

'Hazel.'

'Hazel. Okay, if she's out there we'll find her. But we'd better check the camp first. If you're up to it.'

Which we did. And which I wasn't. Bernie went into the shack alone, while Mal and I sat in the Hino.

The roaring swarm of flies told me that Bernie was checking the bodies. He came out a minute or two later, shaking his head.

'Unbelievable!' he muttered. 'He did a good job. Poor old buggers. I covered them up; least we can do is give them a little dignity.'

I nodded my appreciation. Not everyone out here would have been so sensitive.

'Let's see if there's anyone alive around here.'

A quick search of the camp revealed neither dead nor living. A slower search, this time out as far as the horse yards, told us that Hazel's little bay was missing. The maze of hoof prints around the yard made it impossible to track. But if Hazel had managed to get away, I was sure she'd head for the gaol.

When I said this to Bernie, he glanced at Mal, who nodded his agreement, then we climbed back aboard the Hino.

'Okay,' said Bernie, 'let's go!'

Ghost Roads

I took them cross country, and we hit the track not far from where we'd had our disastrous encounter with Blakie. I caught a glimpse of poor Camel in the distance, crouching forlornly by a small fire. Sweet drove up and filled him in on our plans. After the vaguest of acknowledgments from the battered, bearded one we set off to find Hazel.

I took them via the Long Yard shortcut, but the track faded into a faint set of wheel marks, then disappeared altogether in a patch of whippet grass. I decided to give directions from the back of the truck, just as the late Tony D'loia had done, and it was as I was changing places that I spotted the first hoof prints in the sand.

Her horse? I wondered. Maybe.

A little further on, at the northern gate, I picked out a foot print. Not just a foot print, *the* foot print, the only one in the world I knew at a glance. The crack in the heel, the long, skating arch.

'She's been here!' I cried. 'We're on the right track.'

Bernie gave me a cheery thumbs up.

I climbed aboard, grinning with relief, confident that she was still alive.

My confidence took a downward spiral a few kilometres later when we found the horse itself, lame and alone. We doubled back, searching for the spot where she'd abandoned it. We dismounted, fanned out. We did eventually pick up her tracks, but it took us a good hour to do so, and even then it was only because I'd guessed where she was going. She was heading for the gaolhouse, but taking the longest, toughest route, covering her tracks and cutting across country.

I was puzzled. What was the point? Me she could fool easily enough. But Blakie? Blakie could have tracked a bird through the air.

We pushed on, Mal taking a turn at the wheel now. I took them up through the foothills, over the jump-up, then round the western side of the ranges. From time to time, when something caught my attention, I'd pull him up with a thump on the roof.

Once it was a set of scuff marks, where she'd fallen to the ground. Another time, at the Ngurulu soakage, we came across the remains of a dried-out camel, its teeth little tombstones, its skin rotting away like a carpet left out in the rain.

In the soak itself were fresh holes, but no water.

She was getting thirsty.

Then we found hand prints, stretching for thirty or forty metres. Hand prints! I thought. She's on her knees. Christ, she must be getting desperate. Was she injured? Or worse, driven out of her mind by the horrors she'd witnessed back at the camp?

The anxiety gnawed at my insides. I could feel her fear. Sometimes, touching her hand prints or studying an acacia bush under which she'd rested, I could almost smell it.

I found myself drumming the roof of the Hino in frustration.

I longed to speak to her, to touch her, to reassure her that help was at hand. Christ! I thought, what a godawful nightmare the last few weeks have been for her. First her father, then the rest of her family. Thank God Winnie and the kids were in town when Blakie struck.

We hit the plains and the miles flew by, the wind rattled my eardrums.

The two miners sat in front, neither of them making more than the odd comment. I stood on the tray, clutching the bar and yelling out any change of directions, but our course was usually obvious. Bernie flashed a reassuring smile through the rear window now and again, but for the most part they just stared at the horizon, focusing on the job at hand.

Occasionally they consulted a map. I knew the country better than either of them, of course – I'd grown up among its sun-scoured hills and hollows – and didn't need a map. I wasn't looking for landmarks, I was looking for variations. Things out of place. It was something I'd learnt from Lincoln. Visitors to the desert sometimes remark upon the amazing long-range vision of those old blackfellers, but it's not their eyes. Half the poor buggers are just about blind. It's their minds. So well do they know the lie of the land that they're quick to spot anything up and running.

And that was how it happened: a dead branch beside the track suddenly sprouted wings and burst into a mopoke. As I followed its line of flight I spotted a tiny blur, out on the far side of the burnt scoria that stretched out under the stern gaze of the Brothers Grim.

'Over there!' I yelled, bashing on the roof so hard I put a dent in it. 'Something moving!'

The truck pulled up. 'Which way?' yelled Bernie, his head

half out the window as he shaded his eyes and peered into the afternoon glare.

'Bit more to the left!'

He tried to follow the line of my outstretched arm, then climbed up beside me. 'You've got better eyes than me, Emily.'

'Follow the line of desert oaks until you come to the gap in the cliffs.' The cliffs, coincidentally, that I'd been standing upon earlier this morning as I sat and peered out over the plains over which I now found myself travelling. Jalyukurru.

'She's just below it, see? Near the rocks.'

They were, in fact, a damn sight more than rocks. They were the Tom Bowlers. Karlujurru. Diamond Dove. An appropriate place to find her, given her dreaming, but explaining their significance to my rescuers was the least of my concerns right now.

Bernie Sweet shaded his eyes, scrutinised the horizon. 'Right!' he said, suddenly excited. 'Got her! Got her!'

He yelled some directions at Mal, then stood beside me as we bounced out over the rough terrain.

'What a relief,' he said, and relieved he certainly looked. He was almost buoyant, the wind whipping his smooth, handsome face and working his lips into a smile. He relaxed, leaned against a fuel drum tied to the railing. 'We'll get her into town,' he said. 'She'll need medical attention.'

'She's alive, Bernie. That's enough for me. And I'm going to make sure she stays that way.'

Not that there was danger of anything to the contrary, given the way she was moving. She looked to be in a damn sight better nick than I was. The blur gradually crystallised into a running woman: pumping arms and flowing legs, blue

326

dress, the sun gleaming off her ragged hair. It was my precious Nungarayi all right.

'Hazel!' I yelled.

She kept going. Must have been still out of range.

We closed. I called again, and was surprised when she didn't hear me that time. 'Give her a blast of the horn!' I yelled to Mal, who grinned blearily at me – about the closest thing to an emotion I'd seen from him – and obliged with a chorus of enthusiastic blarps that rang around the red hills.

If anything the horn seemed to stir her into a new burst of energy. She left the track and began heading up the incline, up in the direction of the rocks of Karlujurru.

'Hazel!' I screamed so loudly I strained my vocal cords. 'It's Emily.'

She kept moving. I leapt into the air, gesticulating wildly.

I was in mid-air when it struck me: something doesn't tally here.

Such was the force with which the intuition hit that I momentarily lost my balance, slipped and skidded in the gravel bouncing about the Hino's floor.

Gravel? Not exactly. I'd grazed my hand in the fall, and took a closer look at the minute fragments embedded in my palm.

Splinters of blue light shot away from the raw skin.

I picked up a handful of crushed rock from the floor.

It was sprinkled with blue fragments, fractured and faceted on one side, smooth, round and gleaming on the other. It was only my seeing it in the context of a mining truck that made me recognise the stone for what it was: crushed core samples.

Awfully fucking familiar core samples. I felt an icy wind blow through my heart.

The pieces of the puzzle flew together of their own accord, and oh! the picture they made. At last I understood what was going on. God knows, it had taken me long enough, but I knew who had killed Lincoln. And Jangala. And Maggie. I even knew who'd killed Marsh's bloody cattle. I knew why they'd been killed. And how.

I knew everything about the string of deaths except how to prevent Hazel's and my own from being added to their number.

Boiling Oil

Hazel was staggering now, but still moving. I could feel the terror that was coursing through her veins: something very much like it was coursing through my own.

But then another emotion flared up and through me like a wildfire.

Fury.

What had I been? Fuckwitted? Blind? Racist, even, against my own people. All of the above and more.

Well fuck em, I thought. Not any more. Not any more. If I was going down I was going down swinging. And kicking, biting, scratching, gouging, raking and making use of whatever came to hand, foot or fingernail. I glanced at Bernie.

'We couldn't have found her without you,' he said, his blue eyes beaming merrily.

'No,' I smiled back, 'don't suppose you could've.'

A blur of movement on his right side.

It was only the fact that I was expecting it that stopped the hammer in his fist from smashing my skull. I rolled with the blow, but it still sent me reeling out over the dropsides.

He thumped on the roof and the vehicle pulled up. I heard him jump down, walk back towards me.

'Nothing personal, Emily,' I heard him mutter.

Jesus, I thought, it's fucking personal to me.

He came closer, and I lay still, my eyes closed but my brain braced and working furiously.

A cry from Mal – 'C'mon, quick! Other one's pissin off!' – called him away, doubtless to return when he'd taken care of Hazel. I heard the door slam, the truck start up.

I opened my eyes. The truck began to move. No time to think. No options. I threw myself forward and grabbed hold of the tow-bar. The rocks ripped bitter weals into my flesh as I dragged myself up over the tailgate. I collapsed onto the floor, my legs shredded, my skin dancing with pain.

How much time did I have? Bugger all. The truck slowed as it hit the rough ground leading up to Karlujurru, but Hazel was less than a hundred metres away.

I crouched in the shelter of the forty-four and scanned the truck desperately, looking for a weapon. Shovels? Crowbars? Sledgehammers? Fucking pointless. They had a gun in there. Shovels and crowbars? All I'd be doing was providing them with a bit of light entertainment.

The forty-four.

I tapped. It was full. I grabbed the hammer, ripped the bung out. Full of super.

I glanced at the blokes up front. All eyes on the next kill, they hadn't noticed me.

What could I use for a torch?

I whipped off what was left of my shirt, pulled the matches out of my pocket and tackled the knots that held the drum. Braced myself. I put a match to the shirt. It was cheap crap. Perfect. Went up like a flare. I got a grip on the forty-four, put a foot up on the backboard and heaved.

Thump!

They heard that all right. Felt it, too. The vehicle slammed to a halt. Petrol came surging out onto the floor and I launched myself out over the tailgate.

Somewhere in mid-flight I flicked the burning shirt back over my shoulder.

I hit the ground rolling. Splinters of pain lanced my back. I'd landed on rock. Rock? Shelter, I thought hopefully. I tumbled into a granite outcrop as sheets of metal and screams and a wall of flame flew about me.

I clenched my eyes. Stars exploded, indigo rivers ran down shafts of red and yellow gold. Metal melted, plastic boiled. I squeezed everything that could be squeezed – my eyes into twisted slits, my knees into my tits, my body into a ball as the air shuddered and shook. Rocks burst. My eardrums threatened to do the same. Burning embers and ashes and sparks of glass lashed my bare back. My bones were on fire, my marrow sizzled. I gasped for burning rags of air. I froze, I cried, I screamed until my throat throbbed.

Time warped. I lay for an incalculable span – somewhere between seconds and forever – tumbling in a vacuum.

Then I crawled away, vaguely astonished that I was able to do so.

A dirty black cloud boiled above me. The sun had gone a streaky green, the sky greasy.

I climbed out of the blackened little hollow that had saved my life. Attempted to stand. Wobbled for a while, then made it to my feet. The chorus of pain that screamed from every corner of my body told me I was still all there.

I staggered up to where I'd last seen Hazel, giving the burning vehicle a wide berth and a glance quick enough to ensure there were no survivors. I didn't hang around – there were some bloody awful odours coming from the inferno and they didn't all smell like burning oil and rubber. I studied the wreck for a moment, and made out the charred remains of a corpse. I couldn't tell which one of them it was. It looked as though he'd made it out of the cabin, burning as he crawled, but in his thrashings had rolled back under the truck and been consumed.

Hazel was some thirty or forty metres away, lying face down in the scree on the outskirts of Karlujurru.

I staggered up the slope and put a hand upon her shoulder. 'Hazel…'

She sprang about, wild eyed and sucking air, her mouth twisted into the beginnings of a scream.

Then she saw who it was and the relief swept across her face.

'Oh Emily…'

I fell into her arms and we kissed each other's battered faces.

'It's okay, Haze,' I whispered. 'It's okay…'

'Those *papalurtu*…'

'We're safe now, darling. I burnt the bastards.'

'They killed… them old people.'

'I know. Took me long enough, but I got it in the end.'

We huddled desperately against one another, then she looked at me and shook her head.

'Jesus, Emily,' she muttered, 'thanks for helping em track me down.'

'Sorry about that.'

'Thought I shook em off till you showed up.'

'I only just figured em out meself. Took your wind-chime, didn't they?'

Her eyes crinkled suspiciously. 'What?'

'Your wind-chime. That was what they were after.'

'How'd you know that?'

'Because they took mine as well. Tried to make it look like the Sandhill Gang.'

'I was waterin the horses when they come in. Watched em kill the old ones.' She paused, stared at the west, shook her head. 'Oh Emily, I don't understand. That feller went about it as cool as if he was butcherin a beast.' She shuddered and gagged, resumed her tale with a whimper. 'Poor *olgamin*, she try to run. That silly little waddle of hers, you know? He got her with a crowbar. And the wind-chime – yeah, one of em was smashin it up in the back of the truck when he spotted me.'

'I've been such a fuckwit.'

'I don't understand. Those stones, what are they, gold or something?'

'The blue band's labradorite. Pretty, but not valuable. The interesting bit's the boring-looking stuff at the other end. Olivine, Jack reckoned at first glance. I took a closer look at a chunk of it today. He wasn't far off the mark. It's dunite.'

She looked at me blankly. 'Dunite?'

'Don't you remember it from that old mining book we used to read? *Gouging the Witwatersrand*?'

'Dunite. Maybe I remember the name. What's it worth?'

'On its own, nothing. But alongside of it you got norite, labradorite. Band of anorthosite in the upper strata. You beginning to see a pattern?'

'You always been the pattern part of the outfit, Emily. Me, I never get past the shapes and colours.'

I kissed her forehead. 'That's why we fit together so well,

Haze. Must admit, though, I probably read about these things more than you do. I was brushing up on my reading just the other day, before they flogged my book. The little crystal on your window ledge is part of the pattern too.'

'I thought it was some sort of fool's gold.' The Moonlight mob had been forever bringing minerals into Jack, hoping they were of value. This one was.

'It isn't pyrite,' I told her. 'It's sperrylite.'

She shrugged. 'Oh, you know, Emmy… All those rites an lites. Might as well be starlight to me.'

'It's platinum, Haze. A crystallised form of platinum. Blakie gave it to you, didn't he?'

'*Yuwayi*.'

'That's what this is all about. Platinum. Worth more than gold. Worth killing for. Or so these scum suckers reckoned. Boss was a South African, too.'

'What's that got to do with it?'

'Well, some of them have a certain… panache when it comes to working with blackfellers, for one. But they've also got…'

'The Bushveld.'

I nodded. 'Still the largest platinum reef in the world. Mostly in a dunite matrix. Bloke knew what he was looking at. I reckon I know where he was looking, too.'

'So do I.' She waved an arm at the rocks above. 'Right here. How'd you figure it out?'

'The painting in the gaolhouse.'

'The diamond dove?'

'It's a map of the area. Should have twigged straightaway, but I didn't start using my head until I saw the original.'

'What do you mean?'

'The outcrop on Jalyukurru. I was up there earlier today. Then I spotted the crushed labradorite in their truck and it all came together. Still got a lot of unanswered questions, though. What else can you tell me? Have you ever seen those blokes before?'

She nodded. 'That boss feller, African one you said…'

'South African. His name was Sweet, the prick. No sweet sorrow in that parting.'

'When we got our land back, lotta people come talkin to my father. Wanted to do deals, make money. He was one of em. Come out a few months ago, spoke about lookin for gold. Just a small show, he said. Bit of diggin. Few ton of ore, maybe a few ounces of gold. Never said nothin about no platinum.'

'No, he wouldn't. He was sounding you out. He'd want to keep his cards close to his chest, wait until he already had a mine of sorts up and running. If he'd come out and announced a find as big as I think it is, you'd have had lawyers round here thicker than blowies on a hot turd. Better to worm his way in, work his way up. Mill it on the sly. Drip feed a few royalties.'

'Old man wouldn't have a bar of that. Not at Karlujurru. No way.'

'Which is why they killed him. Sweet didn't want another Jabiluka on his hands.'

'Jabiluka?'

'Top End. Another king's ransom kept in the ground by hard-headed blackfellers. Remember your father disappeared the day he died? This is where he came. Spotted the drill-hole. Trouble was that they spotted him too, followed him back home. Thought they got rid of the problem when they killed him, of course. Freddy Ah Fong wasn't likely to cause trouble. Massie had told them that much.'

'Who?'

'Some government jerk. Sweet went and saw him in March.'

'How do you know that?'

'I saw his name on a list. Impala Productions. Didn't mean anything to me at the time, although it should have. He mentioned it to me the first time I met him. Massie probably gave them an unwitting tip or two on how to stage a murder: he's got a big mouth and a taste for the salacious.'

'The what?'

'What they did to… Kuminjayi's body. Try to make it look like a business killing. They knew Blakie'd cop the blame.'

Hazel shuddered.

'But things didn't go the way Sweet thought they would. First you and your mob came back. Then he spotted the wind-chime on my veranda – and a book on my kitchen table – and began to get nervous. Worried somebody'd make the connection. The wind-chimes were fragments of a core sample.'

'God, the things Blakie picks up.'

'He must have souvenired it from the drill-site.'

'Suppose so. He's always bringin in things like that. They got a fascination for him. Spirit stones, he calls em. Come up out of the earth.'

Blakie. I couldn't put it off any longer. 'Hazel, I have to tell you. About Blakie. I'm sorry, I… well, if there are such things as spirits… he's one of them now.'

'What?' She stared at the ground, massaging her temples,

her mouth a puzzled O. A slow spasm of despair worked its way across her face. 'Them whitefellers?'

'Shot him.'

She shook her head, bewildered, aghast. 'Jesus! World's fallin apart!'

I squeezed her hand. 'We'll put it together again.'

'But kill him?' she rasped. 'I'm surprised they could even see him.'

'Christ,' I muttered, unable to look her in the eyes. I ran a hand through my hair. 'I feel… Hazel, it's my… I mean, he died trying to save my life.'

She frowned. 'Tell me.'

'I come across him in the camp, trying to work a bit of magic on Jangala… got the wrong idea. Like I been doing lately. Well, I ran, he followed. Those fellers picked me up and he attacked em.'

She studied me for a moment. 'Then he died for me too. He woulda known they was looking for me. He was my friend, that crazy bugger, even if our lingo was more stones than words. He always liked you, Emily, you know that? Said you had a good appetite. Said you an him had that in common.'

An appetite for what? I wondered. But I guess I knew – answers, stones, Hazel, a lot of things. And it made me feel even worse.

Blakie Japanangka. I couldn't exactly mourn him – I'd never known him. But I did feel racked by the possibilities of what might have been if I'd ever given him half a chance.

Hazel reached out and dragged me into a rugged embrace. I could feel her heart beating through her battered body. Her breath as hot and humid as a Darwin December.

'Aaaiiyy…' she murmured, shaking her head. His death seemed to have affected her more than anything else that had happened thus far. 'Like a creature from another world. A walkin dream. Sometimes nightmare. Drove us crazy, but he kept us straight. Bit like you, really.'

I felt her tears run down my cheek, lost myself in the smoke and honey-scented hair.

'It's all right, Hazel,' I whispered. 'It's over now.'

Earlier that afternoon I'd promised myself if I managed to find her we'd be okay. I had, and we would be. We'd work our way out of this nightmare. I'd never leave her again. Beautiful visions skimmed across the surface of my mind: a life of simplicity and peace. Red sand, yellow grass. We'd settle down on Moonlight, get the place going. Start a school, build homes, plant fruit trees. Become a community again. Fulfil Lincoln's dream.

A sharp intake of breath, a quickening of her pulse: the shiver shot through us like an electric current. I felt her fingers tighten on my shoulders.

'Oh *kalu*,' I heard her whisper.

I opened my eyes in time to see a long shadow slithering over the rocks to my right.

'That Blakie. The things he does.' The voice was as deep, dark and cold as a mineshaft. 'And fuck me if he isn't about to do some more.'

I looked back over my shoulder.

Sweet. He was a couple of metres away. His face blistered, his brow burnt, his clothes blasted to shreds.

But he had a gun in his hands and a crazy glitter in his eyes.

338

The Iceman

'You're a persistent animal, Sweet. I thought I blew you up.'

'You should have had a better look.'

I flashed a cold stare at him, clutched Hazel.

'I will next time.'

He actually seemed taken aback. 'You think I'm going to give you a next time? You've already caused enough…' he glanced at the burning wreck and snarled, 'complications.' He waved the barrel at us. 'On your faces!'

Neither of us moved.

I stared at him, a bizarre question floating up through the panic in my chest. Not a question to which I expected an answer, but I felt compelled to ask. 'What the fuck are you, Sweet? What kind of… creature does shit like this?'

I looked into his eyes, searching for something, anything: a trace of emotion, humanity… reluctance, even, at what he was about to do.

There was nothing there. The masks he'd so adroitly adopted – Outback Samaritan, Kindly Neighbour, Benevolent Boss – had been shucked off, and there was nothing in their place. Just another mask. His eyes were like blue steel. The shitbag was about to drill us with all the emotion he'd feel if he were drilling a lump of granite.

He pointed the rifle at me and pulled the trigger. The

explosion crashed into my eardrums, the bullet just about brushed my hair.

'Now get down or the next one will be between your eyes.'

Why didn't you put that one between my eyes? I wondered as I stretched out on the ground beside Hazel.

Ah. The Blakie set-up. If he shoots us, they'll be able to tie our deaths to the gun. He's got other plans. Presumably bash us to death and dump us at the camp, two more victims of Blakie's insane rampage. Nobody would go near the camp for years after that: he could have a mine up and running almost before anybody noticed.

Beside me I could hear Hazel softly sighing.

No. It was more of a song than a sigh. Where had I heard it before? When she was talking to the diamond dove out at the waterhole. So this must be... What? I wondered. The swan song? Or dove song, more like it.

She turned to look at me. In her big brown eyes I could see the reflection of the sky. And the reflection of Sweet, steadying himself, raising the rifle butt into a clubbing position.

Wait for it, I told myself. Wait for the right moment. Fling yourself into him, knock him off balance, gain a few seconds.

He saw me coming. 'No you don't, you little kaffir bitch!' he spat, and kicked me in the head with a size twelve steel-cap. Bolts of pain, scattered lacerations, a rush of salt between the teeth.

I glared hazily at him, my head as groggy as a payday at the Black Dog. He planted the boot in my back and pushed. My ribs felt like they were breaking.

Beside me Hazel was still singing. Tapping on the rocks

now as well. Christ, I thought, what do you think this is, Hazel? The black and white bloody minstrel show? This monster's about to kill us. You'll have plenty of time for singing in the next world. Maybe you'll come back as a diamond dove.

My little show of resistance seemed to have pushed Sweet over the edge. He dropped a knee into my back, pinned me down. Leaned in close. 'What am I?' he hissed into my ear. 'What am I? You spend twenty years hammering underground or frying in a fucking furnace overhead, then ask me that! A find like this, it's what we dream of! You think I'm going to give it up so this lizard-eating swill can indulge their primitive fantasies?' His voice shifted up a gear, moved from the sibilant to the demonic, from ice cold to red hot. 'Or *yours*?' He stood up, raised the rifle once again.

I twisted my neck to glare up at him. 'Fuck you, Sweet…'

He paused, smiled. And the smile turned to horror as Hazel flicked the snake into his face.

It was a king brown. Not a particularly big king brown, as king browns go, but as king browns go, it went.

Crazy.

It must have looked like a fucking dragon to Sweet as it flew into his face thrashing, its body whipping, its great mouth working furiously. He staggered backwards, a turbocharged groan rocketing up from his guts. He lost his footing and tumbled down the slope.

'Where's the gun?' yelled Hazel.

I looked down at Sweet. Shit! Still in his hands. He was a determined bastard.

I watched him wheel away in a cloud of dust and coils, his face twisted, his eyes rolling wildly.

But he steadied himself, levelled the rifle, drew a bead on the snake and shot its head off.

Have you been bitten, you prick? I thought hopefully. How long does venom take to kick in? Are you about to keel over and die? Those cold mineral eyes shifted in our direction.

As did the rifle.

'Down!' I yelled as the weapon roared. He missed, but he'd obviously abandoned the Blakie ruse. He came charging up the slope.

'Come on!' Hazel shouted, and we raced off in the only direction open to us.

Upwards, into Karlujurru.

Springs of Rushlit Water
Washed to Rainbow Ford

As a refuge it left a lot to be desired – if he got us up against the cliff face it could easily turn into a death trap. But it was all we had, and we hit it like a couple of runaway wallabies, with Sweet barrelling along behind us. We ran down scattered alleyways and slopes of layered slate, we skidded and slipped across gullies and scree, we belted out over a dry creek bed and came to rest in the shelter of a turtle-shaped boulder.

Hazel gasped for breath and grabbed my hand. 'What now?'

'Fucked if I know.' Try to hide until nightfall? It was hours away. He said he'd called the cops, but if you believed that you'd believe in astral travel and the brotherhood of man. Climb the cliffs? He'd pick us off like a couple of sick pigeons. 'Get a few more minutes' life if we're lucky.' I could hear Sweet on the other side of the boulder. 'C'mon!'

We cut loose, then hit the gravel as another bullet buzzed through the shrubbery before us. It had come from a higher angle, that one. I glanced back and saw that he'd climbed to the top of the boulder we'd just abandoned.

And that he was lining us up for another shot.

I dived, rolled, knocked Hazel to the ground as the bullet

nicked my waist. It should have stung, but in the cacophony of fear and pain that was already rocketing through my body I barely noticed it. We flattened ourselves on the rocks. Long seconds passed, then I risked a glance. Sweet had disappeared. I could hear him making his way round the bottom of the boulder.

That was to be his strategy from here on, his way of overcoming the meagre assistance afforded us by the rocks of Karlujurru. He'd seek the higher ground. As far as strategies go it wasn't exactly a startling innovation, but it didn't need to be. He had the gun.

We relied upon our ears. To expose our eyes would have been to risk his putting a bullet between them. We'd lie low. Very low. Whenever we heard him scrambling for a vantage point we'd bolt.

But it couldn't go on for long. We all knew that. There weren't enough places to hide. If we hit the open plains we'd be dead in seconds. And he was corralling us: the gorge into which we were gradually retreating was narrowing. Another fifty metres and we'd be up against the wall.

We came to a fork in the path and paused to consider our options. I glanced up at the terracotta rock face. Should we try to outflank him now, before it was too late? Or hide, bury ourselves in branches and sand, let him overtake us?

We were crouching there when the inevitable occurred: another shot blew out and Hazel gasped and tumbled over.

Blood poured from a wound in her hip. I dragged her into a recess, ripped her dress apart, tried to staunch the blood. Tried to staunch the screams.

I stretched my body out over hers, stroked her temple, whispered into her ear: 'Easy, Haze, take it easy, darling...'

I could hear Sweet barging up through the scree; I caught a glimpse of his face through a tangle of lancewood. He'd slowed down. The cool had come back, the race was over. He had us now and he knew it. He looked relaxed, confident, eager, like a salesman set to clinch a deal. Time for the coup de grace. He began whistling. A thin, tuneless dirge floated over the slopes.

Jesus, I thought, this is fucking hopeless. I'm fucking hopeless. What have I achieved? For all my battling and brawling and buggering about, for all my poking my nose in and getting everybody off-side, what have I actually managed to do? Jack shit. Get a few people killed – one of them about to be myself – and increase his share of the profits.

Hazel was lying quieter now, but panting deeply, choking with pain. The blood was building up under my pathetic excuse for a bandage. I tightened it, put a hand upon her shoulder. 'Hazel, he's just below us and coming fast. Can you move?'

'I'll try,' she gasped. I helped her to her feet. She took a step, grunted and crumbled. It was no good. The bullet had struck bone.

'Emily!' she rasped, raising herself up onto an elbow. 'You get out of here, ya silly bitch. I just slow you down.'

'Haven't got any more snakes up your sleeve?'

She grinned through a grimace, then eased herself back down, rested her head against a stone, let her gaze drift up into the hills.

A change came over her. I could almost feel it coming in, like a change in the weather, a shift in the wind. She scooped up a handful of sand, let it slip through her fingers, watched it float away. She breathed deeply, looked strangely at ease and peaceful.

What are you looking at? I wondered. Or for? The spirits that inhabit this place? Are you getting ready to join them? What were they anyway, the dreamings that passed through these rocks? There was a stack of them, if my memories of Lincoln's campfire soliloquies served me.

Mountain Devil. Mudlark. Magpie. Wildfire. Jack used to say it sounded more like a day at the races than a pantheon. But this was an important place, the intersection of God knew how many paths.

And then, of course, there was the main one, the engine that drove them all. The eponymous Karlujurru. Diamond dove. Strange to think that such a tiny creature could hold a site of such significance. Strange that it could hold Hazel.

Strange that it could be Hazel.

I looked at her lying in the blood-stained gravel. My diamond dove: it was her dreaming and her medium, her bush name, her bridge to what there was of the other world. For all of her gifts and bounties – for her rocks and snakes and her China eyes, for her painted maps and hidden galleries – she was first and foremost a diamond dove.

It was her equanimity that struck me most. Here we were, both apparently about to die, and yet she didn't seem disturbed. Her mind was on something else. On me, I suspected. I could feel her reaching out, trying to speak to me in a language more subtle than the tongue could manage. Trying to give me something.

The echo of tumbling rocks drew my attention away. I caught a glimpse of Sweet's burnt blond hair bobbing through the rocks. Fucking bastard, I thought. Had Hazel and I come so far, only to finish up like this? What are you anyway, Sweet? No doubt now. You're nothing. Nobody. You're Dante's demon encased in ice, a desiccated brute with a wasted heart and blue metal eyes, the last of a line of thugs who've been stamping on people like us forever.

People like us – the Moonlight mob. My mob.

I'd said it for the first time. A bit late, and a rapidly diminishing bloody mob it was, but I was part of it.

I heard an explosion. I wasn't sure where it was coming from, but it made my recent demolition job on the Hino sound like a pastor's fart. Then I realised it was coming from inside my head. A charge of pure rage, coming full bore with a force that sent me screaming over the rocks like a berserker, then across the top of a stone alleyway and grazing the head of the startled Sweet. He swung the rifle upwards, but I was gone before he got me in its arc.

I skimmed across the other side of the rocks and rolled, somersaulting and skidding down the far side. I landed on my feet and kept moving, arched forward, forearms powering, skimming from rock to rock, zig-zagging and weaving, too smooth to slip, too quick to get a bead on.

I was vaguely aware of a thin blue film of racing sky, of the echo and torque of ricocheting lead, of the rocks that rushed beneath my feet. I took a last, desperate leap across a boulder, flew westward and wallward and landed on a bed of sand at the foot of the cliffs.

My body came to rest but my mind was spinning like a dynamo. Crunch time. Nowhere else to go. I could hear him pounding through the gravel. I looked around me, desperate for options.

There were none. I was completely penned in, a sheer cliff

at my back, unscalable rocks all around me. Sweet would take a minute or two to reach me, but the outcome was no longer in doubt.

I picked up the only decent rock in sight, settled down to wait.

The next few seconds were astonishingly clear, engulfed in the silent riot of the senses that appears whenever you sit still in the desert. Ants glided over dirt as gracefully as sailboats. Blue-grey shale and silver siltstone pressed against my back.

And suddenly, on a pile of stones a few feet above me, there alighted a bird. A small grey bird with stars on its wings and ringed eyes. A diamond dove. The spirit of this place. Unknowable in itself; but if I know anything about beauty, it reached its purest expression in that delicate assemblage of feather, beak and bone.

She hungry as a hawk, that one. Mebbe dove.

Blakie had said that about me. Blakie, who saw things other people didn't see. Was I diamond dove myself?

The bird gazed at me. I looked back into its eyes, and found myself floating over a translucent pool: I saw speckled fish, yellow sand, springs of rushlit water washed to rainbow ford.

And strangely, unexpectedly, I saw myself and Hazel at Moonlight Downs. We were walking along by the creek in a kind of waking dream. Around us there flowed a weird, ethereal music. It seemed to be coming from the rocks themselves, eddying over dry watercourses and white claypans, riding on drifts of bushfire wind. Country music, perhaps, in the blackfeller sense of both words. The voice of the Jukurrpa.

The Jukurrpa. Perhaps it was the same sense of impending doom that sends old ladies scuttling to mass on a Monday morning that had me pondering metaphysics at this juncture.

I remembered, suddenly, asking Lincoln about it once.

I was thirteen years old and beginning to examine the world through the microscope of my own smart-arsed rationality. And he'd answered me, even if his answer was better pitched to satisfy a Medieval alchemist than a hormonally charged teenager.

I remembered he'd cautioned me for breaking some rule or other. God knows which one. I was the community's wild child, forever getting into trouble. Lincoln's dreaming had a stack of rules – if he'd written them down they'd have been thicker than Wisden's Cricketers' Almanack. I think it was the time he caught me cooking fat under starlight. He hadn't punished me, of course, hadn't even criticised me. He never saw that as his role. Just mentioned it as something you shouldn't do. I don't know why I reacted the way I did. I'd been having a bad day. Maybe I had my rags in, maybe I had a few too many books under the belt, maybe I'd just decided it was time to cut loose from the confines of the hillbilly shit-hole in which I imagined I'd been raised.

'What difference does it make?' I remembered challenging him. 'What difference does it make? What I cook or where I cook it? What I eat? Where I walk?'

'Is Jukurrpa,' was his casual reply. 'Dreamin. That's it.'

He was sitting on a toprail at the time, doing a bit of repair-work on his girth straps. The heels of his riding boots rested on the midrail. I was standing in front of him, hands on hips, my hat low and my tolerance lower.

'Is dreaming!' I yelled. 'Well that tells me a lot! Is dreaming! And what the hell is dreaming, Lincoln?'

'Dreamin?' He looked puzzled, as if the question – or the possibility that life could be lived with anything other than the integrity he embodied – had never occurred to him.

He thought for a while, looked around, then picked up a newly polished buckle from his tackle and held it up to the setting sun. 'Is just a 'flection,' he said.

As he moved the buckle a cage of light – a set of interconnecting circles and curves and burnished planes – flew across his shirt and ran up into his eyes. He squinted, grinned, moved it away from his face.

'A reflection?'

'Line o' light. Like a soul. You look at somethin right way – anythin – buckle, bird, stone… look *into* it, you can see.'

That's it? I remembered thinking, livid with youthful stupidity. It's just a reflection? A line of light? That's the divine plan, that's the cosmic truth that underpins our lives? Bullshit!

I hadn't understood him then. But I understood him now. Or saw not so much what he meant as the line of light itself, reflected in the dove's eye. It was like a trajectory, traced in gold.

A trajectory along which – acting on God-knows-what instinct – I threw the rock.

It curved slowly and gracefully along the line of light and bounced harmlessly off the cliff face. Dropped into the sand, a few splinters of granite and a puff of dust the only apparent outcome.

The dove disappeared. A handful of stones, the ones

upon which the bird had been resting, tumbled away. Gravel trickled. Things went quiet.

Jesus, Emily, that was a fucking brilliant idea, I thought. What are you going to do now, bite the cunt? A premonition, or memory – something I'd seen in a painting, the story of a diamond dove and a white devil – was the only answer I could find.

The rifle barrel came sliding round the corner, followed closely by the devil himself.

'Missed!' he smiled, lowering the weapon at me. Then he tilted his head back and began to laugh, kept laughing until, suspicious for a reason I didn't understand – a premonition of his own, perhaps? – he glanced up to where my rock had struck.

The boulder that had been pressing down on the stones there gave a slight wobble, then toppled forward with a shuddering roar, bringing with it a thunderous little land-slide and wiping the smile off his face.

As far as I could tell.

Which, given that he had a ton of granite where seconds before he'd had a head, wasn't all that far. His heels tattooed the earth in a fierce little reflex action, then went still. He hadn't even had time to scream.

I studied his boots for a moment. 'Bullshit I missed.'

The Diamond Driller

I staggered back to where Hazel lay gazing out into the crazy topography of Karlujurru, still whisper-singing.

'He's finished,' I said.

She turned round to look up at me. 'I know.'

'Just like your painting. An avalanche.'

'Not surprised.'

I knelt beside her, tore a strip off her shirt and tried to improve the bandage I'd fashioned.

'So what do we do now, Haze?'

'Dunno,' she shrugged. 'Whatever happens, it'll be okay. You know the trouble with you, Em?'

'Lot of troubles with me, Haze. Take your pick.'

'You worry too much.' She studied me for a moment and smiled.

Nice to be so positive, I thought. Miles from nowhere, buggered and battered and bruised beyond belief, no water and you've got a bullet in you. I closed my eyes as the terrors and tremors of the last few hours welled up inside me, colliding with my consciousness.

My head spun, my body felt like it was giving in to the chorus of torments inflicted upon it of late. The world went black.

'Jesus H. Christ!'

A rough male voice. How long had I been out for? I put a hand to my head, opened my eyes, tried to focus.

The first thing I saw was Camel, standing in front of me. Next to him was Earl Marsh, a gun in his hands, his face as blistered and burnt as ever beneath the sinister shades.

Evidently it was Marsh who'd spoken. He was looking up at where Sweet's body was oozing out from under the rock. Camel followed his gaze and his eyes narrowed viciously.

Shit, I thought. Will this never end? 'Mr Marsh,' I croaked, 'I hope I've completely misjudged you.'

'Why?'

'Because I don't feel up to another fight.'

Another voice, a familiar one, came from behind me. 'Don't think that'll be necessary, Emily.'

I turned my head around to see Jojo kneeling beside Hazel, patching her up, a first-aid kit on the ground beside him. She was sitting up and smiling. Down near the burning Hino I noticed a helicopter, its rotors still turning slowly.

'Hello Jojo. Might have known you'd turn up – me flaked out and damn near naked. How are you, Hazel?'

'In good hands, I reckon.'

'Eh? Don't go gettin too attached to em. Thanks, Jojo.'

'Don't thank me. Thank Earl here.'

'Thank you, Earl.' Marsh nodded uncomfortably. I turned back to Jojo. 'What am I thanking *him* for?'

'Bringing us out here.'

'And what inspired you to do that, Mr Marsh?'

'You got me thinking, with all your talk about drillin out here. I knew I hadn't, but some bugger had. Thought I knew who. I'd been worrying all along there was something suspicious about the way he died.'

'Mr Marsh, I've got no idea what you're talking about. The way who died?'

'Snowy.'

'Snowy?'

'Snowy Truscott.'

'Who the fuck is…' but the answer came to me even as I asked the question. My old man's late driller mate, the beneficiary of the Green Swamp cricket testimonial.

'They tried to tell me he left the hook off his winch,' Marsh continued. 'Tangled his wheels, rolled the rig. I went an took a look at the wreck. No way Snow'd do that. Done a dozen jobs for me over the years. Knew him as a kid in Winton. Most efficient feller I ever seen. Treated his equipment better than he treated his missus. An he treated her all right, which I oughta know, seein as she's me sister.'

'Snowy Truscott was your brother-in-law?'

'Course he was,' Marsh said gruffly.

'Of course.'

'"Who'd wanner do that to old Snow?" I asked meself. I was talkin to him a few days before he died. Said he had some big job comin up, all very hush-hush, top dollar. But then he let on it were for the South African feller. Wasn't till you accused me of drilling on Moonlight that I twigged. Spotted em out here a coupla times when I was checkin me cattle. Figured they must a found somethin…'

'Oh, they found something all right.' I looked at Jojo, who was coming over to check out the bullet nick in my side. 'And you, Thunderbird 3. You just happened to be out on routine chopper patrol when your telepathic headset picked up my distress signal…'

'I was in the cop shop,' Jojo interjected, 'following up on

last night's intruder, when this rather indignant call from Earl came in.'

'Indignant?' Marsh retorted. 'You blame me?'

'Apparently you and him had just had a little discussion out on the Jalyukurru track.'

Marsh frowned. 'Dunno if discussion's the word I'd use… anyway, when I told your friend the ranger about that South African arsehole, he got the idea in his scone that you might both be on the loose out here. He was… persuasive I ought to come back out'n warn you.' He glanced sideways at Jojo. 'Didn't expect the airborne cavalry to turn up as well.'

Jojo blushed. 'I think you know Emily, don't you Mr Marsh? What were the odds there was going to be trouble?'

Marsh looked down at the burning truck, then up at the fallen boulder. 'Trouble all right. Shoulda warned them instead,' he said with a shake of the head.

An abrupt spasm of grief wrenched at my gut. Should have warned those poor old buggers back at the camp, I thought. Turned my face into Jojo's shoulder.

'Anyway, Mung Bean here,' Marsh went on, jerking a thumb at Camel, who I noticed had a few fresh bruises added to the collection Blakie had left him, 'has been most obligin. Course he owed it to me, after what his fuckin rotties did to me cattle.'

I cleared my throat. 'I was gonna mention that if I ever saw you again. Figured it out, did you?'

He frowned. 'You havin a go at me?'

'Christ Earl, loosen up a bit, will you?'

He scowled at me, then what might have been a smile on other faces rumbled through the granite.

I tried to stand, but things were swimming out of focus.

355

'Jojo?'

'Yep?'

'How'd you get a chopper?'

'Mate in the charter business. Name's Jason.'

'Jojo?'

'Yep?'

'I think I'm gonna pass out again.'

Which I duly did. But even as I was spiralling southwards, I caught a glimpse of a translucent image: me and Hazel, together on Moonlight Downs, walking along in a kind of waking dream.

Springs of rushlit water washed to rainbow ford.

Somewhere above us a dove was singing.